KT-227-906

DEVIL'S FJORD

DAVID HEWSON

CANONGATE

This paperback edition published in Great Britain, the USA and Canada in 2021
by Canongate Books Ltd,
14 High Street, Edinburgh EH1 1TE

Distributed in the USA by Publishers Group West
and in Canada by Publishers Group Canada

First published in 2019 by Severn House Publishers Ltd,
Eardley House, 4 Uxbridge Street, London W8 7SY

canongate.co.uk

1

Copyright © David Hewson, 2019

The right of David Hewson to be identified as the
author of this work has been asserted by him in accordance
with the Copyright, Designs and Patents Act 1988

This is a work of fiction. Names, characters, places and incidents
are either the product of the author's imagination or are used fictitiously.
Except where actual historical events and characters are being described for
the storyline of this novel, all situations in this publication are fictitious and
any resemblance to actual persons, living or dead, business establishments,
events or locales is purely coincidental.

British Library Cataloguing-in-Publication Data
A catalogue record for this book is available on
request from the British Library

ISBN 978 1 83885 376 1

Typeset by Palimpsest Book Production Ltd,
Falkirk, Stirlingshire

Printed and bound in Great Britain by Clays Ltd, Elcograf S.p.A.

MIX
Paper from
responsible sources
FSC® C018072

DEVIL'S FJORD

David Hewson is a former journalist with the *Times*, the *Sunday Times* and the *Independent*. He is the author of more than twenty-five novels including his Rome-based Nic Costa series, which has been published in fifteen languages. He has also written three acclaimed adaptations of the Danish TV series *The Killing*.

@david_hewson | davidhewson.com

C334634137

ONE

He was on the roof of their little cottage mowing the thick and umber turf, briar pipe clenched tightly in his teeth, happy and a little lost in his own thoughts, when his wife called from the front porch to say the killings were on the way.

'Tristan! Grind! Grind! Are your cloth ears listening? All those cars a-tooting in the village! They are here! You must come! Come now, man. Oh, what a time to be mowing the roof! What will people think?'

A strong man of fifty-five. Not tall, not short. Not fat, not thin. Clean-shaven with a good head of sandy-coloured hair edging towards grey. It went with a friendly, freckled face, pale since Haraldsen was by trade and nature a man for the office, never the country. Eight weeks out of police headquarters in Tórshavn. A civilian latterly responsible for systems, newly-retired on medical grounds – his mild cardiac arrhythmia failed to pass the adjusted health diktats put in place by the government health officer – he had now only the part-time job of district sheriff for the fishing to occupy a few working hours each week.

'I do not hear you moving, husband.'

It was a sunny September day. A brisk easterly wind from the Atlantic buffeted Tristan Haraldsen as he went about his work on the shallow turf roof of the cottage. Four fat sheep grazed in the back yard next to a flock of white-and-brown chickens picking for worms in the grass. Out on the water, framed by the two high cliffs on either side of the fjord, past the line of snag-toothed rocks called the Skerries, a small flotilla of multi-coloured boats dotted the bright horizon. Fishermen often gathered at the mouth of the snaking, narrow inlet to the Atlantic from which Djevulsfjord took its name, searching for cod, haddock, redfish and mackerel, anything they could catch and transport down to the market in Sørvágur for ready cash.

The vessels flocked together, like sharks slyly closing on the prospect of prey. This was the end of summer. The season the pilot whale pods were on the move, coming close to land. He was the district sheriff. It was time – the first occasion – to earn his keep.

'Ja, ja, ja,' Haraldsen cried, his attention still caught by the view.

'And I shall be most cross if there is tobacco in that pipe of yours. The very thought you must go and mow the roof to suck on that thing . . .'

'Elsebeth! Elsebeth! I am coming. Of course. The roof needs mowing. The pipe is empty. But I must dispose of the machine first. Mustn't I?'

One hand on the shiny new rotary he'd bought for the move, Haraldsen edged towards the lip of the gently sloping roof. The timber cottage had stood on this gentle hill above the village for more than a century. The couple who owned it before were so traditional they'd let the chickens live inside, roosting on the open rafters above the living room, right next to the attic where the two of them were to sleep. One of the birds had pooped on Elsebeth's head when they came to inspect the property. An omen, his wife had said giggling, then announced she wanted the place.

He was content with this on two conditions. The whole of the interior would be enclosed, none of it open to the rafters. The hens were to live in a coop outside which he would build himself, along with the new ceiling, every last piece.

They were the first jobs he finished when, the month before, they moved from the relative bustle of the Faroese capital to the remote village, a place they barely knew, on the western island of Vágar, an hour away by car. Not an easy drive either. Vágar was shaped like a dog's head. Djevulsfjord sat stranded near the eye, accessible only by a lengthy sea voyage round the profile of the hound or a journey by road that ended after a damp-smelling single-lane tunnel cut through Árnafjall, Eagle's Mountain, emerging close to their new home.

Prices in Djevulsfjord were as low as they might find anywhere in the Faroes. No one wanted to live in such a remote spot it seemed. The population had dwindled to fewer than eighty, scarcely any young couples or children among them. The modern world regarded it as too remote, too locked in the past. Tristan and Elsebeth Haraldsen, childless, with no living relatives to look after or look after them when the time came, relished the challenge. Besides, the lump sum from the police authority pension more than covered the modest purchase price. The small salary of the district sheriff gave them the freedom to travel if they so wished, something neither of them had raised since that early summer day they decided to move from busy Tórshavn to silent, beautiful Vágar and embark upon a new chapter in their lives.

'Furthermore you must get out of those pyjamas,' she added. 'Why a grown man is wearing his bed things at ten o'clock of the morning is beyond me. I know you're half-retired. But if one of the neighbours should see you. The district sheriff of all people. In this condition . . .'

The cottage lay above the small and straggly fishing village. A good ten-minute walk from the nearest house and the harbour where cars and bikes and people on foot now congregated like bees swarming on summer flowers. Even set as their cottage was, on the rise of a moderate green slope, it was not, it seemed to Haraldsen, a likely spot for a man to be seen from afar in his pyjamas.

Elsebeth walked out from beneath the cottage porch. The sight of her never failed to cheer him. She always said of late she wasn't so slim as when he courted her at the Tórshavn dances. He didn't notice. To him she was slender still and young too, just not as much as before. And her face was strong and beautiful, more so now she cropped her brown hair short, not long and girlish, the way it used to be.

'I do not wear these things to go about what little business I have,' Haraldsen informed her. 'Only for the comfort of my own home.'

The roof was a tradition hereabouts and needed attention. In spring, he believed, daffodils would sprout and bloom in the turf above their heads. In early summer came daisies and butter-cups and other wild flowers Haraldsen recognized but could not name though they must have died in the early August drought.

His pipe was empty, merely a comforting thing to suck on, with a familiar taste. The doctors had had their say about tobacco and in the end he'd listened.

His eyesight was clear and strong just like, he felt, his mind. He'd know if anyone was watching and might be offended.

'I am waiting,' Elsebeth declared firmly from below. 'And so are your whales.'

'GRIND.'

Jónas tweaked his brother's arm so hard, so insistent he kept on until Benjamin screeched and pulled away from him.

'Remember what that means, goat? Or you too stupid now?'

Silas Mikkelsen had thrown their mother Alba out of the house the summer before. When he did he was adamant there was no room for the brothers in the fisherman's cottage he'd inherited at the edge of the village. So the youngsters had to move with her into the minuscule shack by Djevulsfjord's harbour. The place was all Alba could afford since Silas was rarely forthcoming with the maintenance. In a sense it wasn't a home at all, just a flimsy wooden lean-to tacked onto the sheds where the fish were boxed and the nets and buoys stored by the tiny and dwindling harbour fleet. The smell of dead, dry fish never left the place. In winter it was freezing. In summer the place felt like an oven.

'Don't call me goat,' Benjamin Mikkelsen muttered.

'Goats grunt and groan and stink. They're thick and stumble everywhere. Goat.'

After that he leaned down and laughed in his older brother's face. Ten and twelve. Eighteen months separated them on paper. But the divide seemed much greater, to them, to their mother, to all who knew the sad little family.

'Goat. Goat. Goat. Goat . . .'

Benjamin punched him hard on the arm.

'Mam!' Jónas raced to the door and flung it open. Alba Mikkelsen was at the rickety table in the middle of the single room that was kitchen, living space and her bedroom with a little cot in the corner. She was a thin-faced woman with high cheek-bones, twenty-nine but she looked older with prominent grey eyes, straggly blonde hair, rarely well-combed.

'Mam. Benji hit me again.'

The accused walked out to take the inevitable blame, hands in pockets. All they had to sleep in was a tiny bunk. Jónas made him sleep on the bottom bed and liked to make a play of farting from the top.

'Didn't,' he wanted to say. But it came out just as 'dint'. He couldn't talk well. 'Learning difficulties' the special teacher at school said. Couldn't think straight, talk straight, walk straight. All the kids ragged him about it. He couldn't much think of anything to say or do in return except hit them from time to time. They'd warned him about fighting twice, though on both occasions he'd come off worse. Going on the record the teacher, Mrs Blak said, and the police would get to hear if he kept on bashing people.

'Told you before, Benji. Don't hit your brother,' Alba Mikkelsen said without looking up from the paperwork in front of her.

'He spat at me too,' Jónas added. 'He—'

Her hand came out and slapped him round the cheek.

'Shut up, child. Even if I believed you no one likes a tittle-tattle. And ain't you the one who's always ragging him? Why's it always you complaining? Leave your big brother alone.'

'He's the one doing the hitting, Mam.'

'Only 'cos you make him.'

Sometimes she found it hard to believe they were brothers at all. It wasn't just that they seemed to hate one another. Their characters were so very different, Jónas smart as a shiny button, the other a slow, dim idiot, too quick to use his fists at times, not that he ever managed much in the way of damage. Maybe a baby got swapped out in the hospital in Tórshavn and she came home with the wrong one. Which had to be Jónas. Cunning, cheeky, mischievous, dishonest. Stupid as he turned out, Benjamin was the more loveable. His father wasn't bright. Alba didn't think much of her own intelligence. But the eldest . . . she couldn't imagine what she'd do with him when he was older and needed to look for a job. You didn't have to be clever to crew the boats but you couldn't be clumsy and Benjamin could scarcely get through the week without breaking something or stumbling to the ground in the street.

Jónas had the same brown hair as Silas. The same round, red-cheeked, chubby face, one that, like him, would probably stay boyish even into their thirties. White, even teeth. The sturdy frame that came from fishing stock. Benjamin was fair and lanky, pop-eyed with a blank face bordering on gormless, crooked teeth that needed fixing, skinny in the arms and already starting to stoop.

Silas's father was a widower who'd died at sea in a storm two summers previous. She was the daughter of Baldur and Eydna Ganting. Not that her parents had shown much interest since Silas walked out calling her all the names under the sun. The boys had to rely on hand-me-downs and charity shops for their clothes. Today, like most days, denim jeans and a checked lumberjack shirt for Jónas. Red shorts and khaki top for Benjamin. They could look sweet even if they weren't.

'I heard voices outside,' Jónas told her. 'They're launching the boats. There's a grind coming.'

'Oh aren't you the smart one?' she yapped. 'Do you think we're all deaf here?'

No one could miss that noise. Cars and pickups turning up, honking their horns in delight. The hubbub was rising beyond the wooden shutters of their home. Summer in Djevulsfjord had been long and hot and poor. This was the first hunt to come their way in a year. No wonder people felt eager for blood.

'You never told us, Mam,' Jónas complained.

'Because it's a grind! You don't need to be told. You're fishing folk. It's in your veins.'

'Can I go?' the boy asked.

'Both of you,' she said, nodding at his brother. 'Take Benji with you. No fighting.'

'But . . .'

'You heard!' she shouted. 'I don't want no complaints.'

He thrust his fists deep in the pockets of his threadbare jeans.

'And if you see your father ask him for some money,' Alba Mikkelsen added. 'I'm reduced to cleaning up the witch Dorotea's kitchen for brass. Tell him I need it for you. Not me. Which is true by the way.'

WITH THE QUIETEST OF grumbles Haraldsen took hold of the rope fastened to the mower, then lifted the machine out over the gutter, positioning himself diagonally, one foot down, one up, to take the strain.

'Elsebeth! It would help if you stopped it banging against the windows. I am new to all this you know.'

In Tórshavn they'd lived in a modern house with grey tiles, good secondary glazing, all the modern conveniences. A settled urban couple who visited the countryside out of interest not necessity. This old-fashioned act of household maintenance, commonplace in Djevulsfjord where turf roofs remained popular, was quite new to him. The coming pilot whale drive would be the first he'd supervised too. It was important the job was performed well, on several fronts. The ministry had been precise about both the safety precautions required of fishermen and people on the shore. It was also adamant about the way the pod was to be killed. The modern world had intruded on their way of life and on occasion foreigners did not approve of what they found.

The whale hunt known as 'grind' was a bloody spectacle, shocking to those unfamiliar with it. Men and women from nations where meat was nothing but a lump of pink flesh in a supermarket carton had never witnessed – or wished to contemplate – the slaughter that preceded it. For the Faroese there was no such comfortable illusion. On scattered islands where food had often proved scarce, sometimes to the point of starvation, grind provided winter-long sustenance to be shared among the village according to a complex formula going back centuries. The dead whale carcasses would be beached and numbered. Each catch was to be marked up as 'skinns', about thirty-four kilos of blubber and thirty-eight of meat. Then, according to the sharing system set out in Haraldsen's books, the skinns would be allotted to the appropriate households and boats. After that came the butchery when entire families, old and sometimes as young as three and four, would set about the dead pilot whales with their knifes, to carve the carcasses and take home their share.

It represented, perhaps, an anachronism in a world of invisible commercial butchery and food flown in from everywhere. But this annual piece of bloody theatre was also a fundamental element in the national sense of identity, one that grew stronger the more the foreign critics attacked it.

'Haraldsen! Have you gone to sleep in those pyjamas?'

'Thinking, dear.'

Nothing much happened in this part of Vágar when it came to crime. A little drunkenness. The occasional case of domestic violence. He'd heard a solitary policewoman patrolled the area from time to time. A stranger, the source of some gossip in the village since she'd been there only a few months. She was of Faroese stock apparently but her family had moved to Aalborg in Denmark when she was a toddler. Quite why a youngster would want to hide herself away on Vágar was beyond Haraldsen. This was a place for older people surely . . .

'Tristan!'

He would make a phone call to introduce himself, he thought as he let the mower ride over the healthy turf of the roof then roll down towards the ground. A cry from below told him she'd got it. Then Haraldsen took one last suck on his pipe – the thing was banned indoors – and put it in the top pocket of his black pyjamas as he went for the ladder.

A bright red pickup was making its way up the snaking lane to the cottage. Tristan Haraldsen believed he knew his new job. He'd read every last line in the manual provided by the Ministry of Fisheries, gone with the assigned fleet foreman from Djevulsfjord for formal training in the government buildings in Tórshavn. This was the man behind the wheel of the pickup:

Baldur Ganting, owner of the *Alberta*, the largest fishing boat in the harbour.

Haraldsen hurried down the ladder, came over and shook Ganting's hand as the fellow climbed out of the cab. Elsebeth was shielding her eyes with her fingers, as if in shame.

'You're mowing,' Ganting said in his gruff westerner's voice. 'In your pyjamas. Are you well?'

'Never better! We heard the news. Whales!'

Ganting was staring at Haraldsen's sheep as they came round the corner of the field, curious to see the visitor.

'Where in God's name did you get those sorry creatures?'

'A nice man from Sørvágur sold them, at a very good price,' Elsebeth said with a smile. 'They are pedigree, I believe.'

'Pedigree?' Ganting shook his head then pulled a can from the pocket of his trousers. Snus. Chewing tobacco, imported from Sweden. He popped a wad beneath his top lip and looked at Haraldsen. 'This is a decent-sized pod of blackfish from what I hear. Perhaps forty or more. Someone new to this . . .'

'I leave the fishing and the blood to you,' Haraldsen told him. 'I'm there to see the rules are followed. Nothing more.'

He slapped Ganting on the arm. The fisherman was a hefty fellow. Taller than Haraldsen with a serious face, half-hidden by a grizzled brown-and-grey beard. He wore a blue canvas shirt and yellow oilskins. A long whaling knife that looked a hundred years old sat in a leather sheath on his left side, the curved blade clearly visible. On his right a marine VHF radio. It squawked then. Ganting answered, and spoke so quickly it was hard to catch the words.

'Well then,' he said when he was finished, 'these whales are ours for the taking if we want them, Mr District Sheriff. All it awaits is a word from you.'

'I'll get dressed,' Haraldsen said. 'And consult the books.'

'The books,' Ganting muttered. 'No time for books. If we're to drive them we must know now. There'll be every boat in Djevulsfjord needed for this job.' A pause. 'Are you happy with that, man?'

Haraldsen checked his email daily. If the ministry had cause to demand hunting be reduced in number or abandoned altogether the news would be communicated to every district sheriff throughout the islands. No such missive had arrived.

'I am unaware of any reason why this opportunity should be allowed to pass,' Haraldsen replied. 'You?'

'None at all,' Ganting said and finally allowed himself a smile.

Haraldsen declared he had to go inside to change and make a telephone call. Ganting watched him leave, then doffed his blue fisherman's cap to Elsebeth.

'I apologise, Mrs Haraldsen. I'm a simple fisherman, rude of demeanour and manners too. I never wished you good morning.'

She laughed and said he was forgiven.

'Grind, you see. It's food. It's money. It's—' he winked – 'why we're here. Will you be joining us now too?'

'If I'm welcome,' she said.

A moment he hesitated then said, 'Of course.'

THE THOMSENS LIVED IN an old sea captain's house just a few steps up from the quay. It was one of the few homes in Djevulsfjord with two floors. Dorotea had the upstairs front room set for tea. From there the place had the best view of the village. Out to the little harbour. Along the fjord to the Atlantic. She could see the long finger of grey cliffs that led on both sides of the water. The ridge on the left, the village side, on the way to Selkie Bay, was known as the Lundi Cliffs, *lundi* being Faroese for puffin. They were the point at which the dwindling foothill of Árnafjall, the peak that separated Djevulsfjord from the rest of Vágar, met the raging sea. A spider's web of winding fell paths led up from the harbour to the cliff's edge and ran round to Selkie Bay.

In season the men would go *fleyging* there, fishing the sky to catch puffins for the pot, stretching a hand net between two rods above the stone hides set there for this purpose, then trapping the little parrot-like birds in flight, hundreds on a good day. Dorotea Thomsen believed she prepared the best puffins in Vágar. Smoked. Stuffed with sweet cake, fruit and spices. Soaked in milk or beer then boiled. In the commercial kitchen she'd had her husband George build out back she would bring in hired help for long hours cooking the birds, selling them on in Sørvágur for a hefty profit. Sometimes she would do the same with gannet chicks which had a good market too once her team of local women, paid the very minimum, split the little fledglings end-to-end, took out the ribcage, head, neck, and stomach, then pickled the tiny carcasses in brine.

It was all sound income, for her at least. Especially the gannets if they could persuade some men to make the extra effort to hunt for the tiny chicks. Not that income was a necessity. Baldur Ganting may have possessed some social authority as the leader of the harbour fleet, but the money lay with the Thomsens. While most in Djevulsfjord struggled for a living, they never went without. George's family had been a kind of aristocracy in the hamlet for

13

a century or more. He'd inherited most of the good agricultural acreage along the fjord and running up to the mountain. Almost every smallholder in the area leased their fields and some their homes from the Thomsens and paid a steady rent or found themselves evicted. Dorotea ran the single village shop, a small business that sold everything from milk to batteries and rope from a converted warehouse near the quay. Between the two of them they had the monopoly of local commerce.

A good number of their tenants were in arrears that hard summer. But the sound outside the window, the horns, the hubbub of animated voices, told Dorotea Thomsen there was no need to worry about being paid. The premises out back were set up to process the harvest of the sea as well as that of the air. Whale meat and blubber aplenty when the grind warranted it. A tenant farmer too lazy or talentless to make his fields work might pay off a little of his debts by offering his portion of the skinn. There was a discount in such negotiations, naturally. A greater one than George Thomsen, a weak and over-generous man, would offer on his own.

Dorotea would put steel in his backbone then. As she had many times before.

At her window in the upstairs room she watched the growing commotion by the quay. The Mikkelsen boys came out, the smart one looking round, his chubby face full of curiosity and mischief. The stupid older brother followed, hands in the pockets of his red shorts.

'Oh you little brats,' Dorotea Thomsen murmured. 'Who really fathered you, I wonder?'

'Silas did,' said a voice behind her. 'Don't you go telling people otherwise.'

Her husband had come upstairs and she never heard him. They were a childless couple which was how she wanted it. They had married out of convenience more than anything. She wanted a better life than her peers. He felt it appropriate for his standing to be attached to a wife and none of the local women he thought more comely seemed interested in sharing his bed, in spite of all the money and relative luxury that came with it.

'You think so?' she answered with a smile. 'I would like more tea. There'll be work to be done later. Bargains to be struck when that meat and blubber come our way.'

George Thomsen was a clean-shaven man of forty-eight, one year older than his wife. Thin and a little weedy. It was good he'd inherited, she always said, for a man like him could never make his own way on the sea or in the fields.

'I don't want you making them hate us any more than they do already.'

Outside, the sound of buzzing outboards was growing, like a swarm of frantic bees gathering over the silver water. Soon the district sheriff would arrive, a new one, a town man from Tórshavn. Once this incomer gave the signal the grind would begin.

'I'll endeavour to remember that. Tea, George. And brown bread with butter and strawberry jam.' She held up her hands. They were big and strong, those of a fisherwoman which, if marriage into the Thomsen clan had not intervened, was exactly what Dorotea would have been. 'Make sure that slut Alba's earning her pay doing the pans for the kitchen. And those cutting knives too. Then we'll be swimming in blood before long and where there's blood there's money.'

'Ja,' he grunted and went back down the stairs.

Dorotea pulled her chair nearer the window and gazed at the stone harbour with its single jetty, the whole now alive with people and boats stirring, large and small.

The Mikkelsen boys watched, the smart one tapping his right foot on the cobbles, always anticipating something.

'Whose prick made that wicked little face?' she whispered to herself. 'I wonder.'

TWO

Sharp black dorsals cleaved the bright water as the boats turned and drove the pod to shore.

A good school. Two thirds adults, the rest young whales, clinging close to their mothers, alarmed at the sudden turnabout in their intentions. The pack had been skirting the mouth of the fjord when Silas Mikkelsen, out in his own boat with two local men for crew, spotted them in the churning margin where the inlet met the ocean proper.

His simple craft was small and fast. The nets for shoal fish had not yet been laid. It was an easy matter to steer round the school, take up position off the ocean side, then call up others on the VHF.

From here he could see the shallow curve of Selkie Bay. No one lived there except the mad artist woman who occasionally occupied a shack by the shore. The place was too bleak and too remote even for Djevulsfjord. The nearest real house was back at the edge of the village, the cottage that belonged to the new district sheriff, close to a fell-track that led to the Lundi Cliffs.

'I'll be wanting my share and more,' said one of the crewmen, a lout from Sørvágur who'd come out with his mate for the money. 'Grind's hard work.'

'You'll get your due,' Mikkelsen said and glared at the pair of them. 'Grind! Cut your cackle and get the gear. We'll gather more this day than we'd make in weeks.'

That shut their mouths.

He'd half-hoped there'd be whales about that morning and came out prepared. In the bows of the craft sat the necessary equipment. There were heavy stones fastened on lines to splash noisily in the waves, driving the school landwards until they beached on the stretch of rough sand along from the quay. More loose rocks for deterring any lead whale that might try to break free. They'd probably be needed too. A pod was like a herd of sheep. His father had drummed that into him when he was a child, ready to puke in the heaving family boat, rolling on the rough seas. The creatures had no individual sense of action, only a communal belief that together they would be safe, and apart in peril. Shoo them ashore with noise and boats and mashing water and they'd strand themselves there, ready to die together too.

He had the equipment for that last part of the journey as well. Blunt blowhole hooks attached to sisal ropes that could be inserted into the wheezing gap in the whale's head and used to drag them through the surf to the sand and shingle. The slender spear that would kill them, severing the spine and with it the artery to the creature's brain, all with a single swift strike one hand's width behind the blowhole, a quick and easy death or so it was hoped. And whaling knives, long-handled, vicious old things, sharp as a razor, ready to finish quickly any that lingered.

The cloth he'd run up on the boat mast was tradition. The rules enforced by the district sheriff demanded it. Fifty years before, it was the only signal the fishermen knew. But now they had VHF radios – mobile phones rarely worked reliably on the waves – and could summon others in minutes. From what Silas Mikkelsen could see there were a good six boats casting off for sea already, looking to profit from this calm and sunny day. Word of grind always spread like diesel on water. Men would sail in from Sørvágur and villages beyond, all for a chance to take some meat and blubber home. And in their wake busy women, ready with their butchery blades, hungry for the taste of fresh whale, something they'd grown up with on Vágar, a treat they'd never want to miss.

The radio on his hip buzzed.

'We have permission,' Ganting said through the crackles.

'Of course,' Silas Mikkelsen replied. 'Why wouldn't we?'

A pause then Ganting added, 'Permission is needed. Do this every inch by the book, boy. Haraldsen's new to these parts.' He laughed and that was rare. 'For God's sake he was mowing his roof when I turned up! In his pyjamas! I ask you.'

'I doubt the fellow's a fool.'

'Never said he was,' the older man snapped back. 'You follow the law when it comes to getting those blackfish ashore and in our larders. I want no trickery, no unnecessary cruelty. These creatures die for our benefit. We give them due respect, just as our fathers did before us.'

Ganting and Mikkelsen's old man had been great friends. In a way Baldur had been a kind of father after he died. Until the marriage fell to pieces.

'Ja,' Mikkelsen said.

'Will they turn?' Ganting asked.

Silas Mikkelsen scanned the pod. Two more boats had come to join him, blocking the school's entry back to the open sea. If the whales had the least bit of sense they could swim around these little craft as easily as a bird might fly from an approaching pack of cats. But nature was nature. They clung together and were easily herded. Just like puffins flying so easily into the fleyging net. Meat was put there for a reason. To refuse to harvest it was as close to a sin as he might imagine.

'They will turn,' Mikkelsen said. 'I could do that with the boat I have alone.'

'Ach!' Ganting grunted over the crackly call. 'And steal for yourself all the glory. I am foreman, the sheriff's voice in these proceeding. You will wait for the others. They come soon. I don't want this lot lost when they get to the Skerries like last time.'

The rocks at the mouth of the inlet were always the tricky part. The sound and splashing of the waves against them could easily turn the pod back to the sea if there were insufficient craft to keep driving the school ashore.

'I am aware I failed you then,' Mikkelsen said. 'And in so many other matters also.'

They never spoke about Alba any more. Life was easier that way.

'So bring that pod in,' Ganting told him. 'Lord knows we need it.'

THE HARBOUR WAS SO busy they had to leave the truck at the back of the shop. Ganting took a canvas bag out of the back then grabbed a metal spear and a large hook attached to a rope. By the time they got to the waterfront the quayside was milling with people, full of a party spirit as if this were a picnic or a holiday.

'Silas has got them past the Skerries. It would take a proper fool to lose them now,' Ganting said as he scanned the inlet.

Haraldsen shielded his eyes against the bright sun and peered at the fjord. Elsebeth did the same. It looked for all the world as if a pack of nautical sheepdogs was herding a flock of black, gleaming bodies through the low grey sea towards the narrow strip of sand between the quay and the Lundi Cliffs. The school stretched a good two hundred metres across, fins cutting through the waves as the pilot whales bobbed up and down, retreating from the oncoming craft. Sometimes one would turn and try to head for the open sea. But the men on the boats were lifting and dropping their stones on ropes, some lobbing rocks too. The racket and the threat of violence soon deterred them. That and leaving the supposed safety of the pod.

'There are young ones,' Elsebeth said, a little worried. 'Must they all die?'

Ganting seemed puzzled by the question.

'They live as a family. They perish as a family. How else? If any manages to escape it's our duty to chase it down and kill the creature as gently as we can. Better than to leave it wandering the open seas alone, only to starve and beach itself on rocks somewhere. You are town people. Perhaps you don't understand. This is a harvest. We kill with kindness. But we kill. We kill them all. No man or woman can live in a place like Djevulsfjord unless they take a life from time to time.'

He hesitated then turned to Haraldsen.

'On which subject I must say something. Please excuse my frankness. It is a fault of mine, I know.'

'No,' Haraldsen replied. 'You must speak your mind.'

'It concerns those sheep you've been sold without full knowledge of their upkeep. That building at the back of your cottage. You know what it is?'

'Ja,' Haraldsen told him. 'An abattoir. Though principally I use it as a shed . . .'

'The fact we have an abattoir does not mean we must slaughter things in it!' Elsebeth intervened. 'We moved here for peace and silence—'

'Some beast of yours must be slaughtered for winter mutton,' Ganting interrupted. 'If sheep were never killed there'd be no point in keeping them, now would there? Besides if you don't take them soon the little things become too old and the best you can hope for is fat and gristle, scarce fit to eat. Sheep are not pets. Not for us. You do the creatures no favour to treat them as such.'

Haraldsen had thought about this already. There were butchers in Sørvágur that would do the job, and salt and dry the meat too. It made a tasty, traditional Faroese supper for the meagre months of winter.

'I will help you,' Ganting added. 'Show you how it's managed. The killing and the treatment.'

'We do not—' Elsebeth began.

'Thank you,' Haraldsen interrupted. 'Let's talk of this later.'

A slim young woman in a knitted patterned jumper and jeans walked over, smiling, holding out her hand.

Haraldsen took it without knowing why.

'You are the district sheriff,' she said with a marked Danish accent.

'I am,' Haraldsen agreed. 'And this is my wife Elsebeth. Tristan Ganting . . .'

She laughed. A striking woman he thought. Her hair was blonde and long and curly. Her eyes bright blue and intelligent. There was a stud in her left nostril, though. Something Haraldsen found odd, a little too cosmopolitan for Vágar.

Odder too when she said, 'Hanna Olsen. I'm the area police officer. It's time we met.'

Ganting smiled and nodded.

'We know one another already. Not through business,' he added quickly.

'No,' the policewoman agreed. 'What business is there in Djevulsfjord anyway? Such a peaceful little place.'

'You're not on duty,' Ganting said. 'So why trouble yourself here?'

'Grind!' she cried. 'Who'd miss it?' She shrugged her slim shoulders. 'I was taking a stroll round Selkie anyway.' Then came a smile so direct he couldn't ignore it. 'June I turned up here and not a single whale hunt since. This is my first. Am I not welcome?'

'Grind,' Ganting replied. 'Everyone is welcome. Whether to participate or not.' He wagged a finger at her, jokingly it seemed. 'But only the participants get a share of the skinn.'

'I wish to observe,' she told him. 'Nothing more.'

'Except for the district sheriff, of course,' he added. 'He gets two per cent and doesn't need to lift a finger.'

Haraldsen laughed.

'That's what the rules say. And I will obey them to the letter. But on that point . . .'

Ganting screwed up his eyes. They were heavy, lined, careworn from the sea perhaps.

'You don't want your share?'

'Just a little,' Elsebeth suggested. 'There are only the two of us.'

'And one long winter coming,' the man pointed out.

'A taste will do,' Haraldsen said. 'The rest I put back into the pot to be divided among the rest of you.'

Ganting did not seem a man who stepped outside tradition lightly.

'You'll kill a whale for us though, won't you?' He lifted the spear in his right hand, the blowhole hook in his left. 'I'll show you how. Man . . . we cannot have a district sheriff who's too squeamish to do the job himself.'

'Ja,' Haraldsen agreed, after a moment. He took the spear in his hand, weighed it. 'I'll try.'

'That's something then.'

Ganting led him inside the fishing sheds to find the right clothing. A few minutes later both men reappeared ready for the final act in the brief and violent drama now starting all around them. Both in full-length yellow oilskins, waterproof from boots to chest.

Just a hundred metres offshore the channel was alive with the thrashing of the doomed pod. By the time Haraldsen followed the crowd to the stretch of dun, coarse sand beside the towering cliffs the first young whale was beaching on the shore.

'MAM'S GOT HER EYES on us,' Benjamin said as they stood at the edge of the crowd, watching the thrashing and frightened shoal of blackfish getting pushed and prodded towards the strand.

'Mam's got her eyes on us,' Jónas muttered, mocking him. 'No she ain't. She's in that old bitch Thomsen's kitchen, you idiot. You're so stupid. Don't know nothing at all. Nothing . . .'

'I know I'm older,' his brother grumbled.

'Fat lot of good that does you. Goat.'

Jónas remembered the last grind clearly. Their dad was still at home then. They lived in his cottage, not far from Grandfather Ganting. Plenty of rows at night, about things a child couldn't understand. But he knew what a slap sounded like. He'd had plenty from his father himself and they were a lot worse than the pathetic little bats of the hand he got from his big brother when he taunted him.

The last time the whales came ashore all the misery that hung about their lives like a black cloud seemed to vanish. People began drinking, got happy. That night there'd been sounds from the bedroom adjoining theirs, mysterious noises, both happy and savage, that he hadn't heard in a long while.

And all because the whales came. Stupid, black, writhing creatures that fled the deep ocean where they belonged and beached themselves upon the gritty shingle alongside the Lundi Cliffs. It was as if the knives the grown-ups used to cut them leaked healing blood all over Djevulsfjord. Something red and sticky that fed into everyone and briefly made them whole.

That time Jónas had stolen into the fishing huts and found an old whaling knife. He'd crept through the forest of legs in the bloody water looking to slash and cut some meat and blubber for himself. What remedy came from these dying whales was surely his to have too.

But the district sheriff at the time, Kristian Djurhuus, a surly bugger, spotted him, came over, grabbed the blade, clipped his ear and told him to clear off back to the quay. A dead man not long after. When he heard the old sod was gone Jónas dreamed of the day they'd bury him beneath the turf in the graveyard by Djevulsfjord's white-boarded wooden church. When the service was done he could go up to the simple headstone, the tiny bunch of flowers someone had left on it, spit at the name and dance on the fresh-turned soil. But Djurhuus came from Denmark it seemed. So they took him back there in a coffin.

And now a new man had turned up. A townie from Tórshavn, as good as a foreigner. A chap who smiled a lot and once gave Jónas a five krónur coin in return for a little banter about how his big motor caravan might get scratched if he wasn't careful. Enough for a couple of sweets. Better than the old one though.

What he really wanted was a blade again. A good one like his grandfather's. A proper whaling knife with a wooden haft and a leather sheath, bronze and silver inlays on a cutting edge long enough to stick in the whale's neck and sever its spine. The kind of thing that got passed down in families. Real families. Grandpa Ganting had got his that way.

But Silas Mikkelsen had only a cheap modern blade and barely spoke to them anymore. No real whaling knife to be proud of was likely to be his.

'Mam said to stick together,' Benjamin grumbled.

'So what?' Jónas grunted and pushed at the bodies ahead of him, small sharp elbows forcing a way through, ignoring all their complaints.

Benji would follow. He always did. If there was nothing else to do he'd get his brother mad again and watch the fun that happened when his fists and arms began to fly.

Close to the front of the crowd Jónas could see the first of the whales stranded on the beach, a tall man placing a hook in its blowhole, getting ready with the lance.

Things got frantic around this time. Maybe it was the blood but people forgot themselves. Did things they'd never think of normally.

Benji was behind him looking a little lost, frightened even in the crowd. When he was like that it only took a word to tip him over the edge.

Not now though. There was better fun to be had. Better things to do soon as well.

On the pebbles by the water's edge, close to a man's feet, sat a bright and shiny whaling knife. Someone must have put it down to go into the surf and help with the hooks and spears.

Jónas Mikkelsen stared at the thing, its fine wooden handle, the soft, worn leather slip for the wrist, the ornate sheath that kept the edge safely hidden. He bent down, picked it up, withdrew the long blade. Bronze and silver there and carvings of fish and whales leaping through waves.

'Not yours,' Benji told him, pushing through the forest of legs to get close to him.

The water was lapping at their feet, cold as it worked through the cheap shoes from the charity shop. A pink stain of blood appeared in the swell of the tide, like paint swirling through water. Soon the bay would be scarlet with the death throes of the pod.

Jónas sheathed the knife and tucked it under his jacket, into his belt.

'Is now, goat,' he said and pushed back into the crowd.

SILAS MIKKELSEN DROVE THE blackfish on, slapping his stone in the water like every other man in the boats, chasing the school ashore. As big a crowd as he'd ever seen now waited on the beach. Plenty of help to dispatch the school quickly. Plenty of hands to cut and butcher for the skinns.

A few of the leading whales had already stranded themselves on the shingle where the sand ran out into rocks. Men were in the water with them, stabbing at the struggling creatures with their blowhole hooks. Two had their spinal lances out already, working their way round to make the sudden, savage puncture that, if delivered correctly, would render the creature unconscious in a second or two, then leave it open to the kill.

His radio buzzed. Mikkelsen swore at the distraction but answered anyway. It could only be one man: Baldur Ganting. His father-in-law saw himself as the head of the village and not just when it came to the grind.

'Yes?' he said briskly.

'This goes well, Silas. Congratulations.'

'I'm glad you approve. Now may I return to my business?'

'Remember what I said about the rules. The new district sheriff is a stranger to us.'

'I know the rules, Baldur! Why would I break them?'

He could make out faces on the shoreline. It looked as if Jónas and Benjamin were there, drifting through the crowd. The dim lad would come to no harm. He hadn't the wit to find it. Unless Jónas started him ticking again . . .

'My sons are loose down there,' Mikkelsen added. 'Did you know that?'

A pause then Ganting said, 'I have other cares at the moment than your children.'

'Me too. And I see no sign of your daughter. Maybe . . .'

A click and the radio went dead. Mikkelsen's crewmen knew their work. The boat was close into the strand, beginning to ground noisily on the pebble and shingle. There was a strong and familiar smell of whale, like nothing else on earth. A physical marine odour quite dissimilar to fish, it overpowered the stink of diesel from their engines, the accompanying salt of the surf and the stench of rotting kelp on the nearby rocks.

Silas Mikkelsen found his lance, checked the old knife on his belt. Then, balancing like a dancer, he walked to the bobbing bows, put one foot on the prow, and stepped out into the sea.

ON THE EDGE OF proceedings Elsebeth stood and chatted with Hanna Olsen, a charming young woman who, though a newcomer herself, knew everyone it seemed. The police officer introduced Father Lars Ryberg the village priest, a burly man, forties, perhaps a fit fifty, grey-bearded like a figure from the Old Testament and with a sourness Elsebeth associated with a certain type of pastor. Introduced by the police officer he'd nodded once then abruptly demanded to know why the Haraldsens had yet to set foot inside his church.

'We're heathen, I'm afraid,' Elsebeth replied with all the politeness she could muster.

Ryberg glared at her quite openly.

'You mean non-believers. It's not the same thing.'

'No,' she agreed. 'It's not. I mean . . . we don't go to church. Not here. Never in Tórshavn either since both our parents died.'

'Ah,' he noted sharply. 'So when it comes to matters of the grave we do serve a purpose?'

The noise of the grind was becoming overpowering, thrashing blackfish, anxious men seeking to kill them. The stink was quite rank too, physical and cloying. It was hard to hear exactly what Ryberg said next though it sounded, to her surprise, as if there were a curse in it.

He had bright yellow waders over his clerical robe and a knife in his belt like most of the other men.

'You must excuse me,' he muttered as he went towards the water. 'I am owed my skinn as much as any fellow.'

'I fear I've upset a man of the cloth,' Elsebeth said lightly when he was gone. 'I hope his master wasn't listening.'

'Djevulsfjord's an odd, close place,' Hanna replied. 'It's easy to offend, even without trying.' She looked back towards the fell-path and the cottage there. 'You bought the old Torfasen place? Why, might I ask?'

'We love the countryside. And the coast,' Elsebeth answered, as if it were obvious. 'All our lives we've spent in Tórshavn. And loved it there, mind. We wanted a spot of adventure. Fresh air. Beautiful surroundings. It went for a very good price.'

'No one wants to live here anymore. In ten, twenty years maybe there'll be no Djevulsfjord to speak of. The life's too hard. The young have mostly gone already.'

Elsebeth smiled.

'Then the old will look after the place. And you?'

'I live in Sørvágur. This is part of my area.'

She told her story succinctly. It seemed simple enough. Her parents came from Vágar but moved to Aalborg in Denmark for work when they were young. From time to time they'd return there for holidays. Hanna had fallen in love with the place from the start. While the Faroes was an independent country within the state of Denmark, with its own language and a currency linked to the Danish krone, Copenhagen maintained control over the police service. Finding her way back to Vágar was simply a matter of joining the police in Aalborg then, when she felt like it, requesting a transfer, a move few officers wanted. The fact she spoke both Danish and Faroese meant the move was a shoo-in.

'And your . . . partner?' Elsebeth asked.

'It's not only the men who go fishing today, is it?' Hanna replied, raising an eyebrow. 'Not that pilot whales are truly such.' Her voice had turned deep, a deliberate effort to adopt the manner of Baldur Ganting. 'Being mammals. Even though we call them blackfish too.'

Elsebeth snorted.

'I'm sorry. I shouldn't have been so obvious.'

'No partner,' Hanna said and there was an edge to her words. 'Not looking. Nor wanting. Nor waiting either if I'm honest.'

This was very sensible, Elsebeth agreed. There was no rush. Hanna Olsen seemed a most level-headed young lady.

At that moment they were interrupted by Dorotea Thomsen bustling about, rubbing her hands as if she was about to do business.

'The shop,' Elsebeth said. 'I have never said, Mrs Thomsen, how grateful my husband and I are for your services. If one had to drive to town for everything—'

'I only serve for the benefit of the community,' Dorotea interrupted. 'The two of you will take part in the butchery?'

'Not me,' Elsebeth answered.

'Nor me,' Hanna added. 'I have other business.'

'And yet you are the wife of the new district sheriff, Mrs Haraldsen,' Dorotea said with a direct and judgemental stare. 'Is there no sense of responsibility?'

'On the part of my husband a great deal. That is his job after all.' She smiled with some deliberate force. 'Not mine.'

Dorotea Thomsen considered this and wondered if either of them would like to make a little pocket money by helping out chopping and boiling, preparing meat and blubber for the salting.

'I pay as much as I can afford,' she insisted. 'Fifty krónur an hour. Cash. It is . . .' She stopped for a moment. There was a cry from the crowd. One of sympathy and pity. Then the sad bellow of a creature in the sea. 'It is a village tradition.'

'What?' Hanna Olsen asked. 'Being paid fifty krónur an hour? No wonder you're the lady of Djevulsfjord!'

Dorotea Thomsen's stout frame was encased in a voluminous brown dress. Her hair was black turning grey, too long for her age. Her pale and flabby face wore much the same expression when pleased or not.

'That's a no then?'

'Just teasing,' the young policewoman answered pleasantly. 'A habit I picked up in Denmark. Sorry.'

'Oh yes,' Dorotea said with a heartfelt sigh. 'You come from there.'

And that was all.

The commotion was getting louder. Elsebeth was a little concerned they might have upset her new neighbour as well as the priest. But not so much.

She walked forward to get a better look of the beach and then her heart sank. Tristan was there, up to his oilskins in the sea. Not that it was water much anymore.

In his hands he had Ganting's long spinal lance. The severe Djevulsfjord man stood next to him in the growing gore. At their feet was a black shape, smaller than the rest and barely moving. Ganting's long hook was in its blowhole. He was speaking to Haraldsen, quite strongly it seemed to her.

Someone came to her side. Hanna Olsen with her Dane-inflected musical voice.

'Dorotea Thomsen doesn't own quite all of Djevulsfjord. Your little place is freehold, I believe. And when it comes to a voice of authority I think you'll find Baldur Ganting tends to carry more weight.'

'What's weight without money?'

'Good point,' Hanna agreed.

Not that Elsebeth was really listening.

'They're making Tristan kill a whale,' she said in a low and mournful tone.

The policewoman craned her neck to see.

'I do believe they are.'

BLOOD ON THE SAND.

Blood in the water.

Blood on the boats.

On the shore men came forward wielding their spinal lances and whaling knives, wading through the scarlet shallows, hooks in blowholes, leading the whales to shingle, stabbing them, one hand's width back from the spurting vent, hoping to deliver a quick, kind death.

As a distant, uninvolved spectator, Tristan Haraldsen had seen the grind from afar. When the district sheriff's job was first suggested to him by the police service, he'd watched videos and spent many hours reading the documentation the ministry gave him to accompany the role. He understood this was more than a hunt, a search for winter food. Grind represented a ritual, a kind of ceremonial sacrifice. One that had to be carried out with respect and responsibility, a sense of dignified intent. Since whaling in the Faroes had caught the attention of a watchful, sceptical world, the little nation had gone out of its way to prove the grind was as humane as any such process might be. More quick and compassionate than raising pigs in muddy prisons or chickens in cages where they never saw the light of day. Not that the foreigners seemed convinced, addicted as they were to convenience and food that barely resembled the creature that perished to provide it. In part the district sheriff's role was to ensure the hunt went well. For the sake of the whales and the reputation of the Faroes at large.

And here he was trying to kill an adolescent whale, failing miserably.

Ganting had led him to the nearest, a young specimen, moving sluggishly on the gritty sand, water spurting from its blowhole as it thrashed around, struggling to return to the sea. The Djevulsfjord man, as comfortable with the grind as it was possible to be, placed his hook in the blowhole and held the young whale tight on the shingle, beckoning Haraldsen to deliver the coup de grâce with his lance.

'Now, man,' he said. 'Now! One swift blow. A hand behind the spout. Strike hard, strike deep. You'll feel the spine stop your blade. Then push and snap it.'

The sounds around him – the dying wails of the pod falling on the beach, the men there, concerned the job would be done swiftly and without fuss – made his head spin. Haraldsen, not a weak man, gripped the spinal lance with both hands then tried to fix the point to the back of the blowhole as Ganting indicated.

He pushed but the spear sliced hard to one side through the creature's shining black skin and seemed to enter nothing but flesh that gave and gave. The poor whale screamed. There was no other word for it. And Baldur Ganting swore.

'You're hurting the thing, Haraldsen. Put the creature out of its misery . . .'

'I'm trying, aren't I?' the district sheriff cried. 'I never asked for this . . .'

'You want your meat but cannot pay the price to get it?'

'I'm a town man. I told you . . .'

'Strike! Strike right this time. Strike firm and stay centre for the spine.'

Another blow. The point slithered on the stricken whale's torn and bloody skin, fell to the side once more and punctured nothing but tissue, soft and yielding.

'Ach!' Ganting bellowed. 'I'll not allow this pitiful blackfish such agonies.'

He reached over, pulled the spear from the little whale's body, positioned the point between the two wounds Haraldsen had inflicted then raised his arms to gain some force and stabbed down with a brute, determined might.

'Dammit,' he grunted then took out his long knife. 'I have to use this now, Haraldsen! You see? Only in extremis under the regulations, not for cruelty . . .'

'Ja, ja,' Haraldsen told him. 'On with it, will you?'

The knife cut through skin, through blubber, through meat. The smell of blood and flesh mingled with the salt of the ocean. Gulls flapped overhead, made frantic by the slaughter. Ganting's sharp blade sliced straight to the spine and severed it. Haraldsen watched as the little whale shuddered once, a spasm running through its whole body, then was still.

Blood from the severed artery began to spurt from the wounds. Gout after livid, pouring gout. He stood back and watched, gorge rising.

'Is it gone?'

35

All around him the whales were dying. Most more quickly than his, though with no less blood. That final tremor through the long, black, beautiful body seemed to mark the end.

'Ja,' Ganting answered and left it at that.

'And if I may go back to the shore now . . .'

'There's work to do,' the man in the bloody yellow fisherman's suit snapped at him. 'No time for banter. If you can assist then do so. If not . . .'

A moment he thought about this. Then Tristan Haraldsen trudged out of the bloody water, through the crowd, to stand on the crimson beach in the midst of strangers, wondering where Elsebeth might be.

He glanced to his right. There were two boys there. Brothers he'd seen round the harbour before. The taller, stooped one stood silent, scared he thought, watching the younger wade knee-deep into the scarlet water with a whaling knife tight in his right hand. There the kid launched himself at another beached whale, a little one still wheezing on the pebbles, ignored at that moment by the busy men struggling to cope with the larger creatures.

Haraldsen could scarcely believe his eyes. The lad looked furious, stabbing at the whale himself with nothing more than a knife, slashing deep cuts into its flanks. Which would have been illegal in an adult, and was doubly wrong for a child.

'Stop!' he shouted.

He placed the lad now. A tyke who lived in a hut by the fishing sheds. The kid had begged some money not long before, in return for 'watching over' his motor caravan. He'd paid for ease of mind, not wishing to stir things with the locals.

Haraldsen looked again and felt once more a little sick. The boy wasn't trying to sever the stricken whale's spine at all. He was slashing wildly at its side, to hurt the poor thing. Red livid stripes, torn skin and blubber down to flesh, were appearing with each strike. If anyone else noticed they seemed too busy to care.

He waded back into the water, found the wild boy, gripped his shoulder and ordered him to cease this very instant.

It was as if Haraldsen wasn't even there.

'I said stop, child!' he yelled and reached out to grab the kid's arm as it came back for one more strike.

In that instant the boy looked at him with more hatred and malevolence in his dark young eyes than Tristan Haraldsen had witnessed in any creature, young or old.

A crude swear word and the blade came up. Haraldsen staggered back to the shore, clutching at his cheek. When he took away his fingers there was blood on them, and behind the familiar sting of a wound.

His cry of pain was heard. Someone came close. Then a familiar voice. Elsebeth. Through his shock Haraldsen could see she was with the policewoman, Hanna Olsen. Both of them stared at him, aghast.

'What happened?' Hanna asked.

'The boy . . . the boy . . .' He looked around. The child was gone, and so was his brother. 'I saw him stabbing the poor whale. And then he cut me . . .'

'Two of them?' the policewoman asked, professional in an instant. 'Like brothers?'

'From that shack,' he agreed pointing to the wooden lean-to by the boat sheds.

'Jónas Mikkelsen,' she said with a sudden viciousness. 'That little bastard's gone too far this time . . .'

Someone shouted, pointing to the fell-path to the Lundi Cliffs. Two small shapes there running up the zig-zag way.

'I'll fetch that little monster,' Hanna swore. 'Where's their mother when you want her?'

'No.' Haraldsen's arm came out to stop her. Elsebeth was removing a plaster from her bag. 'It's just a cut, isn't it?'

'You won't need stitches, Tristan,' his wife agreed, checking the wound.

'And you're off duty, Hanna. I've made a big enough fool of myself today.'

He glanced at the water. The sea was so red it was as if someone had emptied the arteries of the world into this little stretch of water down from the Djevulsfjord quay.

Baldur Ganting came striding out of the scummy surf towards them, his face like thunder.

'I want no more trouble—' Haraldsen began.

'Was it that grandson of mine did this?' Ganting demanded.

'Grandson . . .?'

'Ja,' Hanna Olsen broke in. 'It was, Baldur. I have asked you to control him so many times.'

'If his mother and father can't how shall I? But I'll tan the little bugger's hide when I catch him. I promise you that . . .'

'Not for me!' Haraldsen pleaded. Then more softly, 'Not for me.'

He told them what he saw. The boy slashing dreadfully at the dying whale. The fury and madness in his face.

Elsebeth came and placed the plaster on Haraldsen's cheek.

'Let's approach this with care,' he went on. 'Patiently. The child's not well. I could see that. He's a boy. The bad's not born with him. It comes from somewhere. A sickness. Let's not be rash.'

'You're a gentle type,' Ganting told him. 'I should have recognised that from the outset. Not forced you into the hunt as I did.' He took off his seaman's cap with bloodied hands. 'I apologise.'

Haraldsen nodded.

'And I should have refused when I could. I accept your apology if you'll take mine.'

Two hands stained with whale gore met.

'You're an odd one to have in Djevulsfjord,' Ganting declared with a puzzled shake of his head.

'Ja,' Elsebeth said. 'But he's an odd one anywhere if I'm honest.'

Haraldsen looked along at the bloody shoreline. Every whale seemed dead now. Perhaps embarrassed by this brief commotion the men and women with their knives were starting to look at the corpses on the shingle and measure out their skinns.

'Let's find those lads, wherever they've gone. Then we deal with this calmly, in good time, at our leisure and theirs.'

'A gentle, kindly man,' Ganting granted. 'But I'll go along with that. Let me get their father first. And their mother too if Dorotea Thomsen will excuse her from the kitchen.'

Haraldsen shielded his eyes against the sun and tried to catch those two little figures on the winding path to the cliffs where the puffin were trapped.

There was nothing there now. No sign of them at all.

Can't be far away, he thought to himself, unaware how wrong he would be.

THREE

Just before seven, dusk began to fall like an ink stain seeping out of a sky that seemed to stretch forever. Within the space of an hour the Northern Lights emerged, casting their eerie, garish spectrum on the men spreading out to march across the many twisting paths on the Lundi Cliffs all the way to Selkie Bay. Faint at first, a hazy green streak like the contrail of a celestial airliner or the sweep of a giant child's luminescent paint brush, the Lights stood over them all, majestic, distant, cold. But as night made its tentative descent the colours became more marked and the vault above the still and silent world more lurid. Icy blue sheets seemed to spread from just above the horizon to the very pinnacle of the firmament. Then a crimson stretch emerged behind them, a cruel reflection of the bloody water now leaching away on the Djevulsfjord strand.

High on the fell-path, criss-crossing the hillside yet again, Tristan and Elsebeth Haraldsen found themselves looking back to the bay. The stripped carcasses of dead whales lay half-sunk in the sea, ghostly white skeletons in the odd light, as if a museum had cast its natural history collection of bones upon the strand. The tide was coming in. Some of the corpses would vanish into the fjord as it retreated. Others would have to be cleared in the morning. The island had no predators to speak of, no foxes or wolves or wild cats. Only brown rats or dogs on the loose would be gnawing the last of the meat and blubber off the skeletal remains. Forty-nine blackfish, Haraldsen remembered. He was the district sheriff. They had to tell him that.

'Tristan,' his wife gasped as they came to a breathless halt at the top of a narrow and clearly little-used path back to the height of the cliffs. 'Stop. Please.'

'There must be somewhere we haven't looked,' he said.

She stood in front of him and folded her arms. The curious lights, green and blue and red, coloured the face he'd loved for thirty years, ever since they first met at that dance in distant worldly Tórshavn. The policewoman, Hanna Olsen, had accompanied them for part of their journey that evening before being called away to take a message from headquarters. At one point, trying to make conversation as the stars began to dot the sky, she'd asked how long the two of them had been married.

Without thinking, Haraldsen had answered, 'Forever.' And happy to be so, he'd added before she took his blurted-out statement the wrong way. There was a kind of logic behind the words too. He didn't really remember the time before Elsebeth. Back then he'd only been half a man. It was only meeting her, marrying her, feeling the warmth of her presence in his life, that he'd finally felt himself something close to whole.

'We're on our own. Half-lost, and were one of us to stumble or twist an ankle God knows what the other would do. Now.' She said this with her arms folded which was always a sign. 'We go down that hill. Don't we?'

There was no point in fighting a battle that was already lost.

'If you say so, my dear . . .'

* * *

41

THE SEARCH PARTIES WERE growing larger by the hour. Men and women from villages through the tunnel. Police officers, on duty and off, called in by Hanna Olsen, among them, Aksel Højgaard. He and Haraldsen had been colleagues, not quite friends in the police where Højgaard worked as a superintendent with respon- sibility for Vágar, Djevulsfjord included.

Haraldsen should have guessed he would have turned out. The man was always curious, always looking to be a part of everything that went on. So it was hardly a surprise that they found him there at the foot of the path, with Ganting, Hanna Olsen and the boys' father, talking by the harbour. Haraldsen was so exhausted after the long, strange day, he simply stared at his familiar face as if it were that of an intruder from a world they'd left behind.

'Tristan,' Højgaard said with a nod to Elsebeth too.

'How did you get here?' Haraldsen wondered.

He was a quiet, introverted chap who rarely smiled. About forty, tall, stiff-backed like a soldier, ambitious, a little cold, with a craggy face the women in the office deemed most handsome, almost like a TV actor. Not that there seemed much competition.

'This is my patch, you know. I heard Officer Olsen put out a call on the radio.'

He looked up and down the cliffs in a way that suggested he was no stranger to the wilds of Djevulsfjord. Højgaard was a bachelor and had found his way into the bedrooms of a good number of Tórshavn ladies before he moved to Vágar, or so gossip had it. Not a man to be tied down.

'Two boys missing in wild countryside,' he added. 'It's scarcely a rare event out here.' He pulled a pack of cigarettes out of his pocket and lit one. 'The mother says Jónas has stayed away from home a bit of late, you know. Out on the hills. The weather's good for September. There's no reason to believe they're in some kind of peril.'

'This is enough,' his wife said. 'Tristan shouldn't be exposed to this kind of strain. His heart . . .'

'Don't start, dear,' Haraldsen insisted.

'We're going home.'

'You may as well,' Baldur Ganting said. 'The lads will sleep out then slink back when they're hungry. As Højgaard says. It's not the first time. When I was their age I'd go out for nights on end on those fells. Part of growing up.'

Silas Mikkelsen, the boys' father, was on the phone to someone on the cliffs. Their mother, Alba, had gone off with one of the other search parties scouting around the area near the tunnel.

'How can I go home?' Haraldsen asked. 'This is my fault.'

Silas Mikkelsen finished his call and stared at him, his face narrow, sad, resigned in the odd evening light.

'No one blames you, man. We know these hills and pathways. You don't.'

'Those lads are always a handful,' Ganting added then popped a slug of snus under his top lip. 'Jónas especially. He cut you . . .'

Haraldsen tore the plaster from his cheek. The wound didn't even bleed.

'It was a scratch. He's a child. I want to—'

'Go home,' Ganting repeated, in the tone that Elsebeth had used earlier, one that brooked no argument.

Hanna Olsen was watching.

'I think that's a good idea, Tristan,' the policewoman said.

'And how long will you look?' he wondered.

Aksel Højgaard's eyes strayed to the cliff edge.

'We'll have people out here as long as the light lasts. Another hour or two. After that we resume in the morning when it's safe. Your first grind today. It went well?'

'It did,' Ganting cut in before Haraldsen could object. 'Very well indeed.'

Højgaard nodded.

'Good. You're here to look after the fishing when it happens, Tristan. Back in Tórshavn you sat behind a desk. Scouring these hills is a job for local men and those of us in the police.' He frowned and Haraldsen realised: he was a good-looking fellow. He could see why the women liked to look at him. There was an air of solitariness about him, of mystery too. 'The boys will doubtless turn up in the morning all shame-faced and sorry for themselves.'

'I'll tan their bloody hides when I get hold of them,' Silas Mikkelsen grumbled.

Ganting, his father-in-law, stayed silent. There was a gloomy cast in his features Haraldsen found worrying. That and the fact the mother was absent entirely, clearly determined to be nowhere near her husband.

But he did as they said anyway. Taking Elsebeth's hand, Haraldsen walked with her down the zig-zag path, back to the little cottage where he'd begun that day mowing the roof in his black pyjamas, thinking then how lovely this land was, how it appeared destined to be a paradise for the years ahead.

LIGHTS WERE ON IN the village. Some, it seemed, had shunned the search parties to deal with their skinns. At the back of the Thomsen house the illumination seemed the greatest. Dorotea would be working there, Haraldsen imagined, driving on the small group of hired workers to handle the mountain of meat and blubber they'd soon be selling throughout the Faroes. Their own two per cent part of it probably. He'd declined every piece, insisting the meat go back into the communal pot for general distribution, much to the disgust of some of the locals who'd heard.

On a normal grind this would have been a time for celebration. He'd seen this briefly before when they travelled outside Tórshavn. Every door would be open, passers-by, complete strangers even, invited into the kitchen for fresh boiled whale flesh and beer.

There'd be songs. Perhaps even, in the village hall, the communal round dance if the dwindling village could put together the numbers.

Not now. Two Djevulsfjord boys had vanished. And for the life of him Tristan Haraldsen couldn't dispel the idea that he was somehow responsible. Not for prompting Jónas Mikkelsen to flash his blade at him. But because the ritual had found him wanting. The district sheriff was a failure, a man who botched something every soul in Vágar knew was a duty, part of an ancient ceremony that defined who they were: the killing of a beached whale, a living, breathing creature forced ashore to die.

AS THEY APPROACHED THE cottage Elsebeth pulled out a torch. In the velvet darkness they could just make out the silhouettes of the chickens waiting patiently by their coop. He went over, opened the door and let them in. The wire netting was principally to keep out rats, preventing them from eating the eggs. And to deter any stray dog that fancied hen for supper. Not that Haraldsen had seen any.

Elsebeth followed him. As he stopped to watch the four sheep in the little field behind the house, sprawled asleep on the wiry grass, she hooked her arm through his.

'Ganting reckons I need to kill them soon,' he said glancing at the little brick building at the end of the plot. 'That's what the abattoir's for. Not a shed to keep our stuff from Tórshavn.'

She shook her head and he couldn't stop staring at her. Elsebeth looked so beautiful in the strange light from the sky.

'Baldur Ganting's a local man. He lives the way they've always lived. We came here to be among them. Not to think we're the same.'

He put out a hand and stroked her soft cheek.

'Perhaps that's not as easy as we thought.'

'It was a bad day, husband,' she said, a little impatiently. 'They happen. Those boys will turn up. At least one of them's a rascal and known for tricks like this.' She took his fingers and squeezed them. 'Put this behind you. As for the district sheriff post, Ganting should never have expected that of you in the first place. It's not your job to kill whales. You're there to make sure they do it properly.'

Something the priest Lars Ryberg had told him as they tramped the green fell that night came back to him.

'Do you know how it got its name? Devil's Fjord?'

She thought about this.

'I assumed it's because of the location. The Skerries at the mouth of the inlet. The rough sea they get sometimes. Must be a devil of a place to live if you're a fisherman. Their faces rather suggest that, don't they?'

Haraldsen had thought this too. But he was wrong.

'No. Father Ryberg told me when we were out searching. That's not why.'

The way the priest had come out with this was curious. Haraldsen had never asked. Ryberg had simply looked at the Northern Lights emerging above them, green and scarlet by that time, and told him.

'They have a myth . . .'

'Oh for pity's sake,' she said with a laugh, leading him back to the cottage. 'Vágar's full of myths. You know why Selkie Bay's so called?'

'I do not.'

'Because of some old story about a seal washing up there, taking off her skin, and underneath was a beautiful, naked woman. With whom one of the local fishermen fell in love on the spot, fetching ladies being hard to come by hereabouts.'

'You excepted.'

She grinned and tugged him towards the cottage.

'Compliment taken, thank you. They're country people here, Tristan. Dare I say it . . . simple folk. They believe things the rest of us laughed away long ago.'

'What happened to the Selkie?'

Elsebeth pushed open the back door. It was never locked. Why bother?

'The fisherman adored her so much he built a cage for her, since he knew that one day she'd pine for her seal's fur and the ocean. Together they lived happily and had seven children, all of them with webbing between their fingers and their toes.'

Into the kitchen. The kettle went on. No new email on the laptop, a window into an outside world which seemed quite foreign at that moment.

'And?' he asked, finding himself a biscuit.

'And one day the fisherman decided their love was so strong a cage was a cruel and unnecessary thing to keep man and wife and family together. So he took it to pieces, went out back and wrought the thing into fencing for his sheep.'

Another biscuit. She was watching the kettle boil, not looking at him.

'This story will not end well,' Haraldsen murmured.

'For the Selkie it does. When the fisherman returned from selling his catch in Sørvágur she'd gone. Her naked skin was on the kitchen floor. And wet marks leading to the open door. Paw prints of a seal. She'd removed her human guise and the fur grew again, you see. Because that was what she really was. A creature of the ocean. And that's how Selkie Bay got its name.'

She poured water over the tea bags then came and kissed him once on the lips.

'Let's go to bed,' Elsebeth said.

'If you promise not to shed your skin. Ever.'

'Ever.' She smiled. 'This prison is too comfortable. And your story?'

'Father Ryberg's.'

'His then.'

Haraldsen picked up his mug and deposited the tea bag in the bin. They did this every night. The folk of Djevulsfjord weren't the only ones with rituals.

'One day God and Satan were fighting in the heavens. The little people on Vágar could see. It was why the sky was bright with all those strange lights.'

'So much for the Aurora Borealis,' Elsebeth noted. 'And science.'

'This was before science,' Haraldsen explained. 'Before Latin came here too.'

'And?'

'The Archangel Michael was God's champion in this battle. He smote Satan with his sword. Hit him so hard the Devil was cast out of Heaven and struck Vágar with such force the bony edge of his wing cleaved through solid rock as he landed, making that channel outside our door today. So we live in the Devil's Fjord, you see. The place Satan made for us. Somewhere he's never truly left.'

She held up her mug with both hands in a kind of toast.

'I think a geologist might have something to say about that, don't you?'

'True,' he agreed. 'Not that we number many geologists among our neighbours.'

That made Elsebeth think.

'We have so few. All the young are fleeing, aren't they?'

'A man wants a wife and no modern lass from elsewhere's going to come here, I guess.'

'We only looked at the outside when we came here. Not the in.'

A sharp observation. She saw so much more than him.

'Which was my fault. It was my enthusiasm . . .'

'*Our* enthusiasm,' she corrected him.

'Ours then.' A pause. 'I prefer your story to mine. At least there's some love there.'

'Time for bed, Haraldsen. Your black pyjamas. Remember?'

For the first time in hours his face brightened.

'Pyjamas! And tomorrow, when those boys are safe home from their escapades, I will finish mowing the roof as a man should.'

Minutes later they lay in the big double bed they'd had shipped from Tórshavn. It was so peaceful listening to the night birds, the snoring of the sheep and a few faint voices in the distance as the search for Jónas and Benjamin Mikkelsen came slowly to a close.

After a while the evening turned silent, or as near to it as the invisible wildlife of Djevulsfjord would allow.

Still he couldn't sleep and nor could she.

FOUR

The next morning was bright and a little chilly. Tristan Haraldsen, still in his black pyjamas, bare feet cold on the wet grass, stood outside his small, brick slaughterhouse, drowning in thoughts both concrete and abstract. Notions so absorbing he had not yet got around to sucking on the meerschaum pipe clenched between his teeth, on the orders of Elsebeth and his doctor entirely absent of strong black tobacco save for the lingering smell.

The sheep were out of their pen, grazing, chuntering the way they did when they were happy. The chickens were loose too. It seemed just another morning in Djevulsfjord. Yet this small, insulated world had altered overnight, in ways he had yet to comprehend.

'Tristan.'

Elsebeth's quiet, concerned voice broke the daydream. She slipped beside him. Her hand came and took his.

'Now listen to me, husband. You're in your nightclothes. Nothing on your feet. Like this you'll catch your death of cold. Come inside. Have coffee. Breakfast. Then we'll walk into the village.'

'The Mikkelsen boys . . .'

His voice was muffled by the old briar he was chewing as he spoke.

'If they're not home already I'll warrant they will be soon. Hunger drives on little chaps like that.'

She came closer still and kissed his cheek. Soft lips on morning bristle.

'What need have I of children when I've got you?' she whispered in his ear.

He laughed. In part because she expected it. Then, still thinking, he tiptoed across the sodden grass, though it soaked the thick pyjama bottoms, as he followed his wife inside.

TWENTY MINUTES LATER HARALDSEN, now shaven, hair combed and in his day clothes of thick brown corduroy trousers and heavy plaid shirt, walked by his wife's side, holding hands as was their habit. They needed milk. They also craved information.

Dorotea Thomsen stood behind the counter as usual. The grocery van from Sørvágur had yet to arrive. The little warehouse by the harbour stank of boiled whale and the proprietor's equally formidable perfume. Fat arms leaning on the till, dressed in a billowing white shirt and black trousers, eyeing the quay outside, she seemed to have nothing to do but talk.

Father Ryberg was the only other soul in the store when they arrived. He bought the last loaf there, got it half price when he complained the bread was two days old, then started to rifle a stack of old newspapers and magazines for more bargains.

Through the window of the wooden shack Haraldsen and his wife could see Baldur Ganting in the cabin of his grey-and-white, twin-engine fishing boat, the *Alberta*. Silas Mikkelsen stood working on the deck, handling ropes as if they were preparing to cast off.

'Shiny boat old man Ganting's got there,' Dorotea said after she told them the milk would be another hour, maybe more. 'All bought with someone else's money, of course. I do so hope he can pay it back. So long as we get the field rent too, of course.'

The priest sniffed and chose a copy of a celebrity magazine. With his tidy grey beard he seemed a touch fearsome.

'A man must learn to live within his means,' Ryberg muttered.

'And pay his debts,' Dorotea added. 'We're still waiting on you settling your monthly charges, Father.'

He didn't like that.

'The church is a tardy payer. For the very good reason that its congregation is so mean. A churlish flock is its own worst enemy.'

The woman's smile broadened.

'But we're merchants. Not priests. Money makes the temporal world go round. I'm sure you appreciate that.' She reached beneath the counter and took out an old-fashioned lined accounts book then flipped through the pages, turned the thing around and tapped her finger on a long list of entries. 'I would like to draw a line through this before the week is through. God may have patience but the Almighty doesn't have bills to pay.'

Ryberg harrumphed, stumped up some coins for a popular magazine with a semi-naked pop star on the cover, lifted his beret for Elsebeth, then walked out of the shop.

'Two boys missing and the fellow never so much as mentions it,' Elsebeth said, quietly furious. 'Strange for a priest.'

'The man has a beard,' Dorotea noted. 'A cleric with all those grey whiskers around his chops. What a sight. We never had a priest with a beard before.'

They didn't know what to say.

'All the same he was out last night searching over the fells. Were you?'

'We did what we could,' Elsebeth told her.

'I heard you chased them off. Without you none of this would have happened.'

'I did not chase them off,' Haraldsen declared. His fingers strayed to the wound on his cheek. It was nothing much at all. 'There was a misunderstanding.'

'That's what it was? Father Ryberg misunderstands his ability to pay for his fripperies. And you, the newcomers from Tórshavn, struggle to understand how Djevulsfjord works. Strange it's always the foreigners who lack the simple skill of comprehension here.'

Elsebeth had already told him that something had happened with her the day before. She and Hanna Olsen had teased Dorotea Thomsen, lightly they thought. This was, Haraldsen believed, an odd and uncharacteristic mistake on his wife's part. The woman did not seem the sort to own a sense of humour except when it came to comments of her own.

'The boys,' Haraldsen asked. 'Is there any news at all?'

'One's a fool and the younger one's a thief,' she answered. 'I caught that little ragamuffin Jónas rifling through my cabinets only last week, trying to steal food right from under my own eyes.' She folded her beefy arms. 'Gave the wicked little bugger a good belt. Whacked him good and proper, then threw him out, and that simpleton brother of his.'

'I can think of no circumstances that merit the striking of a child,' Elsebeth declared. 'Why on earth would he want to steal food? The child's not likely to starve here, is he?'

Dorotea Thomsen hooted.

'How would you know about children? You've got none. Me

neither. There. We have something in common finally. That husband of mine's no use beneath the sheets either.'

'And to hit a boy without the consent of the parents,' Haraldsen complained beneath her mocking gaze.

Dorotea scowled at him.

'You think those two care? Silas Mikkelsen's too busy struggling to keep out of debt. As for Alba . . . she didn't have a word to say when I belted the little brat. Doesn't want to lose work in my kitchen, does she?'

'Last night,' Haraldsen repeated, trying to steer this conversation back on track. 'Did they find nothing at all?'

Not a trace of the boys, the woman said. And if there were she would surely have heard.

'There's parties up in the hills. The men are checking the coast again,' she added, gesturing at Ganting's boat. 'Don't see Ryberg joining them today. Probably home trimming that pretty beard of his . . .'

Mikkelsen was on the quayside, still messing with the ropes. There seemed to be some delay, one that Baldur Ganting did not appreciate.

'They think the pair of them headed up Árnafjall. If those stupid little buggers played up there at night-time God help them. Good men have gone over the Lundi Cliffs chasing puffin. Ganting picked up a body there himself a year ago.' She frowned at a memory returning. 'That was one of his own too.'

'What?' Haraldsen demanded.

'Kaspar. His son. Alba's brother and there's a tale if you ask me. Kith and kin. Nothing so close as blood they say. The story is he was wandering out there drunk or worse. Tripped. Fell.' She made a tweeting sound then mimicked a pair of wings with her stubby fingers. 'Maybe Kaspar thought he could fly like the birdies. Who knows?' She peered at them. 'You've been here how long, the two of you? A couple of weeks. You're not up on local gossip, are you?'

'No. We're not, thank you,' Elsebeth replied and dragged him outside.

THE DAY WAS BRIGHT and cold with a stiff wind off the sea and clouds the colour of a blackbird's egg. The smell of dead whale seemed stronger than ever alongside the salt marine tang, the cloying stink of rotting kelp and the sharp chemical aroma of diesel. Silas Mikkelsen finished counting notes out of his pocket. Then he set off for the pumping station.

'I swear I'm glad we never met that dreadful woman before coming here,' Elsebeth said. 'Truly I . . .'

'There's always one, love. She's hardly typical.'

'I suppose,' she admitted.

'Ganting lost a son.' Haraldsen shook his head sadly. 'And now two grandchildren are missing. No wonder the man looks at his wit's end.'

Mikkelsen was talking to the local who worked the diesel pumps. The boat's engine came to life. At a snail's pace Ganting edged along the harbour towards the fuel station.

'The father looks as if he hasn't slept a wink as well. I must do something, Elsebeth. I can't just sit here.'

She thought for a moment, then, jointly as always, they agreed. Haraldsen was to approach Baldur Ganting and offer what assistance he could. She would stay in Djevulsfjord and help where it might be needed.

'Unless you want me with you,' she added.

He looked at Ganting's longliner. The *Alberta* did seem new and expensive, befitting the foremost fisherman in the Djevulsfjord fleet.

'You know you hate boats, love.'

'I don't hate them, Tristan. It's just that they make me throw up.'

Haraldsen kissed her cheek. Then again. 'Leave the sea to me.' The smile vanished. 'I'll hope to do better than yesterday if Baldur Ganting will allow it.'

Elsebeth thrust her hands deep in her pockets as he left her, wondering if he had warm enough clothes to brave the ocean.

Djevulsfjord was one of the quietest places she'd ever known. But at that moment the peace was fractured. The brutal racket of heavy engines came from nowhere overhead. A helicopter flew low over the harbour, nose dipping as if sniffing for prey. One word on its dark blue side, 'Politi'.

The police were out in force. About time she thought.

FIVE

High on the mountain Benjamin Mikkelsen awoke, bones aching, shivering from the cold. He was in a damp cavern hidden away close to the western peak of Árnafjall, the place Jónas had led him during that long, strange night before. More tunnel than crevice, the cave now smelled of smoke and meat and damp. There was no sign of Jónas. Just the crackling of a dying fire against the rock wall ahead, flames beneath a makeshift spit. A naked, elongated body hung on it, flesh ripped from the charred limbs that hung like broken sticks above the embers.

The boy took fright, snatched one quick and careful look around, then ran for the mouth of the cave where the blue sky shone and a single gull wheeled idly against the brightness.

Just a few steps from freedom a leg came out and tripped him. Benjamin fell hard to the rough, rock floor.

'Where you going, goat?' Jónas asked, clambering to his feet out of the shadows. 'And don't you think of fighting back, either. More than me to deal with if you start trouble.'

THREE KILOMETRES AWAY, PAST the Lundi Cliffs and a steep-sided cove the locals called Freyja's Pool, by the ribbon of coal-black sand that defined the fringe of Selkie Bay, Hanna Olsen stood in uniform, rocking back and forth on the soles and heels of her heavy trainers.

Along the headland flocks of puffins swooped and rose in clouds of black-and-white dots set against the sea and sky. The Atlantic seemed peaceful on the surface but animated by a constant swell, as if the ocean resented the loss of the sleek black creatures stolen the day before. A few fishing boats dotted the horizon. Somewhere, she guessed, the white skeletons of the grind were being picked clean in the cold, clear water. Food feeding food. Elsewhere in the Faroes the clean-up after grind was more organised and controlled. But this was Djevulsfjord. The isolated little fishing hamlet ran to its own rules while the rest of the island barely noticed.

The police helicopter from Sørvágur skirted round the corner of the cliffs, banking low. Wheeling puffins scattered like dust clouds ripped apart by the force of its rotors. Then the machine turned seawards, following the line of headland out to Djevulsfjord.

Hanna had left the search party to take a look around on her own. The locals regarded her as an intruder twice over. Not one of them and police besides. She'd dressed in civilian clothes: thick wool sweater and jeans. She was lost as to what to do, where to go next. Then she heard footsteps not far away and saw Superintendent Højgaard striding across the hard shore grass. It looked like he'd been talking to George Thomsen among the men scouring the footpath along the beach. Højgaard didn't seem to be treated as an outsider at all. But then Vágar was his territory, his fiefdom. Everything that happened here must have run across his desk. Not that she'd talked to him about that much. There'd never seemed the opportunity or perhaps she lacked the courage.

He marched on until he was next to her.

'You know the weather forecast?'

Weather never interested Hanna Olsen much. There seemed little point. It always did what it liked.

'Can't say I have.'

He pointed to the western horizon. A line of puffy clouds was gathering there, grey-bottomed, innocent from afar.

'There's a storm out there. If it comes inshore we're done.'

'The Mikkelsen boys?' Hanna asked since this seemed more important. 'Any news?'

Højgaard grunted something unintelligible underneath his breath.

'If they're still out on the fells somewhere when the weather turns—' she added.

'No news my end,' he interrupted. There was a cold, hard smile on his face. 'Other than all the customary parties are out looking. What about you, Officer Olsen? Anything you want to tell me?'

BALDUR GANTING ASKED ONE question only before allowing Haraldsen on the longliner.

'Are you fine with the sea, man? Because you're best ashore if not. There's a swell on the way that'll get to the weak. It'll be worse as the day wears on. By night we'll be lucky if the ocean's fit for a boat at all.'

Then he rubbed some snus beneath his stained upper lip and waited for an answer. No, Haraldsen told him. While he had proved himself hopelessly unskilled when it came to dispatching pilot whales, he was not in the habit of falling seasick. From Tórshavn he'd used boats aplenty. The ferries to Denmark. Local pleasure craft.

'This ain't pleasure,' Silas Mikkelsen muttered. 'You had women nearly crying at the pain you put that young blackfish through.'

Nearly crying. That didn't happen easily. Not a mention of his boys. Perhaps this was the Djevulsfjord way. Avoid the obvious and the awkward always.

'I can only apologise for yesterday so many times. I'd like to help find your sons if I can.'

'The police have sent parties up in the fells,' Ganting said. 'George Thomsen is taking some men up beyond the Lundi Cliffs. Anything to get away from that evil wife of his—'

'If you don't want me,' Haraldsen interrupted. 'Just say . . .'

Ganting looked up from the open wheelhouse.

'The boat's best with three men. You'll find spare oilskins in the cabin. Do as you're told and if you feel sick make sure you puke over the side. Any of it on the deck and you clean it up yourself.'

Haraldsen said thanks and stepped on board. The two men watched as he found the heavy yellow fisherman's garments in the cabin and put them over his everyday clothes. When he came back to the deck Ganting glanced at the churning waves, and said, 'The ones in the hills look for living things. If we find something out on the sea it's likely to be bad. You understand that?'

'Ja.' Haraldsen nodded. Then, before he could think found himself saying, 'I gather it's not the first time. I mean . . . one hopes there'll be no more reoccurrences of what happened with your . . .' Stumbling over his words, shocked by the fiery gaze in Baldur Ganting's eyes, he still couldn't stop himself. 'With your son . . .'

'Cast us off,' Ganting barked at Silas Mikkelsen.

Five minutes later they were sailing past the Skerries, Freyja's Pool on their left, swelling open ocean ahead, the *Alberta* bucking up and down, side to side, like a drunken horse.

Not a word did the men say. They just scanned every inch of cliff and coastline as they went.

Tristan Haraldsen wondered if he'd be true to his word about throwing up. The chop of the police helicopter's rotors came and went, a mechanical racket above the growing howl of the wind and the low roar of the angry waves.

'Look,' Mikkelsen said eventually.

He was pointing out to sea, a gesture which, through its direction, made Haraldsen's heart sink.

Black fins sheared through the distant waves. Up and down, almost serpent-like in their gleaming sinuous motion.

'A grind lost,' the younger man moaned. 'We could have used the money them blackfish bring. This year's cursed all round.'

A SHARP STONE CAUGHT Benjamin as he careered to the floor. All he had were cheap hand-me-down shorts too small, a year too young for him. Jónas always got the better clothes like the strong denim jeans he wore now. In the bright summer light streaming through the cave mouth the older boy could see the damage the sharp flint had wrought on his bare knee: a long cut across the skin, blood welling up, dark and thick.

No crying. It was important Jónas never saw that. Tears only egged him on. Then Benji would fly at him with his fists. And lose. He always did. Always took the bait as well. Couldn't stop himself.

'Going home to see Mam now,' he muttered all the same. 'You said we could.'

The night before, getting more and more lost as they wandered up the steep fell, Jónas pushing him on, kicking him when he slowed, he'd got that half-promise out of his brother. Down the steep incline they could see the lights of the search parties, the torches sweeping everywhere, across the tough arctic grass, out to the stone hides of the puffin hunters on the cliff. Benjamin heard the men and women calling their names over the whistles of Scops owls and the timid cooing of rock doves.

The sea had been a kaleidoscopic flood of colours. Green and red from the Northern Lights. Shimmering silver from the starry sky. A few boats busied around the harbour, the beams of their lamps sweeping along Djevulsfjord, past the Skerries, out to the ocean, round to Selkie Bay. For a while he could see the lights of the village itself. There was a dim and waxy yellow glow behind the window of the old shed where they lived near the quay. Mam must have been there, crying probably. That almost made him mad enough to use his fists. But Jónas had cut someone, the newcomer, the district sheriff. They both would get the blame. They always did. So he kept up with his brother as he walked and after a while even the lights of Djevulsfjord were gone.

All that was left then was the night, the sea with its odd colours, the crisp fell with its scent of herbs and mountain water and above them the steep hillside of Árnafjall where the sharp peak cut a ragged tear out of the disc of a bright full moon.

Jónas knew where they were going. It was an hour of hard, steep walking before they came to the cave. The place was empty but hadn't been for long. There was a pile of clean, warm straw and the faintest smell of a cigarette. Jónas took most of the makeshift bed and threw a little damp hay his way. His brother somehow knew where to look for water too and recovered two packets of crisps from a hole in the rock near the back.

They had to stay hidden, or so his brother insisted and he had a kind of reason why. That way the folk down the hill, their mother, their father, all of Djevulsfjord, would know what they might lose. All those people would weep and cry for their return and hug them more tightly, love them more deeply, when they walked back down Árnafjall the next day, wide-eyed as if it were all a dream.

It seemed, to Benjamin, a high price to pay for a little affection that might soon turn bad. And he wondered who'd been in this dismal cave before, smoking a cigarette, leaving a little food behind.

The night came on. The sound of people searching the paths below receded.

'They give up easy,' his brother grumbled, then told him to sleep and never think of going outside.

Benjamin had tried to get comfortable on the hard ground, struggling to make the best of the straw he'd been given. The day had been long and odd. He was tired and still he couldn't take his eyes off the starry sky outside. Finally exhaustion closed his eyes. No dreams came. Only the bright morning and that ill-fated dash for the door.

Scrabbling on the floor now, knee bleeding, pain all down his leg, he stared at the cave mouth ten steps away. It might have been in faraway Tórshavn for all the use it was.

'Eat,' Jónas ordered. 'There's meat. Be still and take what pickings I left you.'

The smell of charred hare from the fire made his stomach rumble and ache. Jónas was good with snares and traps. He'd catch anything that moved. Mice. Rats. Sparrows. Starlings. Even once a young seal pup on the black sand of Selkie beach.

They never died quickly or easily. Not unless Mam caught him and then there was a spanking. All the same Benjamin understood there was more to this than his brother's handiwork. Someone else had brought that hare, maybe built the fire and the spit.

He rubbed at his knee to still the blood and pain and crawled across the cave floor. Most of the creature was gone, ripped in caked shreds from the carcass. There was just a bit of leg left. Jónas watched, quietly laughing, as Benjamin tried to retrieve a few shreds of dry flesh from the long charred bones.

'When do we go home?'

'When I say.'

'Need to go outside.'

'You pee and shit at the back of the cave like the goat you are. Hear me?'

It smelled as if someone had done that already.

'Mam'll be mad.'

'Mam can go screw herself. Know what that means?'

Benjamin fell silent at that. His brother might have been the younger one but all the same he'd been party to knowledge that was still beyond him. Uncle Kaspar had told him things. The two of them had been so close. There were grown-up matters Jónas understood and whispered about sometimes. Benjamin knew one thing about them only: they were dark and no good ever came from darkness. Grandpa Baldur said that and he was a man who knew right from wrong.

'When can we go home?' he asked again, trying not to sound as if he was pleading.

'When you're told,' Jónas answered, staring at the sky beyond the cavern mouth. 'And don't think you can come at me with those skinny fists of yours. I'll maybe let it look like you win when Mam's around. Not now. I'll kick your stupid head in.'

That, he realised, was true.

'Who tells us?'

'Shut your mouth.'

His brother seemed almost frightened by that question. Just a little. But that was enough to be worthy of note. Nothing scared Jónas Mikkelsen normally. Not a whack from Mam or a scolding from their dad when he could be bothered to show.

Benjamin looked at the scrap of hare meat in his hand. Leg, all sinew and leathery muscle. These tough creatures that lived on the hard bare fells could run as fast as a horse or so Grandpa Baldur always reckoned.

He could see a mark in the fibrous tissue. Maybe from the whaling knife Jónas had stolen. Or the cruel tether of the wire snare that brought this animal to their fire.

'I want to go now . . .'

'Shut up! Shut your stupid trap!'

His brother was on him straight off, scuttling across the hard rock cavern floor like a spider chasing a trapped fly.

The shiny blade of the whaling knife flashed in Benjamin's face.

'Be quiet, goat. Or you're the next I cut.'

The only noise then was from the world outside. A strange and distant racket, a thunderous chopping roar of rotors.

'That's us they're looking for,' Jónas said.

The boy bit on his meat and stared at the black wood embers of the fire. He watched his brother go to the mouth of the cave and pick up something from behind the rocks there.

It was a phone. An old one. As Benjamin watched it began to ring.

* * *

HANNA OLSEN FOLDED HER arms and went quiet as the helicopter swooped overhead. Then it vanished round Árnafjall and the clamour diminished.

'The money that thing's costing,' Aksel Højgaard moaned. 'All for those Mikkelsen toerags.'

She suspected he'd been watching her down by the harbour the day before when she was making out that was a social visit. In any case it was none of Højgaard's business. Those hours were hers, gifted to . . . what exactly? A pipe dream. A grim dark itch that refused to go away.

'Do you think those kids are dead?' he asked.

That was what some of the locals were muttering already. She'd talked to George Thomsen, a nervous man in thrall to a wife with a vicious tongue and a bullying nature. But Thomsen had grown up in Djevulsfjord. So he knew these parts, much better than she. The Lundi Cliffs, he said, were criss-crossed with wells and dangerous potholes. There were the occasional signs warning people to keep to the path. But sometimes people strayed, chasing puffins, looking at the stone mounds that were the hunting sites, all of them close to the precipitous, unguarded edge. Still, no bodies had been found. Had the brothers fallen onto the rocks below they ought to have been spotted either by the craft running out from the Djevulsfjord quay or the police helicopter that kept scanning the coastline. The gulls feeding on their corpses would surely show the way.

But on occasion it took time to locate lost parties on Vágar. Days. Weeks. Sometimes, Thomsen said, and she wondered if there was an edge to his words then, they were never seen again.

'Why did Tristan Haraldsen move here?' she wondered.

The question appeared to offend Højgaard.

'You're asking me?'

'He doesn't seem particularly suited. A town man in a place like that.'

'If he'd asked my advice I'd have told him to steer clear.' He frowned. 'Djevulsfjord doesn't take kindly to incomers. You go in that place and the way they look at you . . . They can't wait for strangers to turn round, go back through that grubby little tunnel and leave them to whatever it is they're up to. Wasting away mostly. The place is as good as dead.'

'They seem content enough with you.'

'I'm the closest thing to law they know. They don't have any choice.'

'What about me?'

He laughed. It wasn't kindly.

'I asked, Højgaard. What about me? I'm supposed to be the district officer.'

'You're a woman and a foreigner.'

With a bold swift gesture he moved closer, reached out and felt the fabric of her sweater between the thumb and finger of his right hand. The gesture was so unexpected she wasn't sure how to respond.

'Why did you do that?'

'They make good sweaters here on the Faroes. Black wool from black sheep. Nothing dyed. All organic and sustainable, I gather. Not this cheap Chinese shit.'

'I know what they make here,' she snapped. 'And they cost a fortune.'

'What else do you have to spend your money on? No man. No

life. You could at least dress better, Hanna. You're half good to look at. You seem to wish to hide that.'

She was blushing and hated that he was seeing this, amused by it.

'Have you found any trace of him yet?' Højgaard asked.

The helicopter had returned, sweeping up and down the coast once more. The roar of the engine blanked out her thoughts. Either that or Højgaard's unexpected question did the job.

'Him? You mean the Mikkelsen boys?'

He shook his head and sighed.

'Your brother Søren. Who else?'

ELSEBETH HARALDSEN SOON FOUND that no one wanted her assistance in Djevulsfjord. Eydna, the missing brothers' grandmother, seemed a kind of recluse, only opening the door to her cottage to explain that she was about to close it. The village women were content to leave the search for the boys to their menfolk. The general expectation everywhere was that this was a prank on the part of Jónas Mikkelsen, a rascal with a dark streak, known for his mischief.

So she returned to the quayside and watched Baldur Ganting's longliner disappear past the Skerries out to sea, Tristan at the stern, scanning the craggy coastline. It was tragic and disturbing that Ganting's son had died the year before. Life was cruel with its coincidences sometimes.

She hoped this would not prey on her husband's mind. He was a gentle, sensitive man. The way the Mikkelsen boys vanished and his cack-handed stabbing at the poor whale the previous day had got to him.

To her astonishment it seemed the latter that dismayed the locals the most. Missing boys appeared to be one of life's hazards. Clumsy attempts at dispatching whales during the grind, an act Tristan Haraldsen had never considered before in his life, were of an altogether more serious nature.

'Perhaps we will never understand this place,' she muttered to herself as she walked up the steady incline back to their cottage.

Tea, she thought. Some work in the garden. Washing grass cuttings from black pyjamas with a quiet curse under her breath. There was always plenty to do.

Five minutes along the way she found the boys' mother outside the church, crouched on the verge of the gravel lane, hands round her knees, eyes pink with tears, long fair hair all over her damp cheeks.

Elsebeth had never spoken to the woman. Now seemed a poor time. Nevertheless it would be wrong to avoid her. Ignoring bad in the world never got you anywhere. So she walked over.

'Can I help? Is there anything I can do?'

'Such as what?'

She didn't look up. The voice was that of a hurt child.

'I can make you a cup of tea if you like. We can talk.'

Alba Mikkelsen clambered to her feet, straightening her crumpled grey skirt as she did so.

'You wouldn't want me in your house, missus. I'd leave a black mark on it.'

'Nonsense. I . . .'

She stopped. Father Ryberg was marching down the path, seemingly a man in a hurry. He flew through the gate, stroked his silver beard and eyed the mountain. The fellow had his boots on and looked ready for a walk.

'No news of them, I presume?' he asked.

'What do you think?' Alba asked.

'I think that was a reasonable question. Worthy of a reasonable and polite answer.'

'Not that we know,' Elsebeth said.

'My boys . . .' Alba whimpered.

'In God's hands . . .'

'Are you going to look for them?'

'My business is my own,' Ryberg grunted then set off at a pace down the lane.

Still Elsebeth persisted.

'Alba. Please. There must be something I can do to help . . .?'

Her blue eyes glinted with anger.

'And what would you know about helping people here? You and your man turn up like it's a holiday or something. Him the district sheriff and he can't even kill a whale. Maybe if he'd done that my boys wouldn't be missing . . .'

'I'm sorry. We both are. Though to be honest I don't see how—'

'Sorry? Lot of use to me that is.'

Then, uncertainly, like someone in pain, she walked, half-hobbled back towards the quay.

Elsebeth thought of following but realised she was out of words. Sometimes there was nothing to be done and thinking otherwise made matters worse, not better.

THERE WERE THREE MEN in the police helicopter that had flown out of Sørvágur airport that morning. A pilot and two policemen as observers.

Trained officers, used to checking for missing boats in the

71

choppy seas mostly and the occasional tourist lost in the remote green hinterlands where visitors sometimes wandered.

Over and over they scanned Djevulsfjord and the surrounding fells, seeing nothing of interest.

A final pass from the harbour, over the cliffs, on to Selkie Bay.

'What's that?' the pilot asked, pointing out to sea.

The two officers put their binoculars to their faces and looked out at the swelling ocean. On the western horizon the familiar anvil shapes of cumulonimbus clouds were building. Air traffic control had been in touch already warning that the meteorological office was predicting thunderstorms before the end of the day. Perhaps they would come inland. Perhaps not. In any case the helicopter would need to return to refuel soon.

'Foul weather coming,' one of the officers said.

'To hell with that,' the pilot muttered and turned out to sea for one last sortie.

'We are supposed to be looking for those boys, Karl,' the second policeman cried. 'And I doubt they are swimming so far beyond the Skerries.'

'True,' the first officer agreed. 'I believe we're owed another perspective however.'

The pilot did what pilots sometimes liked to do with awkward passengers. He put the helicopter nose down and set the craft into a steep dive down towards the water.

'Throw us around and we will be sick,' the first policeman warned.

'You know the rules,' the pilot reminded him. 'All puke belongs to those that puke it. Besides . . .'

He levelled out fifty metres above the swelling ocean, turned a lazy leftward curve. Then the helicopter rose abruptly, engine roaring, the pilot's keen eyes set back on the fells.

'The rules about puking will alter if this continues,' the officer closest warned.

'No time for that now.'

The pilot cursed himself. He should have thought to fly out to sea earlier. The distance and the change in position opened up new views of Árnafjall. They revealed something he hadn't seen before.

'Use your eyes,' he said, pointing ahead. 'Get your glasses there. Two shapes high up, moving through the grass. Coming down hungry I'll be guessing. You'd think Djevulsfjord would take care of its kids better than that. Can't be many of them left in that dump.'

The men did as they were told.

'There's them lads,' the first said and soon the second agreed.

'Well, at least they live,' the pilot muttered. 'Though I'll bet someone will be giving them a good hiding before the night's over.'

The first officer was on his radio straight away, to Aksel Højgaard as they'd been ordered. The second was idly staring back at a curious sight in the sea.

It was the half-scavenged corpse of a whale, white bone, black and bloody flesh still clinging to its skull.

'They got plenty of meat, I reckon,' he murmured, almost to himself as the helicopter flew towards the peak, establishing a firm line of sight to the Mikkelsen boys. 'I'd have been down for that grind myself if it wasn't for duty.'

'Enough yakking,' the pilot told him. 'We're going back.'

He turned for Sørvágur.

The first officer took the glasses away from his face.

'I believe we're supposed to maintain sight of those little lads.'

'We cannot,' the pilot replied. 'This bird does not run on an empty belly. Note their position. Tell Højgaard.'

'No signal,' the first officer said, waving his phone.

'Then . . .' He pointed the nose back towards safety and fuel. 'Radio back to base and ask them to do it. Now.'

HØJGAARD CAME UP TO her so close she could smell the tobacco on his breath.

'Oh come on. You were doing so well in Aalborg. Not a blemish on your record. I checked. If you'd stayed there you'd have been promoted by now.' A wink. 'You had a boyfriend. A fiancé, I believe.'

The thing in the sky retreated once more.

'I never realised you were so interested in me,' she said finally.

Of course he'd know about Søren. She was stupid to think otherwise.

'I was on holiday when that fool Rasmussen gave you this posting. You were here by the time I got back. This is unfortunate. We should have had a conversation. Perhaps I would have sent you elsewhere.'

'A conversation about what?'

'About motives. You give up your career. Your life,' Højgaard continued. 'All to come to this dump. To arrest drunk drivers and the odd wife beater. It doesn't take a genius to realise why.'

'No,' she said. 'It doesn't. My brother came here and then . . . vanished. He sent me a selfie against the beach.'

Højgaard clearly didn't know this and asked if he could see it. Hanna kept the picture with her always. She found her phone – a new one now, not the one that received the shot – and showed him.

A smiling figure, clean-shaven, handsome with long fair hair. Behind his muscular torso stretched the coal-black sand of Selkie's beach. The only other living thing in the picture was the flashing outline of a puffin vanishing off to the right. She'd looked at this photo so often trying to understand. In a way this was all that remained of him. Dots on a screen. Bits and bytes stored somewhere she could never picture. They never changed, unlike the image she had of him in her head. That metamorphosed constantly, shifted, faded, then returned looking different. It was hard to place the real Søren at all.

One day, she understood, that shadowy memory would make the inevitable transition from painful present to melancholic past. He'd be a headstone that was never erected. An obituary that remained unfinished. Gone.

'He was younger than you.'

'Eighteen months. Kid brother. I used to look after him.' A smile then and she looked him straight in the eye. 'If anyone touched him at school they paid. I saw to that.'

'And then he grew up.'

'Meaning what?'

'Meaning he went and lived in that drug den in Copenhagen for a while. Christiania.' He pulled a sour face. 'The free state. Do what you like. Forget the consequences. As if that's possible. Is that why you never raised him with me? Embarrassment?'

She put the phone away.

'You must spend a lot of time in front of the computer, Højgaard. Let me raise him now? Is there anything new you can tell me?'

'Only the little you read already thinking no one would see you'd been going through the files. I notice, Hanna. Trust me.' He closed his eyes for a moment as if pretending to remember something. 'Søren Olsen. Just out of jail for—'

'I don't want to hear this!'

He smiled and said, 'So I gather.'

The police in Denmark had been understanding. Not her fault they said.

'Søren strayed,' she said. 'That's all. He was young. Naive. Easily led.' The memories were coming back. 'I paid for the ticket to Vágar to get him away from those creeps. He wanted to reconnect with his roots.'

'I'm sorry. The lack of certainty must be—'

'Three weeks he was supposed to be on the road. The picture's the last thing I got.'

'You won't find him here,' he said very firmly. 'If there was anything to be known about your brother I'd know it.'

'You seem very sure of that.'

Højgaard smiled.

'I'm trying to help. Your brother must have gone his own sweet way a year ago. There's nothing for you to chase here. Not even his shadow. Why not go and be useful picking up halfwit tourists in Tórshavn. More your kind of thing. I'll fix it. No reason for you to be here. Not today. Not tomorrow. Wherever your junkie kid brother washed up it wasn't Vágar. My guess is you'd be better off looking in Copenhagen. Dopeheads don't hang around a place like this long.'

Hanna Olsen walked away, back to her mountain bike.

'I trust you're listening,' he said, catching up. 'I've another officer who can move to this patch. Someone born and bred who's lived in Vágar all their life. Someone—'

'Someone you can boss about?' she cut in. 'Tell them what to do?'

'No need to change an officer for that.'

'Søren never flew out of Sørvágur. There's no record of him taking the ferry to Denmark or Iceland.'

He shrugged.

'Your brother knew enough people, didn't he? Plenty of little boats shuttle between the mainland and Vágar. There's smuggling goes on. Coastline like this. People like these. Not a lot you can do to stop it. Maybe your brother didn't use the airport and the ferry for a reason. Junkies. You never know what they're up to.'

'He was better,' she said through clenched teeth. 'He'd given up all that shit. He was going to take a few weeks holiday here, then come back and start again. I was helping him.'

Højgaard wasn't even listening, just scowling at the black beach. Looking for missing kids appeared to be beneath him.

'It must be killing you,' he said.

'Shall we get on with our work?'

'Such as it is. But you have to wonder.'

'Wonder what?'

The smile once more, cruel and mocking.

'What if you were to come across something? An answer? And what if that answer turned out worse than not knowing after all?'

She climbed on the bike, was about to hit the pedals and head for the path.

'Wait,' Højgaard barked.

'Why?'

But no answer. He was on the phone.

HIGH ON ÁRNAFJALL JÓNAS Mikkelsen followed the helicopter moving against the rolling clouds on the horizon like a giant iron bird. It was veering off to the right as he tugged his brother's arm and dragged him behind some grey rocks.

'Hide that big, stupid head of yours, lump,' he ordered.

'Why?' Benjamin asked.

The bunched fist came up. Then, in his left hand, the whaling knife.

'Because I said.'

'Mam'll be waiting for us.'

'Ja. And the rest of them. I'm not done yet.'

The sound of the helicopter changed. Jónas popped his head out from behind the rock and looked. It was heading back down the coast, towards Sørvágur. Perhaps the thing hadn't seen them at all.

He waited a minute or two then stood up. Benjamin did the same.

'Follow,' Jónas ordered.

Benjamin didn't move.

'The path's over there,' he said, pointing back towards Djevulsfjord.

'What path?'

'The way home.'

'You piss off if you want, goat. I'm not going yet.'

The rock hides for the puffin hunters were a good kilometre

below them. Close to the edge, high walls, well-built with dark stone, a place no one could see inside.

'Third hide on the left he reckoned.'

'Who?'

Jónas chuckled.

No answer.

'Mam said we weren't to be alone up here.'

'Mam said. Mam said. Mam take off my shitty britches.'

He headed off towards the cliffs.

'Who?'

'Come and maybe I'll tell you. Your choice, goat. I got stuff to do.'

PHONE CLUTCHED TO HIS ear, Højgaard turned towards the horizon. The helicopter was there already, returning to Sørvágur. He listened, then walked away from her and seemed to tap a message into the phone.

'They've spotted two boys,' he said when he came back. 'Close to the puffin hides above Freyja's Pool.'

He pointed to the eastern end of the bay. A single footpath wound up from the rocks at the end of the beach, turn upon turn, to the closest end of the Lundi Cliffs.

'You can get there on your bike. I'll walk back to the harbour and round up a team. Get onto those fells as soon as you can. When these boys are found I want an officer there. Not just locals.'

This sudden show of concern surprised her.

'They won't harm them, Højgaard. They're just . . . kids.'

'I want someone there.'

Hanna Olsen looked up the path. It seemed to her the wrong one to choose and she said so.

'There must be a more direct way surely—'

'You know these hills better than me?' he snapped. 'You take that track. I'll go another way, back to the harbour. If you see something you get on the phone to me.'

'Your way might be shorter. If I'm on my bike I could get there—'

'Like all the Danes, aren't you? Presumptuous. Convinced you're dealing with simpletons . . .'

'I come from here!'

'No. You think you do. Get moving.'

She watched him go. Perhaps he was right. The route she was taking was more hilly but possibly less circuitous. Either way one of them would find the Mikkelsen boys. This strange saga, at least, would be brought to an end.

SIX

Baldur Ganting's longliner pulled out to sea, the better to get a view of the slopes of Árnafjall. Højgaard had called with a rough approximation of where the boys had been spotted from the air. Silas Mikkelsen was scanning the area with the only pair of binoculars the boat had.

'Nothing,' Mikkelsen said.

Ganting grabbed the glasses from him.

'There can't be nothing. That helicopter saw them.'

Tristan Haraldsen stayed close to the wheelhouse awaiting instructions. The rollers were turning choppier by the minute. A wind had come up seemingly from the ocean itself, cold and strong. Haraldsen remembered a little of his meteorology from school. This was the thunderstorm's gust front, a boundary between hot and cold air. Dangerous for shipping, especially for a boat this size not far from the rocky coast.

'Well . . . is it nothing for you too then, Baldur?' Mikkelsen demanded in a petulant voice, a tone above its normal register.

'These boys shouldn't be out there in this weather,' the older man grunted. 'We'll have lightning within the hour and all manner of downpours.'

He handed the glasses to Haraldsen and told him to try.

They weren't the best binoculars. Old and poorly maintained. The district sheriff set about the task methodically, as was his habit. He started at the point where Árnafjall's slope slackened beneath the rocky outcrops at the summit, then worked the glasses down, moving his vision horizontally from Selkie side to the Djevulsfjord direction. He could see the gorse bushes struggling with the growing wind. There were sheep in places, wild probably. The odd black mouth for a cavern and then, at the ridge of the cliffs, several puffin hides set quite close together. From this distance they looked like stone moles on the face of the peak.

'I see . . .'

Something moved, close to one of the largest hides, built directly above the sharp-edged cove of Freyja's Pool.

'What?' Ganting demanded, snatching the glasses from him. 'Where?'

The policewoman, Haraldsen thought. Hanna Olsen, blonde hair flying behind her as she pedalled a mountain bike, hard off the seat.

'Miss Olsen. She's looking for them.'

Haraldsen stayed at the stern, hands firmly clasping the steel rail. The two fishermen were quiet in the boathouse. Concerned, Haraldsen believed. The weather was changing, quickly as it sometimes did anywhere in the Faroes. The storm clouds out to sea were now larger and seemed not too far away. The anvil shape had acquired a menacing blackness to it. From time to time they could feel and hear the grumble of distant thunder, like rocks moving around the heavy, leaden sky.

The *Alberta* sailed the coast, from close to Djevulsfjord's harbour, round the small, steep-sided rocky bay of Freyja's Pool, on to the black beach of Selkie.

From time to time Silas Mikkelsen would mutter something

dark about missing another grind for this seemingly ill-fated venture. The pod of pilot whales was tantalisingly close at times. Haraldsen no longer needed the assistance of the experienced men around him to see them. The black fins of the creatures broke the thrashing waves so close to the boat that he felt he might reach out and touch one.

Then the pod was gone and Ganting turned the boat once more. Away from Selkie, back towards Djevulsfjord. There was no point in wasting time and fuel. The boys were somewhere else. Hopefully skulking somewhere on the slopes of Árnafjall, fearful of the beating they might get once they came home.

Towards Freyja's Pool they sailed. Haraldsen thought of what they'd heard from the gossiping Dorotea Thomsen that morning. That the previous year Baldur Ganting had recovered the body of his own son from this spot. Looking at it as they hove past he wondered how. And in this strange, almost hypnotic state that was beginning to grip him a memory came back. One of the stories they told at school, a Faroes myth.

Freyja was the Norse goddess of extremes. Of sex and love, of war and death. He dimly recalled reading once, in a book about Faroese mythology, that she was reputed to have come to Vágar and bathed naked in the tiny bay, surrounded by its sharp rocks and steep cliffs, believing that no mortal would see her.

In the way of ancient fables she was, of course, wrong. A young man from what must once have been Selkie was out hunting puffins with his nets, invisible to the goddess tucked away in his rock hide. Seeing the beautiful, immortal woman fly down into the pool, disrobe, and reveal her loveliness, he could only creep to the cliff edge, look down and stare.

The sight of her, the legend said, was enough to fill any man with lust and wonder. But Freyja had a guardian, a wild boar, Hildisvíni, loyal, strong and brave. In battle she would ride him, dispatching enemies with her sword while his sharp white tusks dealt with others.

As the local fisherman gazed at the beautiful goddess with a growing passion from the cliffs above the pool, Hildisvíni noticed and came a-creeping up behind.

One moment the hapless boy was stricken with a heated sense of desire the like of which he'd never known. The next he heard the snuffling of the beast behind him, then turned only to be skewered by its rapier tusks and tossed like autumn wheat, over the rock edge down to the water where his corpse crashed, a sacrifice to the goddess below.

So furious was Freyja at being spied upon by an ordinary mortal that, still naked, she leapt astride Hildisvíni and the pair of them flew furiously into the air. Over the village in Selkie Bay the boar opened his fearsome mouth and, like a dragon, roared flames on every man, woman and child there, burning everything, flesh and bone, wattle and daub huts, wooden fishing boats, to ashes.

That, the story said, was why the sand of Selkie Bay remained black as coal, and no sane soul had lived there for as long as anyone could remember.

He wondered why the story had stuck with him. Perhaps because of the curious notion of a pig that could spit fire.

Ganting's loud, coarse voice broke the reverie.

'Are you with us, man?' the skipper demanded. 'Or simply dreaming?'

* * *

BEFORE HE COULD ANSWER the boat bucked and rolled with fresh violence on the growing swell. Then, a good thirty metres from the cruel sharp rocks at the pool mouth, it lurched forward and the little cove was gone from sight.

Freyja, the boy and Hildisvíni was a cruel story, Haraldsen thought, as so many myths were. But Baldur Ganting's own flesh and blood had perished in this self-same spot, for reasons that seemed odd and obscure. That was a genuine tragedy, not the product of an ancient, over-active imagination.

As they approached the Skerries the sea calmed a little thanks to the influence of the fjord.

'What next?' Haraldsen asked.

'Next we moor and join the men in the hills,' Mikkelsen replied. 'This weather will do for us if we don't get ashore soon.'

Ganting himself remained silent. Lost in his own gloomy thoughts.

'Tell me what you wish of me. I'll do it. I still feel somewhat—'

'You're not responsible,' Ganting interrupted with a swift brusqueness. 'Kindly cease saying that, man.'

'Ja, but—'

'But nothing,' the fisherman went on. 'This is our business, not yours. We will deal with it as we always do. I'll dock the boat. Go find that wife of yours. Think about what you're going to do with the sheep. When you want them slaughtering and salting for the winter, let me know. I'll do it by way of thanks for allowing us the grind since you took none of the skinn.'

There it was again, Haraldsen thought. These men could divide their world into two separate parts without a second thought. In the first a couple of boys were missing. In the other, the daily round of life, of meat and death and labour, went on regardless. This was, he accepted, reasonable. Sensible even. It was also quite beyond him.

The sharp needles of the Skerries went past, the *Alberta* rolling only gently now. The small harbour loomed. Though no mariner, he could tell the tide was coming in from the way the lively waves were lapping at the shore.

Thirty metres from the wall Baldur Ganting's phone went. He passed the wheel to Mikkelsen who edged the boat towards the quay.

It was a short conversation with a single question from Ganting. Then without a word he returned to the wheelhouse, grabbed control from his son-in-law, fired up the boat's engine and turned it round full into the heaving waves, towards the black storm clouds on the horizon.

Haraldsen found himself forced to the port side and had to hang on hard to stay in the boat at all.

'What is it?' he asked when he'd got his breath back.

'The police. They seen 'em,' Ganting said, eyes on the dark line ahead. 'They seen 'em good and proper somewhere above Freyja's Pool.'

Silas Mikkelsen stayed silent. Haraldsen made his way to the wheelhouse.

'So why are we heading out to sea?' he asked.

Ganting glared at him and said not a word. Then he notched up the engine further. The nose of the boat rose and bucked on the roll of waves ahead as they started back the way they came.

* * *

STEEP, STEEP, THE CLIFFS were steep. Coarse grass and dying late-summer flowers. Sheep shit in brown desiccated lumps that stuck to your shoes if you let them.

Jónas led. Benjamin followed, ankles hurting from the incline, bare legs caught by spiky mountain vegetation.

He didn't whine too much. No point, he thought. He was the older one. It wouldn't have been right. The phone had rung. The magic phone, or so Jónas seemed to think, summoning them to something his brother didn't care to explain.

Somewhere their mam sat, worrying. Crying probably. She did that a lot when she thought no one could see. Benjamin might have been the stupid one. People told him that often enough. But he noticed her weeping even if others, his younger brother especially, didn't.

They turned a low knoll clothed in arctic willow. Benjamin snapped a leaf or two and chewed the bitter leaves. Grandma Eydna said they cured toothache. He didn't know about that. But they didn't taste nice.

The boy spat them out. His brother turned and glared at him.

'What stupid thing you doing now, goat?'

'Both goats now, ain't we? Clambering up and down the mountain like this.'

You don't answer back.

How many times had Jónas said that, hard bony fists bunched, threatening to break his nose? Benjamin was bigger, stronger. But Jónas was quick and fearless, and that counted for so much more.

His brother stopped, came straight up, raised his knuckles in Benjamin's face.

'Screw with me now, goat, and I'll kill you. Rid the world of

87

your useless carcass. That I promise. Got business in these hills. Understand me. Ja?'

High on Árnafjall. No one to see. Anything could happen here. It was only the presence of their mam that kept him in check back home in the cramped, damp quarters of the little shed by the quay.

'What we doing here?' Benjamin whispered.

His brother laughed.

'You? You're following me like always. Useless piece of shit. Go on. Walk down that hill. Go home on your own. See if I care . . .'

'Mam—'

'Mam said don't go out on those hills alone.'

He did a good impression of Benji's voice when he wanted.

'Shift, goat!' Jónas bellowed and dragged him down the path.

HE'D NEVER LIKED THE places they trapped the puffins. They'd always seemed like tombs from the days of the old people. Vikings and primitive folk who came before. Stone enclosures, rock upon rock, stinking of age and the piss of men and beasts, beer cans and dog ends on the floor, worse sometimes too, they stood at intervals along the Lundi Cliffs, staring out to sea.

Once – just once – he'd come hunting with their uncle Kaspar. This was early that bad summer when they were still a family, just. Arguments were rare and for the most part he felt they were happy. Jónas had been bullying him as far back as Benjamin could remember, always with the same sly and cunning trick. Wind him up then, when Benji lost his rag and started to yell and throw his fists about, one of two things happened. Either Jónas flew at him hard and vicious with his sharp and bony knuckles. Or he ran to the nearest grown-up, a parent, Mrs Blak the teacher, the priest, the district sheriff, and whined about how his big brother was a crazy creature, too dangerous to be let out of the house.

The folk of Vágar were there to cope with what life served them. Grandpa Ganting had told him that when he complained about the way Jónas got him into trouble and did far more by way of punching and kicking than Benjamin ever tried. You either took it, the old man said, or you stamped and kicked back. Which was not Benjamin's way. He retaliated, never started the fight.

There'd been words exchanged from time to time though. The niggles and the sly, persistent blows would stop for a week or so. Then, when Grandpa Ganting and the rest of the men got tied up in a summer grind or winter slaughter, Jónas would come back at him with a vengeance.

That happened the day they killed the puffins. He remembered it clearly now as they bore down on the rocky shelter beneath the fading, late-afternoon sun.

The nets, the swift way the birds were snatched from the bright air. How they squeaked and squealed when their little necks were wrung. Kaspar swearing if one of them caught him with its beak.

And Jónas.

Madder than ever. Running round trying to get to the struggling bodies first, anxious to be the one who took their little lives.

Kaspar strangled them as easily as if he were plucking carrots out of the meagre patch behind the cottage. Not Jónas. There was a pleasure in it for him, a black glee Benjamin failed to understand and was determined not to share.

Not even when his uncle ordered him to kill one of the birds as if it was a test at school: do this sum, get it right, pat yourself on the back . . .

He was never good at sums either. Couldn't bring himself to wring the terrified creature's neck. Got punched hard by both of them for that.

As Jónas raced ahead of him, determined to be first to the narrow dark entrance of the shelter, Benjamin saw this day from the year before so lucidly in his mind's eye it almost felt as if he was back there.

The memory made him shiver.

Jónas stopped by the entrance and waited for him to catch up.

Bony fist up, he snarled, 'You stay here, goat. None of your business and never will be.'

Don't be long, Benjamin thought but didn't say. I want home. I want off these hills. A bath. Clean clothes. Some proper food again.

There was someone inside. Unseen. Hiding too. But Benjamin could hear the man, his low and grunty tones.

Nothing was going to get the boy through the black hole of a door into the darkness where they'd wrung the puffins' necks.

Nothing at all.

SEVEN

A long ride it was, so hard in places she had no choice but to get off the bike and push the thing up the narrow brown path that led up to the Lundi Cliffs.

At the top, when the ground became more even, she'd made a breathless phone call to Aksel Højgaard. The man was on voicemail. Hanna uttered a short curse about senior officers, took a couple of lungfuls of clear mountain air, then got back on the saddle.

The boys were probably heading home after their brief adventure. There was no good reason for them to be around this part, so close to Selkie Bay with its black and empty beach.

Still she rode on, enjoying being alone for once. Her brother had vanished somewhere hereabouts. In the past few months Hanna had spent every spare waking hour searching around Selkie and the surrounding countryside looking for some small sign. A lost piece of clothing. A hat. A shoe.

All in vain.

The breeze was stiffening into a horizontal blast. Black clouds had edged in from the western horizon. There'd be no Northern Lights, no moon either. The sky was already too thickly-cloaked for that.

A lone boat was out at sea. Ganting's. It was a safe bet, she thought, that the new district sheriff would be on that. He seemed a persistent man.

She had his number too. It came with the job.

By the largest of the puffin hides she stopped and leaned the bike against the dry wall rocks. He answered on the third ring.

'Haraldsen,' he said politely over the roar of the engine and the thrashing of the angry waves.

'Hanna Olsen. I imagine you are with Ganting on his boat.'

'Ja. They say the boys are somewhere on the cliffs.'

'The helicopter's gone back to Sørvágur. I'm looking on my own from the Selkie side. Have you seen anything?'

'I have a pair of binoculars. Let me look again.'

Somewhere in the background, over the roar of the ocean, she heard a curse.

'I think I have you, Hanna. I saw you up there earlier. I thought you'd spotted something.'

'I believed I had,' she agreed. 'But perhaps I was wrong. They may have seen sense and headed off for the village.'

'All I see now is you. Nothing else. I'm sorry . . .'

A noise then. She walked round the circular hide, phone still to her ear, trying to make sense of it. Small feet rustling through stiff fell grass. Voices too. One young, one older, both raised though the sound was muffled since it came from within the hide and so she could barely hear.

'Benjamin!' she cried. 'Jónas?'

No answer but there were people there. Two, three. It was hard to tell.

She looked at the black mouth to the hide and felt a sudden shiver of fear run through her.

'Haraldsen,' she said, looking out to sea again, 'they're here. Perhaps trying to avoid me. I don't know. Get in touch with the search teams on the fjord side. Tell them what I've told you. You've no need to waste your time any more on the sea. I'll bring the boys in—'

Silence then.

'Haraldsen?'

ON THE LURCHING BOAT, arm firmly round the handrail, he watched in growing puzzlement.

There were shapes on the cliff, barely distinguishable from this distance.

'Someone, Hanna. There's someone near you—'

Then a heart-stopping moment. She vanished abruptly behind the rock hide, brought down, it seemed to him, by a blow from a shadowy figure mostly blocked from view by the stone wall.

Before he could speak again the *Alberta* bucked like a wild horse. He fumbled the phone into his oilskin pocket and clutched hard on the rail with both hands, fighting to stay on board. Ganting was screaming something from the cabin, inaudible over the roar of the storm. For a good three or four minutes they seemed lost in a maelstrom of wind and water, one so fierce Haraldsen found himself wondering, for the first time in his uneventful life, if the end had truly come. Then the vessel seemed to calm itself, found more peaceful water, and Ganting edged her round to face the cliffs again.

Through the old binoculars there was no sign of the stricken Hanna Olsen, or anyone else. He was wondering what to say or do about this when a small shape pitched out onto the gentle slope. There it could do nothing but roll helplessly down the hill, towards the ragged edge.

'There's a lad gone over,' Haraldsen whispered and found himself clutching for his own life as the boat began to buck and bob on the wild ocean once again. 'Ganting! Mikkelsen! Look!'

The child was tumbling head first down the cliffs, arms flailing, legs too, fluttering like an angel stripped of wings, plummeting to the unforgiving rocks below.

Imagination gave the boy a voice over the roaring ocean, one that could not possibly be real.

Nevertheless it was there, deafening in Tristan Haraldsen's head: a terrified shriek, an angry, fearful scream.

BALDUR GANTING WAS FIGHTING the wheel once more, trying to steer into the narrow cover of Freyja's Pool. They could see the child now. A rock ledge a good five metres above the thrashing waves had broken his fall.

'He moves,' Silas Mikkelsen cried, trying to stay upright in the prow. 'I saw him, Baldur. The boy moves.'

'You think?' Ganting bellowed back and struggled to bring the vessel in closer.

Haraldsen edged his way along the handrail, towards the front. It was as if he no longer existed. These two men, well versed in the ways of the sea, were focused on one thing alone: the crumpled shape on the rocks ahead of them. There was no other way to save the child but the boat. No helicopter could fly in this weather. No climber would be able to abseil down this treacherous cliff face in such conditions. It was their job alone and they knew it.

Ganting stuck his head out of the wheelhouse and yelled, 'I can perhaps get in once without foundering, Silas. You position yourself up front and grab the lad when I come in. Then hang on for dear life. I'll be pumping this motor for all she's worth and praying we can get out of there.'

'Ja,' the younger man replied and without another word took one step forward.

For a second only he took his grip off the handrail. At that moment the fiercest, most cruel wave dashed against the stern. Up pitched the boat's nose until they were staring at the cliff itself, and the black sky above. Silas Mikkelsen was airborne, screaming. Then gravity took hold. The *Alberta* fell down, bucked once more as the bawling man tumbled back towards the deck.

Even above the roar of the waves Haraldsen could hear that crack and knew what it meant. A broken limb. Perhaps more. Mikkelsen lay thrashing on the timber planking.

'Wait for me,' Haraldsen cried and felt his way further along the deck then took the mooring rope in his hand.

'I cannot keep this boat here much longer,' Ganting cried. 'Forget Silas. Get the boy.'

It must have been the most extraordinary seamanship. Somehow Baldur Ganting had worked the longliner into the very heart of the cove where the water was a little calmer. Mikkelsen lay groaning on the deck, his right arm at an awkward, painful angle.

'Get the lad, Haraldsen. There'll be no second chance today.'

A modest man. One of few accomplishments. He'd never risked much, never sought much. Yet at that moment Tristan Haraldsen felt his life finally had some purpose.

The child had moved, his father said. There was still a chance to save him.

Haraldsen launched himself at the prow as the vessel made

one final rolling approach to the hard rock ledge. The nose hit a spear of craggy stone not a metre right of the child. Splinters of wood and fibre glass spat into Haraldsen's face as he placed his right foot on the boat's forepart then his left on the ledge.

'Poor thing,' he muttered, scooping two hands beneath the boy who lay face down, blood staining the pale young cheek that was visible.

'Now!' Baldur Ganting bellowed and Haraldsen, the child held horizontal in his arms, leaned backwards, trusted to something, any benign influence that might have braved the storm, and lurched, half-fell towards the boat.

What happened after was a blur and would remain so. All he was aware of was the sea, the black sky, the crash of the *Alberta* against the merciless rocks, and a terrible burden in his arms.

BY THE TIME ELSEBETH Haraldsen returned home after the abortive effort to talk to Alba Mikkelsen, the weather was vile and cold and quite in touch with her mood. Better to stew in the close quarters of the cottage than shiver alone on the quayside. The couple no longer owned a car. When Tristan retired they had part-exchanged their Volvo estate for a two-berth, diesel camper van. They liked the name, an Ace Capri. The vehicle was elderly but smart: white with a blue stripe on the side. Its compact accommodation was comfortable for trips around the islands, staying at farm campsites, and a longer holiday they'd taken in Jutland across the water on the ferry.

How practical it was for Djevulsfjord Elsebeth wasn't sure. When the weather got worse and snow arrived they could find themselves trapped altogether, reliant on Dorotea Thomsen's little shop and nothing else. But then the same might apply if they bought an old Jeep or Land Rover. Tristan's attitude towards driving was simple and practical, just as it was to life in general: if the outlook was so treacherous it demanded special consideration then special consideration should be given as to whether the journey was worthwhile at all. And usually the answer was, firmly, 'no'.

Still she liked the Capri. It made a portable nest for the two of them, a refuge like Djevulsfjord where they could retreat from the bustle of the modern world. A statement that said: we have entered a new era in our lives together and it's one where a boring, conventional, reliable Volvo has no place. The vehicle stood to one side of their cottage by the kitchen window. Now, as she walked up the drive, she was surprised to see a small motorbike in the drive next to it. A tall and sturdily-built woman perched on the saddle cradling a scarlet crash helmet. She was forty or so with mannish cropped red hair and an unsmiling, rugged face.

Elsebeth walked up and introduced herself.

A strong handshake followed then the visitor did the same: Inga Dam.

'You're the wife of the new district sheriff? The man from Tórshavn?'

'Among other things.'

'Where is he?'

The question surprised her.

'Out with all the other men. Looking. There are two boys missing. Where else would he be?'

The woman scowled and put her helmet on.

'Give him a message. From people who care about these islands and their creatures.'

Elsebeth waited.

'There are more whales close by Djevulsfjord,' Inga Dam said. 'I can see the beauties from my studio window. The grind . . .'

'I think the grind is not uppermost in anyone's mind around here at the moment. Do you live in the village? I haven't seen you before.'

'No I do not. I sculpt. On my own. A shack the other side of Selkie.'

'I didn't know anyone lived out there.'

'Perhaps that's because it's none of your business.'

Elsebeth struggled for the right thing to say at that moment, then asked herself: why bother?

'Give your husband a message.' There was a fierce, almost intimidating expression in the woman's face. Unpleasant in the extreme. 'Death and Djevulsfjord go hand in hand. Only a fool thinks otherwise.'

'My good lady . . .'

'Don't patronise me! The wife of the district sheriff. Do you think that gives you airs and graces?'

Elsebeth blinked.

'Not for one moment. I was merely trying to be polite.'

'No room for that in this hole either.' She pulled on a pair of leather gloves. One black finger stabbed out as the woman threw her leg over the saddle of the motorbike. Inga Dam's sleeves were marked with white dust and rock fragments. It was easy to imagine her toiling away angrily at a slab of marble, a mallet and chisel in her hands. 'Tell the district sheriff this as well. Those bastards have had their fun. No more grind. I don't care how many black-fish they see out beyond the Skerries. No more grind. Or there will be consequences.'

'Is that for you to say?' Elsebeth asked.

'Yes. It is. The meat's tainted, for God's sake. Ask any doctor with half a brain. Their flesh is so full of mercury and all other manner of shit you're not even supposed to eat it.'

She'd heard this too. The chief medical officer of the government had said so years ago. It made no difference at all. People ate what they wanted, just as they smoked tobacco knowing the risks.

'My husband will take all facts into consideration and act within the law.'

'Sweet Jesus,' Inga Dam cried. 'He'll be the only one here who does.' She kicked the bike into life. 'I suspected you two were out of your depth. It never occurred to me how much.' The black finger stabbed at her again and flakes of shattered stone fell from her sleeves. 'If I look out of my windows and see one more bloody corpse upon the beach there'll be a reckoning hereabouts. That I promise. Those responsible will be held to account.'

'Miss Dam.' It was hard to stay calm. 'We're newcomers. My husband is here to see the rules are kept when it comes to the grind. If you object to the fact it's legal you should take it up with the authorities. We are surely innocent of your anger, well-placed or not.'

'Innocent! *Innocent!*' It was close to a scream. 'You're a pair of fools. There are no innocents in Djevulsfjord. Not a soul among the folk here. They do what they want regardless of your husband's wishes. Well, I've seen enough. Those blackfish are living creatures too. They deserve protection and by God they'll have it.'

Then she started the engine, blipped the throttle a couple of times so it roared in anger, before edging the machine slowly past the Ace Capri, down the pebble drive, off towards the track that led up to the Lundi Cliffs and on to Selkie Bay.

Had there been the opportunity Elsebeth would have asked how environmentally friendly her smelly bike was. And how thoughtful to forsake the tunnel and the asphalt lane round to Selkie – a long way round it had to be said – and tear across a path meant for walkers not machines. But it wasn't possible and perhaps that was for the best.

Elsebeth went inside, through the open door, found the bottle of sherry in the kitchen and poured herself a glass.

Her fingers shook as she lifted it to her lips. Glass in trembling hand she walked into the living room. No one locked their houses hereabouts. There seemed no reason. But someone had been here. The door was ajar.

Elsebeth's first instinct was to check for theft. But nothing seemed to be missing. The most valuable portable thing they owned was Tristan's laptop which still sat on the desk in his tiny study overlooking the back garden. The wallet he habitually left on the mantle of the fireplace was untouched. The usual marks of a burglar, or so she understood them to be from what he'd talked about after work, were absent: vandalism, vile acts, drawers removed from sideboards, their contents scattered across the floor.

Only one thing was different. Across the plain pine table in the study, next to the Haraldsens' own inkjet printer, someone had churned out a selection of photos and arranged them very carefully in a sequence.

It was a grind. Yesterday's. Thrashing whales. Scarlet water so bloody the ink had soaked through the flimsy paper. Men were wandering between stricken black shapes looking for the quickest place to land a final, killing blow.

In the midst of the pages was a picture blown up so much she could see the dots. It was Tristan struggling with the spear, Baldur Ganting by his side, cross, barking what looked like orders, glaring at him angrily.

No sign of the Mikkelsen boys. Nothing but a dying whale, her husband, Ganting, the long weapon and blood turning the tide and the sand scarlet, dappling the surface of the page with its soggy spread.

There was a ring around Tristan's face, marked in black felt tip. Next to it what looked like a crude drawing of a whaling knife, unsheathed, the blade aimed at his eyes.

SHE DIDN'T USE THE computer much. She didn't like the things. They seemed intrusive. But someone, a woman called Inga Dam, had intruded into their lives. It was reasonable enough to find out who she was.

Not least because the name rang a bell and it only took the most cursory of searches to realise why.

The computer had popped up with several pages and a photo: the same tall woman she'd seen outside on the bike. On this occasion she was in a glitzy evening dress, looking almost elegant, holding up a champagne glass and smiling for the camera. Next to her was a sculpture. Or she assumed it was that. To Elsebeth, who was no fan of modern art, it looked more like a shapeless lump of white stone.

'Call that a statue,' she said to herself, pointing at the screen. 'I could do that myself.'

Inga Dam was that rarity, a Faroes artist who'd become known to the world outside. The newspapers had reviews of her shows in London, New York and Paris. Two years before she'd designed the Faroese pavilion for the Venice Biennale. To Elsebeth it looked much like a very large and winding intestine with lots of dark corners and installations filled with plants and strange artefacts in transparent plastic: dead animals, body parts, filth and, in one, the black sand of Selkie Bay covered in rubbish from the sea. People were supposed to walk through it and discover themselves and their connection with nature. Dam was, the article said, a ferocious environmentalist convinced the earth was headed for disaster.

'The woman's filthy rich and barking mad,' she said and hoped she didn't sound jealous even though no one else could hear. A home and studio in Copenhagen. Another in Tórshavn.

'And this,' she said, jabbing a finger at the screen. It was a short article, one that had received no cooperation from the woman herself. In fact it said she wished to keep her studio in Selkie a secret, to make it a place she could retire to out of the gaze of the public.

'As if she's a bloody star,' Elsebeth found herself cursing beneath her breath. 'As if . . .'

There was a photograph of a small shack, one that looked barely legal. A motorbike, the one she'd ridden to Djevulsfjord, was parked outside. It didn't seem much of a discovery.

'You're a very poor detective,' Elsebeth said to herself.

Still she typed some more and there it was. A long article on a Danish environmental website about the grind. Not a flattering one. The pictures were gory and made the locals happily engaged in the butchery look like ghouls. A few Danes were quoted condemning the slaughter. And one local. Inga Dam, who described it as little short of murder.

'What a word to use,' she said going through the article again. 'They're fish. Not people. Why not save your sympathy for them?'

The post ended with a quote from the woman. A rather chilling one Elsebeth thought as she read it out.

'The grind is nothing less than the Faroese holocaust. A mindless slaughter carried out by the cruel, the bloodthirsty, the ignorant, the savage. There is more nobility in a single whale than you will find in the heart of any of the men who rape and pillage our seas, who trap birds and wild creatures on our hills, who steal the holy life out of our land and oceans for nothing more than their pleasure. If the law will not stop it then good men and women shall, by whatever means we deem necessary. The butchers have been warned!'

Indeed they have, Elsebeth whispered.

She didn't want Tristan to see any of this. He was in a delicate enough state as things stood. So she screwed up the printed pages Dam – it surely could be no one else – had left behind and threw them in the bin.

Though perhaps, she thought with a shred of amusement, she should have kept them. A piece of original artwork by the genius of Selkie Bay.

A second sherry was on her mind when the phone rang.

'Husband?' she asked, in a tremulous voice.

A pause then the crowing tones of Dorotea Thomsen came out of the earpiece.

'Not your beloved, dearie. He's out on that boat of Ganting's. Best you get down here, I reckon. Looks like it's all turning turtle. You don't want to miss it. Oh no.'

AFTERWARDS HARALDSEN BELIEVED HE must have fainted. Something was missing in his mind, the way it measured time, the means by which one logical thought led to another. Where they were precisely when he came round he had no idea. The cliff still loomed above them but further off. The jagged rocks that surely spelled death for all were retreating now. Ganting must have been as happy on the ocean as on land. The man seemed to speak to the waves, to read their intentions. Carefully now, edging through the tempest, he steered his battered vessel out towards the Skerries, shattered timber and fibre glass showering everywhere as it lurched through the vicious waves.

Tristan Haraldsen could do nothing but clutch the precious bundle he'd snatched from the rocks, hold the child close to him hoping that neither of them would be swept out to sea.

Then he saw Silas Mikkelsen scrabbling over the deck of the heaving boat, broken arm hanging to one side, gaunt face a picture of grief.

'Don't, man,' Haraldsen cried. 'This is too dangerous. Stay where you are. I have the child.'

Halfway across the lurching timbers, still crawling towards Haraldsen and the little figure hunched against the deck wall, Mikkelsen held a hand out, pleading.

'He is my boy. My son. How fares he?'

Haraldsen clutched the small cold body to him much as he had since he plucked it from the ledge over Freyja's Pool. His head didn't feel right.

'How fares . . .?' Mikkelsen cried again then to Haraldsen's horror tried to struggle to his feet.

'Get down!' he yelled. 'Baldur! Ganting!'

The man in the cabin didn't move. He looked in the midst of a battle with the wheel, fighting the thing with his wrestling hands and arms as it struggled to break free and doom them all.

'Ganting,' Haraldsen shouted once more nevertheless. And then the wave hit. A wall of solid icy water, grey and foaming. It came over the boat side three times higher than the vessel's mast, caught Mikkelsen as he stood amidships, arms out, begging for sight of his son.

Haraldsen could think of nothing to do but crawl more tightly into the deck wall, one arm round the child, the other clinging desperately to the nearest drain gap.

Suddenly the fury abated. He understood why and that knowledge filled him with dread. The *Alberta* was no longer at the mercy of the sea. The force of the storm had ejected it from the ocean and now the little boat was briefly aloft in the maelstrom, calm for a moment before the madness returned.

He saw Silas Mikkelsen then, one arm bent and waving, the other clutching helplessly at nothing but salty air. He was flying too. A good metre off the deck. The vessel turned slowly to one side. Another vast wave fell upon them. There was a scream, a man in torment. All Haraldsen could do was cling on to his small cargo and hope to hold to the deck wall.

How long it lasted he never knew. A second or two, no more,

though it seemed to go on forever. Everything about that moment – Mikkelsen disappearing in the grip of the giant wave, Baldur Ganting clinging to the wheel, the awesome relentless nature of the brute force that had them in its grip – would stay with him till his dying instant. And perhaps that was not so far away he realised, thinking of Elsebeth, hoping she was warm and safe somewhere in Djevulsfjord, knowing the moment that wish occurred to him that, if he died, she'd abandon that strange and foreign place without a second thought.

This notion disturbed him as he held the boy's small body tight, waiting for the inevitable.

It came. The boat fell back to the sea like a brick hitting ground. The crash was so loud he wondered if his ears might burst. Freezing water soaked the two of them, ran inside his oilskin, down his neck. Still Haraldsen clung on.

A long time it took for him to dare to look up. Despair there and joy. Ganting was still in the cabin, dealing with a wheel that seemed less crazed than before. Silas Mikkelsen was with him, a broken form slumped on the floor, not moving, perhaps unconscious, dragged there somehow.

Haraldsen waited until he was sure the world was calming. When he dared he raised up his neck and peered over the side. The Skerries were close by and with them calmer water. Along the line of cliffs he could just make out the outer wall of Djevulsfjord's little harbour.

The raging waves fell back into a steady, more familiar rhythm.

'Baldur,' he cried at the tall man in the wheelhouse. 'How is Mikkelsen?'

'I am busy!' came the angry cry in return.

Ganting turned from the wheel and gazed at him, a mixture of both pity and contempt in his craggy fisherman's features. Then he nodded back the way they'd come. Haraldsen plucked up the courage to raise himself a little and stare over the stern.

A black wall of storm sat on the churning waters, running straight out from Freyja's Pool, something from a nightmare, a line of darkness that might have been the very edge of the world. He knew then it was a miracle they'd survived this cruel and vicious tempest at all, and that every breath he took from now on would be witness to Ganting's wondrous talent as a mariner.

'The father's hurt bad,' Baldur Ganting said simply. 'What about the boy?'

Haraldsen still held the child in his arms, young pale face streaming with water turned to the deck. There'd been no sign of movement, not the slightest indication of life since he'd scooped him from the rocky ledge.

'The boy!' Ganting cried again. 'Does he live?'

'I think not,' Haraldsen said softly, almost to himself, and plucked up the courage to turn the little body towards him.

The boat's passage seemed almost normal. The horizon ahead, the village, the harbour, no longer bucked up and down beyond the sharp prow.

He placed his fingers on the lad's neck, feeling for a pulse. The pale skin there was as cold as ice. Two blue eyes stared blankly at the grey sky, as if surprised, rain on the pupils. A bloody bruise marked his forehead. He wasn't breathing.

'Which child is it?' Ganting bellowed again, his voice close to cracking.

'The younger . . .' Haraldsen let go, feeling some strange object pressing against him from the child's chest. 'I don't . . .'

Words deserted him. They were close in to land, in the lee of Árnafjall which protected them from the harshest of the weather. Ganting seemed to know this without thinking. He jammed a piece of wood into the ship's wheel to lock it then stepped across the still form of Silas Mikkelsen and stumbled across to where Haraldsen and the child lay on the deck.

'Oh, child,' the old fisherman moaned, his face wet with the sea, his eyes glassy with salt water and a sudden burst of tears. 'The poor little bugger.'

The longliner was free and rolling loose in the swell. Ganting seemed lost. Haraldsen stood up and went swaying against the swelling tide to the wheelhouse, determined to keep it under some kind of control. He knew what he'd seen anyway. There was no point in looking at it more.

Behind him Baldur Ganting let loose a wail so full of pain and grief it sounded as if the world itself was crying.

From Jónas Mikkelsen's chest, hard fast in his rib cage, protruded the same whaling knife the child had stolen the day before, seemingly prompting this present tragedy.

Haraldsen knocked out the wooden lock on the wheel and turned the boat for home.

EIGHT

Five hours later the last blue flashing police light left the quay. Two ambulances had made their way through the Árnafjall tunnel, one to remove the body of Jónas Mikkelsen, a second to take a semi-conscious Silas Mikkelsen to the hospital. He had a broken arm, a broken leg, internal injuries yet to be determined, and by all accounts a shattered mind. A puzzled Hanna Olsen who'd staggered down from the hills was treated by a police doctor brought in by Aksel Højgaard then sent home to Sørvágur to recuperate from a minor head wound.

Tristan Haraldsen had watched all this in helpless silence, shivering inside his yellow oilskins on the harbour side. One sight in particular would stay with him from the moment they docked with the sad corpse of Jónas on the deck. Alba, the mother, the wife, had wailed like a banshee when they brought the bloody little body off the boat, throwing herself at Jónas's corpse in a manner so hysterical Haraldsen thought the dour and equally upset Ganting, compressing all that pain inside himself, might hit out at her before long. When she saw the injured Silas being taken off on a stretcher it looked as if she might lose what little composure she still possessed. Yet not a soul came to speak to her, to offer a word of comfort, and when Elsebeth tried the young woman rejected her furiously as if it were an insult.

Of the missing Benjamin Mikkelsen there was no sign, though

already the whispers had begun. It was no great secret that the older, slower brother had often been taunted into violence by his younger sibling. The assumption was that Jónas had jeered at him once too often. That Hanna Olsen had somehow stumbled upon the argument and been attacked by Benjamin from behind. Since she had no idea who'd struck her this seemed, for most of those gossiping quite openly by the harbour, to make some sense. After all . . . who else could it be?

Haraldsen thought the idea questionable at the very least and was glad to find Elsebeth of the same mind. A child killing his own brother, even an awkward, bullying one. Such things didn't happen, not much in the outside world let alone in the Faroes where crime was as rare as Catholicism. Besides, though he did not elaborate on this at the time, he had seen something, someone by the rock puffin hide, a shape behind Hanna as she fell. A shape he felt to be too tall for Benjamin Mikkelsen, and too full of a deliberate violent intent. A man it was surely. Though who, he couldn't begin to imagine.

Still he kept his thoughts to himself. The people of Djevulsfjord were closing in on themselves, drawing a veil around the little village by the water. There was no energy left to mount another search for the elder boy. That would wait until daylight and from the sound of it the effort would now be more a formal criminal investigation. From what he understood and had briefly witnessed, poor Benjamin Mikkelsen was a child who probably suffered from a developmental disability like autism, one that might go unnoticed and unchecked or simply see the lad labelled 'thick'. But slow was not the same as stupid. If Benjamin had fought his brother with such terrible consequences he'd surely feel himself hunted with greater ferocity. Even more so if he wasn't the one responsible since, whoever the third party was, the fellow would surely have the boy in his sights too.

These ideas roamed and fought and argued in his head until it ached. To no good purpose. There was nothing else to be done or said by the quay. The Haraldsens had wandered the cold damp night trying to talk to the locals with little success, feeling more and more like dazed spectators trapped in a continuing nightmare they could not begin to comprehend.

'We should go home,' he said eventually when there seemed nothing else to be done.

She didn't say a word.

'Elsebeth. We must cope. We always cope, don't we?'

Again the silence, so he asked, 'Is something wrong? Beyond the poor waif and his brother?'

'No,' she said very quietly. 'What makes you say that?'

'It's just . . .' He didn't know. They never hid things from one another. That was a bargain they'd made from the very start. Honesty above all else, even if it was uncomfortable on occasion. Like him being told he could no longer smoke his pipe. And the niggles from time to time about his heart, which were nothing really.

'Soup. That would be nice.'

'We have none,' Elsebeth replied in a low and mournful voice that was not like her at all. 'And it's time you got out of those oilskins of Ganting's. You don't even know you're wearing them, do you?'

'A few other things on my mind,' he said rather hastily.

But it was true. He'd quite forgotten he had them on. So there and then, on the quayside, he stripped them off and found his own clothes mostly dry beneath. The longliner was empty as he stepped on board to replace the yellow fisherman's suit in the cabin. The boat seemed badly damaged, broken timbers, shattered fittings everywhere. Haraldsen didn't linger long on deck.

'The shop will have some soup,' he said. 'Surely.'

GEORGE THOMSEN WAS RESTOCKING the shelves when they arrived.

Elsebeth was in a quandary. She wanted to tell her husband about the strange visit from the woman called Inga Dam, and the even stranger gift she'd found on the desk. But a boy had died. Another was missing. And Tristan Haraldsen seemed confused, exhausted, lost for what to do except believe that some of this was his fault. Now was not the time.

'Soup, if you will,' she said taking the lead as they entered.

Dorotea winked at her husband.

'There. See. I was right. Told you there'd be custom. My ears for business are as good as ever. I knew it was worth staying open on this lively day. Whatever goes on in the world outside people must always eat.'

'Soup,' Haraldsen repeated with an unaccustomed vehemence. 'I would not call it lively. A young boy has died.'

'Tristan . . .' Elsebeth whispered. 'Tread lightly.'

'I am treading lightly,' he insisted. 'Thank you very much.'

Thomsen cleared his throat then went back to stacking the shelves with flour and detergent.

'Yes,' Dorotea noted. 'The bright young Mikkelsen boy's gone. They'll bury him next to that wicked uncle of his, I imagine. Two or three days at the most. No one waits on funerals in Djevulsfjord.'

'If the police allow it,' Haraldsen pointed out.

She gazed at him, baffled.

'Why wouldn't they? Aksel Højgaard knows who did it. The superintendent is well familiar with that pair. Saw him talking to the younger one only yesterday morning before the grind. That stupid big brother of his slew him. He may be still at large but that shouldn't stop us putting the young one in the ground, should it?'

'The lad has only just died—'

'Dead is dead,' George Thomson declared, staring at the soap powder. He was picking off an old price and putting on a new one.

'You two doubtless won't have noticed,' his wife added. 'You haven't been here long enough. But that pair were always a nightmare, headed for trouble. It was in their blood. The times we've had trouble with them in here—'

'Only Jónas,' her husband interrupted from the shelves. 'A terrible thief and a liar to boot. The older lad never did us any harm. Just stood back with that stupid look of his as if he didn't know what to do next.'

'Well . . .' She laughed. 'He's surely made up for that now, hasn't he? I have tomato or mixed vegetable only by the can. It may be out of date but I doubt you'll notice.'

'Vegetable,' Elsebeth said before Tristan could speak.

Dorotea Thomsen shrugged and passed it over.

'What a day. We never have them like this except when outsiders come.'

'Which means what?' Haraldsen asked.

'What I said. Was it unclear somehow?'

'Benjamin's still out there . . .' It was rare for Tristan to lose his temper. But not unknown. 'He's as much a victim as anyone surely . . .'

'At the risk of repeating myself I must say I never thought for one moment he might be up to harming that awful brother of his.' George Thomsen seemed finished with the shelves. Everything he'd stacked very neatly. 'Not seriously. Lord knows the evil little bastard used to torment him enough. He loved to get that poor simpleton ticking. Did it to everyone round here and the rest of us boxed his ears enough. Not that it did any good. All the same . . .'

'And the hoodlum clouted a grown policewoman round the head as well,' Dorotea added.

'I don't know about that,' Thomsen went on. 'Benji isn't a bad lad at heart. Only when that brother of his got him going. Maybe it was Jónas bashed her and his brother him after. Seems more likely.'

'Then why's the idiot gone running?'

He came back to the counter and slapped his hands together to shake off the dust. Everything he'd been stacking seemed to be old and covered in it.

'Because, wife, he's an idiot. Look at the parents. Silas isn't the brightest button in the box and as for Alba—'

'If he *was* the father,' she interrupted. 'With that one who was to know?'

There was a prolonged and awkward silence. Elsebeth could see Haraldsen was close to fury.

'I believe we shouldn't speculate,' she said. 'Thank you for the soup.'

'No need for that tone of voice,' Dorotea Thomsen told her. 'We know Djevulsfjord. You don't. Children grow up quick round here. They've got to. This isn't Tórshavn. With all your niceties.'

'I had a word with Aksel Højgaard,' her man added. 'He's sure as sure can be it was down to the older lad.'

'Strange,' Haraldsen said with a shake of his head. 'How would he know anyway? He wasn't there.'

'Højgaard was adamant.' Dorotea was sensing victory. 'It's Benjamin they must find. Though he's a Djevulsfjord lad so he could live up there for weeks on his own if he wanted.'

'Don't be ridiculous,' Haraldsen objected. 'He's a child.'

George Thomsen stuck his feet out. He was wearing a pair of sturdy hiking boots caked in grass and mud.

'A child of ours. He's as much at home out there as he is in front of his own hearth. We all of us used to go out for nights on end in them hills when the summer's on us. You can find food, berries, eggs, hunt for hares and birds and roast them. Plenty of water. I done it often enough when I was their age. Gets you out of the house and away from your father wielding a belt when he's full of beer. Those Mikkelsen boys went up to Lundi, Selkie, Árnafjall often enough. Even that idiot lad could hide up there as long as he likes till the weather turns. No one's going to find him if he don't want it. Got to look out for the holes, mind. They're everywhere. Fall down one of them and no one's going to see you again.'

Elsebeth Haraldsen didn't know what to say, any more than her husband.

'Besides,' Dorotea added, 'who else could it be? There was just those two brothers up there. Them and that police girl who says she didn't see a thing till one of them whacked her.'

'There was someone . . .' Haraldsen began. Then stopped himself for some reason.

'What do you mean . . . someone?' Dorotea Thomsen demanded.

'Tristan?' Elsebeth said quietly. 'We should go.'

He didn't move.

The boat was bucking beneath them at the time. The binoculars were old and far from clean. When he worked in the police he'd sat in on a few interviews. Officers always asked witnesses for hard detail, for certainty, and often became frustrated when they couldn't get it. Now he understood why. Memory and vision were flimsy, unreliable things. He wasn't sure what he'd witnessed at all and certainly wouldn't be able to attest to much in court if it ever came to that.

'I saw something,' he murmured all the same and knew on the instant how pathetic that sounded.

Elsebeth packed away the soup in her bag, a clear sign it was time to leave.

'Good night,' she said and shoved him through the door.

The rain had turned to drizzle with the scent of ice in it. The wind had fallen to little more than a steady breeze. It was as if the weather felt it had done its work for now and was saying, like the rest of Djevulsfjord: enough.

NINE

The evening was long and filled with awkward silences. When he worked, and she did part-time teaching in a Tórshavn school, the days had mostly taken care of themselves, and holidays, lately in the Ace Capri, were always busy too. But now they had no jobs – the district sheriff wasn't much of a post at all. These uncomfortable, unwanted hiatuses in their hours together were becoming common, and neither knew what to do with them. Finally Haraldsen grew embarrassed by his inability to make interesting conversation so he retired to the study he'd made next to the kitchen. Questions kept dancing all around his head. They would stay there until he did something to quell them.

Sitting at the desk in front of his laptop, reading glasses on, waiting on the sluggish internet connection, seemed as good a way as any to pass the time. Outside the chickens were clucking happily in their coops. The sheep had been checked. In their little haven just outside the village all seemed still. Or distant. Or simply unfathomable.

One other thing appeared out of place. The printer was bleating to have a cartridge changed. He couldn't recall using it in days, not since he'd churned out some fishing reports forwarded from Tórshavn.

By habit and nature, without talking this through at all, they'd always reverted to the same response when life brought them challenges. A quiet stoicism shared gently and then filed away as 'one of those things'. It had been like this when Tristan's heart had, as he'd put it, 'started to act up'. She'd listened to the news from the doctor, and how it meant early retirement, and said, 'Ja'. It was the same when their parents died, when friends were lost or filed for divorce. Even, in the early days of their marriage when cash was hard to come by and money problems reared their head.

The two of them went through the facts, ruminated over them in silence, said whatever was necessary, then retreated inside their own thoughts. In some odd way this was more reassuring – more loving – than the alternative of endless discussion that led nowhere except, perhaps, to the unwanted conclusion of argument.

Tristan Haraldsen never brooded, never lingered on bad thoughts or allowed them to fester. He did what he could to manage them, then waited for the following day to offer new challenges and opportunities. None of this seemed an acceptable position any more. Jónas Mikkelsen, a ten-year-old village scallywag, was dead. His brother, older in years but not, everyone said, in mind, had already been judged guilty of his killing.

It seemed an astonishing sequence of events. Unreal and quite wrong. Though in a sense all such questions were still academic. First they had to locate the absent Benjamin who, according to the Thomsens, could hide on the green hills around Árnafjall perhaps for days without being seen.

These events were so foreign, so unlike any he'd ever before encountered, Tristan Haraldsen felt unable to process them in any meaningful way. Which was why he'd slunk away from the equally silent and pensive Elsebeth to the computer where idly searching round for facts to quell the doubts and fears and questions that kept running round his head was meant to offer some kind of comfort.

He was halfway through something he'd found when the door opened and she came in.

'What are you doing?' she asked bringing the bottle of beer to refill his glass. Then she tidied away some spent paper by the printer, quickly scrunching it up and placing it in her pocket.

'You can leave the rubbish here,' he said. 'I'll empty the bin later.'

'It's alright.'

'We require more ink. I didn't know you needed to print something.'

A pause, then she asked if he liked the beer.

'You know I do, thank you,' Haraldsen said, grateful for the break from the screen. 'No need to linger. I feel tired but not sleepy. If you wish to go to bed . . .'

She smiled and patted his head.

'Tristan. By now you must know. Whenever anyone wants rid of me, I stay. What are you doing?'

'Just . . . nothing.'

He was so bad at lying. The guilt must have been written on his face.

'You've spent a long time doing nothing.'

Rumbled in an instant, as usual.

'I'm sorry, Elsebeth. I thought I was taking you somewhere quiet and peaceful. And now . . .'

'I was unaware you took me here. My recollection is this was a joint decision. Equal on both our parts.'

He took her hand and squeezed it. Warm skin, getting wrinkled.

'Funny,' he told her. 'If we'd had kids none of this would have happened.'

The question seemed to interest her. Elsebeth pulled up a seat and sat next to him at the desk.

'What do you mean?'

'I mean that if we'd been blessed with children I rather imagine we'd have stayed in Tórshavn. Where they were. We'd have been part of a bigger family. Instead of coming here.'

'Here is different,' she agreed. 'The people seem more like . . . pieces of the same jigsaw. The same tribe. One getting ever smaller. Perhaps a little fearful of the future.'

'Well put,' he agreed. 'As always.'

Elsebeth was a reflective woman and never made her thoughts known quickly. So it took a while before she said, 'So, I repeat my question. What are you doing?'

'Nosing about.'

'You're the district sheriff. Your job's a little one. We're retired here, aren't we?'

'Not today. Or yesterday.'

'They pay you a pittance to see the whales go to their end with as little pain as possible. Nothing else. You don't work for the police any more. And when you did you were an office manager. Not an investigator. Also your heart—'

'My heart's nothing. I rather wish I hadn't told you.'

There she glared at him.

'Of course you would have told me. I'm your wife. When you have something on your mind I'm meant to hear. So . . .' She folded her arms. 'What is it?'

'Beyond the obvious?' he asked. 'A child dead? His brother

missing? Supposedly his murderer? Or the one responsible for his death at least . . .'

That look in her eyes stopped him. It was the same expression, one of concern and care and foreboding, he'd seen when he first told her the department medical officer had spotted a blip in his annual check-up.

'There's more to it than that.'

'I hear him,' Haraldsen replied in the gentlest of voices. 'From Ganting's longliner, the *Alberta*'s deck.' His voice cracked. 'I hear him still, love. Jónas Mikkelsen. And see him. That poor boy screaming in terror as he fell down the cliff into Freyja's Pool. In that scream it's like there's a question—' he tapped his head and the sandy hair turning grey – 'in here. Asking . . . why?'

'And you think you can find the answers? The district sheriff? The man who's supposed to watch the grind and see it done the way it should be? Nothing more?'

He thought about that for a moment.

'I define my duties. Not some civil servant in Tórshavn. Or Aksel Højgaard. The plain fact is I was a witness to these events. In part their cause. I believe I have an obligation to try.'

She picked up the beer glass and took a sip. Haraldsen knew when she disapproved of something. There was no need of words.

'Move over,' she said, budging him out of the seat as she reached for the keyboard.

He'd minimised the page in question the moment she came close. She knew it too.

She squeezed his hand again and said, 'One of the reasons I love you is you're the least devious person I know. That's not the same as being a bad liar, by the way. Though you would be if you were so minded. I believe deceit is quite beyond you and that's not something one can say of many men.'

He stayed silent.

'And now you're nosing around about your neighbours. Which is not the Tristan Haraldsen I know at all.'

'I told you. I hear him screaming! I see him tumbling down that cliff! And besides a child does not kill another child. It's unthinkable.'

She scowled.

'Is it? If Jónas used to bully his brother something rotten like they say. If there was bad blood between them already . . . It may just have been a fight gone wrong. An accident. The boy went over the cliff . . .'

'With a whaling knife in his chest? Some accident. I saw something. Someone. Not a child . . .'

'What then?'

'I don't know!' he blurted out with such vehemence he felt guilty on the instant. 'A man.'

'Or a woman?'

'Possibly. Why do you ask?'

She said nothing then.

Haraldsen closed his eyes for a moment. It wasn't just the scream. He couldn't shake from his head a bloody, visual memory of the day before. The pod of blackfish in their death throes on the strand near the quay. The wives on the harbour cobbles close to tears demanding the menfolk end their agonies.

'Perhaps you're right,' he confessed. 'The way people think here, violence is a part of life. They kill the whales. They slaughter their lambs. Their chickens . . .'

Her fingers brushed his hair.

'It's where meat comes from. They simply see what most of us wish to avoid.'

That was true to an extent. Yet there was more to it.

'I think there's a feeling here,' he said, 'a belief, an old belief, that the way to deal with some intractable problems is to act and bring them to an end. To cauterise a wound. Or sever a useless limb. However painful that might be.'

Haraldsen was aware this conversation was upsetting his wife. Yet it was important. Some things had to be said.

'Benjamin did run away, didn't he?' she replied. 'Why would an innocent child do that?'

'A child's as likely to flee out of fear as guilt, surely. I know we're ignorant of parenting but surely we understand that? Or perhaps he was running *to* something, or someone, not away from it.'

'What do we truly know of these things, love?' she asked. 'How many murders were there in the twenty-five years you worked with the police?'

He'd thought about this already. Quite a lot. And checked it online.

'Two. Both domestic. A couple of decades apart.'

'Quite. And you were an office manager. They concerned you not a whit.'

'Two *reported* murders,' he added. 'Both in Tórshavn. Where one could hardly hide such a dreadful act. Here . . .'

He gestured at the window. No Northern Lights tonight. Instead the sky had cleared on the horizon, to reveal the last of a beautiful late sunset like a wild, imaginative painting, leaking golden blood into the sea.

'Here's supposed to be paradise,' she said gently.

'I'm sorry, Elsebeth. I can keep this from you no longer. There's something you must see.'

You're not needed any more.

Aksel Højgaard told Alba Mikkelsen that as they lifted Silas into the ambulance. She'd done as he'd asked. Gone and fetched what photographs she had of Benji, though why she wasn't clear. Everyone knew what he looked like. And how many twelve-year-old boys would be out roaming the fells in the wild anyway?

He'd wanted pictures of Jónas too and that she found even odder.

'Why'd you need all this?'

'Because I do,' he replied. Højgaard flicked through the photos. Most were from the summer before, back when they were still a family, just. The boys on the beach. The boys at the grind. A handsome one of Jónas grinning on the sand, stark naked, giggling with his hands in front of him, trying to hide while she took the embarrassing photo.

'I want them back.'

'Noted,' he said and pocketed the pictures.

She just about found the courage to say, 'They took my Jónas away and didn't even let me see him.'

'Best that way. What's the point?'

'He's my boy.'

Silas wasn't conscious when they took him. Or if he was he didn't make any effort to recognise her. He looked terrible. Broken limbs, blood everywhere.

'I want someone to drive me there,' she insisted. 'Sørvágur.'

'They've gone to Tórshavn,' he said, watching the ambulance go.
'Tórshavn then.'

'And how will you get back? At dead of night?'

Questions. That's all anyone threw at her. She didn't know.

'They're my family, Højgaard.'

'Ask your father then,' he said then climbed in behind the gurney
and the medics before closing the door in her face.

She did ask Baldur Ganting. The last thing on his mind was a
trip to Tórshavn. The *Alberta* was damaged. As always he was
thinking of the days to come, how to make money, how to save it.

'Silas won't be working for months. You know what that means,
daughter?'

'I am more worried about my Benji lost in the hills.' About
mourning for Jónas, poor, always-angry Jónas, dead, by his brother's
hand they said.

'And what use is your worrying, girl?' he snapped then went
back to the longliner to look at the shattered deck and the gear
they'd lost.

She wasn't much good at ordering her thoughts and there
seemed so many of them to marshal. Which came first? Which
last? What mattered more than something else? She'd no idea.

None of this was her fault though Alba expected the blame
anyway. That was how things worked.

'What am I supposed to do?' she asked in a voice so full of
pain and weakness it sent the few locals still lingering round her
scuttling elsewhere on the quay.

She knew what most of them would say: work. That was
Djevulsfjord's answer to everything. Climb on a boat and find
solace beyond the Skerries. Scour the hills for puffins to net or

hare to trap. Beg Dorotea Thomsen for part-time pin money gutting chicks in her kitchen or boiling blubber for the distant middle-class people in Tórshavn and beyond.

The only regular income she had was for cleaning the priest's place, the manse next to the white wooden church. Doing his washing and ironing. Two and a half hours a week she got paid for that though often he managed to squeeze another hour out of her for nothing.

Alba did not like Father Ryberg or the way he watched her, stroking his grey beard from time to time. She sat through his Sunday morning sermons out of duty alone. To miss them would be to incur his wrath. To make the men and women of Djevulsfjord stare at her even harder than they did most days. The lost woman. The single mother. The outcast.

If it kept on like this maybe she could run away again. Catch the bus through the Árnafjall tunnel to Tórshavn like she did the year before. Not take a job on the ferry to Denmark this time. Maybe . . . maybe steal enough for an air fare somewhere. Copenhagen. Sweden even. Whatever that was like. There'd always be jobs cleaning for people too idle or too rich to do the job themselves. A hotel would surely pay a legal wage greater than Ryberg's stingy thirty krónur an hour.

How could that be worse than the life she had in the fjord, eking out a grim existence for herself and the two boys, one a tyrant, the other an idiot? The first now dead and the other probably headed for detention when they found him. Whatever the future held it looked like being one she'd end up facing on her own.

Alba Mikkelsen had no illusions about herself. She was skinny, not bright. Attractive enough to get men interested provided she gave them what they wanted. Silas wasn't the first in that regard. Simply the first who'd promised, in the white village church, to look after her, in good times and bad, through sickness and in health.

That was a lie, sworn on the Bible. God was a man. On their side, not hers.

Once they'd found Benji and told her she couldn't be his mum any more – and that would happen, she felt sure – then she'd be free to take herself off wherever she felt like. Nothing left in Djevulsfjord to keep her there except pain, regret and misery.

'Need money,' she whispered to herself. 'Can't run without something in my pocket.'

That's what she'd done the year before when Silas belted her once too often, and as a result found herself mucking out cabins and toilets on the ferry to Jutland.

'Need to . . . to . . .'

She shook her head, tried to think straight. How could she even consider running? There had to be a funeral. Jónas going in the brown Djevulsfjord earth. He was an evil little bastard and doubtless got up to stuff Alba never knew about. But dead . . . that seemed impossible. Only the morning before, looking forward to mischief at the grind, he'd seemed so full of himself. As if he knew something was up.

Her eyes welled up and she rubbed them with the back of her hand. You weren't supposed to cry out in the street in Djevulsfjord. Weeping was for the home. For the bedroom. Preferably on your own.

'If I'd known . . .' she muttered through her tears and saw the way the people of the quay moved further down the cobbles. 'If I'd have known!' she cried.

'Known what?'

The old, familiar, taunting voice. Dorotea Thomsen was out, poking her nose in everywhere as usual. She came up close and bent her big and fleshy face to peer in Alba's. 'Known what those young sons of yours was up to?'

'They were good boys in their hearts,' was all she could think to offer.

Dorotea folded her flabby arms in front of her chest.

'Well, that's not much use now, is it? No point you thinking about the past, Alba. Enough to worry you in the future, if you ask me.'

'Yes,' she whispered.

'Speaking of which I gather Silas isn't likely to be out of hospital in weeks. Maybe he'll be stuck in that wheelchair. Can't work the boats again at all. You thought about that?'

'My little boy is dead.'

'I *know*. And the other one done for him. The past. Can't change that. The future . . .'

It was impossible to argue with the woman. The Thomsens as good as owned Djevulsfjord. If they wanted, they could cast you out like God did Satan when he made the place with his horny wing.

'I did my best. I loved them both.'

Dorotea Thomsen scowled.

'Love. Can't feed a soul with that, can you? Can't light a fire. Can't build a house on love. No use at all that frippery, child. Only trouble comes of love. You want strength and money and all that comes with them.'

'I was their mum. That was my strength.'

'Not enough then, was it?'

Another time, in another world, she'd have walloped the fat old cow right there and then. Took out all the fury and the grief on her, nails scratching, fingers flying. But not in the life she'd been given. That was never going to happen.

'A funeral's going to cost,' Dorotea added. 'You talked to Lars Ryberg about that yet?'

'He only died this afternoon.'

'Got to go to Sørvágur for an undertaker. Those bastards will sting you good and proper too. Don't matter if it's a young 'un or someone in their dotage.'

Dorotea took her arm for a moment and seemed to try her best to appear friendly.

'I must remind you, girl. You signed a contract on those rooms I rented you. Two months' notice. Money's due whether you're there or not. Two months. Paid weekly. I'm a businesswoman. Can't afford to do favours. Still want my money come Monday, I'm afraid.'

'You got work?' It was the question she wanted to be asked.

She chortled at that.

'Not the usual. All the meat and blubber from the grind's taken care of. We won't be needing casual labour maybe not till spring.'

'Then . . . how . . .?'

'What about your mum and dad?'

'My mum and dad are in hock to you up to their elbows already.'

'Well . . .' Dorotea Thomsen withdrew her arm and put a finger to her cheek. 'Let me think on it. While I do I guess there's only one place left then. Back in the days when people starved it was always the church they turned to. That's where charity comes from. You talk to Ryberg. See if there's any extra . . . duties he can offer.' She sniffed the air, ready to go. 'Good luck with that.'

She watched her waddle off back towards their nice house by the harbour. The lady of the village. The one you never scorned. She was right though. A funeral would cost. No money coming from Silas for months ahead. All the dreams: a funeral for Jónas, a future for Benjamin if she could somehow think of one, a ticket out of Vágar if everything came to naught; all these things depended upon her having something no one in the world was going to give her.

As evening fell she left the quayside, walked up to the priest's timber cottage and stood outside looking at the place. It was like the man himself: gaunt and bare. The brightest part was the downstairs windows freshly-painted with white frames, a contribution he'd demanded of one of his parishioners during the summer. Ryberg levied his parishioners like a minister of old. He scrounged food and favours constantly, nudging his flock into acts of reluctant generosity they would never bestow on one another.

Respect for God meant respect for his priests. Or so the lean bachelor always said.

And respect came in many forms.

But he had his bony fingers on the purse strings of the church. There was money there somewhere. There had to be.

HARALDSEN WENT BACK TO the computer and pulled up the cutting he'd found earlier. It was from the previous summer and headlined: 'Djevulsfjord man dies in tragic cliff fall'. Then a line in smaller type beneath that read: 'Father finds him during boat search'.

He scanned it again and said, 'Remember. This is written from

Tórshavn. A reporter they sent to the scene the following day. As much a foreigner as us. Everything reported third-hand at best. From whatever the locals . . . and Aksel Højgaard chose to say.'

Elsebeth dragged her chair right up to the desk and started to read the piece out loud.

'Kaspar Ganting, a much-loved son and brother of Djevulsfjord, was pronounced dead yesterday after his body was recovered by his own father in Freyja's Pool, a cove at the foot of the Lundi Cliffs, one of the remote area's most scenic natural features. He was twenty-five, a fisherman and jobbing labourer in the village. His father Baldur Ganting farms and owns the longliner *Alberta* on which Kaspar worked regularly. The young man had lived at home since leaving Vágar College seven years before.

'Father Lars Ryberg, priest in the village, paid tribute to Kaspar yesterday and asked for his family to be left in peace to mourn him. He described the dead man as a "paragon of virtue" who had contributed to every local social activity with a selfless and dedicated enthusiasm. A much-loved brother to Alba and uncle to little Jónas and Benjamin.'

Haraldsen tapped the screen.

'But that isn't right, is it? Not if Dorotea Thomsen is telling the truth. The man was a rascal. How a priest can . . .?'

'What do you expect him to say?' Elsebeth asked. 'The poor creature had just been found dead. Is the man with the Bible supposed to add to the family's misery by spouting out the truth about him to the world at large?'

Haraldsen nodded and agreed this was a good point.

She read on.

'The circumstances of the death have now been established

after a thorough investigation by Vágar police. The dead man, like many a Djevulsfjord local, was fond of walking the hills of a summer night. At nine in the evening Kaspar announced that he was minded to go looking for puffins and eggs above Freyja's Pool and afterwards, given the fair weather, to sleep out on the hills, a habit many in the fishing village have at this time of year, so pleasant is the summer climate. It was not the first time he'd taken such a decision so none in his family thought this remarkable.

'Kaspar then took his puffin net and walked alone to the cliffs that lead across the seaward foothill of Árnafjall towards Selkie Bay. Somewhere along the path it appears he lost his footing and tumbled more than eighty metres onto the rocks at the base of the outcrop.

'His family were sure he had decided to stay out on the hills for the night. So his absence was unquestioned. However the following morning locals in Djevulsfjord were alerted when gulls were seen in frantic activity near the area. A boat captained by the man's own father went out to investigate.

'After a dangerous and demanding sortie into the treacherous waters and rocks near the cliffs Kaspar's body was recovered around midday and immediately returned to his home village where the police were called. Father Ryberg paid tribute to the many local men and women who have called upon the Ganting family – parents Baldur and Eydna and a married sister Alba – to offer their condolences. The funeral is due to take place in Djevulsfjord next Wednesday, with a respectful turnout from the village expected for such a popular fellow.'

Haraldsen closed his eyes. He couldn't begin to imagine the agonies Baldur Ganting must have gone through revisiting this same nightmare that very day, and finding the body of his grandson in the process.

'So was this nosing about worthwhile?' Elsebeth wondered. 'Does this fit in with your role as district sheriff?'

'I may know very little about habits here in Djevulsfjord. But I'm sure as sure can be no local man goes hunting puffins and eggs at nine o'clock at night. And the idea a fellow like that . . .'

'You don't know what he was like! You've only Dorotea Thomsen's word for it!'

'I may not be a detective, wife. But I recognise the improbable when I see it.' He gazed at her over the glasses he needed for the computer. 'And so do you. Ja?'

She scowled. Then shrugged.

'Now you may wish to leave me because what I am about to do is, in theory, beyond the law.'

'Oh, Tristan! Leave this and for pity's sake come to bed.'

He didn't answer, just hammered on the keys.

THE ADDRESS FOR THE internal website of the police headquarters in Tórshavn was one he knew by heart. As office manager there he'd used this same laptop when working from home.

'What in God's name are you doing now?'

'Seeing how efficient our technical people are when it comes to removing retired colleagues from the system.'

The logon form came up. He typed in his old password.

'This is shameful,' she said. 'Prying into matters that are none of our business.'

Haraldsen found himself looking at the page that had greeted him every day for most of the last five years, ever since someone from Copenhagen came over and installed the new network, then found a young man fresh out of the Faroes university computer department to run it.

His inbox contained three emails from colleagues wishing him good luck on his retirement and offering invitations for beer. All of them had arrived after his departure from the building.

A few keystrokes took him into the records section where he typed in: Kaspar Ganting.

There were two files there. One listed a series of seven complaints lodged within the space of four months, the last just two days before his death. They accused Ganting of theft, aggressive and threatening behaviour and logged three reports of sexual harassment at dances in Vágar. But since the accusations had arrived anonymously in the form of paper printouts sent by post to Tórshavn there was, the report concluded, little the police could do.

'They must have interviewed him,' Elsebeth said.

'If they had it would be here.'

She hesitated then asked, 'Why not?'

'I don't know.'

'All these charges . . .'

It was hard to explain.

'They're not charges, love. They're accusations. Without a name to put to them.'

'And no police officer would even have had a word with him? What about one of your beer-drinking mates? If one of them had been on the case?'

Haraldsen thought about that.

'If anyone should have been looking at this it was the station in Sørvágur. Aksel Højgaard.'

He knew what was coming next.

'So you are going to raise this with him?'

'Perhaps your new friend Hanna . . .?' he suggested.

'Hanna Olsen wasn't there at the time. And this is none of her business.'

'Never mind. Let me take a peek inside the Sørvágur records then.'

'Tristan!'

There was very little to look at. Simply a document stating that the complaints had been handed to the responsible superintendent to consider and he had recommended no action due to the lack of evidence and witness names.

A noise outside disturbed them. The sheep stirring for some reason. Elsebeth leaned forward and looked at the screen.

'Well, well. Signed off by Aksel Højgaard. So your friend from Tórshavn knew about this all along.'

'I never said Højgaard was my friend.' Haraldsen scrolled down the screen but there was nothing more to see. 'Merely an acquaintance. They dispatched him to Sørvágur five or six years ago, I believe. His family come from Vágar originally if I remember correctly. There were manning problems or something. He never came back.'

Haraldsen then looked at the second file on Kaspar Ganting. It was the autopsy performed after Baldur Ganting had identified his son. The conclusion was clear: accidental death caused by multiple injuries due to a fall.

'See,' Elsebeth said triumphantly. 'This is where your suspicious nature leads you. Nowhere.'

He read the details carefully. As the paper predicted there was no sign of illegal drugs in his corpse and little trace of alcohol, insufficient, the medical examiner said, to impair his senses.

Ganting had fallen a long way to his death. His body suffered terrible injuries meeting the cruel hard rocks of the cliff near Freyja's Pool. The pathologist suspected he might well have been dead from an impact along the way before reaching the bottom. A head wound that showed clear signs of rock fragments would have rendered him unconscious if not killed him, even without the dreadful lacerations to his chest that came from the ledge on which he landed.

'He must have hit himself on the way down,' Elsebeth suggested.

'Or someone hit him. Much the way someone struck poor Hanna Olsen today.'

'You don't know that, Tristan.'

He scrolled to the bottom of the document.

'And they never found a puffin net,' he said.

IT WOULD BE WRONG to reply to the emails from his former colleagues. All that would do would be to alert them to the fact the young man recruited to run their system from the university was a little lax when it came to maintenance. And deny him entry another time, of course.

'Kaspar Ganting was a Djevulsfjord boy,' he pointed out. 'He would have clambered those cliffs chasing puffins and their eggs as soon as he could walk. Crossed them like a mountain goat, like those two nephews of his did yesterday. He was a strong and agile young man from all accounts.'

He pulled up some photos on the laptop. Elsebeth had taken them the previous summer when they took the Ace Capri to Vágar for a walking holiday and become so entranced by the scenery they'd begun to dream about moving there when retirement came.

'This is the footpath,' he said, finding the sequence he wanted. 'The one where I saw Hanna Olsen. Probably the one Kaspar Ganting took too.'

There Elsebeth was, pretty as a picture, on what looked like a scorching summer day. Sunny blue sky, peaceful azure sea. Not a cloud anywhere. This being the Faroes the weather was never quite that kind, of course. So she wore a navy windcheater and a headscarf and stood arms folded, beaming at the camera, happy as a lark.

The track was broad grass, clearly-marked. It ran a good six steps back from the cliff edge. A cautious man, not fond of heights, he remembered walking it and recalled thinking about that precipitous drop, determined that neither he nor Elsebeth would go near.

'Tell me,' he said, 'tell me please. How does a man like Kaspar Ganting, as sure-footed as a goat, sober, intent on something – though I doubt it was birding – how does he fall to his death in a place like that? Truly, Elsebeth. How?'

She didn't answer.

'And how can it be, one year later, that his own nephew should die in the selfsame spot? Supposedly at his brother's hand?'

Elsebeth looked set to cry which made him feel deeply guilty, though determined nonetheless.

'Oh, Tristan. We're both tired and overwrought after this terrible day. Two terrible days . . .'

Her hand went to his head again. Elsebeth's eyes were bleary, with exhaustion and, he realised, the beginning of tears.

'Do you not feel something's wrong?' Haraldsen asked.

'Everything can seem wrong if you look hard enough. The wrongest thing I see right now is my dear husband.'

'Jónas Mikkelsen ran away from the strand because of me. Had I not—'

'This isn't your fault. We should leave it.' Elsebeth bent down and kissed his cheek. 'Please. No more.'

Not since the time they got lost on holiday in Jutland – entirely due to Haraldsen's faulty map-reading as he later realised – had they been so close to a genuine, heartfelt squabble. The very proximity of that pained him.

'Perhaps you're right,' he said.

She reached out and closed the laptop lid.

Haraldsen got to his feet, stretched and said, 'If I were a praying man I'd put my hands together for that poor lad out there somewhere now. And his father in hospital.'

'I'll make some bedtime tea. And get you clean pyjamas. The red ones. The black ones are in the wash.'

'The black ones are more comfy . . .'

'And covered in grass cuttings since you insisted on mowing the roof in them. I had to brush a load of clippings out of the bed thank you very much.'

'Ah.' That seemed a long time ago. 'I must finish that some time. A tidy roof is a necessity . . .'

'But not in your pyjamas this time . . .'

Haraldsen pulled the empty pipe out of his cardigan pocket and sucked on it.

There was something more she was about to say. But Elsebeth stopped and they both knew why. It was the noise from outside again. The sheep in their pen were bleating their little hearts out, a sad refrain of fear and puzzlement the likes of which neither of them had heard before. Then the chickens joined in too with a chorus of worried clucking.

'Stay here,' Haraldsen said and went for the door.

TEN

Father Ryberg was at the fireplace in his tidy living room when Alba Mikkelsen came in.

'You didn't knock,' the priest complained.

She stood on the threshold of the bare, bachelor room, puzzled. When she came to clean he'd never asked her to announce herself before. Just watched her walk in, thinking. Looking. He was a priest. He was a man as well.

'I thought you'd be out searching for that lad of yours,' Ryberg said.

'They said they'll start again tomorrow. Police. Like he's a murderer or something.'

She hadn't seen him out with the teams that afternoon. Only the first night when they went missing.

'I don't know where the money's going to come from. Not for anything. Dorotea Thomsen's bloody hovel. I'm not going back in with Mum and Dad. Not if I can help it. No room there for Benji when they find him . . .'

Ryberg sighed as if she were stupid.

'Your boy will go into one of the homes in Tórshavn if they find him. Maybe across the water in Denmark. You don't need to worry about that.'

'I'm not *worrying*. He's my son. He should be with me. So I can look after him.'

He had cold eyes but she knew exactly what he was thinking at that moment. Probably what most of Djevulsfjord was thinking.

You couldn't look after the boys when there were two of them. Now the youngest's dead you think they'll let you screw up raising the daft one who can barely dress himself as well?

'I can look after him,' she insisted. 'Benji's just slow. You need to be patient. Jónas never was which is why they fought . . .'

'He killed his brother.'

No, she thought. She still couldn't believe that. Not that there was any point in saying that to Lars Ryberg. Or probably anyone else in Djevulsfjord at that moment.

'I'm going to need some money. For the funeral. For Benji when they find him. For the bills. Dorotea Thomsen—'

'She sent you here, did she?' he snapped behind the beard.

'She said the church is about . . . charity. About looking after the flock.'

'Some flock,' Ryberg grumbled. 'They get back what they put in. Not been much of that since I came here.'

'I need to earn more money,' she begged. 'I'll work for it. Do more cleaning. Whatever you want. I got all the hours in the day. Got no pride either. This place beat that out of me long ago. You just say . . .'

That came out wrong, she thought, and regretted it immediately.

He was grinning, white teeth breaking the silver whiskers.

'Well, you know how to earn it, don't you?' he said tugging at his belt.

The priest walked back into the hall, then did something so strange she wondered if she were dreaming. Father Lars Ryberg

141

took the old, long key off its hook beneath a painting of Christ on the cross, and nodded upstairs.

'I'll be going now,' she said and did.

ELSEBETH WAS THERE BEFORE Haraldsen could go outside, hands outstretched, flapping. 'Enough, Tristan. It's just a stray dog or something.'

He stopped by the door, hands on his hips.

'I know this has been an odd day, dearest. But truly to see you in this state simply because I desire to check our chickens . . .'

'Discuss these matters with our young policewoman friend,' she added. 'Let her set your mind to rest. Your heart—'

'My mind, I believe, is in much the state it's always been. My heart, as I keep saying, is nothing serious.'

Outside the sheep bleated again. There was a puzzled, half-frightened cackling from the hens cooped up for the night next to the butchery.

'For me then,' she pleaded.

'This is our home,' Haraldsen said with a sternness he did not truly mean. He grabbed the torch from the kitchen sideboard and his jacket off the hook. 'I shall see what's out there.'

'You do not even have a gun!'

The shrill nature of her voice was quite foreign to them both. And the thought that they of all people might need such a weapon. Common as it might be among the locals who would shoot as much game as they could – they'd heard evidence of that often enough – the possession of a shotgun was something the two of them had never discussed for a moment. They might as well have discussed the acquisition of a spacecraft.

'You worry too much. Stay here,' Haraldsen ordered and marched outside.

NIGHT HAD FALLEN COMPLETELY. Stars were beginning to make their presence known through the clearing sky. The autumn constellations of the northern hemisphere had arrived. Andromeda, Aquarius and Capricorn. Among them stood the bright sparkle of the North Star.

With a brisk and unfaltering stride he marched over towards the brick and wooden abattoir and the chicken coop next to it. There were sounds he recognised. The distant screech of an owl. The sheep back to mumbling again.

Then something stirred rapidly behind him. He turned and found himself shining the torch directly into Elsebeth's face.

'You don't think I'd leave you out here on your own, do you?' she asked, a shaky kind of annoyance behind the question.

They heard it then. Someone nearby, movement in the field.

'Hey!' Haraldsen called. 'You! Stop now. Stop what you are doing and talk to us, please.'

Silence and they waited, a little afraid but not so much they'd go inside.

Finally, frantic, not certain what he was doing at all, Tristan Haraldsen raced forward and began to shout.

'Benjamin Mikkelsen! Benji! Do not be afraid, child. There's no need. We are your friends. We will help you, boy. Benji!'

He stumbled on one of the stones laid out to mark the path and nearly fell over. Elsebeth was with him straight away, holding his arm.

'This is madness, Tristan. Come inside, love.'

He shook her off and began yelling again, loud enough to reach the stars he felt.

'Benjamin! *Benjamin!* I do not believe you harmed your brother. I know there is another out there. Come here, child. Come stay with us tonight. We'll keep you safe.'

Silence, then three bright chirps from an owl.

'Whoever it was . . . whatever . . . has fled,' she said. 'And thank goodness for that.'

'You think it good?'

'I do. It was probably a dog.'

'A dog.'

Something clattered in the breeze. When he shone the torch they saw. The chicken coop door was open. Haraldsen took a deep breath, bent down and went inside, his wife behind him.

The hens were where they were supposed to be.

'If only chickens could talk,' Elsebeth suggested.

'No dog,' he said. 'A stray would have been among these birds and killing them.'

The flock had come from a farmer outside Sørvágur, along with instructions on their upkeep, diet and how to keep out the dreaded red mite. They were pure whites and he knew the heaviest layer because she was the biggest and most vocal and always sat on the roost beside the door, above the same nesting box she used day to day.

'You collected any eggs today?' he asked, aiming the torch beam into the box.

'No,' she answered. 'Not yesterday either. There never was the time.'

He reached down and felt the empty nest box, then showed her the bare straw in the beam of the touch.

'Then either we have a local dog that likes to take his supper home. Or a hungry thief.' He thought about what he'd read. 'That boy's out there. Nearby. He'll be living off raw eggs and anything else he can find.'

Haraldsen went back into the garden and started to call his name over and over again.

Benjamin, Benjamin Mikkelsen.

Out to the stars and the endless sky.

He did that for a good minute or two until Elsebeth linked her arm through his and said, 'And do you think he'd come, dear? For a stranger baying at the moon?'

'Benjamin,' he cried. 'You have nothing to worry about. I am the district sheriff and I'll make sure they treat you kindly. Fairly too. For what it's worth, lad, I don't believe you hurt your brother. Not for a moment. Not for a . . .'

His voice was breaking. Elsebeth made a little whimper next to him and he realised in that instant she might be about to cry again.

'We can deal with this tomorrow,' she begged. 'When we can both try and think straight.'

The district sheriff was supposed to keep an eye on the mete-orological forecasts. One had come in while he'd been at the computer.

'The weather changes fast here, love. Storm one moment. Clear the next. Tomorrow I think it may well turn again.'

The mobile phone in his pocket throbbed and warbled. He looked at the message there. A summons from Højgaard to the

Sørvágur police building the following morning at nine. Nothing more than that. The superintendent expected to be obeyed without question.

'What is it?' she asked.

'A meeting. In Sørvágur tomorrow. I will need the Ace Capri. Will you be alright here on your own?'

'I'm not a child, Tristan. Do you not want me there?'

He hesitated, then said, 'It's business. Perhaps unpleasant. I'd rather . . .'

'Very well.' To his surprise she didn't seem upset at all. 'Let's go to bed.'

IT WAS ALMOST MIDNIGHT. He couldn't remember when they'd been awake this late. They lay in the big divan along from the rafters where chickens had roosted the year before, one pooping on her head as she came through the door that time they'd first looked round. There were no more unusual sounds from outside. No easy words between them either, which was new.

Both understood why this was, not that they realised they shared the knowledge. Elsebeth was nagged by the fact she'd received the threatening message from Inga Dam and never told him. It would have been wrong at that moment. He was too energised, too overwrought to receive yet more distressing information.

The solution lay within her own hands. In the morning perhaps she should go over to Selkie Bay, find the Dam woman, and have this out with her face-to-face.

She kissed his bristly cheek and asked him if he really hated the red pyjamas.

'I know they're not as fluffy as your black ones and with winter coming on I wouldn't want you to be cold.'

'They will suffice,' was all he said.

'When I'm next in Tórshavn I will get you another black pair.' He seemed lost in thought. 'Or you could buy your own, Tristan. There's always that possibility.'

'No.' He kissed her in return, closed his eyes and folded his arms over the duvet. 'You're so much better at these things than me.'

'If you say so. Goodnight.'

For his own part Tristan Haraldsen wanted to tell her his own secret, the other story he'd come across hunting around in the files on the web. But Elsebeth was worried enough and he'd no desire to add to her concern. Probably for no good reason. Probably.

The previous district sheriff was called Kristian Djurhuus. A bachelor of fifty-eight, originally from Sørvágur though he'd spent the best part of three decades as an inspector in the Copenhagen police before returning to the Faroes. A dour-sounding man, he'd been in the habit of sending the occasional email to the police headquarters in Tórshavn, most of which were rerouted to Aksel Højgaard. A few remained on the system and they were not the kind of thing Haraldsen felt was consistent with the district sheriff's role. They hinted at potential tax-dodging among the Djevulsfjord fishermen, some smuggling perhaps and other misdemeanours that were only suggested. The name of Kaspar Ganting was mentioned too when he moaned about drunkenness and thuggery which the authorities seemed willing to ignore. Given that the little fishing village was as remote a place as one might find on Vágar this was, perhaps, understandable. If the police had to navigate the single-track lane of the Árnafjall tunnel, a forty-minute journey from Sørvágur, they'd hardly turn out for the odd boozy brawl.

None of this would have mattered were it not for two facts Haraldsen spotted in the logs. Djurhuus had died one night in that self-same tunnel not far from their own front door, supposedly while riding his unlit bike. Run over by a vehicle, perhaps a commercial one, the police were uncertain because the driver was never found. Djurhuus was regarded as a Dane, not a local, and so the story had merited no more than a few paragraphs in the papers, where it was recorded as one more drink-driving fatality.

The investigating officer – if indeed the inquiries into Djurhuus could be described as an investigation – was, naturally, Aksel Højgaard. His predecessor had died a week after Kaspar Ganting's body had been retrieved from the foot of the Lundi Cliffs by the unfortunate man's own father.

Running this over in his mind Haraldsen found himself wondering out loud, 'Why in God's name would a man ride a bike through the Árnafjall tunnel? At night without so much as a light?'

His pulse raced. His heart pounded. Elsebeth stirred beside him.

'What did you say?' she asked in a drowsy mumble.

'Nothing,' he told her. 'Nothing at all. Just . . . rambling in my sleep.'

He wasn't sure she heard that. Or the words that came before.

Tristan Haraldsen hoped not. Something was up in Djevulsfjord. Something the district sheriff before might have spotted too, and perhaps paid for with his life.

ELEVEN

At seven the two of them rose, dealt with the chickens and the sheep, had breakfast, then fell into an uneasy silence.

'You would not want to come,' Haraldsen announced finally over his boiled eggs.

'Perhaps not.'

'Højgaard was very clear. The invitation was for me, in my official capacity.' She sniffed at that. 'There are better things for you to do here, Elsebeth. That poor mother with her lost child. The parties will be searching for the brother. You're very good at offering consolation.'

'Only to those willing to accept it. I don't think our neighbours much seek consolation from the likes of outsiders like us, do they?'

'True,' he said and got his jacket.

'If there's anything you want me to pick up in Sørvágur?'

The place had a small supermarket and a petrol station which doubled as an off licence.

'Bread, milk, butter, some meat,' she said. 'Also fill up the Capri with diesel if you please and the two spare cans in the shed for safety. Perhaps while you're at the garage you can buy us some beer as well.'

It was all said with such a distanced lack of enthusiasm he felt quite strange.

'You're not sulking because I'm leaving you on your own, are you? If so—'

'I don't sulk, husband. When have you ever known me sulk?'

From time to time, he thought, but judged it was best not to mention as much.

'I'm sure the parties out looking for poor Benjamin will be grateful for some help, love.'

'I have things to do, Tristan. You've no need to fill my day for me. Thank you very much.'

'Very well,' he said. 'So be it.'

Elsebeth watched him manoeuvre the Ace Capri out of the drive then down towards the dark mouth of the Árnafjall tunnel. They were both disconcerted about the manner of their parting, she felt. There were secrets between them and that was new.

ONE HOUR LATER HE sat down in the single-storey brown wooden cottage that served as Sørvágur's police station and absent-mindedly reached for his pipe. Only to discover he'd forgotten it.

'No smoking in here,' Aksel Højgaard said, realizing what he was searching for. 'Not on government premises. You can go outside for that.'

Hanna Olsen, in uniform now which made her look older and somewhat more remote, sat at the end of the table and said nothing.

'I seem to recall I've seen you smoke here.'

'That's different.'

'So it seems,' Haraldsen replied and took out his pen and note-book to fiddle with instead.

The town lay at the end of a narrow bay, surrounded by modest rising hills, nothing like the towering peak of Árnafjall. Around a thousand people lived there if his memory served right, more than ten times the population of tiny Djevulsfjord. All the same it looked like their own hamlet writ large, a collection of low timber bungalows in many colours, white and green and blue and ochre, so close to the airport that visitors often walked the twenty minutes to their chosen boarding house by the water.

Twenty-four hours after Jónas Mikkelsen's death, Haraldsen was still unable to set his mind straight about what had happened. The violent storm upon the water. The shock of recovering the wounded child's body. Then the strange information he'd uncovered the night before about Kaspar Ganting. And the secret, the thing he'd kept from Elsebeth, probably so badly she'd suspected something was up. The fact his predecessor as district sheriff had died a violent and unexplained death not far from their home.

They were in a small bare room with a long dusty window looking out on a black timber church with a white spire. It was as if the previous day's storm had never happened. Gulls floated against the horizon, suspended over the lazy waves. A few fishing boats were making their way out to sea. Past the inlet a line of morning mist was fading like smoke dispelled by the breath of an invisible giant.

Even a good four hundred metres from the ragged shoreline Haraldsen could taste the hard salt tang of the ocean in his throat, behind it the cloying stink of dead whale. There'd been a grind here lately. The whitening ribbed skeletons of the victims lay on the beach, dogs scavenging around the carrion. The arrival of the pilot whales seemed to have occupied Sørvágur much more than a strange death in Djevulsfjord, a remote, and ill-considered community hidden away behind the far-off peak of Árnafjall, reached reluctantly, and only by the narrow, foul-smelling tunnel.

'Are you any closer to finding Benjamin Mikkelsen?' he asked when he could think of nothing else.

Højgaard almost looked affronted by the question.

'Think of what you just said, man. How would we know if we were close?'

'I imagine . . . I imagine it depends on how hard you're looking. And where. I heard no helicopters this morning . . .'

The superintendent waved away the idea immediately.

'Helicopters cost a fortune. If the boy's anywhere he's hiding in a cave and there's a warren of them. I have a small unit out from our rescue group. They're looking for signs. I do not expect an early resolution.'

Still the policewoman stayed silent.

From what Haraldsen remembered of his police days, the most Vágar had to deal with was the odd motoring offence, usually to do with alcohol, and the occasional domestic dispute. It felt quite odd to hear Højgaard relate what he believed to be the train of events that led to Jónas Mikkelsen's death, and the injuries that had led to the boy's father being rushed to hospital, so badly hurt he might be confined to a wheelchair for many months.

Jónas it was who jabbed at Haraldsen at the grind then fled for the hills with his brother. They stayed there overnight and at some point the following day the two had an argument inside the puffin hide. One of the boys had heard Hanna Olsen approaching and struck her from behind. A struggle had taken place which resulted in Benjamin wounding his younger brother with a whaling knife then, accidentally or deliberately, pushing him over the cliff.

'Not a pretty story,' Højgaard concluded. 'Still, that's Djevulsfjord for you. But I am confident that is the only explanation and shall put it down in the log. The Mikkelsen lad will doubtless confirm it if we ever find him—'

'If?' Haraldsen asked in astonishment.

'If,' Højgaard repeated. 'Those hills are perilous. Mines and rock falls. We've known grown men vanish up there before.'

'So I believe,' Hanna Olsen threw in.

Haraldsen shook his head.

'I'm sorry?'

'Not now,' Højgaard snapped.

'Superintendent—' she seemed determined to continue – 'do you have any evidence for these suppositions?'

'Suppositions?'

'I mean this as no criticism, but you have no murder squad,' Hanna pointed out. 'No call for one. I worked murder in Aalborg where there was a need. Where we had certain procedures—'

'This isn't Aalborg.'

'No. But murder's murder. I was assaulted also . . .'

'I said already. It was one of the Mikkelsen boys who attacked you from behind. They were well known for fighting and the older lad was big enough and strong enough to take you down.'

She shook her head. The yellow hair was tucked back in a ponytail and there was a seriousness about her Haraldsen hadn't noticed before.

'That's not how I remember it. I thought I heard a man there . . .'

'You thought?' Højgaard responded. 'Yet you saw nothing. We've been through this.'

'I saw someone,' Haraldsen insisted. 'From Baldur Ganting's boat. It looked too big to be a boy.'

Højgaard scowled, a natural expression for his narrow, unsmiling face.

'How big?'

'I don't know. The figure came out from the puffin hide. We were in that rough sea. Ganting's binoculars were old.'

The superintendent laughed and turned to the police officer at his side.

'So tell me. How would evidence like that fare in an Aalborg murder inquiry, Officer Olsen? Would your squad of detectives in Aalborg take seriously something someone thought they saw at a great distance from the deck of a boat in the middle of a stormy sea?'

'I believe Mr Haraldsen worked for the police—'

'He was a pen-pusher! A counter of paper clips! Not a serving police officer.'

'Nevertheless, I do not believe what I saw was a boy, Højgaard. In fact—'

'You have no facts.' The man held up his hand, demanding silence. 'I've been through all the statements. I know what they say. The truth is Officer Olsen never saw her assailant. You were far distant on a vessel that nearly came a cropper on the rocks. What weight may I or anyone give to what you think you saw?'

'A little surely,' Hanna thought. 'The district sheriff was there. He witnessed something. Also . . . also I smelled tobacco smoke. Cigarettes.'

'And? Do you think these young louts had never smoked a cigarette?'

'I don't know.'

Højgaard shook his head.

'No. You don't. Of course they would. Besides, it's irrelevant. I went there myself. I looked inside that puffin hide. There was no trace of cigarettes. No evidence of a man. No footprints. Nothing. All this I oversaw personally. Do you think I take a violent death here lightly? Which is it you question? My professionalism or my honesty? Or both?'

There, Haraldsen thought, he had them. Neither would wish to make such an accusation lightly. Nor did they possess a shred of evidence or cause to argue for it.

'Well, we can ask young Benjamin when we find him,' Hanna said and from her face Haraldsen could see she felt this was a weak response. 'We must do that, Højgaard. I'm sure you agree.'

The superintendent stared at her: cornered.

'We look. But how much time is decent to devote to this? To a lost boy from a damaged family?'

'As much as is necessary to find him, I'd say,' Haraldsen replied with heat. 'The child's been on his own for two nights now. Whatever happened on the Lundi Cliffs . . . he must have witnessed something terrible. I believe—'

'The search continues though I have reduced it to two men. You, Olsen, will not be a part of it,' Højgaard broke in. 'How many times can we return to places we've looked at before? Say he harmed his brother, perhaps in what started as nothing more than a childish fight. All the same he must know how it turned out. He may have fallen down a pit. Dead. Perhaps at his own hand.'

The casual ease with which he spoke silenced them for a while.

Finally Haraldsen asked, 'Then why did you summon me? It seems that you've solved the conundrum, in your own mind at least. For myself I would rather be out looking for that poor mite on those hills. Not sitting here listening to dry theories.'

Højgaard picked up a pen and clicked the top.

'You're the district sheriff. I know your responsibilities begin and end with the whales. Nevertheless you worked for the police service. You understand how things are managed.'

Haraldsen nodded in agreement.

'As district sheriff . . . is there anything you've noticed in your time in Djevulsfjord that I should be aware of? If so now's the time to say it.'

'Such as?' Haraldsen wondered.

'It is my duty to ask.'

'I cannot think of a single thing I'm aware of that will be of assistance,' Haraldsen replied with a sigh. 'Beyond what I've told you already which you seem to feel has little merit. I'm sorry. I wish I could offer more.'

'Well.' Højgaard seemed oddly pleased to hear that. 'It was only right I should have this conversation with you. There are more schools of blackfish around. Perhaps when the grind is in progress they'll start to gossip. If there is more to be known. Of that I'm unsure. Djevulsfjord's a squalid little place. Full of squalid little people. One should not expect much of them.'

Tristan Haraldsen didn't move.

The superintendent motioned at the door.

'I'm busy today. My superior in Tórshavn requires an update. You may leave.'

'I can't help but wonder. Did my predecessor Kristian Djurhuus share this kind of intelligence with you?' Haraldsen asked. 'Before he died?'

The room turned quiet again, and chilly, Haraldsen thought. He had pressed a button Aksel Højgaard didn't wish touched at all.

BALDUR GANTING AND HIS wife Eydna had raised two children in their wooden cottage close to Dorotea Thomsen's mansion. The place had just two bedrooms. Kaspar and Alba had been forced to share the smallest until she married Silas Mikkelsen. It was not an unusual arrangement for the fishing folk of Djevulsfjord. The families that lived off the sea did so in the knowledge no riches lay beneath the grey, uncertain waves.

On the frequent occasions poverty loomed there was always money to be borrowed from the Thomsens. For the most part it was a circular loan, taken from Dorotea Thomsen's left hand only to be placed in her right in return for food and rent. But that was how things lay in Djevulsfjord. It had been the same for Ganting's father and his father before him. The only difference was that they were in hock to a woman of commoner stock who had taken the Thomsen name on marriage. But George was not cast in the paternalistic mould of his ancestors. A weaker, more diffident specimen, he acceded to whatever his wife demanded and left the business to her. So the natural kindness and consideration with which the Thomsen dynasty had customarily favoured the tenants of their personal fiefdom had been replaced by a stony-hearted, money-grabbing ruthlessness.

Seated in a kitchen chair, jabbing at an ancient pocket calculator with his fat and clumsy mariner's fingers, Ganting was starting to think of funerals. They never came cheap. To remind himself of the process he'd taken a walk round the Djevulsfjord graveyard next to the timber church and stared at Kaspar's simple headstone. The cemetery was populated by the handful of local names that had belonged to the village for a good two centuries – their own, Thomsen, Mikkelsen and a few less common ones. There'd be fresh earth dug there soon for little Jónas. It all cost more than he could afford. The boat needed repairs too. Then there was Alba, now close to destitution since Silas would not be giving her a penny from his hospital bed. Ganting knew he'd be back to Dorotea before long, trying not to grow furious under her withering eye. The loan always came. It would be repaid too, one way or another.

'Ma,' said Alba, lifting her head up from the table, barely looking at the untouched plate of toast and a single fried egg in front of her. She'd knocked on the door late the night before, teary-eyed, stood there in silence. Her mother let her in, made her a cup of tea, and then she'd gone off to her old bedroom without a word. Got up late the next morning too, long after her parents had breakfast, only coming down when the social people knocked demanding a meeting. They were gone now, back to Tórshavn, leaving a trail of awkward doubts and questions in their wake.

'What is it, love?' Eydna Ganting asked as she washed some dishes. 'Eat something will you? That egg'll go cold.'

Thirty years they'd been married, in the church up the lane. Like him her cheeks were leathery and lined from the salt air and the hard outdoor life. Never was Eydna Ganting broken though, even if she had to bend to fit life's cruel and unexpected pressures from time to time.

'Are we going looking for Benjamin or not?' Alba asked in her thin and childlike wail.

'I told you,' Ganting broke in. 'We went through this. Ja? Aksel Højgaard has men on the hills. They got radios and things we can't use. He wants us off there so they get a clear run.'

'Benji's my boy!'

'And don't we know it!' Ganting cried, with more heat than he wished. 'The police say this is up to them. They won't thank us for getting in their way.'

'Sounds like you don't want him found.'

He didn't answer straight away so she said it again.

'Course I want him found,' he said finally. 'I'm his grandpa, aren't I? No pretending it's not going to be awkward when that happens. What with all that's gone on.'

'I can't just sit here on my arse, Dad!'

Eydna smiled at her.

'Sometimes it's best a woman stays close at home, love. No good interfering in matters best left to men.'

'If they find you on them fells they'll send you straight back here,' her father added. 'You know what Højgaard's like. You don't cross him.'

She didn't argue. There never seemed much point in that.

'So what do I do then?'

'You can stay with us for a while,' Eydna said.

'What's the point? Dorotea reckons I can't get out of the rent for that dump of hers. She still wants her money. I got none.'

Her father stared at the uneaten food on her plate. Eggs from the coop out back and fish he'd caught, bread made by Eydna, those were the things the Gantings lived off. Buying stuff from outside was a luxury. This year he didn't even have any sheep to keep them through the winter.

'I'll talk to the woman,' he said. 'Don't you be worrying about money and rent and work and suchlike. More important things to occupy our minds. Eat your breakfast for God's sake.'

'I'm not having you running up more debt with that bitch on my behalf,' Alba told him.

'Don't—'

'No, Dad. I mean it.'

The social people from Tórshavn had turned out to be a bossy woman and a timid man. They'd offered their condolences in ten seconds flat then got down to business. If Benjamin was found – never 'when' but 'if' – he'd have to be taken into care whether it was judged he'd harmed his brother or not. Alba was not a fit mother, as events surely showed. Silas wasn't in a state to be a proper parent even if he was so minded. Also there were rumours, the sniffy woman from the social said.

Alba didn't ask what rumours, any more than her parents. That was a place none of them wanted to go. So they did what the folk of Djevulsfjord usually managed when big men and women came calling from Tórshavn. Nodded, said alright and waited for them to leave, hoping they'd never come back.

'When they find my Benji they'll still let me see him, won't they?'

Eydna came over and stroked her daughter's lank hair.

'Eat something, love! There are men out on those hills. They'll do their best.'

'And if they don't find him? Then what?'

'Stop worrying yourself unnecessarily,' Ganting told her. 'Benjamin's a Djevulsfjord lad. He can eat his fill on Árnafjall from the berries and the herbs. Get himself some eggs. When he's thought about things. When he's not scared . . . Where else has he got to go?'

So long as he didn't fall down any of the holes up there. Or tumble off the cliff like his brother.

Eydna picked up the toast in her wrinkled fingers.

'Squash that egg on there. You know you like—'

'Don't want,' Alba grunted, pushing away the food.

Ganting got up, walked over to his daughter. Eydna's eyes were on him. They were pleading: *leave her alone. Not now.*

Perhaps his wife was right, not that it mattered. Some things needed saying. Asking.

'You must eat something,' Ganting said. 'Have a bath and a good wash. We'll get you looking like you used to when you were a girl. When Kaspar was around and we were just a happy little family all together.'

Alba just stared at him and said, 'Happy? That was happy?'

'I miss those days,' he added. 'Your mother does too. I don't know where we went wrong . . .'

'Who said we did?' the young woman muttered.

'I said. I don't need anyone else to tell me. Your brother gone. Jónas. Benjamin lost. Silas in the hospital. I'm the father in this house. I must have done something to bring this down upon our heads. I don't know what—'

'Silas kicked me out with the kids and you two didn't do nothing. Just took his side.'

'You ran off,' Ganting said. He didn't want to raise it, didn't want to be cruel. But it was important not to hide things sometimes. 'You ran off to the ferries and left him with the boys. And then—'

'He hit me, Dad! He beat me!'

'So you said. Some men do. Doesn't mean a lot . . .'

'Did he hit you, Mum? I never heard that.'

Eydna Ganting went back to washing the dishes.

'I asked a question,' Alba cried. 'If you won't answer . . .'

Eydna turned the tap on full just to hear the sound it made. Alba, furious suddenly, got up, walked over to the sink and turned it off.

'I asked a question.'

'No one sees inside a marriage.' Eydna didn't meet her eyes when she said it. 'No one wants to. What happened between the pair of you was yours to deal with.'

Alba went back to the table and stabbed her knife through the egg then smeared the yellow over the hard brown toast, her narrow blue eyes darting anxiously round the tiny kitchen.

There was a knock at the door. Eydna answered it. George Thomsen was there in what looked like a new black suit and shiny shoes. He took off his flat cap and said, 'I'll be looking for the man of the house if he's in.'

Ganting went to the door and waited.

'I thought I'd best come down and ask you about the *Alberta*, Baldur,' Thomsen said. 'You'll be wanting timber and fittings to get her out on the water again and they need ordering in.' He glanced at Alba, eyes down at the table. 'People have seen more blackfish and we're never going to have a good grind if you're not out there to lead it. This place needs a Ganting as foreman. It always has. I'll put the necessaries your way. No need to worry about payment right now though it's best we keep that between the two of us. Don't want the house dragon finding out, do we?'

Ganting grabbed his jacket.

'A boat. Bloody whales,' Alba spat at her father. 'I got a boy dead and needing burying. The other one missing and that's all you can think about.'

'Very generous of you, George,' Ganting said, putting on his cap. 'I will respect your wishes, naturally.'

When he'd left his wife pulled a chair up to the table and took her daughter's thin, cold hands.

'Your father's a remarkable man. Decent and honourable. Better than any of the others round here. I wouldn't have married no one else and Lord knows I had the offers.'

'Ain't got eyes in the back of his head though, has he?'

'Oh Alba, Alba . . .' There were tears starting in Eydna's eyes. 'We're going to be needing one another in the days to come. Don't start that again. No digging up the past. It'll only make things worse.'

'Got no choice,' Alba Ganting said then slid out from under her embrace and got her thin windcheater from the door.

'Where are you going?' her mother asked.

'Home. It isn't here, is it?'

'It is, girl. It always will be!'

Alba opened the door. It was a fine day, sunny, bit of wind, bit cold. She wondered how Benji would fare on those hills. He was more capable than people thought. He could find food if he wanted. All the same she wanted him back. Wanted to hug and hold him the way she should have done before.

'Don't you even think of running away again,' Eydna warned her. 'The morning bus has gone by now and damn me I'll stand by the evening one to stop you if you try.'

'Not running. How could I?'

If only she'd taken the kids the year before. That might have worked. Though what they'd have done while she was mopping out the puke and piss from the bogs on the overnight runs to Jutland she'd no idea.

'Got one son to bury and one to find, haven't I? What kind of mother do you think I am?'

Alba Mikkelsen didn't wait to hear the answer.

Halfway to the harbour her cheap little phone rang. It was Father Ryberg.

'I fear we left on unfortunate terms yesterday,' he said and sounded a little nervous for once. 'A misunderstanding. It's important we speak, Alba. There are pressing matters we must deal with. This funeral of yours . . .'

'Not mine. My lad's.'

A pause then, 'I see this is not a good time to talk. Never mind. I'll make the arrangements regardless. Those going to a better life should not be delayed upon their journey. I'm sure you'll agree . . .'

'Dirty old bugger,' she muttered as she cut the call.

HØJGAARD PUT DOWN THE pen, folded his arms and leaned back on his chair.

'What do you know about Kristian Djurhuus?'

'I know he was in my job for four or five y-years,' Haraldsen stuttered, struggling to speak out in a way that did not reveal his illicit dipping into police records the night before. 'I'm sure he had tales to tell.'

'Why?' the superintendent asked. 'He was the district sheriff, like you. A part-time post, a sinecure with minimal responsibility.'

'You might have told me how he died . . .'

'How he died?' Hanna Olsen asked. 'The previous sheriff was before my time—'

'Kristian Djurhuus was a delusional drunk,' Højgaard cut in. 'He took to booze during all that time he spent in Denmark and came back here thinking he could be lord of the manor. More fool him.'

'He was killed—'

With a wave of his long arm Højgaard demanded silence.

'You have been doing your homework, Tristan! Shame it's not on something more interesting. Here . . .'

He placed his hands together like a schoolteacher then recited his version of events. Djurhuus was riding through the Árnafjall tunnel full of booze. A passing vehicle struck him. He was dead when they found him the next morning.

'Jesus,' Hanna whispered. 'No one ever mentioned . . .'

'That's Djevulsfjord for you.' Højgaard glanced at his watch. 'They'll know who was behind the wheel. They'll never tell. Djurhuus never made a single friend while he was there. The man was a fool, out of his depth.'

'One other thing,' Haraldsen ventured. 'The brother . . .'

'We are looking for Benjamin Mikkelsen! How many times must I say this?'

There was a heat and intemperance to his response that Tristan Haraldsen found interesting. Aksel Højgaard was not a man who was rattled easily.

'Let me finish, please. I didn't mean Benjamin,' Haraldsen continued, undeterred. 'I was talking about Kaspar Ganting. Alba's brother. Baldur's son.'

The superintendent sat stony-faced in his chair, then muttered a single word.

'Dead.'

'The week before Djurhuus was found,' Haraldsen continued. 'Dead in the same place as the grandson too. Freyja's Pool. I'm no detective but this strikes me as curious.'

'Really?' Højgaard asked.

'That was around the time Søren vanished,' Hanna said and sounded a little breathless.

'Søren?' Haraldsen asked. 'Who's Søren?'

Højgaard wasn't listening.

'You have a date for that, Officer? I thought he caught a ferry here and simply disappeared. If you can tell me what day of the week he was last seen, where, what time—'

'You know I can't . . .'

The superintendent got to his feet, marched to the door and threw it open.

'Your brother has nothing to do with any of this. Any more than Kaspar Ganting or that idiot Djurhuus. Now . . .' He looked at his watch ostentatiously. 'I must attend a meeting in Tórshavn. The Gantings have been pestering about when they might bury the boy. The sooner the better. We're not in a place to keep a corpse on ice for weeks on end. I see no reason to keep hold of the mite. Tomorrow appears to suit—'

'Tomorrow!' Hanna's voice was high and fragile, quite unlike her. 'They're going to bury Jónas Mikkelsen tomorrow? How can you even think—'

'The Jews and Arabs bury their dead in the space of a day.

Perhaps they passed through Djevulsfjord years back. Who knows? I wouldn't be surprised.'

'Christ, Højgaard. This is a murder case. Manslaughter at the very least. The rules of evidence mean—'

'Danish rules,' he said in a chilly, bored tone. 'The bureaucracy you loved in Aalborg does not apply in the Faroes. The family want the boy in the ground. We have the knife that killed him. If the hills don't take Benjamin Mikkelsen we'll have the hand behind it soon as well.'

She was lost for words. There were plenty running through Haraldsen's head at that moment but he realised they were unlikely to have much effect.

Højgaard held the door open for them.

'Ryberg will be making arrangements I imagine.'

There was no opportunity to argue, even if there'd been any point. Defeated, down the corridor they walked, both deep in silent thought.

Outside in the car park he stared at the grey sea and said, 'That poor lad gone only yesterday. Tomorrow in the earth. I can scarcely believe it.'

'We need to talk, Tristan. A coffee is in order.'

'Yes,' he replied. 'I believe it is.'

TWELVE

Elsebeth was in the kitchen when she received a call from Haraldsen saying he was going to be longer than expected. In truth he'd no idea when he might be back since there were discussions to take place with Hanna Olsen, and perhaps another visit somewhere or other and the shopping to be done, though when he'd get round to that he didn't know.

'It's alright, Tristan.'

'I'm sure I'll be back before long,' he said down the crackly line.

'I'm sure you will. Don't worry.'

'And I will remember to get the diesel. And some beer . . .'

'How are they doing with finding the Mikkelsen boy?'

A pause then he said, 'Not much in the way of progress.'

'They are looking?'

'After Højgaard's own fashion. I take his point, a little anyway. It is difficult, love. Those hills are vast and the lad must surely know how to hide if he wants.'

True enough, she thought.

'All the same. That poor mother . . .'

'Højgaard says the young one gets a funeral tomorrow.'

'What?'

'Tomorrow . . .'

'But that's so soon . . .'

'He says that's how the family want it. The dead don't linger long in Djevulsfjord. They die, the living grieve, then get on with their lives. Or so it seems.'

She tried to make sense of that idea. It seemed both improbable but entirely in keeping with what they'd come to learn about the place.

'We must be there. For the service.'

'Ja. We must. Let's talk more when I get home. Are you . . . are you finding something to occupy yourself? That is not too much worrying?'

Something in his tone sounded close to patronising. She wasn't used to that. Nor did she welcome it.

'What do you mean?'

'I know . . . I thought you seemed upset last night.'

'As did you. In the circumstances.'

'I'm sorry I had to leave you this morning. I get anxious. Can't help it. Don't fret, love. I'll be home before long and—'

'Oh that is *such* a relief.'

'I meant to say—'

'I am a fully functioning human being, Tristan Haraldsen. Quite capable of managing thank you very much. At least I was last time I checked. Sweet Jesus!'

And with that she slammed down the phone. Which was not like her.

Elsebeth waited a long minute to see if he would ring back. Then spent a similar amount of time considering whether to phone him herself and, while not apologising – that would be both unnecessary and rather strange – take time to smooth out any troubled waters between them.

But eventually she decided to leave it there. Haraldsen wasn't himself at that moment. The previous night he was the one who'd been behaving oddly. Evasive was the word that came to mind. Sly even, a term she would never have associated with her husband before. True, she didn't tell him about Inga Dam and the strange message left on the desk, churned out from their very own printer. That, she reasoned, was a sensible precaution in the circumstances, a product of his odd demeanour. His fault if she cared to think of it that way.

'The last thing Tristan needs in his present frame of mind is one more strange complication gifted to them by this new home of ours,' she said out loud. '*I* surely have no reason to feel ashamed. None at all.'

It was almost convincing. She'd meant to set off as soon as he left but there'd been the animals and chickens to care for, the house to clean, soup to be made which was better than the muck Dorotea Thomsen had sold them. All distractions designed to deter her from what she really wanted to do, and she knew it. Now his tone had made the decision for her.

The mountain boots bought that summer were clean and newly scraped of mud from all the recent walking on Árnafjall. Her best fell jacket, a dark green, all-weather one, was freshly waxed too.

It was important for the wife of the district sheriff to keep up appearances. Who knew who she might meet on the hills? A search party? Benjamin Mikkelsen himself with any luck?

One person for sure if only Elsebeth could manage to locate her. It was time to have things out with the strange and menacing sculptor across in Selkie. Miss Inga Dam.

* * *

170

THERE WAS A CAFÉ by the harbour, little more than a hut with tables outside. The woman who ran it was busy selling cooked breakfasts for three tourists, German by the sound of them, caked in mud and muck from tramping across damp fields and starving too. Tristan Haraldsen insisted he buy the coffee, and a couple of buns. Then they went to sit outside at the most distant spot overlooking the harbour.

The residual stink of the recent grind apart, the place smelled differently to Djevulsfjord. Sørvágur was scarcely a town but the place possessed an industrial bustle missing elsewhere on Vágar. Here were fish wholesalers, a processing factory and two small smokehouses. So there was employment that paid better than working longliners forced to brave the sea beyond the Skerries and come back all too often with little or nothing to show.

Alongside the commerce came a reminder for Haraldsen of what life was like back in Tórshavn. The place was busier, noisier. Instead of Djevulsfjord's sharp clean air there was an ever-present aroma of diesel, car fumes and factory smoke, the occasional roar of a commercial jet, the constant buzz of traffic.

A heavily-built man in a business suit walked past, tipped his hat to them and said, 'Officer Olsen, good morning. I am sorry to hear of the news from that place beyond Árnafjall. Little good emerges from there. Still, if you hear of anyone in need of advice you know where to find me . . .'

She smiled and said something both sympathetic and non-committal. The man waited for more, appeared disappointed not to receive it, then tipped his hat again and was on his way.

'The local lawyer,' Hanna said when he was out of earshot. 'Jørundur Restorff. Never have I met that first name before. You?'

'It is approved, surely,' Haraldsen noted. 'If he's a lawyer it must be . . .'

'I imagine so,' Hanna replied.

He laughed at what he'd just said.

'These laws on what you should and shouldn't name your children. Really. The things we worry about. Though I suppose no one wants a son called . . . I don't know . . . Parrot. Or Seaweed or something. Do they?'

'In Aalborg I arrested an American drug dealer called Pacifica once,' Hanna told him. 'Pacifica Aurora Hartmann.'

'A boy or a girl?'

'Neither.' Hanna took out her police phone and checked it for messages. 'It was a woman. From California. All of fifty-five years old.'

Haraldsen frowned and said, 'The world's a curious place beyond these islands. Which is why, when they come here, they think us strange too. Sometimes the way they look at us I feel as if I'm in a zoo. The creature behind the bars.'

Hanna stirred her coffee, tasted it, pronounced the cup good if a little on the weak side.

'People here mow their rooftops,' she observed. 'Lots of places would find that a touch peculiar.'

'If a roof is made of turf how else is one supposed to deal with it?'

'Preferably not in black pyjamas,' Hanna noted giving him the look.

'Ah. Word gets around. That point has been made by my wife,' Haraldsen declared. 'Does Jørundur Restorff have much business in Sørvágur? A lawyer?'

The policewoman shrugged.

'Property and wills. Land disputes and the odd drunk driver. Or wife beater. It's a living, I imagine. Better than any the Gantings or Mikkelsens could manage.'

Haraldsen would finish only half the coffee, he decided. It was too modern and bitter for him. Besides, he and Hanna Olsen were dancing round one another, avoiding the subject. Of which there seemed to be more than one.

'I don't imagine any of them have the money to employ a lawyer,' he said and that glint in her eye told him she was thinking the same thing. 'Not unless they borrow it from Dorotea Thomsen. I rather fear that family feel they're in hock to that woman enough already. A shame since that boy of theirs . . . Benjamin . . . he will surely be needing advice once he's found.'

'Once . . .' Hanna pushed her coffee away too.

'Tell me Højgaard really is looking,' he begged. 'Those two lads ran off because of my cack-handed efforts at killing a whale. Had I not—'

She let down her hair and shook her head. Then walked to the counter and got the woman there to top up her coffee mug with not one but two shots of espresso. *Two shots*. He was, for a moment, captivated by the sight and the presence of her. Hanna Olsen was quite unlike even the most forward of the young ladies he used to encounter from time to time in office life in Tórshavn. It seemed odd that she should leave busy Denmark, a place for the young surely, and cast herself adrift in secluded Vágar.

'No, Tristan,' she said when she came back and plonked two crunchy Italian biscuits on the table. 'They didn't run because of you. At least, if that was the initial cause which prompted Jónas to head for the hills it certainly wasn't what detained him that night. Or, I believe, led to him being found in Freyja's Pool.'

'Then what?' he asked.

'I don't know. I wish I did.'

A long silence then. Nothing to break it but the steady putt-putt of a small boat returning to the harbour, nets draped across the stern, two men busy on the deck cutting and gutting their catch.

'If Benjamin Mikkelsen's found he will be placed in an institution,' she went on. 'Locked up for years. Possibly for good. Blamed for his brother's death. That I don't doubt. You heard Højgaard and he's the superintendent around here. Judge and jury in matters that never come before a court.'

She drank her coffee, both hands around the cup. Strong fingers, Haraldsen noted. But more lined and wrinkled than he would have expected in one her age.

'Perhaps Højgaard's right,' he said quietly. 'I was in a state when I saw what I thought I did. It was a long way away. I'm really not sure—'

She leaned forward and parted her blonde hair so they could see.

'Do you think a child did this?'

It was a cut and a bruise. Not so small. Not so big either.

'I don't know,' Haraldsen answered. 'After these last few days I'm not sure what to think any more. About anything.'

Hanna Olsen nodded, looked around, made sure there was no one close by them.

'You and Elsebeth are good people,' she said. 'That has been obvious from the start. Clear from what I've seen in the files too.'

'I didn't realise we were of such interest to you.'

'Good people,' Hanna repeated. 'Strangers on Vágar. Strangers certainly in Djevulsfjord.'

For a moment she seemed vulnerable. Alone.

'May we speak frankly?' she added. 'I have no one else to talk to. And yet . . .'

'What's this about your brother? Søren?'

'What's this about your predecessor too?'

His head was starting to spin again. These intrigues were not his style.

'I don't understand. You're a police officer. If you've been through the files surely you must know of the fate of Kristian Djurhuus. He died as Højgaard said in an accident last year. I doubt road traffic fatalities happen much in Vágar. There must be more you can tell me there.'

Her eyes were cold then and very keen.

'Kristian Djurhuus is not in any files I've seen.'

A car drove along the harbour road, slowing as it approached their table. The window came down. It was Højgaard at the wheel. His long face turned to stare at them. Then he stuck his head out of the window and called, 'You have time to chat with the locals, Officer Olsen. I'm pleased by this. We're here to serve the community. I hope, mind, Haraldsen is paying. Now I go to Tórshavn. Be good and dutiful in my absence.'

ELSEBETH DIDN'T SEE ANOTHER soul when she took the winding path from behind the cottage, up the steep green hillside towards the cliffs and Selkie. If there truly was a search group out looking for the missing lad they were somewhere out of sight. Perhaps back near the puffin hide where his unfortunate brother had been stabbed and Hanna Olsen assaulted. That was a good way distant from the track Elsebeth had chosen. Not that she could see any men close by, or near the cliff edge. Only a single boat out in the bay close to the Skerries, an unfamiliar one, perhaps from Sørvágur or further afield. The men of Djevulsfjord seemed to be shunning the sea at that moment.

They'd only walked to Selkie once and that was the summer before. The place, with its shiny black sand, seemed depressing somehow. It sat on a low silted estuary that ran beneath the bare bleak rocky face of Árnafjall, a side too steep and exposed to the elements to attract much in the way of vegetation let alone pasture for sheep. Only a little-used dirt track led down to the black sand from the road that ran the other side of the peak into the tunnel near their home. That, as far as she understood, was barely used except by a few hardy swimmers and surfers in the height of summer. Even they were few since the waters of Selkie were notorious for strong and unpredictable currents and sharp breezes that might catch the unwary.

Nothing much lived round here or wanted to. Not even the mythical creature that had given the place its name. Except for a strange and angry sculptor who seemed more in tune with black-fish than her own flesh and blood. There were many lonely places on the Faroes where a solitary soul might hide. But as she rounded the final turn of the track from Djevulsfjord and saw the shallow black line of Selkie glittering in the weak, late-summer sun it occurred to her that few would have the haunting starkness of a place like this. If one wanted to hide from the world, there was no better place to be.

'And where is the woman who dare walk into my house to leave threatening messages for my husband?' Elsebeth demanded, stopping to let the wind blow hard against her face as she climbed down the last winding portion of the path, to sea level a few hundred metres from the beach.

The sweep of sand lay in front of her, empty or so she thought at first. Though now she looked it was not entirely absent of life. Out on the water, maybe half a kilometre or more, dark and shiny dorsals were breaking surface, like thorns rising from the deep. Had Djevulsfjord been its normal self surely Tristan's permission would be sought at that very moment and another grind coming together in the rush of boats and men and excited watchers on the shore.

'Where are you?'

There seemed to be nothing here but the shingle estuary, the ebony beach, the waves, the meagre grass in the shifting dunes.

Think. Be what Tristan hopes himself to be. A detective.

She returned to the road and continued along it, back towards Árnafjall, until she found what she was looking for. Tyre marks, just two, from a motorbike, it had to be. They led off into the tufts of vegetation in the dunes. Elsebeth followed them, aware that she was getting further and further away from anything that might count as civilization in these parts.

Eventually the tyres veered sharply to the right, round a low hill.

There was no sign. Not an electricity cable. Not an asphalt lane by which any conventional vehicle might make entrance to bring furniture or goods or services. Inga Dam, it seemed, did seek a kind of hermit's life out here.

The disturbed sand ran round the shallow rise, back towards Selkie. Then she saw it. A fisherman's hut, that was all, faded blue timber planking the colour of the late summer sky. The front gave out onto the side of the bay where the whales were now beginning to gather in some numbers.

Elsebeth walked round the side until she found a door. It was next to a long, panoramic window stained with salt from the surf. Behind it were pale shapes, strange and huge, organic forms that looked as if they belonged in a museum not in this desolate little building on the edge of Selkie Bay.

She rapped on the door and tried to peer through the glass. The place looked empty. All this way and Inga Dam was probably out shopping. Or in Tórshavn or Copenhagen. Or a plane to some fancy engagement in London or New York.

A hand touched her shoulder from behind. Elsebeth leapt in shock then turned to face whatever had come out of nowhere to find her.

'What the hell do you want?'

It was the woman. Red hair. Furious face. A kind of knife in her hand, covered in what looked like putty and white dust, a smock over her skinny form, one that ran down to her knees and was covered in stains of paint, blue and yellow and scarlet.

'This is my home!'

Courage, Elsebeth told herself. She was not in the habit of being intimidated, least of all by someone who sneaked up on you unseen.

'At least I am only looking from the outside,' she said as calmly as she could. 'At least I don't walk through your door and print out menacing messages for you to find. Like a coward.'

It was a palette knife in her hand. Blunt. Part of the woman's work she guessed.

'What do you want?'

'To talk. Is that so much to ask?' She nodded at the bay. 'Out here if you wish. But talk we will, Miss Dam. I will not leave till we have words.'

'NOTHING IN THE RECORDS? That can't be possible?' Haraldsen said when the superintendent's Ford had vanished past the black-and-white sheep that lined the fields around the airport. 'I worked with files. It was my job. I'm sure . . . I'm damned sure.'

It was rare for him to curse and she seemed to pick this up immediately.

'Damned sure of what?'

'There are files in Tórshavn. I've read them, Hanna. Only last night.'

'Oh . . .' She raised her cup in a toast. 'Sneaking. I see. You could go to jail for that.'

'I know. I could show you how to access them too,' he suggested. 'It's not hard. They'd been archived, for sure.'

'Archived. Is that normal?'

This thought had occurred to him too. It was for closed cases. All the same some record of the original incident would usually have been left for the local officer to view if it was needed.

'In all honesty I'm not sure. It may simply be an oversight.'

'*Two* oversights,' she pointed out. 'In that office you just attended there's not a word about your predecessor. Or Søren either. Who came here around that same time.' She took out her

179

phone and tapped at the screen with busy fingers then held it up for him to look at. 'I mean here. Vágar. Can you see?'

It was a young man with long fair hair much like hers. A vacant face, Haraldsen thought, with the expression of someone who wasn't quite sure of himself. Though that was, perhaps, a lot to try to glean from a single picture on a phone.

'Selkie,' she said. 'The black beach.'

'It's not the only black beach around.'

'It's Selkie,' she insisted. 'I'm telling you.'

Then he listened to her story. About Søren Olsen, her kid brother, eighteen months her junior. Haraldsen was not happy to hear that his first impression had proved correct. The poor lad was lost for a while, messed up in the drugs scene in Copenhagen, on the fringes of the criminal world on the mainland. Hanna had paid for a trip to Vágar to help him out. He'd never come back.

'Why?' he asked. 'Why Vágar?'

'It's where our parents came from. I thought . . .' Her eyes misted as they turned to the grey sea running out to the pale horizon. 'I thought that might help him.'

He touched the phone again.

'Did the picture he sent you have a location on it? They usually do these days.'

'No.' She looked impressed he'd asked that question. 'Mostly they did. But not that one. Not any of them that he sent me after he got off the ferry.'

'So perhaps he didn't want to be found.'

'Perhaps . . .' She came close and gripped his arm very tightly. 'What, in my position, would you do?'

He knew the answer she expected.

'I would find someone who'd believe you.'

Hanna Olsen raised her empty mug and chinked it against his.

'This window you have into the police network. The files. Your archives.'

He understood what was coming and dreaded it.

'You want me to look for your brother? For Søren?'

'Yes,' she said. 'And I want to be there when you do.'

Elsebeth, he thought.

A web was closing round them. Himself, his wife, Hanna Olsen, perhaps Alba Mikkelsen and Baldur Ganting too.

'Tonight,' she insisted. 'We will sit down together and see what we can find.'

'I don't know . . .'

She took his hand and squeezed it.

'Good people. I saw that from the start.'

THIRTEEN

Højgaard was in a place he had to visit from time to time, always briefly which suited both men in the room. It was the office of Chief Superintendent Rasmussen, his immediate superior, a bureaucratic fellow in headquarters at Tórshavn, fond of his uniform and the comfort that came from knowing he was of a rank to avoid the cold and wet and inconvenience of duty outdoors.

In theory Rasmussen headed the chain of command over Højgaard and the whole of Vágar. He could direct any investigation personally on the ground if he so wished. In reality he was simply a man behind a desk, a bureaucrat Højgaard kept informed as he saw fit, and that as rarely as possible. The appointment of Hanna Olsen apart – something Rasmussen had waved through while Højgaard was on holiday – the running of police operations on the island was something he was happy to leave to the immediate officer in the field. In this respect Højgaard had served him well. No trouble came to his desk, no complaints, no loose ends, no difficulties that required effort to resolve.

Detail was something Rasmussen found quite inconvenient. It was, he was fond of saying, a modern blight upon the service, quite unnecessary for the efficient supervision and running of a methodical police force. An amateur chef who liked to interrupt case meetings with his latest recipe, he often compared operations of all kinds to the preparation of a meal. Too much seasoning, too many ingredients, too much forethought only went to spoil the dish, hiding the principal element, disguising it with fripperies. It was like making curry out of fresh blubber. Or dowsing salted winter lamb in a drizzle of French herbs. The point was lost, the heart of the matter camouflaged in needless complexity. The people of the Faroes were simple folk at heart, Rasmussen frequently declared. That innocent lack of complexity and clutter was both their strength and the basis of their island character. To treat the men and women of even sophisticated Tórshavn as if they were the boulevardiers of Copenhagen or Oslo was to misread their unique disposition, unspoiled as it was by cosmopolitan and international airs.

This was a fond lecture of his, frequently delivered. Højgaard had learned long ago to nod and agree with such advice, before thanking the man for his sagacity.

Today, though, he was not going to hear it. Events on the island across the water had reduced Rasmussen to near despair. He was aghast at the news from Djevulsfjord, a place he'd visited once only in his fifty-eight years and found not to his taste in the least.

'Tell me this again, Aksel,' he begged after Højgaard ran through his version of events. 'I can scarce believe it.'

After the second recounting he said, simply, 'Jesus.' Then pulled a bottle of the local akvavit out of his desk and poured himself half a plastic cup. The strong aromas of caraway and cardamom wafted across the room. Højgaard declined to join him on the grounds he was driving.

'And who,' Rasmussen asked, 'would dare to stop you if you weaved around the road a little on your way home? I'm not

ignorant of your reputation and your power around there. Still
. . .' He swigged at the clear liquid. 'If you so wish . . .'

The matter of the dead Jónas Mikkelsen had, Rasmussen
declared, disturbed him more than any case in all his thirty-four
years with the Faroes police. To Højgaard's inner amusement,
he'd looked ready to throw up when he was faced with the morgue
photos of the savage injuries to the young boy. Even without the
grisly proof of Benjamin Mikkelsen's handiwork, the very idea of
what had happened seemed fundamentally upsetting to him, like
a tear in the steady, quiet life of the island.

Murder was so alien he had never encountered it in his entire
career, since both the distant killings of years before had fallen to
another officer. Even instances of serious assaults were rare, and
usually involved drink, a fractious foreigner or both. The news
Højgaard had to import was, he declared, 'just plain wrong'.

'Nevertheless,' the superintendent had to point out, 'that is the
news. And we must deal with it.'

'No. You must, Aksel. More up your street than mine. I can't
. . . I can't begin . . .'

It wasn't just that the culprit was a twelve-year-old child, albeit
one from a deprived background in a remote village few ever
thought about let alone visited. A good part of Rasmussen's
concern was somewhat broader and decidedly less emotional. It
had to do with public relations and something he talked about
obsessively from time to time: image. It was bad enough that the
islands were getting a vile press from foreigners for the grind with
all the accompanying blood and slaughter, a rite they failed to
understand both from a practical point of view and a cultural
one. If the media were to latch onto a salacious tale about child

fratricide in the normally quiet islands the few flights to the little airport in Sørvágur would be full of inquisitive foreign journalists. Reporters. Rasmussen hated them. They never looked for the good in life, only the bad. Every last one would wish to dump ignominy and hatred on the little nation in the North Atlantic, a distant, solitary country that was happy if it managed to avoid publicity altogether.

'I want this matter dealt with,' he ordered. 'Killed. Silenced. The only bloody foreigners who are welcome here are the ones who spend their krónur then bugger off. Tourists or businessmen we don't want them hanging round long, certainly not if they're hacks sniffing round for dirt to dig. Do I make myself clear?'

'Perfectly,' the superintendent replied. And if the small search efforts were to bear fruit and find young Benjamin Mikkelsen alive?

Rasmussen's face creased into an unpleasant snarl and he muttered a low and uncharacteristic curse.

'What am I supposed to do with the boy?' Højgaard asked. 'What do you recommend?'

'I recommend you get the murderous little thug out from under our noses immediately,' Rasmussen pointed out in a rising falsetto. 'We have no institution on the Faroes to care for homicidal children. How could we? Why should we? Such creatures have never before existed. Bloody Djevulsfjord . . .'

'Not that we know of, sir . . .'

'This is the Faroes. We're not that kind of people. Ship the little sod off to Denmark. Or Norway. They have experience of that kind of monster. Not us. Ye gods!'

'If we find him. The hills are endless. The weather will close in before long. For my own way of thinking . . .'

Rasmussen waited, fiddling with the shiny buttons on his uniform, then, when he could wait no longer, asked, 'Your own way of thinking . . .'

'I have a feeling . . . an instinct . . . We won't see the child again.'

'Let us hope you're correct. I know that sounds a terrible thing to say . . .'

'I doubt any on Djevulsfjord would disagree with you there. They are . . . practical people. Perhaps it's the place. The fact they've nothing but the boats and the fishing to sustain them and that not so much these days. They're not in the habit of chasing after lost causes. Better to bury the dead and get on with things.'

Rasmussen looked shocked by that and said something about the wickedness of some of the wilder places in Vágar and beyond.

'Not that there's anything the likes of us can do about it,' he added. 'We're police officers not moral guardians. If their priests and their own consciences can't point out what's right and what's wrong they should not expect the likes of us to do it for them.'

'Perfectly put,' Højgaard agreed.

'This funeral? Tomorrow you say?'

'It will be.'

'Not an hour too soon. Get the mite in the ground. Tell the family to keep their traps shut. I will deal with the local rags. We'll bury Jónas Mikkelsen *tout suite* and make sure he stays that way. Agreed?'

'Agreed,' Højgaard said and got to his feet.

'If I never hear of that blasted place again I'll feel all the better for it, Aksel. I won't be sitting in this chair much beyond Christmas, you know. There'll be a successor. The seat is largely in my gift.'

He walked to the door, opened it and held out his hand.

'A quiet life is all I ask. You will do your best to deliver that, won't you? It will be in both our interests.'

A message came in on Højgaard's phone. It was from the two men who'd spent the day trudging the heights of Árnafjall. While Rasmussen watched and listened he called back. There was, they said, no sign of Benjamin Mikkelsen anywhere. One more hour he ordered. Then they were to go home and await instructions.

'Very good,' Rasmussen said when he was off the phone. 'We have better things to do than chase a wayward child across the fells of Vágar.'

Outside, as Højgaard walked off to his car, there was a second phone call, one he'd been half expecting. It was from Ryberg. The priest, it seemed, was worried.

INGA DAM'S COTTAGE WAS, unlike its owner, quite fetching. The interior timber walls were painted a range of pastel shades all variations on the ocean's blue. Photographs of animals, mostly threatened ones, Elsebeth thought, were everywhere. Gentle music, some kind of Nordic folk instrumental, was playing in the background. By the windows of the front studio stood a massive marble slab half-worked, the surface covered in chisel marks, the floor around littered with stone shards and dust.

'What's it going to be?' she asked since it was impossible to tell from the shape.

The sour look on the woman's face told her this was the wrong question.

'What it is now. A piece of stone. Only different. What do you think?'

Elsebeth blinked and told herself to maintain an even temper, hard as that might turn out.

'May I sit down? May we hope to have some kind of reasonable conversation even if it may never be described as amicable? I didn't come here for an argument.'

'Then why?'

'For . . . illumination. On both our parts perhaps.'

She sniffed at that, muttered something Elsebeth couldn't hear, then ordered her to take a seat by the long window and vanished into the kitchen. A few minutes later she returned with two cups of a herbal tea, the scent exotic, quite unlike anything Elsebeth had ever known.

'It's unusual . . .'

'Forget about the tea. Small talk. I don't do it.' She nodded at the ocean. Her short red hair was dusty from working on the marble, just like her fingers. She didn't seem to notice or if she did to care. 'There are pods out there. You see them? Free and wild those blackfish are. If your husband and those monsters in Djevulsfjord get their way it won't be long before they're stripped and bloody carcasses on the beach.'

Stay calm, she told herself. Do not rise to the bait.

'A young boy's missing. His brother's been found dead. I think they have matters other than fishing to occupy them at the moment.'

Inga Dam sipped at her tea and said, 'Violence breeds violence. Blood breeds blood.'

'Is the life of a poor child not more important than that of a poor dumb whale?'

The woman held her mug very tightly and stared at her in astonishment.

'Of course not. The blackfish choose nothing but to swim in the ocean. We are sentient beings. Rational supposedly. We make ourselves this way. Those children were raised by parents in that damned place round the bay. Not that a soul in Tórshavn cares what goes on behind Árnafjall, do they?'

'Those boys did not choose to be born there, Inga.'

It was time to address this woman by her first name, whether she liked it or not.

'True . . . Elsebeth.'

Djevulsfjord had been left to find its own way in the world. And if the world could come to understand what that way was . . .

Then what? Elsebeth wondered. Who cared about the lives of a handful of fisher folk in a little hamlet quite remote from everyday life even in Sørvágur? Who, in the busy world, had the time? Or the reason?

'My husband was handed the job of district sheriff because his heart problems were deemed too serious to allow him to continue working for the Tórshavn police. He didn't ask for it. I am starting to think he doesn't want it. Baldur Ganting—'

'The Gantings . . .'

At the mention of the name the mug went down. Inga Dam picked up a chisel and hacked off a chunk of white marble. Angrily. With force.

Elsebeth didn't follow.

'Baldur seems a decent man,' she said. 'A sad man. A man made by difficult circumstances I dare say. A hard life. Losing his son Kaspar. Now his grandson and the other lad missing.'

Inga Dam just stared at her, nothing on her pale face that Elsebeth could read.

'Ganting virtually forced Tristan to try his hand in the grind,' she went on. 'He didn't want it and he won't do that again. Nevertheless his job is district sheriff and he will try to do it honestly. That's how my husband is. I worry about his health so the last thing I want is someone entering our house and leaving unnecessary . . . *vile* threats for him to find. I . . .'

She couldn't go on. The very thought of it was making her too angry for words.

The chisel struck the stone again. Clumsily this time. Inga Dam missed the intended point and the blade shifted round, caught her near the wrist. She yelped with pain. A splash of blood marked the pure white marble.

'That needs washing. And dressing,' Elsebeth said immediately and got to her feet.

'You'll be a nurse now, will you?' Inga Dam spat at her clutching the wound, quick tears in her eyes. It looked long and deep.

'I was a teacher for a while. The first-aid officer for my school. I know when a cut needs attention. Inga. *Inga.*'

She shrank behind the statue and for the first time it occurred to Elsebeth that perhaps this woman was weak and frightened and vulnerable, and disguised all this with a mask of aggression and false strength.

'I never asked you here. You should go.'

Instead Elsebeth folded her arms and stood her ground.

'On the contrary. You summoned me by leaving a nasty message for my husband. I will not leave until you've promised that won't happen again. And I've seen to that cut.'

Tears. A glistening line that ran from her wide, sad eyes and began to trickle down her cheeks.

'I never asked . . .' she whispered.

'So you said.'

Close above the roof a sea bird shrieked. Somewhere beyond the bay, miles away in Sørvágur, Tristan was doing God knows what. A child lay on a morgue table in Tórshavn. A funeral was being planned by faceless men in an undertaker's office, perhaps watching a weeping Alba Mikkelsen, asking how she might find the krónur to pay. While Benjamin stayed lost in the hills and blackfish gathered along the coast, tempting the likes of the Gantings back to sea if only Baldur's boat was fit for the sortie. Yet here, in Inga Dam's remote studio, it was as if all the world outside was but a dream, a story in someone else's head. That was why the woman buried herself in this place. Perhaps the people and the places beyond its pale blue walls held some terror for her Elsebeth Haraldsen couldn't begin to imagine.

'I am going into your kitchen,' she announced. 'I assume you keep a first-aid kit there. If you would care to follow then I will deal with that wound, then hear you promise to leave my husband alone. After which I will happily get myself out of your hair so you can go back to taking out your fury on that lump of stone . . .'

'Not anger. *Do not call it anger!*' Inga Dam screamed at her with such heat Elsebeth stepped back in shock and wondered what she'd said.

INGA DAM'S KITCHEN WAS like the rest of the place: bright and colourful, a little eccentric and marked by the untidiness one found in the homes of people who lived alone. Next to a small table with a dirty plate that bore a few uneaten salad leaves there was a gas stove with a cylinder by it. On the shelves and tables stood an array of candles and a few electric lamps. The place clearly had no power. However else Inga Dam lived when she was away from Vágar, this solitary hut was the hideaway of a hermit.

By the small and rather grubby sink there was a white box with a red cross on it. The seal was still on. The thing must have been years old. Inside were bandages, plasters, a tube of antiseptic cream.

Like a naughty child summoned by a cross teacher Inga Dam came in, held out her hand, stifled her cries as Elsebeth washed the wound clean with water from a large bottle by the window, then dried it carefully, applied some cream and wrapped it in a bandage.

'If I were you,' she said, 'I'd get that looked at by a doctor. The hospital in Tórshavn. It's quite deep.'

'I will live,' Inga Dam said very slowly.

There was something new in her eyes and it wasn't the hurt Elsebeth expected.

'I'm sorry if that was painful.'

'It was nothing.'

Of course it wasn't, you silly woman, Elsebeth thought. But perhaps there was a bigger hurt somewhere, one so large it covered such a local pain.

'Now. Can I be sure you'll leave my husband alone? We've trouble enough . . .'

'You think they won't go for the blackfish?'

Never a straight answer from this one.

'Baldur Ganting's boat's been damaged, I gather. It hit the rocks when they picked up that dead boy. I think they were all lucky to get out alive from that. His son-in-law, the lads' father—'

'Silas Mikkelsen. I know him. I know more about that crew than you ever will.'

Doubtless true, Elsebeth thought. But how much of that knowledge would you share?

'The father's in hospital, badly hurt. So I think they won't be fishing for a while. My husband . . .'

There was a photograph above the canister of gas, taped to the wall, crooked. That seemed a little clumsy.

Elsebeth looked at it and felt cold all of a sudden.

It was the harbour in Djevulsfjord. A sunny day. Whitening skeletons lay on the beach, gulls frozen in the air above them. Baldur Ganting was there, Silas Mikkelsen, a few locals Elsebeth recognised but didn't know by name. From their exhausted faces and the bloody detritus on the strand it was clear a grind had just happened. Clear too what the figure apart from the fishermen, a tall, burly man with a grey beard and a lined and forbidding face was doing. He had a clipboard in his hands and a book that Elsebeth recognised. It was the manual on fishing rules that Tórshavn had given Tristan when he got the job.

'You knew this fellow?' Inga Dam asked in a low and broken voice.

'No. He must be—'

'Kristian Djurhuus. The district sheriff before. You know what happened to him?'

She didn't and it occurred to her at that moment she ought to. Tristan's offer of the job had come out of the blue. He'd never expressed any interest in fishing at all. In truth it was probably the last thing he ought to be doing with his enforced retirement.

'We never—'

'A good man. A Dane at heart. He came to hate all that shit and nonsense when I opened his eyes. The blood and the killings. He saw those demons for what they are. If . . .'

Inga Dam stopped. The tears were in full flood now. Finally Elsebeth realised and wanted to kick herself for being so slow.

'It wasn't anger,' she said. 'It was grief. I'm sorry. I didn't mean to pry. I just want my Tristan left alone.'

Inga Dam wiped her eyes and nose with her sleeve and that sent blood that had strayed from the wound spreading across the marble dust along her arm. A very artistic, painterly effect, Elsebeth thought.

'One summer I had him, my Kristian. One beautiful summer. He came to see the world the way I did in the end. No one ever did before. No one ever will now.'

'I'm sorry . . .'

The woman left the kitchen without another word. Elsebeth looked at the photo on the wall again, the men there, some known by name, some by their faces only. One, she realised from the clippings Tristan had shown her, was the late Kaspar Ganting, perhaps snapped not long before his death. Another next to him, about the same age, tall, muscular, smiling unlike the others, was a complete stranger.

When Inga Dam came back she was carrying two crash helmets and set of keys.

'Put this on,' she ordered, throwing a helmet right at her. 'There's something you need to see.'

With that she walked out and not long after Elsebeth heard the sound of the bike coming to life.

Not knowing quite why, she got out her phone and

took a photo of the faces on the wall. Perhaps it would come in useful. Or simply drag them into the darkness ever more quickly.

'Are you coming, woman?' Inga Dam yelled from beyond the door.

'It seems so,' Elsebeth replied, then followed her outside.

FOURTEEN

Alba Mikkelsen could think of one thing only: finding her Benji. No one else seemed much bothered. The two policemen who'd stopped by to say hello when she was down by the harbour looked as if they couldn't wait to pack it in. They even came in ordinary shoes. Couldn't set foot outside the lines of paths that ran around Árnafjall into all the tough bracken and gorse that dotted the hills, around the caves and all the places a lad like Benji might hide.

On her own, old leather boots so worn she could feel the blisters growing and the blood starting to run through her broken skin, she'd trudged those tracks herself, hour after hour, behind the cottage of the district sheriff, over the narrow tunnel, poking her head into that thing's black mouth as well. Her mother was right. The bus for Tórshavn had gone. There'd be one more in the afternoon.

Not that she'd take it. Not with Benji missing. Poor Benji. Thick Benji. A confused lad two years older than his brother but with half the brain. Though Jónas had too much of that about him if she were honest. He was always up to tricks, most of which she never latched onto. Or if she did it was too late. Him and Kaspar had made a terrible pair, taunting, teasing, nicking, rummaging through people's vegetable plots and sheep flocks trying to cause trouble. Her brother had kind of adopted the lad from the moment he could get persuaded into mischief. Wasn't hard. Silas had never seemed much interested in the boys unless they were biddable, easy, willing to go along with everything he wanted. And Jónas was never going to be that kind of kid. After last summer she'd thought Kaspar's absence might calm him down. It did too. But only for a little while. When the warm weather came back and he could spend most of the day outdoors, bunking off school, heading off to the fells whenever he felt like it, the old Jónas was back. Not that she ever really knew where he went, especially of late.

All these thoughts and doubts and worries, along with their accompanying nagging guilt, ran through her head as she rambled across the mountain, right up to the bare southern fells, then back to the puffin hides on the Lundi Cliffs. There she'd stopped and stared at the black semicircle of strand on Selkie Bay and the snag-toothed rocks below. White horses were breaking on the Skerries with the tide. There was a pod of whales not far off beyond their needle points and her father would be cursing like mad he wasn't in a position to chase them.

Standing there, breathless on the cliffs, she realised she was next to the very puffin hide they said the lads had been hiding in. Just a pile of stones, God knows how old, a place to bury yourself away from the flocks of birds that gathered on the cliffs each summer, and flew into the fleyging nets so easily, in such great numbers.

'What were you up to?' Alba whispered to herself, then ducked down through the low stone door and walked inside. It was dark and damp in there, and the smell she knew already. The stink of cigarettes so rank it was as if someone had been there lighting a fag not long before. Someone had been pissing here too. Just the kind of thing Jónas would do. Only two weeks before she'd caught him taking a leak on George Thomsen's rhubarb patch behind the big house and the boy had run away laughing, so quickly, vanished for a whole night, waiting till she got worried so that when he finally came back she didn't even whack him round the ear.

'Stupid, stupid . . .'

She raced outside – there was nothing to be learned in that vile little hole – and stood on the clifftop wondering whether to howl with rage or grief or just let all that bile inside spew out of her.

Staring at the Skerries and the black fins breaking surface there, thinking about the strange sequence of events two days before, the beast came and rose inside her, like one of those monsters from the myths they used to recount at school.

Alba Mikkelsen walked forward and stood on the cliff edge, staring down at the craggy rocks so far below. The waves crashed on them, taking away her dead son's blood and guts for all she knew. The ocean ran and ran, forever to the grey horizon, uncaring, uninterested, like everything else in the little world of Djevulsfjord.

And so she screamed and yelled and howled and spat every word they hated, the nastiest ones she knew. Screeched at herself, at Jónas, Silas, her dad, at the green fells, the filthy puffin hide with its stink of piss and tobacco, at the day, the sky, the sea and, more than anything, the ragged line of houses back by the harbour, a prison from which she'd escaped briefly just the once, and that didn't turn out well at all.

'My boys! You took my boys! I fucking hate you all!'

Gasping for breath, tears stinging her eyes she edged her toes over the tip until half her feet balanced over nothing, wondering if the rocks below were calling for her. It would be so easy. One last step out into the cold and salty air. A few seconds, then a swift and brutal end to all the agony.

She'd have done it too. But Benji was still out there. And whatever he'd done to his brother he surely had his reasons.

'Too easy,' Alba Mikkelsen said and trudged back to the path.

SHE WALKED TO THE village, slowly, step by painful step, looking all round her, wondering if she might see a figure in the hills, hiding in the caves maybe, frightened, needing his mum. But there was no sign of a soul out on the Árnafjall fells. No one in the tunnel by the district sheriff's cottage either even though she stood in the black mouth and hollered out his name over and over until her throat hurt.

Exhausted, lost for what else to do, she went back to the shack, kicked open the door, kicked off her boots, sat down, put her head in her hands, decided not to weep because there wasn't the time, the opportunity, the strength. The blood was coming through the holes in her threadbare socks. A couple of blisters were rising and those she'd have to pop.

One low curse she uttered and then a voice came out of the darkness by the boys' bunk beds.

'Some way to talk that is, Alba Ganting.'

'Mikkelsen,' she snapped back. 'Mikkelsen. I'm married. That hasn't changed, as far as I remember. And this is my home. You don't just walk in—'

'No. This place is mine.'

Dorotea Thomsen came out of the gloom and stood in front of her. George, the weak-willed husband, was trailing in her wake. He at least looked a bit shame-faced.

'This isn't the moment, love,' he said. 'The poor woman—'

'Yes. Poor,' Dorotea cut in. 'Living off our charity.'

'You said you'd give me some time!'

'Ja. But that was on the house. Now there's the funeral to be paid for. Your father's boat wants mending. All those debts keep mounting.'

'Jesus fucking Christ woman!'

Alba was on her feet, waving her bony fist. You didn't swear in Djevulsfjord. Not like that. Did lots of things that were worse from time to time. But never cursed bad out loud.

'No call for such language,' George Thomsen chided her. 'No call for that at all.'

'What do you want? *What do you want?*'

Dorotea squinted at her.

'To help you. That's what we always do. Help those less fortunate than us.'

'Who are mostly less fortunate *because* of you.'

'George,' Dorotea said, 'I don't think I want to hear any more of this. Tell Alba Ganting—'

'Mikkelsen!'

'Your man's gone,' Dorotea yelled, waving a fist at her. 'Don't you get that? He don't want you. No one does.'

'My boy!'

Silence, then the woman just laughed in her face.

'Your dad's got big bills coming to get his boat back in the water. Can't do that without us—'

'You bastard, George Thomsen,' Alba yelled at him. 'You said you wouldn't tell her.'

'Didn't . . .' he mumbled.

'Didn't need to.' Dorotea had that look she loved. Triumphant. 'I know what's happening in Djevulsfjord. I know everything. Don't you get it? While you lot struggle to get by we keep the wheels a-turning. Come up with money and goods when you're hard up. Nothing goes through this place without me seeing it. Nothing goes out either.'

'We should leave the girl,' he said. 'Now's not the time.'

'Best she knows where she stands.' Dorotea threw a piece of paper on the table. 'This is a fresh contract, Alba. You don't need to read it. I know you're not so good at that . . .'

'I can read! I'm not a moron.'

'It's legal,' George Thomsen told her. 'Even I can't understand all the stuff in there. Lawyer drew it up for her.'

'Legal . . . I got my boy's funeral tomorrow.'

Dorotea brandished the paper.

'If I pay for it. And the priest. And the hospital bills on Silas. If not you're going to have to go begging to the social people in Tórshavn and God knows when or if they'll help you out. Either way you're screwed. Question is who you want screwing you. Someone local who knows the kind of woman you are and doesn't mind putting up with it. Or some distant bastard in a council office who's only going to hear the worst. Maybe lock you up too like that son of yours. Don't think it'll be together either.'

Alba's voice was failing, and so was her strength.

'I'm not what you think . . .'

Another laugh then, hard and guttural.

'Aren't you? Sign this. I'll pay for everything. I'll let you stay here. I can get your father's boat back in the water in a day or two if I want. If I don't I can't see him having a penny income all winter. Can you?'

The paper. The damned paper was waving in her hands.

'What does it say?'

'It says you work for me. Doing what I tell you. Cleaning. Mucking out the sheep when we want it. In the kitchen. Full time. Hours flexible. Whatever I want them to be.'

Tears, they kept begging to come and she was determined the woman wasn't going to see that.

'You mean like I'm your slave?'

'Employee,' George Thomsen insisted. 'It's just that she puts money in one envelope for you. Then takes it out with another.'

'And I never get to leave?'

Dorotea Thomsen shook her head.

'Djevulsfjord's your home. Why would you want to do that? Where could you go?'

She chuckled and the way her heavy jowls moved reminded Alba of the pig her father had kept once and slaughtered bloodily on a wooden frame in the back garden for winter.

'Let's face it. You tried running once before, didn't you?' Dorotea declared. 'Look how that turned out.'

'I will not be your slave,' she said, knowing now the tears wouldn't come.

'You are already,' the woman announced. 'Like the rest of this hole. It's just that you're too stupid to know.' A nod of her head. 'Never mind. George. Watch. You're the witness.'

There was a pen tucked into the pocket of her floppy purple

cardigan. She took it out, popped the top, bent down and signed the contract. Then showed Alba the name there: her own.

'No—'

'You saw her sign, George. Didn't you? And let's face it like all the Gantings she's barely literate. No one's going to argue.'

'No!' Alba cried.

'Husband . . .'

George Thomsen didn't say a word. He looked terrified. Perhaps by both of them.

'This is a legal document,' Dorotea told her, folding the paper and putting it into her pocket. 'I'm doing this for your own good, Alba. I'll see the funeral happens. I'll get your father's boat back in the water. You, in turn, will pay me back.' The chuckle again. 'For years to come. Now . . .'

Alba blinked. She couldn't think of anything to say. Any way to object.

Dorotea Thomsen placed two notes on the table. Two hundred krónur. More than twice the money Alba had in her possession just then.

'It's for your own good. Just to prove it's meant in good faith I'll give you this as a signing-on bonus.'

'Didn't sign . . .'

She just smiled.

'I know you won't go telling stories. You're not that daft. Who are they going to believe? You or me?'

She wanted to say it again: tomorrow I have to bury my boy. But there didn't seem any point.

'By way of thanks I've got a stack of filthy fish trays out the back of the kitchens from the grind. I'd like them washed and scrubbed clean. Can't leave stuff like that around for long. Do that and you never get rid of the stink. Waste of money.'

She banged her clenched fist on the notes on the table.

'Two hundred krónur, Alba. When did you last have that much in your pocket?'

'When I was working the ferry out of Tórshavn. When I was . . .'

She wanted to say: happy. But it wouldn't come.

Dorotea was smiling so hard it looked her fat face might break.

'That worked out well, didn't it?' She clapped her hands. 'No time like the present. Those trays won't wash themselves. But take tomorrow off if you want. Like you said. Things to do.'

INGA DAM RODE HER motorbike the way she doubtless approached life. With a deliberate recklessness, devoid of thought for others or the consequences. Elsebeth clung on tightly from the pillion seat, arms around the woman's waist as they took the winding path from behind Selkie up to the heights of Árnafjall. Perhaps, she thought, Inga wanted the shortest route to Djevulsfjord, one that didn't involve the circuitous journey round the peak and through the tunnel. Or she was hoping to see something along the way. If the latter was the case they were both disappointed. There was no sign of Benjamin Mikkelsen or any search party out to find him, not by the stone puffin hides set like ancient graves along the broad path that crossed the cliffs, the tracks that led up to the cave networks beneath the mountain heights or on the pale sweep of beach before the Skerries.

Close to home, as they lurched across grass and gravel, Elsebeth's phone buzzed and, with tenuous fingers, she managed to read the message there. It was Tristan, apologising for his lateness and lack of communication. She was not encouraged by the unusual vagueness of his tone. Ever since the grind the little village, and their own lives, had been affected by something she failed to comprehend except that it was dark, unwelcome and malevolent. Almost as if the slaughter on the strand had somehow cursed them all, an idea she was not going to broach with the woman clutching the handlebars and twisting the throttle in front of her, since Inga Dam would, without doubt, concur.

To Elsebeth's surprise they sped right past their little cottage, the sheep grazing at the back, chickens pecking round the wire-fenced pen. A picture of rural bliss that no longer rang quite true. She'd assumed that was where Inga was taking her, but no. Another three hundred yards and finally they were on asphalt, headed for the shady entrance to the Árnafjall tunnel, a dark place only just wide enough to take the Sørvágur bus and if you met that halfway through it was wonderful fun to have to reverse to let it past. More than half a kilometre long and she hated every second of being inside it, feeling the weight of all that rock above pressing on your head.

The bike came to a halt on a patch of mud close to the tunnel mouth. Inga Dam kicked down the stand, leaned the machine to a halt and leapt to one side, dragging her helmet off as she did so.

A car drove past. Aksel Højgaard was behind the wheel. He glanced at the pair of them, no smile, no expression on his face whatsoever.

'The superintendent seems to have much business in Djevulsfjord,' Elsebeth observed.

'His own. None of any good to other folk I'd warrant.'

There were shiny tears in Inga Dam's eyes. They must have been there all the way. Now they did look like anger.

'Why are we here?' Elsebeth asked when it became apparent the woman was going to say nothing more without some kind of prompting.

She strode to the entrance and stopped a couple of paces before the darkness began. Afraid to go further, Elsebeth thought. Which was curious because she doubted there were many things Inga Dam was scared of.

'This was where they killed him. A year ago.' She kicked a pebble into the darkness and listened to its dying echo. 'Not long after another grind. Kristian hated those damned things. Hated everything about this place.'

'Except you.'

That startled her.

'Except you, Inga. I'm sorry. I assume you're going to tell me what happened. I assume that's why we're here.'

The woman's eyes stayed on the burrow through the mountain, nothing else, as she spat out her story. Elsebeth listened, not believing at first. The idea Tristan's predecessor had been killed – accidentally or not – on their doorstep seemed incredible. Incredible too that Tristan had never even known how the man had died. That no one in Djevulsfjord had so much as mentioned it in the time they'd been here. It was as if Kristian Djurhuus had never existed, which was, Inga Dam thought, what they wished to believe.

'They hated him,' she went on. 'All of them. They hated the way he made them follow the rules. How he wouldn't turn a blind eye when they wished it. Not my Kristian. He was a good man. An honest man. A man of the world. That was why they detested him most of all. He wouldn't do their bidding. Not like . . .'

She stopped, her gaze still set on the black mouth in front of them.

'Not like Tristan, you mean?'

'I didn't say that.'

'His job is almost a sinecure. A favour to a retiree from the civil service. All he has to do is see the grind carried out according to the rules. As far as I'm aware – as far as he is – that's what he did. You may not like the hunt. I don't myself. But it is legal. What else are we supposed to do?'

She came up very close, helmet in hand. There was a hardness to her, and it didn't just come from spending her working day attacking marble with the blade of a sharpened chisel.

'You think these people care about the law? About anything but themselves?'

'They don't seem to care much about young Benjamin Mikkelsen so I don't—'

'I was in Paris when they ran him down. I didn't even know he was dead until I came here two weeks later. I thought . . . I thought Kristian had perhaps found someone else. I was barely around for him. Why shouldn't he?'

Elsebeth held out her hand.

'I will tell my husband what you've said. If we work together—'

'Then what? Kristian's dead and gone. That policeman Højgaard couldn't care less. He says it was just an accident.'

'Perhaps it was . . .'

There was contempt in her face at that moment and it stung.

'He knew something. He'd found out something about this damned place. He wouldn't tell me. I think he thought it was too . . . dangerous.'

Elsebeth Haraldsen felt cold at that moment. It was as if they all stood on the edge of the Lundi Cliffs like young Jónas Mikkelsen. One step forward and you began to tumble. One step back and the view ahead, which was important, perhaps vital, might disappear.

'Come and talk to us. To me and Tristan. He'll be home soon. That police officer, Hanna Olsen, will be with him. She's not from here. If only—'

'You need to leave,' Inga Dam snapped. 'I know this place. Too well. There are monsters behind all this beauty and they will devour the innocent. The fools. The gullible.' She held up her hand in the shape of a gun and pretended to fire it in Elsebeth's direction. 'You and your husband, I fear, are all three.'

There was nothing Elsebeth Haraldsen could think of to say.

'I'm going straight to Sørvágur. There's a flight out to Copenhagen this evening. I will be on it. If you had any sense you'd join me . . .'

'How can we?'

'It's simple. You do it. You're like the rest of them here. Shackled to something you never question even when it's a myth. A brazen, perilous lie. Well. It's your grave. You lie in it . . .'

She climbed on the bike, kicked the thing to life, put her helmet on, looked once in Elsebeth's direction, shrugged and then rode off.

Back the direction they came. Not through the tunnel which was surely the obvious way to go.

Elsebeth was not afraid of the dark. Nor of ghosts or the memory of a man she'd never known. According to Inga's own version of events Aksel Højgaard had been adamant the previous sheriff had died in an accident, a hit-and-run, something which was rare in the Faroes but scarcely unknown.

'I will not be frightened out of my home by anyone. Never.'

She walked to the mouth of the Árnafjall tunnel. The place was unlit. There was surely no need for anything but the head-lamps of the small amount of traffic that used it. But she had her phone with her and there was a way you could use that as a torch if you wanted.

Two steps closer she took until she began to smell the narrow vein through the rock. Damp and diesel. All the same it was close to their house and someone, they assumed the lost Mikkelsen lad, had been nearby the night before, stealing eggs from their chicken coop.

Then something else stopped her and it took a moment to realise what it was.

Smoke, she thought. Tobacco. The same black leathery smell she'd met in the puffin hide on the Lundi Cliffs.

HØJGAARD PARKED HIS UNMARKED police car next to the graveyard. A meandering path led to a gate in the fence by one of the many fields the Thomsens rented out to whoever could afford them. On the other side stood the priest's two-storey home.

He walked past a small flock of quiet, timid sheep, on into Ryberg's small, unloved garden. A spiral of dark smoke was working its way from the chimney up towards the fading sky. The back door was open. The priest was in the downstairs living room, in front of a dying fire.

'You took your time,' the man complained.

'It is my time, Lars, after all. A police officer's got lots on his plate.'

Ryberg looked half-mad.

'The game's up. I'm burying the Mikkelsen brat tomorrow then I'm off.'

Højgaard took two steps into the room and looked around. Ryberg had been here for five years. The priest before him, a more friendly man, a bachelor who loved the sea and fishing, had managed almost a decade before he returned to Denmark. That one had worked on Baldur Ganting's boat for nothing but the smallest share of the catch. So enamoured had he become of the ocean that he'd decorated this room in its honour. An old ship's wheel sat on the wall above the fireplace. Photographs and paintings of fishing expeditions and the grind were pinned to every spare inch of space on the striped, fading purple wallpaper. Ryberg was simply too lazy to remove them. Next to a large leather armchair a small capstan had been turned into a coffee table. Around it, still intact, was a length of heavy sisal rope.

Højgaard sat down in the adjoining chair and poked the thing with his toe.

'I'll never understand why you didn't redecorate this place. Put your own stamp on it. Being a bachelor I imagine—'

'Don't screw about now,' the priest snarled. 'I've burned everything. Papers. The lot. Nothing comes back to me if this shit gets out.'

'Was that really necessary?'

'Who knows? I want out of here.'

'What?' Højgaard snapped his fingers. 'Just like that?'

Ryberg came away from the fire, waving his pale bony hands.

'Yesterday I nearly had my way with the Mikkelsen girl. She didn't much like me trying. But next time I may not take no for an answer. You want that?'

Højgaard's face fell, so quickly Ryberg stepped back a pace.

'Oh, Christ. You idiot.'

'She's been waggling that bottom of hers around this place long enough without me touching it. Why shouldn't I enjoy what everyone else does?'

'If you'd wanted some company you only had to ask.' Højgaard thought about this. 'Oh, I see. You think this is a way of shutting the door behind you. Making me give you what you want.'

'If that little whore started to blab your bosses might wake up finally. They could pull me in. And if they do that . . . I talk.' The priest winked. 'Man of God. Not cut out for lying. There. I made your decisions for you. Get me away from this hellhole before I do something to Alba Mikkelsen that makes her run screaming to Tórshavn.'

Højgaard sighed.

'For pity's sake, Lars. Do you honestly think anyone in Djevulsfjord willingly calls us about anything?'

'I believe . . .'

The priest fell silent as Højgaard leapt to his feet. The two were around the same height and the same build. But the superintendent was a few years younger and possessed the natural aggression of his trade.

'It's unwise to threaten a man like me,' he said and jabbed a hard finger at Ryberg's black priest's jacket.

'The walls are falling, Aksel! Benjamin Mikkelsen's still out there on those hills. He knows something. He must. I can sense it.'

Højgaard laughed.

'Best ask the man upstairs then. You're the fellow for that.'

'Don't taunt me.'

The policeman nodded.

'No. That would be wrong. Here . . .'

He walked to the sideboard, picked up the bottle of cheap whisky there and poured a large glass.

'Drink up, Lars. That always helps, doesn't it?'

'You bastard!'

'Drink, I said!' He held out the glass until the priest took it in his shaking hands and with his uncertain lips gulped at the amber liquid. 'You're a weak man. You always were . . .'

'Everyone's weak in this hellish place except you. I want out of here. For good. No one coming after me either.'

'Drink,' Højgaard said more gently. 'You're a terrible worrier. Perhaps it goes with the job. I have everything in hand. You'll get what's outstanding. All debts will be honoured.' He clapped his hands. 'The ones you owe as well. By which I mean tomorrow. The funeral. You have to be there.'

More of the cheap booze from the garage in Sørvágur went down Ryberg's throat.

'Do I?'

'If the village priest flees this place the night before a burial people will be asking questions everywhere. More so than if Alba Mikkelsen started screaming rape. The sooner that Mikkelsen kid goes in the ground the better.'

'And when you find the brother?'

Ryberg blinked and looked at the ashes in the fireplace.

'None of your concern.'

'Jesus, Aksel! I've risked a lot for you. I could lose everything.'

'But you won't. Trust me, Lars.' Højgaard took his arm in a tight and certain grip. 'You can't run now. After the funeral. Then . . .'

He smiled and fell silent.

'You're thinking,' said Ryberg.

'I'm always thinking. You want Alba Mikkelsen, don't you?'

'I've not had a woman since I took a weekend off to Aalborg. That little whore cost me plenty—'

'Spare me the details. Tomorrow, get your things. Put them in a little case. What money you have. Passport. ID.'

The priest was looking at him like a hungry dog, waiting on food.

'They could still come after me.'

'They have to find you first. And Father Lars Ryberg will be gone from the face of the earth. I will organise a new you. Someone with money. A way out. A way you can start afresh.' He squeezed Ryberg's arm. 'Imagine that. No Djevulsfjord. No Vágar. A new life, a new name, new opportunities somewhere a long, long way from here.'

'Where?'

'Where do you want?'

He thought for a second and said, 'Bangkok.'

'Bangkok it is,' Højgaard replied without a moment's hesitation. The priest's grey face broke with a rare smile.

'You mean it?'

'Every word. I never let people down. Haven't you noticed?'

'I knew I could rely on you,' Ryberg said, taking Højgaard's right hand and pumping it up and down. 'And yourself?'

'What about me?'

'What will you do?'

A shrug then the policeman said, 'Why should I do anything? You're leaving. Fleeing they'll say. All blame will come the way of Lars Ryberg, a man who paraded himself as a priest. A man who's vanished from the face of the earth . . .'

'I *am* a priest.'

'You were. Tomorrow we'll put an end to that nonsense.' He reached forward and stroked Ryberg's heavy grey bristles. The man recoiled. 'Shave off that beard. As soon as you've buried that kid.' Højgaard nodded towards the hall and the staircase. 'Whatever money you have . . .'

'I've hardly enough to get me to Sørvágur. I'm in hock to that Thomsen bitch.'

Højgaard groaned.

'Dorotea Thomsen is the last thing you need worry about. Find whatever you want to take with you. Like I said, pack your passport and ID. That way I can persuade my superiors you're travelling under your own name. We'll make sure you're not.'

Ryberg looked both grateful and ashamed.

'I never meant to do real harm. None of us did. Surely?'

'We didn't,' Højgaard agreed. 'And what harm there was . . . it wasn't to anyone that mattered, was it?'

'That little bastard Jónas . . . he was the devil himself. The Mikkelsens. The Gantings. Jesus . . .'

Højgaard was silent again.

'What are you thinking now?' the priest asked.

'I am thinking of you, Lars. The man you must leave behind. His story. The narrative I will require to explain your disappearance. What fiction you invent when we get you out of here . . . that's yours to make.'

'I'll send a postcard,' Ryberg grunted.

Højgaard gripped him hard by the collar. The glass fell from

Ryberg's fingers and shattered on the tiled fireplace next to the sooty ash from the papers he'd been burning.

'Don't think of that for a moment. If I hear from you again it will not be in your best interests. Now . . .' He nodded at the stairs. 'Go and find your case. The things you want to take with you. After that . . .'

He smiled.

'After that . . . what?'

'We need to talk about the funeral. It will be your last. You should make it special.'

The priest thought for a second then nodded and shuffled off for the stairs.

Aksel Højgaard watched him go. He'd always liked the capstan seat. It was as well that Lars Ryberg had never got rid of the thing.

Bending down to look at the side he could see that the heavy sisal rope was real. Nothing attached it to the centre except a loose knot, easily freed.

Højgaard unrolled the thick cord loop by loop and wound it round his arm. There were footsteps across the creaky floor above him.

The papers in the fireplace were ashes, records of christenings and funerals and other such trivia he imagined, most of it of no relevance at all. Among the blackened leaves stood the sooty poker Ryberg had been using. It looked as if it might have been fashioned from an ancient whaling spear.

He took it and liked the way the thing hung neatly in his hand.

* * *

THERE WEREN'T SO MANY fish trays. The job would be done in twenty minutes. Dorotea watched all the time, arms folded, smug by the door, while her husband retired upstairs where the sound of radio music soon drifted out to the dank courtyard behind their house. This was, Alba understood, not about cleaning a few fish trays at all. It concerned cementing the relationship between them. Dorotea saying: before you simply owed me, now you're mine.

They were all peasants in Djevulsfjord anyway, beholden to the Thomsens the way folk in the village always had been. Alba had simply made the unexacting transition from serf to slave. All on the basis of a forged signature she could never deny because she was Alba Mikkelsen and the vicious woman watching her was right: no one would believe the estranged wife of a poor fisherman over the moneyed lady from the mansion.

'Done,' she said when the last blue plastic box was wiped clean.

It was a statement. Not a question. Even slaves knew when to say no.

'You got a big day tomorrow, Alba. Like I said. Don't need to turn up here. I'm no tyrant. You can catch up on your hours at the weekend.'

'Too kind,' she grumbled, then stowed the mop and the clothes and the disinfectant in the outside shed and walked out without another word.

The afternoon bus was just leaving for Tórshavn, stopping at Sørvágur along the way. When she was a kid she'd liked to sit in the fields with the black-and-white sheep outside the airport watching the planes come and go, wondering what the world was like beyond the grey-green landscape of Vágar. Once the school had organised a trip to Copenhagen and for a while she'd thought she'd be on it. Flying like the sea birds. But then Dad said they didn't have money for the fare. So she stayed behind, the only pupil left in the classroom with Mrs Blak, a kindly woman who came from Jutland originally and didn't seem to understand much about Vágar at all. Anyway, the child Alba had thought, if she was a bird at all it was a puffin, fated to flutter along the Lundi Cliffs on her little parrot wings until someone with their fleyging net, Silas or her dad or Kaspar, came and swept her out of the sky, down to the cold, hard earth. Then did anything they liked.

What looked like the car belonging to Højgaard was parked up by the priest's house. The rest of the village seemed deserted. It was that time of the afternoon. People were either out shopping in Sørvágur, tending their sheep, maybe braving the sea in a boat looking for a shoal, or just idling.

'I will find you, Benjamin,' she said to herself as she strode back to the shed where the three of them had lived inharmoniously since Silas kicked them out. 'One way or another I will find you and we'll leave this place together. We'll have a life. I promise. I . . .'

The door to the ramshackle hut was open. That was odd. She never locked it but she always shut it surely, even when her mind was in a flap after Dorotea Thomsen's incessant bullying.

Alba walked in and knew straight away what to look for. The money on the table. The two hundred krónur placed there like a set of handcuffs chaining her to the Thomsens seemingly forever.

It was gone, of course. Some bugger had stolen their way into her shack and nicked it. She stared at the empty space it left and spat and cursed and tore her hair. Thought of running up the road to the priest's house and finding Superintendent Højgaard. Yelling at him until he did something. But what?

No one stole from other people in Djevulsfjord. It was unthinkable. Everyone knew everyone. You'd be able to see the guilt written in their familiar faces.

So . . . who?

She sniffed. She wiped away the tears. There was a smell in the room as well. A human one. Sweat and body odour. Something else too, a fragrance that was half-familiar.

Alba looked around. What she saw there was so unexpected it took her a while to realise, to accept, it was the source. She got up and walked to the bunk bed where the boys had slept, Jónas on the top as he'd demanded, his tall, ungainly brother at the bottom. The smell of them, sweat and the rest, was still on the threadbare sheets and thin wool blankets. On the mattress of the upper bed there was a bouquet. Clumsily made, a circle of Lady's Mantle, dark green leaves, pale green flowers, with a bunch of rose-pink ragged robin in the centre, the star-like flowers already shedding their spiky petals on the thin, worn sheet.

A wreath gathered on the wild hills from Árnafjall. She knew that straight away. They'd grown up with these flowers as children. Picked them for their parents for birthdays in the summer. Pressed their petals into books to stare at in the long dark days of winter, reminders that the sun would come again.

'Oh, Benji,' she whispered, the tears starting to flow in a flood down her cheeks. 'Why come here and run, boy? Why? Just stay . . .'

The shack was at the end of the harbour landing. He must have sneaked in from the cliffs unseen then vanished.

Around the room she ran, shouting it, bellowing as loud as her lungs would let her.

Benji, Benji. Just stay . . .

Her voice echoed off the dusty timbers, the tiny, grimy windows out onto the yard and the deserted harbour beyond. She ran to the door, looked round, saw no one. Raced to the cobbles by the harbour, looked back at the hills. Just green and grey and empty like they usually were.

'Just come to your mum,' Alba Mikkelsen whispered. 'For God's sake . . .'

Back inside she sat at the empty table, wondering what he might do with the money. Two hundred krónur he couldn't know how to spend, even if there was some place to use it.

FIFTEEN

Five strides into the Árnafjall tunnel and the place was cold, so black Elsebeth Haraldsen's eyes hurt from the effort of trying to pierce the gloom. She fumbled for her phone and, after a few futile efforts, managed to turn on the torch app. It cast a white light ahead of her, weak, barely a beam and all it revealed was the green algae on the walls and the black tarred road. A few steps forward and she began to meet the detritus: cans of beer and soft drinks, a burger wrapper, crisp packets, a dead bird, and cigarettes, lots of cigarettes. Another dead bird. Then the sound of something scurrying away in front of her. Something small but not so small. She knew her fauna of the islands, they all did. No rabbits, they'd all been destroyed. No cats, the same since they wrought such damage on the birds. A brown rat or a mouse or a hare that liked the dark. They were the only three wild mammals that managed to survive the climate and the hunts.

'A rat,' she said out loud and the thing scurried away even further.

Two more steps. The tunnel ended on the far side of the mountain half a kilometre away, hidden in shade at that hour. So the world beyond was barely visible, a circle cut in shadows, nothing more.

Something moved and this was bigger.

'Benjamin!' she called in a voice she hoped was loud without being threatening. 'Benjamin Mikkelsen! It's Mrs Haraldsen here. The district sheriff's wife. Please come out. I know you're here!'

She didn't. She wasn't sure of anything at all, whether it was wise to be going deeper into the narrow tunnel with just the puny light of the phone to pierce the dark. Then she leapt in shock, as if electrified, wondering what cold and clammy thing had touched her, fingers reaching up desperately to remove the thing from her bare neck. A drip of freezing water fell from the ceiling and ran down her right cheek.

Some kind of plant or algae. That was all it was. Disgusting but quite innocuous.

'Be sensible, Elsebeth,' she told herself. 'One more minute in here and then we're done.'

Something was moving again, too loud, too large to be anything but human.

'Your mother's worried sick about you, Benji,' she called out. 'We all are. What happened with your brother . . .'

What do you say? What words were there?

You didn't kill him really. I don't believe that even if everyone else does. The police among them.

'We can put things right. But we have to talk to you. Your mum . . . and . . . Christ!'

She didn't like screaming. It wasn't like her. But she couldn't stop herself again. More freezing, stinking water had come down from above and she felt sure she heard a noise and this time there were footsteps, real and close, fast-moving.

'Benji!' she called.

The torch showed nothing in its blue-white beam. The steps

kept echoing around the narrow vein through the rock, both close, both far away, and she couldn't begin to tell where from.

'For pity's sake child . . .'

Somewhere near here Kristian Djurhuus had died, knocked off his bike by someone who never stopped. Drunk they said but left for dead. Perhaps injured, bleeding, whimpering all night long till they found nothing but a cold body in the morning, shrugged their shoulders, never came up with the vehicle that hit him.

'I know you're . . .'

She could pinpoint him then. The steps were behind her, heading back to the village end of the tunnel.

'Don't run. Don't run!'

Elsebeth turned to follow and didn't look behind.

'LIGHTS,' HANNA OLSEN ORDERED as the Ace Capri fell under the shadow of the peak then drove at a steady thirty kilometres per hour into the tunnel.

'Oh.' Haraldsen hadn't been concentrating. His regime when driving was to take everything at a snail's pace on the grounds that this usually allowed time and distance to correct his not infrequent mistakes. 'Of course.'

In truth his mind was anywhere but Vágar at that moment. He was thinking of routines and procedures in the police station in Tórshavn. How they were so fixed over the years that no one would much know how to deal with anything new or different should it come their way. Some months before he'd retired they'd had a visit from a very senior officer in the famous police head-quarters in Copenhagen. A handsome, tall, rather theatrical man who'd talked of all the threats of the modern world – terrorism and money laundering, international mobsters and the smuggling of hard drugs – then waited as those assembled for the lecture asked questions.

There were three only and all concerned his journey and how much he was appreciating the Faroes. The fellow had left not long after, scratching his head in amazement. No one had the opportunity to tell him: such things did not touch the family of green islands nestling in their corner of the cold Atlantic, or the people who lived upon them. They were apart from all the chaos and corruption of the modern world. Or thought themselves so. As to murder . . . the man mentioned the crime almost in passing, as if he assumed the taking of a life was a matter-of-fact occurrence for every police force around the world.

But not in Tórshavn, and never in Vágar. At least, Haraldsen had thought with a sense of growing alarm, not that anyone knew.

'Lights, Tristan!'

God, they were already into the maw of the tunnel and he still hadn't found the switch. There was a shriek from the left as metal met stone.

'Lights!'

He found them. The Ace Capri rolled a little then achieved some semblance of equilibrium in the centre of the narrow lane.

'It is not,' he declared for her amusement, 'a Haraldsen vehicle if it has no scratches upon it.'

Hanna Olsen didn't laugh. She was thinking about her missing brother, he guessed. From their conversation earlier it was obvious this was why she came to Vágar in the first place. And now they would try to make an illicit journey into the network in Tórshavn in the hope of uncovering a little more about his fate.

What would Elsebeth make of that? He was still aware of the coldness between them that morning. The feeling on both their parts that secrets had been kept. This was unwelcome, wrong, a subject to be dealt with frankly. Though not with a police officer around.

'As agreed,' he said, setting up a steady pace down the tunnel, 'we will spend no more than an hour on this. If there's something to be found that should be time enough. If—'

'Tristan—'

'I don't wish to raise your hopes—'

'Tristan. Your lights. They're on dip. They should be on full beam in the tunnel.'

'I was not aware I was here for driving lessons, young lady.'

'Full beam!'

Her voice was anxious and full of fear or so it seemed.

He squinted ahead, did as she asked anyway, and turned the Ace Capri's headlights up to full. Which was not much, if he was honest with himself. It was an old vehicle, much loved, a veteran of trekking all around the Faroes and a good part of Jutland too.

'There's someone there,' Hanna said. 'In the tunnel. Someone. Can't you see?'

'BENJI!' ELSEBETH HARALDSEN CRIED again then stepped out into the centre of the dark, dank vein beneath the mountain, blinking at the circle of daylight ahead. 'Benji . . . stop.'

Run, she thought. As fast as him? How could you? And whoever had been hiding in the shadows, desperate to avoid her, was surely younger, faster, more determined.

She couldn't help thinking of the dead district sheriff too, gasping out his final hours somewhere near. A man Inga Dam loved. A man she believed murdered though why the troubled sculptor of Selkie Bay had no idea. Though it did occur to her that perhaps the woman had more to tell than she'd revealed. Lost for what to do, Elsebeth stood close to the tunnel exit, shivering, wondering when Tristan would come back.

'Mysteries . . .' she murmured then heard something behind her: a familiar engine followed by the squeal of tyres on damp asphalt, the teeth-jangling scrape of metal against stone.

When she turned the bright white lights were nearly on her, so close Elsebeth could think of nothing but to shield her eyes.

There are monsters behind all this beauty and they will devour the innocent.

It looked like one was here.

SIXTEEN

'Tristan?'

Elsebeth was in bed, sprawled across the sheets, quite alone. Her head hurt. Her arm was in a sling. An annoyance, one she felt was unnecessary. She sat up, removed the stretchy fabric carefully, and rolled back her sleeves. Bruises, blue and yellow, ran down from her right shoulder to the elbow. She felt her head. A lump on the same side. The memories were coming back. Headlights in the depths of the tunnel, the screech of brakes, a sudden desperate urge to throw herself to one side which mostly worked . . .

'Bloody hell, husband,' she muttered, remembering those last moments and the paintwork of the Ace Capri. 'You ran me down.'

More images flooded back, as if somewhere in her head a valve had opened. Inga Dam in tears in her pale-blue timbered hut, talking about the dead district sheriff, marble powder running down her arms. Then the tunnel. A place, it seemed to her, that possessed some secrets. Which was why she'd entered. The smell of smoke and something else, a human stink. The sound of footsteps, running. A vague shape fleeing out into the bright daylight when she turned, not knowing a vehicle was coming from behind.

'Tristan?' she said again.

She walked to the bedroom window and peered out. The thickest fog she'd seen in years had descended upon Djevulsfjord.

It seemed to occupy the entire world beyond the glass, a grey-white brume so dense she couldn't make out the chicken coops or the old slaughterhouse, so damp it formed a cloud of mist across the window panes. The light had that brightness about it that hinted the sun might burn through and, in the end, deliver a summer's day. Or not. There was a saying they heard all the time in the Faroes: if you didn't like the weather then wait five minutes for it to change. But the climate was always fickle. Sometimes it did. Sometimes it simply teased. Djevulsfjord, more than any place she'd known, seemed prone to meteorological uncertainty. The village might stay in this strange state of limbo all day.

'But there's a funeral coming,' she whispered and just the thought made her feel down again.

Jónas Mikkelsen's. It was important they were there. It was important too that Benjamin, his brother, who was surely skirting the village, hiding in the tunnel, stealing eggs from time to time, was found before another tragedy occurred.

'Tristan,' she said again, more loudly. 'Where in God's name are you?' She checked her watch. Already half past ten. 'I'm hungry and for the life of me I don't know whether this will be a late breakfast or an early lunch. Where . . .?'

She marched downstairs. The living room was empty. The grey shroud peered back at her from every window.

'Husband. *Where are you?*'

'Elsebeth?' asked a faint voice in return.

The study.

Elsebeth walked in. He was rising from the computer, sucking so hard on his empty pipe she could hear the noise of it. Hanna Olsen was by his side. She looked as if she'd been crying.

'You should stay in bed,' Haraldsen said, coming to take her arms, then thinking twice of it.

Elsebeth was rarely ill and on those few occasions hated the whole experience. The lethargy, the inability to do anything, the boredom, all these tedious side effects were far worse than any pain she'd known. And then there were the questions, all of the ones Tristan was throwing at her at that moment. About how she felt, what hurt, what didn't, and why she wasn't back in bed where she was supposed to stay, a tedious invalid until the curfew went.

'The doctor advised . . .'

'What doctor?'

He turned his head to one side, narrowed his eyes and peered at her.

'You don't remember?'

'Of course I remember. I just woke up so I'm being a little slow. I was in the tunnel. Someone else was there. I damned near caught them. It was the Mikkelsen boy I think.' She tapped his chest. 'Then you came along.' Another tap. 'And ran me down!'

'You were in the dark! How was I to know?'

She'd upset him with the accusation so she apologised and kissed him once, quickly, on his whiskery cheek, noting that he had yet to shave.

'What do you want?' he asked.

'Bacon. Eggs. Toast. A mug of tea. Oh and you need a razor on those cheeks.'

'I've been . . . busy.'

'Doing what?'

Hanna Olsen got to her feet. Her eyes were pink.

'Elsebeth,' she begged. 'Please go back to bed.'

'No, I shan't. You didn't actually hit me. Did you, Tristan?'

'I believe it was what they call a glancing blow. The Capri took the worst of it.'

'Is she still drivable?'

'Just. Elsebeth . . .'

'Well then.' She sat down at the laptop. 'It seems we got off lightly. Now it's crystal clear the two of you have been up to something behind my back. What it is . . . I'd like to know.'

There was a photo on the screen. A young man, burly with muscular arms covered with tattoos. Someone she'd seen before and it took a moment for her to realise.

'Who's that?' she asked.

'My brother,' Hanna said. 'Søren.'

'Where is he now?'

No answer.

'My phone, Tristan. Did it survive?'

He went into the kitchen and fetched the thing. The glass was scratched but the screen flickered into life when she turned it on.

'Where is he now?'

'I don't know. He came to Vágar last summer. He'd been in trouble back home. He . . .' She shrugged. The tears weren't far away. Much like Inga Dam, Hanna Olsen possessed a hard but brittle veneer, one easily shattered by grief. 'He vanished.'

The phone came alive. She hunted for the photo album. Then Elsebeth held up the picture she'd taken in Inga Dam's kitchen: a group of men by the harbour in Djevulsfjord, Djurhuus the previous district sheriff, now dead, among them. The aftermath of the grind. Kaspar Ganting and a man who was clearly Søren Olsen.

'I can tell you one place,' she said. 'He was here.'

Hanna pulled up the spare office chair and took the phone, stared at the picture, said not a word.

'Also,' Elsebeth added, 'I have other news to impart. Since it seems we are now all like detectives together.'

'What news?' Tristan asked warily.

'Your predecessor. A man called Kristian Djurhuus. He died in that same tunnel. Run down by a stranger the police have never found. Murdered, according to the woman who was his lover. Though why . . .'

It was, she thought, quite a revelation and deserved some kind of acclaim. As well as a good cooked breakfast after that. Instead Tristan and Hanna Olsen said nothing, just glanced at one another with clear expressions of shiftiness on their faces.

'You knew.' Elsebeth felt astonished at first, and then quite infuriated. 'For the love of God, Tristan. You knew and never told me.'

'I'll get the kettle on,' he replied and fled for the kitchen.

THE FUNERAL WAS FOUR hours away yet Baldur Ganting, to his wife's concern, was still in his field clothes: grubby, blue, denim overalls that hadn't seen the wash in weeks, a green plaid shirt, no socks, no slippers though a threadbare blue fisherman's cap was pulled low over his ears. He sat at the kitchen table obsessing over his slaughter knives, blades long and short, sharpening each in turn with a whetstone as if there was a killing coming. She didn't understand. They hadn't been able to afford any sheep for the winter. There was nothing for them to cut and salt and store.

Money was short in any case without all this extra expense. Not that he would dream of discussing the matter with her. A man was meant to take care of his family. It was his job, no one else's, and over the three decades they'd been married Ganting had always managed year in, year out. There'd been times when the animals had died or the grind failed which meant they went into autumn with nothing much in place for the harsh months to come. Those winters had seemed interminable with little to eat but root vegetables, eggs and a boiler chicken as a treat for Christmas.

Often the kids had gone to school in clothes so old, ill-fitting and darned Eydna wept quietly in shame as they climbed on the bus. How he managed to get them through at all she failed to understand, but the Gantings never quite starved, never wanted for bare essentials. Survival was a skill a Djevulsfjord family learned early because the alternative was endless misery or worse, getting even further into hock with the Thomsens. Yet more disgraceful throwing yourself on the mercy of the social people in Tórshavn. There, in that last desperate place, lay a degree of humiliation a man like him could never stomach. She could take the sideways looks of the mothers in Sørvágur when they saw Alba and Kaspar's fall-apart clothes. But it was different for women. Men were supposed to be hard, stoic, beyond feelings. Which was hard to remember now his mood, bleak at the best of times, seemed to be turning more dark and silent with every passing day.

The news from the hospital about Silas was bad. He wouldn't be back on his feet for a month or more, and even then would be unable to work. To make matters worse two boat builders had come over from Sørvágur that morning to look at the *Alberta*, only to stand by the harbour shaking their heads. The damage was far worse than Ganting and George Thomsen feared. More extensive and costly to fix. The boat wouldn't be seaworthy without a day or two of hard labour on it by the craftsmen. The idea of Ganting without his *Alberta* was unthinkable. Only the evening before pods of whales had been seen offshore and they wouldn't linger long. Not that anyone could go chasing them in this fog even if Ganting had a boat.

She knew what he was thinking. Tomorrow the mist would surely lift and every man and woman in Djevulsfjord would be happy to race to the strand, tugging their children with them, if a group of blackfish was spotted beyond the Skerries. Lingering memories of a funeral or not. But they would look to Baldur Ganting to lead them out to sea and gain permission from the district sheriff. That was his role, social and formal under the government rules. Without a vessel of his own he'd be forced to beg a position on one belonging to another family, which was a kind of slight, not that any would mention it. There came the matter of pride and shame again. To be nothing more than a crewman for the grind would be as bad as missing the hunt altogether.

Alba had called by, sullen as usual, lost in her own thoughts. She now sat by the dead kitchen fireplace toying with her mother's unfinished knitting: a cable jumper with a Celtic knot. She'd asked idly if they were alright. A question, Eydna believed, better directed at her than them. She seemed even more distracted as usual, her hair a mess, her eyes blank.

'You need to smarten up for the funeral, Alba.'

'That's right. Pick on me. Seen what Dad looks like? Like he's about to go out on the grind.'

'Things to do,' Baldur Ganting grunted and swept the long slaughter knife down the stone again. 'No one's going fishing in that weather either. You're sea folk, daughter. You ought to understand that.'

They always gossiped in the kitchen if there was news to share. So Alba picked again at the knitting then told them: the night before a doctor from Sørvágur had come out on an emergency call, summoned by the policewoman from Denmark.

'The new sheriff's wife,' she added. 'Apparently she got hit by her man's van in the tunnel while she was walking through it.'

'Jesus.' Ganting put down the knife. 'What in God's name was she doing hanging round in there?'

'Dorotea don't know that, Dad. She don't know everything about everyone. Not quite.'

Eydna could scarcely believe what she was hearing.

'Never mind all that. Is the poor woman hurt?'

'Nah . . .' Alba said and went back to playing with the needles and yarn. 'She got lucky. Someone has to, I suppose.'

'She seems very nice from what I've seen. They are strangers though. God knows what they're doing here—'

'He's the district sheriff,' Ganting cut in. 'Got to have one of them or we can't go out on the grind, can we?' The long, scythe-like knife went up and down the grey stone again. 'Not that he's got much of a clue but that's hardly his fault. The police wanted him out of Tórshavn and sent him down here far as I can gather.'

Not a word about the funeral, Eydna thought. They never did talk about awkward things head on, except when there was an argument and she hated those. Still . . .

'You need to smarten up, both of you. We're saying goodbye to little Jónas. The priest won't like it if you turn up looking like a pair of tramps.'

'Like anyone's going to see us in this shitty weather,' Alba murmured.

'It won't be foggy in the church now, will it?'

They both went back to what they were doing.

'I want you two dressed proper.'

'The hospital are putting Silas in a wheelchair,' Alba cut in. 'Bringing him here in an ambulance. Hope to hell he don't expect me to pay. Got enough to deal with.'

Silence again for a while then she added, 'Dorotea Thomsen gave me a job. Full time. That way I get to keep the shack. For me and Benji when he comes back.'

They'd stopped talking about Benji pretty much. There didn't seem any space what with the service coming up and all the other worries. Eydna had realised there'd be no one out heading for the hills that day; she'd struggled to find the hen house when she went out to feed the chickens, so thick was the mist.

'How much are you getting?' Baldur asked.

'Enough. I won't need to worry.' She hesitated then added, 'None of us will.'

Ganting put down his knives and stared at her.

'Us?'

Alba clattered the needles together and glanced at the kitchen clock.

'Got to go now. Like Mum said. Got to change.'

He stood up to stop her as she headed for the door.

'What do you mean?'

'I mean I'm working for Dorotea Thomsen from now on. I'm kind of . . . what do they call it? Indemnity for all the money we owe her. Like her hostage . . .'

'Alba!' her mother cried. 'You never talked to us!'

'Well I'm telling you now . . .'

'We're your parents,' Ganting roared. 'We don't take charity from you.'

'It's not charity, Dad! It's what gets us through the day. And if I'd asked you'd never have let me! Too bloody proud. All of us. Except me. Listen.' She came over and took his arm, tried to peer into his bleary, confused eyes. 'I'm not blind. I know the state we're in. I know I got us there.'

'Don't say that,' Eydna told her.

'Why not? If it wasn't for me . . . well . . .'

'I can keep my family,' Ganting muttered, shaking his head in disbelief. 'Not a woman's job to do that.'

'And I got a family too. What's left of it. Wasn't getting a penny from Silas before. You think he's going to be paying me mainte-nance from a wheelchair?'

There it was, Eydna thought. It had been hanging round the little kitchen all morning. A storm cloud waiting to break.

'So you won't be running away again then?' Ganting asked.

'Can't, can I, Dad? Happy now?'

'Alba . . .' Eydna didn't know what to make of it. 'You could have talked to me.'

'What's the use?' she snapped. 'You'd only have gone running to him to beg his permission and he'd have said no. I didn't want to. I didn't mean to. Dorotea kind of forced me into it . . .'

Eydna shook her head.

'All the more reason—'

'All the more reason to let her get away with it. She won't kick me out. Won't kick you two out. That husband of hers will see your boat gets fixed. I get to live in that shithole another year or two at least.'

'You should have talked to me!' Baldur Ganting bellowed, his voice like an animal in pain.

'No, Dad.' Alba tried to push past him but he held her back. 'I didn't have to. You've got me where you want me now. All of you. Stuck here. Can't leave. Trapped like a blackfish on the beach.' She grabbed a knife from the table and brandished it in his face. 'Just let me go, will you? I got a son to bury.'

Baldur Ganting snatched the thing from her fingers.

'And us a grandson. Don't forget that.' He scooped the rest of the blades into their leather holders, marched to the door, pulled on his socks and old boots there. 'Had enough of listening to woman talk. Time I damned well used these things.'

HARALDSEN RETURNED WITH THREE cups of tea and a cooked breakfast for Elsebeth. She quickly dismissed all questions about her health, both from him and Hanna Olsen who had, it seemed, recovered her composure. The state of the weather almost helped in some way. So dense was the fog beyond the windows they felt cocooned in the wooden cottage, set apart from the world outside.

'You knew,' she said again as she jabbed her fork into the very yellow yolk of an egg fresh from the garden, 'I cannot believe you didn't tell me.'

'It's not quite as straightforward as that,' he insisted.

Then, between the two of them, Haraldsen and Hanna Olsen went through what they'd learned.

The summer before had been a bleak one in Djevulsfjord.

Kaspar Ganting had died in an apparent accident on the cliffs. One week later Kristian Djurhuus, the then district sheriff had been the victim of a hit-and-run driver in the Árnafjall tunnel. Around the same time, Hanna Olsen's brother, a troubled young man from Denmark, vanished while visiting the Faroes. The police had found no trace of him. Yet it was now clear from the photograph in Inga Dam's cottage that he had been in Djevulsfjord and perhaps met Kristian Djurhuus, the Gantings and Silas Mikkelsen.

'And no one in Tórshavn mentioned any of this when you were offered the job, Tristan?'

No, he agreed. But then he hadn't talked to anyone about the position until the following spring. There was no need for a district sheriff during the winter months. As for Søren Olsen . . . he was a missing foreigner whose disappearance didn't seem to ring any alarm bells, except in the mind of his sister who abandoned her career in Aalborg to come looking for him.

'Not,' Hanna added, 'that I've had much luck.'

'They should have told you,' Elsebeth insisted to her husband.

'Perhaps.'

'Someone . . . someone here in the village should have mentioned what happened to Djurhuus, surely,' Hanna added. 'Dorotea Thomsen at least. She survives on gossip.'

'They don't talk to us,' Elsebeth found herself saying. 'Not unless they want to. We're . . . foreigners to them. Just like you.'

Elsebeth stabbed a finger at the laptop.

'And now you're rummaging around the files again. A place you're not supposed to go.'

The two of them glanced at one another then sipped at their tea.

'Have you found anything?'

Still the silence.

'Have you found anything, Tristan?'

He sighed and clicked on a tab in the browser. She edged her chair in towards the screen and started to read while picking at the food. It was a short and archived incident report. A record of the death of the previous sheriff, with a brief note that he had been struck by an unidentified vehicle in the tunnel and died of his injuries, probably after spending the night in agony after being injured.

'That's it?'

'That's it,' Hanna agreed.

'What about a post-mortem?'

'There must have been one,' Haraldsen told her. 'The law demands it. But it's gone. This is all there is.'

'And what information there is resides deep within the archives in Tórshavn,' Hanna added. 'If it weren't for Tristan I'd never have found it. There's nothing in Vágar at all.'

Elsebeth ran a finger down the screen, unable to believe this was all that remained of the life of the man who'd come so close to Inga Dam, a troubled woman who had perhaps never achieved that degree of intimacy before and would struggle to renew it with someone else.

'They told Inga he was drunk. Shouldn't there be some proof of that?'

'There should,' Hanna agreed.

'She said . . . she thought Kristian Djurhuus had been sending reports to Tórshavn about people in the village. He had suspicions . . .'

'Of what?' Hanna wondered.

'I don't know. He wouldn't tell her. This was one week after Kaspar Ganting died? Around the time your brother was here? On holiday?'

Haraldsen muttered something she couldn't interpret.

Elsebeth glared at him.

'I am tired of being in the dark, Tristan. I've shown you what I know. Proof Hanna's brother was here. I've told you what I learned from Inga Dam about your predecessor. We have never hidden matters from one another . . .'

'You don't need to say it—'

'But . . .'

'Hanna?'

The policewoman got Haraldsen's message, stood up and grabbed her jacket.

'I'm supposed to be on duty,' she said. 'I'll wait outside if you need me. There are calls I can make.'

WHEN SHE WAS GONE Elsebeth took her husband's hand.

'Thank you for breakfast—'

'I could have killed you last night. And here you are going on about food.'

It occurred to her that marriages did not always thrive on frankness. What was left unsaid was sometimes as important as confidences shared. They had spent most of their adult lives together, happily too. But was it possible a part of that content-ment lay in keeping one's private thoughts hidden at times? When Haraldsen was tempted to be impulsive she was usually inclined to allow it, unless the limits of common sense were about to be breached. Equally she was, at times, a little too cautious, to the point of being excessively faint-hearted. Not that he would mention it, just get on with things behind her back and overlook her surprise if the results became known.

It had to be said.

'We've never much argued, Tristan, have we?'

'Happily, no,' he agreed.

'Perhaps we should have. Perhaps we allowed matters to remain silent when they deserved an airing.'

He smiled and in that shy, small expression she saw the nervous young man who had first asked her onto the floor at that dance in Tórshavn, a distant place in a distant time.

'The time has come,' she said, 'for us to be candid with one another.'

He tapped the pipe on the desk as if it still contained tobacco. 'Tórshavn wasn't so bad, was it?'

'Not at all. I will happily go back there. With you.'

'Except we're both as quietly stubborn as a pair of timid mules,' Haraldsen added. 'We must find Benjamin Mikkelsen first. We must try to understand what happened to him and his brother. And his uncle too. And my predecessor, Kristian Djurhuus.'

She was puzzled he'd stopped there so she waited. But still he didn't go on.

'And . . .?' she asked.

'And?'

'And young Hanna Olsen's brother, of course. You can see how cut up she is by his disappearance. Perhaps it is coincidence. Perhaps this is all a set of strange coincidences. The fellow just happened through and moved on elsewhere. But we must ask, Tristan. Mustn't we?'

His eyes strayed to the laptop. Then she understood. They had been seeking answers already. That, as much as the picture of Søren she'd shown them, was the cause of Hanna Olsen's tears.

They sat there in silence until a voice from behind sounded, loud and firm.

'I will tell Elsebeth,' Hanna announced, returning to pull up a third chair at the table. 'If you are finished with your private talk. I didn't listen to that. Rest assured. But I assumed this would come round to me in the end.'

SEVENTEEN

The boy thought he knew this world, every path, every stone, every cave and crevice in which to hide. But the fog had descended overnight while he slept dry and quite warm beneath a covering of bracken in the mouth of a narrow gallery carved into the side of Árnafjall not far from the tunnel. Now it was hard to discern what was just a few feet in front of his face.

It had taken him a while to find his way back to the plot behind the cottage that belonged to the district sheriff. But the chicken coop there was sufficiently far from the house for him to sneak in without being heard. That morning, thanks to the mist, everything was even easier. Benjamin had crept through the grey-white cloud, opened the coop gate, wandered inside the hen house, picked up the bird nearest the door. Its feathers were warm and had that same delightful smell he remembered from Grandpa's place. Two eggs there. He took them, snuck out to the lee of the mountain by the tunnel, cracked them one by one and swallowed each raw.

'Jónas,' Benjamin Mikkelsen murmured to himself, thinking about his dead brother, 'I never did no stealing with you. Watched though. Watched plenty while you nicked things. And the rest.'

The taste he'd got used to now, so much he was beginning to like it. You could live off eggs like this for ages, that and water scooped from clean puddles on the hills. Sleep in the caves beneath warm bracken.

The clot of the last yolk was still raw and snotty at the back of his throat. He thought about that for a moment and nearly gagged.

'Didn't need you anyway, brother,' Benji said, his voice muffled by the thick damp cloud. 'Don't need no one now. Not even Mam.'

'Then why'd you sneak back into the shed and leave them flowers, stupid?'

It wasn't Jónas talking. He knew that. At least he felt pretty sure. It was another part of him arguing back, the way the devil whispered in your ear. The grim-faced priest with his horrible beard had warned them all of that, time and time again. Djevulsfjord. Devil's Fjord. It didn't get that name by accident.

'Why'd you take that money on the table then, goat? If you ain't no thief—'

'To stop *him* having it! You listening?'

Course not. It wasn't Jónas. Just a voice in his head.

'And anyway,' the devil who sounded just like him added, 'autumn's coming and winter then. And a twelve-year-old idiot ain't living on these hills alone in all that rain and muck and snow.'

'I'll find Mam when I want to,' Benji whispered and felt something stinging in his eyes. The fog. It had to be.

There was the sound of an engine somewhere near. He closed his eyes, told himself not to be so stupid as to talk to his brother. Who was dead. Benji knew that. Knew what dead meant and what came after.

The sound. Growing up in Djevulsfjord he'd heard them all. The rattle of an outboard on a dinghy spotting a shoal off the Skerries. The deep, warm rumble of Grandpa Ganting's boat the *Alberta*, a proper ship that went further and caught real fish, big fish that sold for more if only they could find them.

Other sounds too. Bedroom noises from Mam and Dad's room in the timber cottage Silas had inherited by the sand spit along from the harbour. Sometimes happy. Sometimes not. Sometimes halfway in between and those he couldn't comprehend at all even though Jónas seemed to and always had a wink and a pinch to go with them.

Sometimes they happened while Dad wasn't at home and Mam kept the door all closed and locked, telling the kids to get the bloody hell out of there, play on the beach, make Dorotea Thomsen's life a misery, try to con a few coins out of any tourists stupid enough to think Djevulsfjord was a place worth visiting.

Noises.

He knew this one now. It was a vehicle, not a car, something larger, coming along the tunnel, its engine slow and echoing against the walls.

Benji swallowed down the last of the raw egg, edged along the slope and perched behind a rock, unseen to them all but close enough to see through the fog. There'd been a commotion here the night before. Screams and later the blue light of a doctor's car. That hadn't stopped at the sheriff's house long. So either someone croaked or they weren't sick at all.

Little enough traffic came through the tunnel most days. The buses, the school transport, a few cars and vans. Never seen a convoy.

Curious and a little frightened he watched. First out was a police car, all marked up, the hatchet-faced officer all the village hated and feared, Højgaard, at the wheel. By his side was what looked like a large bunch of flowers set in a circle. It took Benji a moment to work out what that was: a wreath. And then a longer moment to put two and two together and realise what it might be for.

The next thing to come through was an ambulance, one that had windows on the side, and through them he could see a face that was pale and bleak, blind to everything by the looks of it.

'Dad,' he whispered.

One more thing left. He just knew it.

Little heart pumping, damp, cold fingers clinging to the rock hoping it would hide him, Benjamin Mikkelsen worked his way round closer, determined to see.

The vehicle that appeared like a ghost through the grey mist was not quite a car, not quite a van. Long and black with open windows behind, two men in dark clothes, serious-looking sorts, the kind you got in hospitals or prisons he imagined, were seated blank-faced in the front.

Behind them, perched atop shiny silver railings, was a pale and shiny box, more flowers on it. Not many.

Jónas never liked flowers. Never liked anything really except causing mischief. Which he was so good at in the end it took his life.

The fog was really stinging now and the taste of the raw egg at the back of his throat had turned vile.

Benjamin stumbled back to the hillside, caught his foot on a stone, tripped up, fell headlong onto the damp grass, threw up there, all slime and mountain water spewing out of him in a warm and noisome stream.

He didn't know how long it took him to come round. To get his head back after a fashion. But when he did he looked around and saw where he'd fetched up. It was a patch of ragwort, just like the flowers he'd found for Mam the time he'd snuck back home the day before and took the money from the table. For safe-keeping, that was all.

Fingers cold and shaking he began to pick them.

They were burying Jónas. His brother.

'Burying both of us, goat,' said the voice in his head.

THE THREE OF THEM sat in front of the laptop screen not knowing what to say. Here in words and pictures, signatures on police reports, photographs of crime scenes, witness statements, forensic diagrams, medical reports and phone records, was a picture of Hanna Olsen's younger brother. The face on Inga Dam's wall, smiling by the harbour in Djevulsfjord as if he was about to become part of Baldur Ganting's crew. A handsome, strong fellow by the looks of it though the mugshots depicted someone else, a scowling thug, hard eyes on the camera, burly arms scarred with loud tattoos.

Haraldsen, like Elsebeth, was an only child so the idea of siblings was somewhat foreign to them both. Nevertheless he thought it understandable that a sister would see her own brother differently to the rest of the world. But quite so much? Even if they meandered apart, in the slow drift that happened when their parents separated, or so she claimed.

But then Hanna had said many things. And now he didn't know quite what to believe.

Frankness, he thought. That was a promise to his wife, one that could not be broken.

'I didn't say this when we chanced upon these records, Hanna. You seemed too upset. When we spoke yesterday you told me your brother was a troubled young man. A decent lad who fell in with bad company in that hippie, druggie place they have in Copenhagen. Well . . .'

The document on the screen was a court record from Copenhagen, four years before. It told of the arrest and conviction of Søren Olsen on a charge of attempted murder. The details were so unsavoury Haraldsen found himself shivering as he read them, unable to connect the picture of the man painted here with the quiet, decent young policewoman they had come to know.

'He seems to have fallen very far,' Elsebeth whispered, following every line as he ran down the report. 'And with great enthusiasm.'

According to the document Søren was the ringleader of a drugs and prostitution gang in the city. They'd begun a vendetta with a rival outfit. A fight had ensued in which he'd come within a whisker of stabbing a man to death. Only the swiftness and professionalism of the Copenhagen medical service had saved the individual's life, and Søren from a manslaughter charge.

'Three years,' Haraldsen said with a shake of his head. 'All that and he gets three years . . .'

'He got more than that,' Hanna replied with a bitterness she didn't care to disguise. 'That was what he served.' Her tone lightened a little. 'What he was allowed to serve after I spoke up for him. Probation too offered to help him, along with others. Rehabilitation. A life away from Copenhagen. It was the city. The people. If he could only escape . . .'

'Not him?' Elsebeth asked.

The comment hit home.

'Do you not think we're made as much by the places we find ourselves? As much as we're created by ourselves?' Hanna replied.

'More so for the damaged, and Søren was damaged. No fault of his own. I shouldn't need to remind you both of this. Here. In Djevulsfjord.'

'Your brother almost murdered a man,' Elsebeth said.

'When he might have died himself if he'd done nothing! The issue of self-defence . . .'

An argument was starting. That was the last thing Tristan Haraldsen wanted. He let the two women go to and fro for a little while then grabbed back the laptop and rattled the keys again.

'You're missing the point,' he said when they paused briefly for breath.

'We are?' demanded Elsebeth.

'Søren was sufficient a criminal for the records people in Tórshavn to pull his records when he was reported missing. And then . . .' He typed in Søren's name again. There really was just this one file. 'Then nothing. Nothing. It's like Kristian Djurhuus. Almost as if he didn't exist. Do you think they looked for him at all?'

It was a practical question for two practical women who were not so different in temperament.

'They must have done something,' Elsebeth declared. 'A man goes missing. A foreigner, it doesn't matter a jot. If Hanna here reported him—'

'I did,' Hanna said. 'And Aksel Højgaard knows about his case. He taunted me with it.'

'What?' Haraldsen asked.

'It was as if it was a joke. He said they looked into Søren's visit and found nothing. As far as he's concerned he passed through and then went elsewhere.'

Haraldsen closed the laptop. It was all too depressing.

'Perhaps he's right. And we find ghosts at every turn. Benjamin Mikkelsen is out there, still alive as far as anyone knows. We must see his brother buried then find that boy and—'

Hanna reached for Elsebeth's phone and stared at the photo there. Her brother was wearing a hoodie, blue and white, with a logo on it.

'Football,' she said. 'He got crazy about it when he moved to Copenhagen. Went to every match he could.' She put the phone down. 'Went crazy about lots of things.'

There was a hammering on the door.

'Haraldsen!' It was Baldur Ganting's booming voice. 'I am come about the sheep.'

THE FOG SEEMED PALER and less dense. Enough that it was obvious enough what the man was carrying: a set of knives.

'Baldur,' Haraldsen said, quite worried, 'are you alright, man?'

'Fine talk from a fellow who mows his roof in his nightclothes. Those sheep of yours . . .'

Hanna asked for Elsebeth's phone, found the photo of Søren and stepped forward to show it.

'What is this?' he asked. His voice was strange and that wasn't just the fog distorting it. Something had happened to Baldur Ganting. The events of the last few days, the funeral in a few hours . . . 'Why are you showing me a picture of my dead son? I got enough on my plate already. A grandson still out on the fells and no one's finding him in this weather. Why?'

'The other man here,' Hanna asked. 'This one.'

He peered at the photo, shook his head and asked, 'Who's he?'

'That's what I'd like to know,' she replied.

Again he seemed befuddled.

'A tourist or someone. I don't recall. One day last summer. The visitors find their way here. Walk round from Selkie, from Sørvágur some of them the mad fools.'

'He was my brother,' Hanna said. 'No one's seen him since.'

'What?'

'*No one's seen him since.*'

'The sheep . . .'

'I am asking a question, Baldur Ganting! I am a police officer here and I may take you into custody if I feel like it.'

'Hanna . . .' Elsebeth placed a hand on her arm. 'Please.'

'They know something! All these bastards in Djevulsfjord. They know something and keep it to themselves. My brother . . .'

TO THEIR RELIEF AND perhaps hers Hanna Olsen's police phone rang at that moment. Just the sound of it seemed to make her recall who she was, why she was there.

'I know, Højgaard,' she said, a little flustered. 'No I'm not at the church. Something came up.'

A loud and angry voice was audible from the phone as she held it from her ear. Then she announced in a low, hurt voice she had to go, embarrassed by the outburst.

'The sheep . . .' Ganting repeated as she left.

'Not now, Baldur,' Elsebeth said.

'Now is the only time we have.' He lifted the knives and screeched one blade against the other. 'This weather is talking to us. Saying autumn is coming sooner than any of us thought. You got to kill and bleed those animals and salt them for the winter. Otherwise they're no use . . .'

A butcher, Haraldsen told him. He'd take them to a butcher in Sørvágur as he'd said already.

Ganting seemed to take this as a personal slight.

'We don't go giving them people work and money when we don't need to! They're robbers for folks like us. I can get one of your beasts slaughtered in that little house of yours right now, hung up to bleed then salt her myself when she's dried.' He stood up very straight as if to make himself appear more serious. 'The rest I'll do later. Here's the bargain, Haraldsen. You got four sheep. I do all the work and provide the salt in return for one of them.'

'Not now!' Elsebeth cried.

He hesitated and for a second they thought they'd won. But then, voice cracking, he said, 'I got no boat. No money. No beasts of my own save the chickens. A lifetime of debt owed to the Thomsens. I need a sheep to salt for winter mutton else God knows what . . . God knows . . . You cannot come and live here if you don't have the guts to kill a thing from time to time.'

Out of the fog one of the animals bleated and that only made him worse, so close to tears they both felt as sorry to witness it as the man did for his state.

'But today of all days!' Haraldsen cried.

'I can kill one now. Get her hanging. The rest . . . give me a day or two. You'll get meat all winter and I can bag the offal for your freezer.'

'Baldur . . .'

The man looked caught between tears and rage. He wasn't going to go.

Elsebeth dragged her husband to the side of the cottage. They didn't talk long. There didn't seem many choices, or any way of persuading a distraught and determined man like Baldur Ganting away from his intentions.

When they came back Haraldsen said, 'You may take all four beasts. We don't much like mutton anyway . . .'

'I am not here begging for your charity, district sheriff!' Ganting roared. Somewhere close by a bird fluttered away, terrified by his anger. 'What kind of man do you think I am? To take what isn't mine—'

'Jesus Christ,' Elsebeth muttered. 'In that case take all four and sell whatever you don't need. Meat, offal, the lot. Then give us our share.'

He blinked, as if trying to work that out.

'Does that satisfy your pride, now?' Elsebeth added.

'You won't want anything for the winter?'

'No,' Haraldsen told him. 'That won't be necessary.'

Ganting took off his fisherman's hat and scratched his grey head.

'Well, so be it. I will get you a fair price in Sørvágur. Not from that bitch Thomsen.'

Elsebeth groaned.

'The price we'll leave to you.'

'Now . . .' The knives clashed again in the fog. 'You are city folk and probably will not wish to be hearing this. I gather they're putting what flowers they can find in the church. If you would care to see it. Perhaps help. Else—'

'You're sure you want to do this now?' Haraldsen asked.

He frowned, like the country man he was, assessing the effort a familiar task would take.

'I will be back in time to change into my mourning clothes. Well so. You . . .' He grimaced. 'Tórshavn folk are never good around blood. Come back here after we lay little Jónas in the ground. The rest I will deal with as the days go by.'

'A moment,' Elsebeth said quietly and walked off.

He knew where she'd gone and so, Haraldsen suspected, did Ganting, a man who was not insensitive, just dulled and hardened by the life he'd come to lead.

She was leaning on the shed as he joined her. The doomed animals had come to stare at them, expecting food as usual.

'I should never have bought the creatures,' Haraldsen said, winding his arm through hers. 'Ridiculous idea.'

'It was all a part of our fantasy, Tristan.'

'Well, we leave Ganting to it. If we don't get a penny back from those animals I won't mind.'

She unhooked her arm from his and shuddered.

'Just don't ask me to set foot in that shed again, please. Perhaps we should put on our funeral clothes and see if Dorotea Thomsen has some flowers.'

They went inside and changed then, into loose dark country gear, the best mourning wear they could find. The fog was slowly clearing. A few minutes on they heard a sound drifting through the damp and cloudy day and Elsebeth and Tristan Haraldsen found themselves drawn together, arms round each other just like teenage lovers back outside the dance in Tórshavn. A scream it sounded like, back from home. One so real and sharp for all the world it might have been a child.

HØJGAARD LEFT THE HEARSE, its drivers, the contents in the shiny coffin in the back, stuck in the mist by the church to wait on the mourners. The ambulance crew pushed Silas Mikkelsen into the nave where he could stew in his wheelchair for an hour or more. Only then did he take the winding path across the sheep field to the manse.

The weather suited his mood and, he felt, his purpose. A black fake leather briefcase swung at the end of his right arm as he walked the damp grass, whistling an old tune.

The door was open. He marched straight in. No one on the ground floor. He'd little desire to see upstairs so he hammered on the thin wood walls until there were footsteps down the stairs.

Ryberg was dressed for the occasion: all black, clerical shirt, a dog collar, his beard neatly trimmed.

'Do you enjoy funerals?' Højgaard wondered.

'It's not a question of enjoyment. It's work.'

'You get paid a little extra?'

'A little. I say the words. I watch the box go in the earth. Then . . .' His eyes narrowed. 'Comfort the bereaved if I can.'

'I expect there will be much comforting to be done. Alba Mikkelsen's a pretty little thing in a damaged kind of way.'

The priest was staring at the case.

'I trust that's for me.'

'I trust you'll earn it.'

The man in the dog collar glowered at him.

'We are set on this course, man. No turning back. For either of us. But I require my—'

Before he could say another word Højgaard came right up to him and felt his beard, quite roughly.

'Oh my God. Is that perfume I smell? You do have plans for later.'

'Only the ones we agreed.'

'This must come off before you flee.'

254

He placed the case on the table and flipped it open. Then took out a Danish passport. It was in the name of Emil Holm. Age forty-eight. Ryberg stared at the photo and said, 'How the hell did you get hold of that?'

'I'm police here. Did you forget?'

It was Ryberg's ID photo from six years before, when he was still in Denmark, a mugshot from the files in Helsingør. Clean-shaven, guilty.

'I'm an inquisitive soul, Lars. I know all about your little problems there. Why they dispatched you to the ends of the Lutheran earth. Women.' He shook his head. 'Always women. Though not willing ones or so they said. At least you never went near boys.' He hesitated. 'Or did you? I doubt the police found out everything. Did your superiors in the church put a halt to things?'

'We should not be having this conversation.'

'Boys,' he repeated. 'That would be interesting. No? Still . . .' He slapped the passport on the table. 'Your secret will be safe until you're gone. Bury the lad. Do what the hell you like afterwards. It'll never come back to haunt you. Here we are.'

There was a plane ticket in the name of Holm. Direct from Sørvágur to Copenhagen that evening. Then a night service to Bangkok.

'Thailand, Lars. Or should I say Emil. You can take your pick of partner there. And this . . .' An envelope full of brightly-coloured bank notes. 'Fifty thousand Thai baht. As good as ten thousand of our krónur. That should you see started. Of course when it runs out—' he gripped the man's arm very tightly – 'you're on your own. You do understand that, don't you? No coming back. Not ever.'

'As if I would,' Ryberg grumbled then grabbed the passport, the money and the ticket, then the case.

'Not this,' Højgaard told him and snatched the briefcase back. 'This is mine.'

'No traces home to you then!'

Silence between them until Højgaard said, 'I'm still waiting.'

'For what?'

'Why . . . a word of thanks. What else? You wanted out of here. I've made it possible.'

'For your own reasons! Not mine!'

'For our mutual benefit. How long will this damned service last?'

The flight was at eight. There was time for everything.

'I'll have the child buried and the lot of them out of the grave-yard by four.'

'Good.' He relaxed his grip on Ryberg's arm. 'After which you must . . . console the mother. Here. The two of you, alone. Don't take too long about it, will you?'

The priest hesitated.

'Is that . . . is she really necessary?'

Højgaard squinted at him.

'What?'

'If that family of hers ever found me . . .'

Højgaard grabbed him by the collar.

'They won't. You'll be gone. Of course it's necessary. If it wasn't I wouldn't be asking. Don't pretend you've acquired a conscience now. It's too late and I for one will never believe it. Besides . . . you know you want to.' A wink. 'It won't be the first time, will it? Such stories from Helsingør. No wonder they dispatched you to this hole.'

Ryberg kept quiet.

'A man of God will keep his word,' Højgaard added. 'After the service you will see to Alba Mikkelsen. Shave off that beard. Take your things. Drive yourself to the airport. Climb on that plane. No one will stop you. No one in Copenhagen will think you're anything but a middle-aged lecher called Emil Holm travelling to the fleshpots of the East for a little entertainment. Which won't be so far wrong, will it?' He held out his gloved hand. 'Farewell then. I'm sure you'll be too busy with the church and everything for us to talk again.'

'Farewell,' Ryberg muttered and clutched at the money and tickets.

The fog seemed a touch thinner when Højgaard went outside. All the same he made sure to go and see the two ambulance men sipping from their flasks of coffee, the attendants with the hearse, everyone around. To let them know he'd spoken to the priest who was, it seemed, as upset as everyone at the sad ceremony to come.

EIGHTEEN

The shop had one bouquet of flowers left, roses and lilies imported from Africa, Dorotea Thomsen said. Which was why they were so expensive even though the petals were starting to wilt and the white of the lilies betrayed a tinge of rust.

'Don't sell many flowers. Even when there's funerals. The thieves from the undertakers usually grab that business.'

Elsebeth had walked in silence all the way. He knew what she was thinking about: the sheep in the slaughterhouse and Baldur Ganting working there with his knife.

You cannot come and live here if you don't have the guts to kill a thing from time to time.

A truth that had never occurred to them when they first drove through the Árnafjall tunnel in the Ace Capri, believing they were emerging into some kind of paradise, a place to spend their final years of leisure walking the hills, watching the waves break upon the Skerries as the dwindling Djevulsfjord fleet plied the sea.

'We'll take them.' Haraldsen took out his wallet. 'You'll be closing the shop for the service, I imagine.'

'Of course,' she said as if the question was idiotic. 'No business during a funeral now, is there?'

Elsebeth scowled and shot him a look.

'I imagine not,' he replied.

'But I'll open the doors for an hour this evening in case anyone wants something. We have beer in specially. We don't do wakes, not like you know in Tórshavn. It's for the family.' She shook her large head. 'If you can call the Gantings that.'

Elsebeth grasped the bouquet and walked outside. What remained of the mist was now a shade of white tinged with watercolour blue. The light in Djevulsfjord was like that. It changed almost hourly sometimes, even when the sky was obscured entirely. One's view of the place was entirely subjective, dependent upon perspective, the time, the season.

She went and sat on a bench by the harbour. The hulls and cabins of the small fleet bobbed up and down in front of them, white and blue, marooned by the weather and events. Ganting's *Alberta* was covered in tarpaulins, shattered timber planks poking out of the fabric. It looked much like an injured patient waiting on assistance in a hospital corridor after a crash.

'That boy lost on those fells must be terrified,' Elsebeth said eventually.

'Perhaps. Or perhaps not.'

'Tristan . . .'

'Love. If there's one thing we've learned here it's that we've learned very little at all. These people don't live like any we've ever known. The boys, the men, they head off into the hills with their fleyging nets, hunting chicks and God knows what else. You heard. They stay out there day and night sometimes.'

She turned and stared at him and he knew he was being judged.

'In weather like this? When his own brother's being buried?'

'And how would he know of that?'

'Because . . .' She pointed to her eyes. 'He has these. They all do. It's in their faces. We look at this place and see one thing.

They peer at it and see another. Somewhere we never go. I think . . . I think Benjamin Mikkelsen's up there somewhere. Stealing into our garden for his eggs. Hanging round that tunnel. He's watching us and wondering when he might dare come home.' She hesitated. '*If* he dares come home. Here.'

She thrust the bouquet of flowers into his hands. Petals were falling off them already. A gull squawked unseen. The boats creaked as they rose and fell upon the tide. Elsebeth looked him over and straightened the collar of his wax country jacket. It was dark green, the closest they had to black, and matched hers naturally since they always shared the same taste in clothes.

'Look at us,' she said. 'We're hardly dressed for the occasion.'

'Well. We didn't come here expecting to be attending a funeral.'

She faffed around with his collar again.

'If you'd rather not go, Elsebeth . . .?'

'I will not miss this occasion for all the world,' she said very quickly. 'Nor shall you. We owe Jónas Ganting that. Besides . . .'

Elsebeth got to her feet, and the noise of her movement sent a couple of birds cackling into the mist.

'Who knows what we may see?'

DJEVULSFJORD CHURCH WAS THE largest building in the village and the least-frequented. Sundays apart, Lars Ryberg's duties were confined to christenings and the occasional wedding and funeral. White timber exterior, white conical spire, a cross at the lintel, a smaller crucifix over the tiny raised altar at the nave. The place was unheated and little light streamed through the high narrow windows. The Haraldsens, as atheists, had never set foot inside nor seen any reason why they should.

Perhaps that was why heads turned as they arrived. Though only briefly. Djevulsfjord seemed more intent upon its own. The coffin was resting on a trestle covered in gleaming cloth. There was music but it came from tinny speakers and a CD that Ryberg kept for such occasions. The old organ that had sat at the side of the nave for fifty years no longer worked. Besides, Djevulsfjord lacked a musician, and the funds of the Gantings were insufficient to bring in an organist and portable instrument from outside.

The Haraldsens shuffled into the shadowy interior behind a couple they recognised from the grind: a middle-aged man and his wife, whose names they didn't know. Father Ryberg in his clerical robes nodded at everyone as they arrived. Dorotea Thomsen stood by his side retrieving any flowers people had brought and setting them in a loose arrangement by the font. Most bunches seemed local, straight from the gardens or the hills. A wreath on the coffin apart, the only bought-in blooms seemed to be their own.

There was this old platitude in the mystery books Elsebeth Haraldsen sometimes read: how the criminal always returned to the scene of the crime. But it was a cliché, she felt sure of that. The congregation here, strangers most of them, was so quiet, so serious, so devoted to the moment that it was impossible to believe anyone in the church might do a child harm.

Deliberately, she added, trying to think this through as they walked at a snail's pace behind the other mourners.

Jónas had fallen from the heights of the Lundi Cliffs and was found with a grind dagger in his chest.

Benjamin had vanished afterwards and was, everyone seemed now to assume, the guilty party in his death. Even if it was some kind of accident. Blame would always be apportioned in a place like this. Perhaps it was when Kaspar Ganting died the year before. Perhaps – and she knew this thought was running through her husband's head and that of the troubled policewoman she was beginning to like too – the missing Søren Olsen had a hand in that, since he was a man of violence however hard his sister fought to hide the fact.

Maybe Inga Dam's lover, Kristian Djurhuus, uncovered all this and found, for some reason, his beliefs rejected. By Aksel Højgaard she imagined. Who else? And then . . .

Dorotea took the bouquet from her and placed it by the other bunches, petals streaming from the heads with every step she took.

Tristan wound his arm through hers and they sat down on a hard pew at the back, somewhere they could see the Gantings seated together to the left of the small coffin shining brightly under an electric lamp standard brought in for the occasion.

Alba was at the end of the row, nearest to the boy. As Elsebeth watched, heart ready to burst with pity and bewilderment, her skinny mother's arm reached out and touched the polished wood, ran a finger down the grain, then returned to her lap.

Silas, the estranged husband, sat hunched in his wheelchair, head down across the aisle. Nothing appeared to pass between them, not a glance, a word. Yet they must have married here. Must have watched little Jónas baptised in the wooden font behind them, his brother two years older at the time, a quiet infant, Elsebeth guessed. Not bright. The whole village said.

'Not his brother's murderer either,' she whispered under her breath.

Her husband raised an eyebrow and she fell silent again. Eyes on Alba, always Alba, trying to imagine what thoughts were running through the poor woman's head.

The recorded organ struck up louder. A hymn she remembered from her childhood. The congregation, perhaps twenty people, little more, rose slowly to their feet.

The words still lingered in her memory from those Sunday morning visits to the chapel with her parents. They sang this when her mother went into the ground too, one year after her father.

Hear, Smith of the Heavens
God I call on thee,
To heal me . . .

EYES STILL LOCKED ON Alba Mikkelsen, standing shakily next to the shiny coffin, she couldn't sing. It was impossible. So Elsebeth did what came more easily. With the conscious rhythm of her breathing, slowly, deliberately, she began to weep.

A HEARSE. THAT WAS the name for the long black car that had rumbled out of the tunnel, Jónas in a box at the back. He remembered now. They'd had one when Grangran Ganting died and got put in the ground. One when Great Grandpa went the same way he guessed though he was too young to remember that.

'Too stupid more like, goat,' he found himself saying in Jónas's guttural growl.

The voice had been following him round ever since the Lundi Cliffs. Sometimes it got so loud he had to stop and stuff grass in his ears until it went away.

'I can stop that working too, big brother,' it said.

Which was, Benjamin thought, true. The voice wasn't Jónas. It was him thinking that way. Wondering if maybe his kid brother's personality, or what remained of it inside his head, might wake up, alive and come and take possession of him somehow. There'd been stories like that they'd got told by the fire on long winter nights when the television wasn't working and all they had to mess around with was books and their own imaginations. Ghostly tales, scary ones he'd listen to while Grandpa recited them. About demons and monsters and things that came out of the sky and the sea. Djevulsfjord had plenty of stories. Jónas used to make them up at night, lying on the top bunk in the shed. At least he thought they were made up. Sometimes they weren't about monsters at all. They were about people, ones Benjamin knew, and he wasn't sure whether they were real or not because they involved things, grown-up stuff he'd kind of heard about but didn't really understand.

You do know what they do in bed, don't you? When a man sticks it in a woman? When she start yelping like Mam does from time to time?

No, he didn't. And he wasn't sure he believed Jónas when he told him. There were so many stories, and some of them weren't about what happened beneath the blankets either. Some were about whaling knives and blood and people getting killed. Except stories had endings and Jónas never did that with some of them. He just teased and taunted.

Then when Benjamin said, 'What? You mean that?' He'd say, 'None of your business, goat. You're too stupid to understand. I deal with the shit round here, me and Kaspar. You keep your dumb nose out of our business.'

Then Uncle Kaspar was gone and that was another time the

long black car came with a shiny box in the back and people standing round a hole in the brown earth by the church, all sad faces saying nothing much at all.

He'd asked questions then as well and just got told to shut up by everyone.

Too stupid Benjamin Mikkelsen. Not your fault you was born with half a brain but the half that's still left ought to be smart enough to tell you when to keep quiet.

Jónas said that quite a lot.

'But you're dead, brother,' Benjamin whispered. 'Not me.'

Dead and buried soon.

Thinking about that made his eyes sting again.

Flowers. There were always flowers around funerals.

He wiped his runny nose with the sleeve of his jumper. He was well filthy now and must have had the most awful stink about him after sleeping rough all this time. Two nights was the most he'd spent out on the fells before, and that always with Jónas and Kaspar along because Mam wouldn't let him out on his own. Now he almost seemed to be living there, nicking food, picking wild berries, drinking the icy fresh mountain water. Peeing and crapping where he felt like.

'Can't live there forever, goat,' Jónas-not-Jónas said. 'Too thick and too scared for that.'

Flowers.

He sniffed away the snotty nose again then walked over to the patch of ragwort soaking wet from the fog and began to rip more blooms from their thin, sparse stalks.

★　★　★

WHAT HAPPENED IN THE church Alba Mikkelsen didn't really know. That thirty or forty minutes – she wasn't sure how long it lasted – possessed the filmy unreality of dream, with no possibility one would ever wake from its listless, grasping clutches. The canned organ crackling out of the tinny speakers, the lethargic singing, Lars Ryberg saying his part in a bored, fixed drone as if he were reading a letter from the government, not a rite for the dead. Her father sobbing and trying to hide it, smelling of meat in the one threadbare suit he owned. Silas bent over in his wheelchair, eyes on the worn stone floor, lost to everything. And her mother locked in silent grief, unable to do much at all except stand when she was asked and mouth the words from the book.

There was no eulogy. Jónas, she imagined, would have hated one. Only a brief sermon from the priest. Something about how life was never fair, the small world of Djevulsfjord only a transitory illusion between a temporal existence and the next. The kingdom of a god she couldn't imagine, any more than Jónas would. He'd have snorted at his own funeral, laughed and grown bored, slunk out the side door into the fog and the graveyard, mischief or worse on his mind.

You are not in that box, she thought. *It's just a broken sack of bones.*

The real Jónas vanished into the hills for some reason with his big brother after jabbing a knife at the new district sheriff. Though there had to be more to it than that.

Alba turned away from the altar and the shiny coffin and scanned the pews behind her. All the faces she'd grown up with. None of them weeping except the sheriff's wife, a stranger, whose eyes were tight on hers as she looked.

The music got louder. Ryberg said something about faith and trust and perseverance. Another hymn, the last one.

When the talk and the singing ended, three pallbearers from the undertakers marched in, glanced at her father until he worked out why and stood up.

Silas began sobbing out loud then, moaning about how he wanted to do it.

'Can't,' Alba said, getting up and putting a hand on his shoulder just for a second. 'Can you, Silas?'

Not a word came back, just the same dark hatred in his eyes she'd seen since the summer before when she briefly fled to the ferries, a fleeting moment of freedom that was never going to last.

The coffin was on their backs. Four men, one of them her father. Jónas was only a little lad. Two of them could have managed it.

Outside the fog was lifting. Through the mist she could make out the shape of Ryberg's house across the fields and the low forms of the animals grazing by the path along the way.

Footsteps moving through damp grass.

Voices, low and saying things she didn't want to hear.

Funerals. She didn't know what they were for really. You never said goodbye to a child of your own. They lived inside you, nagging, whispering, taunting you if they were Jónas, saying, 'How did this happen then, Mam? Where were you when I came out of that puffin hide, knife in my guts, rolling down the Lundi Cliffs to the rocks where Dad was, not that he helped either?'

The pall-bearers slowly lowered the coffin onto the grass by the gaping rectangle in the soil. Dad let go first. Put his sleeve to his eyes. Her mother went to throw her arms around him. While Alba stood there all alone, mind somewhere else entirely.

All around them were the headstones of the Djevulsfjord dead. The same names over the centuries. Ganting and Mikkelsen. Joensen and Poulsen, not that there were so many of them left after the young ones fled to Tórshavn for work that didn't involve the cold and wet and boats. Thomsen, too, but only on the fancier graves that looked like little church steeples. Even when they were nothing more than dust that lot wanted to lord it over everyone, liked to show they had the money.

And Kaspar.

She had so many memories of her brother, growing up together in the same bedroom of the timber cottage down the road. Not something she'd wish on anyone else. Girls and boys deserved their privacy.

Kaspar.

His hair was blond, his face nothing like Dad's. He had strong arms though and when it came to the grind he was always the first out on the strand, knife in hand, ready to spear a lance by the first blowhole.

Him and Jónas were thick as thieves. Silas used to watch them, forever gloomy and jealous at their closeness.

They were burying Jónas next to his grave. Which seemed kind of right.

More words from the priest. Then the people around her, all anxious to get this over with, began to walk away from the church-yard, back through the chilly mist to home.

When a big man died in Djevulsfjord, a fisherman, a skipper, they had a wake with beer and even a bit of singing now and again. But not for a kid, and certainly not for Jónas.

A hand took her arm and she found herself face-to-face with Dorotea Thomsen. The last person she wanted to see.

'You're bearing up very well, Alba. I must say I admire that.'

Her husband, George, was lurking next to her, silent, shifty, embarrassed.

'What am I supposed to do? Shout and scream and weep?'

'Some would.'

'Well . . .' There was a purpose for this. There had to be. 'What do you want?'

'Father Ryberg asked if I'd have a word with you.'

'Did he?'

'Busy man. Said he couldn't do it himself. Seems he needs you to go up to the manse. There's paperwork to be done. Records to be filled out.'

'You mean he wants his money?'

'Oh, poppet.' Dorotea stroked her cheek. 'Don't be so callous. Of course he doesn't. We've seen to that. Haven't we, George?'

Her man shuffled on his feet. Shiny shoes. Town shoes, too polished and new to fit in here.

'All taken care of, Alba,' he said. 'Don't worry yourself.'

'A relative's got to sign things off when someone dies,' Dorotea cut in. 'Best do it now. Get it out of the way. Then tomorrow we go back to normal.'

Normal.

What was that? How did it feel? Was there some way of telling it from anything else?

'Alright,' she said and nothing more.

NINETEEN

Not long after the burial ended with a few, unemotional words from Father Ryberg, the grey fog that had hung around Djevulsfjord all day was gone. It was almost as if the dour, silent nexus of grief around the cemetery had somehow repelled it. A child's coffin was in the cold, dark ground, two burly sextons brought in from Sørvágur to shovel earth upon the pale pine lid. Alba Mikkelsen had watched every spadeful take him from her, no tears in her eyes, only bafflement and fury.

The Gantings, Baldur and Eydna, had stood beside her lost for words then, after one last, brief hug between mother and daughter, they shuffled off. Still Alba stayed there, staring at the brown earth and the flowers strewn upon it.

Elsebeth Haraldsen tried to talk to the woman since no one else did. She merely listened to her well-meant pleasantries and said, 'Thank you. I have to see the priest now.' Then went back to staring at the grave. And so the Haraldsens gave up.

Not a word had passed between her and Silas Mikkelsen in the wheelchair. Elsebeth, keen-eyed as ever, saw this and wondered if the two would ever speak to one another again.

'Come, husband,' she said to Haraldsen. 'Let's go home and I will make cocoa. There's a chill out here.'

'Cocoa,' he repeated and she knew from the look on his face he was immediately associating the word with his black pyjamas. They were both praying for night to fall, for this long strange day to come to an end. And as always when one begged this of the hours they would fail to obey with a stubborn determination.

Hanna Olsen was waiting by the rickety cemetery gate. Aksel Højgaard breezed over and nodded at the three of them.

'It's good we were here,' he said. 'It shows the rest of us care.'

The young policewoman didn't look quite right.

'My brother was in Djevulsfjord. I have proof of it. A photograph of him down by the harbour, near the Ganting's boat.'

He seemed unmoved.

'Hardly the time to speak of this, is it?'

'Did you know?' she demanded. 'After I reported him missing—'

'Your brother was a criminal,' Højgaard cut in. 'He flagged up on our system as a serious risk.'

A pause then. They waited.

'We found no sign of him.'

'Kristian Djurhuus was killed,' Haraldsen told him. 'Kaspar Ganting died . . .'

The glazed look in the superintendent's face told them he was already tired of this conversation.

'Don't overcomplicate matters, man. Accidents both. It was a grim summer in Djevulsfjord. I'd hoped they'd be spared more tragedy this year.' He looked genuinely aggrieved at that moment. 'I'm sorry, Hanna. I'm sorry I don't have more to tell you. But that's the truth. We looked. We found nothing. If he came here then he must have travelled through so briefly no one ever noticed. Visitors often do. Hikers. Walkers.' He shrugged. 'What more can I say?'

He pointed to the ambulance men wheeling Silas Mikkelsen back to their vehicle.

'I'm going back to Tórshavn. I thought I'd see Mikkelsen to the hospital. Least we can do.' He stared at her. 'Go home. You seem unduly upset.'

'I just watched a child buried.'

'We're police. We need to keep our distance. Tomorrow . . .' He was thinking. 'Tomorrow take a look around the hills. See if there's any trace of the brother. I rather doubt . . .'

He didn't go on.

'Where do I meet the rest of the team?' she asked.

'You don't. It's just you.'

Then he was gone.

'We will help, Hanna,' Haraldsen said immediately.

She was staring at the grey-green expanse of Árnafjall, a vast and empty landscape that could consume anyone, young or old.

'It's hopeless,' Hanna Olsen muttered. 'Everything is. We're lost here. Outsiders all of us.'

'Højgaard's right for once,' Haraldsen told her. 'Best go home. Sleep on it. We'll talk tomorrow.'

Still she didn't move.

'Søren came here. If he left . . . where did he go?' She shrugged. 'I know. Back to Copenhagen. Or somewhere else. Back to his old ways. His old friends. And forgot all about me. His family.'

'It's possible,' Elsebeth suggested.

'And that's the best I have to hope for?'

They had no answer. So they said their goodbyes until the morning and the Haraldsens walked home. Neither went near the meat shed from which a distinct odour of blood and meat was leaking. But Haraldsen dealt with the chickens and the remaining three sheep as best he could.

Cocoa was waiting on the table when he came in. It was five by then and the sun had finally defeated the haze, emerging harsh and bright over the blue split of the fjord, the grey teeth of the Skerries, and the endless verdant fells around them.

'There were no eggs,' he said as he sat down. 'Taken again, I think.'

ALBA WALKED THE FIELDS around the cemetery, staring up at Árnafjall, calling Benji's name. Wondering if this was what it was like to go mad, to wander round like a crazed woman bellowing at nothing, hearing nothing in return.

Benji. Benji. Benji.

Silas gone for good, the boy was all she had left. Apart from her parents and that wasn't enough.

Benji.

To hell with it, she thought, as she rounded the low hill back to the priest's house. To hell with everything.

One son vanished. The other in the ground. Now some tedious paperwork to be gone through as if Jónas wasn't properly dead without it.

She dawdled all the way to Ryberg's front path thinking she'd rather be spending time skivvying for Dorotea Thomsen than dealing with the dry, sly priest. The front door was ajar. She knocked and walked straight in. There was a small suitcase at the foot of the stairs and a smell about the place, not unpleasant. Aftershave or cologne. She didn't think priests wore them much.

'Father . . .?'

Downstairs was empty but as she walked inside the small and frugal kitchen she thought she saw a shape flit past the window in the jungle that was the vegetable garden out back. The priest before loved that little patch. Ryberg, a man who preferred begging food from others to growing it, never bothered with the place.

'Father . . .?'

He'd never be out there. Ryberg wasn't an outdoors man.

'Dorotea Thomsen said I was to come . . .'

'Wait on me!' yelled a voice from upstairs.

Why not? I wait on everyone else.

The front windows gave out onto the cemetery. It was empty now. The sextons must have finished their work and returned to Sørvágur. The path of fresh brown earth that marked her son's grave stood out among the leaning headstones and the grassy mounds. Soon the busy grass and weeds of Djevulsfjord would plant their seeds and roots in that as well. By Christmas – Christmas without her boys, there was a thought – the last home of Jónas Mikkelsen would be much like the resting places of those around him. Two centuries some of them had been there, not that time mattered to the dead.

'Alba.'

Ryberg's voice made her jump. He'd come down the stairs so quietly she'd never even heard and now he was as close as the man had ever been. Too close. She stepped back into the living room. He followed, dogging every step.

'You look different, Father.'

He did too. Baggy new jeans, a checked cowboy shirt, brown boots that were probably new.

'Your face . . .'

He grinned and stroked his cheeks. They were pink and marked by a few razor cuts but entirely lacking the full salt and pepper beard that for her had been the man before. Now he looked . . . human. Frail. Like everyone else. The face beneath the whiskers seemed that of another man. Worldly. A little avaricious perhaps. Wanting something she recognised.

'I decided to leave this hole,' he said, taking a step towards her. His eyes fell on the old sofa behind them. Once again she thought she saw someone flit past the window. 'Leave Djevulsfjord forever. Just some . . . ends to tidy up beforehand.'

'Paperwork. To do with Jónas . . .?'

'No.' His hand went to her neck, his fingers closed round her throat. Then, as if he was scared too, he touched her hair, pulled on it gently for a moment. 'No, Alba. Not that. Just something I'm owed.'

'I'm going—'

Before she could move he was on her, one swift blow and Alba Mikkelsen fell screaming to the sofa.

FLOWERS. BENJI HAD THEM. Jónas needed them. The dead always went with flowers. It was like a rule. Maybe if they didn't get them they couldn't go to the next place at all. They just hung around like ghosts making the living miserable. That wasn't right. Jónas would have loved it though.

And there were flowers there already. He could see that now from the place he'd sneaked to close to the graveyard, hiding behind a sheep pen in one of the fields near the priest's house. Bouquets on a patch of brown earth. Not a soul around.

Days he'd been on his own now. Days when all he could do was run and hide and steal and watch. In the time since Jónas tumbled down the hillside, all the way to the rocks beneath the Lundi Cliffs, the boy had retreated inside himself. There'd been a reason to it, a kind of logic. If you kept away from all the bad stuff, the blame and the screaming and the beatings, you'd become invisible after a while. No one could ever hurt you, never again. You could live like Benji used to with Uncle Kaspar, fending for yourself, nicking when you needed it, a wild thing out on the fells.

But then the weather would change. Like today. You'd remember autumn was coming and bitter winter behind it. Hard enough living in the shed with Mam and Jónas then. Never enough money, never enough to eat. Out on Árnafjall, pinching eggs from the district sheriff's coop, he'd never make it. If the mountain spirits, egged on by Jónas, didn't steal his life away hunger the cold and loneliness would.

'Mam,' Benjamin Mikkelsen murmured as he tried to make himself small and invisible in the lee of the crooked wooden pen. 'Ma . . .'

He'd seen her leave the graveyard, wander off, heard her calling his name. But fear kept him back. It always did.

It was time for a decision. He was hungry. He wanted clean clothes. More than anything he wanted his mother and she'd been calling for him. So whatever he'd imagined when he was out there on the fells there'd be a home somewhere.

The boy stumbled out of the shadows, walked over the firm damp grass of the sheep field, trying to avoid the droppings. Eyes on the graveyard, the patch of bare earth with its bouquets.

Ragwort and some blue blooms, small, insignificant, weeds really, that was all he had.

'Jónas,' he said, 'you never gave me nothing. But I got flowers for you.'

RYBERG DIDN'T LOOK SURE about this. About anything. He seemed scared. Almost as trapped as her.

Alba crouched back on the sofa, rammed her legs tight together, wrapped her skinny hands around her knees. She felt small and cold in her skimpy, black cardigan and trousers, the best she could find for the funeral.

'I buried my son today. And here you are—'

His fingers clawed their way around her neck, his face was in hers.

'Shut up. Shut up woman . . .'

She did and now she could hear his breathing, smell it. A man in a hurry.

Alba closed her eyes and tried not to think.

Close to her, too close, Ryberg's hard, flat voice forced its way into her ear.

'God never said a thing about the sins of the mothers, did he? Why not, Alba Ganting? What do you think?'

'My name's Alba Mikkelsen,' she murmured, keeping her eyes tight shut. 'You should know. I got wed in your church.'

'That was a child the fool before me married. A child no more. Silas abandoned you because of your base ways. All of Djevulsfjord knows that. Perhaps you have no name at all. Just . . . whore.'

No tears. She wouldn't allow him that.

'I never asked for any of this. I promise—'

'What's a promise worth?' he yapped. 'From a woman who's fallen?'

A part of her still wanted to cry but she'd done enough of that for Jónas.

'I am what this place made me. Just like you . . . ah . . . no!'

Hard wet teeth bit her earlobe. The flowery fragrance on him filled her head. Cheap aftershave barely covering up a stink that was old and fusty.

'There is good and there is bad,' the priest said. 'Nothing in between. And when the black beast rears its head a man like me must listen.'

'Please . . .'

He gripped her shoulders.

'We listen and we let it loose. A devil can't be cooped. We let it free to fly away not fester in our souls.'

'For God's sake . . .'

'Upstairs. Look! Look, dammit.' When she opened her eyes he was pointing to the landing. 'You can walk or I can drag you.'

Close up his skin seemed dead, covered as it was with scratches and cuts from the razor, tufts of whiskers still left there from the beard.

He grabbed her arm, tugged her to her feet, kicked her once, dragged her all the way to the stairs.

Up the narrow wooden steps, into the room on the right, the one she'd cleaned from time to time and had to argue to get paid. There was a single bed pushed up against the end wall, sheets awry as if he'd never made it in days. A small crucifix stood above it, next to the sideboard where she put his freshly-washed and ironed shirts and underclothes. A bachelor's room, lonely, sad and untidy.

'I want to go home,' she said, as calmly as she could manage. 'My boy got buried today. My husband's in hospital. My lad Benji—'

Ryberg started to undo his belt. There was the smell of smoke from the fire downstairs. Burnt paper seeping through the leaky chimney. Except this seemed fresh somehow.

'I don't want to!'

He sneered at that and tugged at her belt.

'Take those clothes off. All of them. You answer death with life. With sweat and semen. With what I give you.'

'No . . .'

She watched him remove his trousers then his long and ancient underpants. The man was ready.

'Do as I say or by God, Alba Ganting, you'll regret it.'

If she had the money to get out to Tórshavn, take the ferry or a plane from Sørvágur even she'd do it. Find another world. Anywhere but here. Except there was still Benji. That one door hadn't been closed.

'On the bed,' the priest ordered.

'I came expecting kindness . . .'

'No. You came here for absolution and I'm the one who'll deliver it. We all know you here, Alba. We understand what you are.'

Maybe she could try meek. The way she did when Silas turned on her.

'I am begging . . .'

His hand came up. There was fury and a kind of madness in his grey eyes.

Give in.

That's what always happened in the end.

She thought of how easy it would be to lie back on his worn sheets, stare at the white wood ceiling, freshly-painted like the windows outside. Think of nothing but Jónas and Benji and how she'd failed them. Offer up a pointless kind of answer to a debt that was not a debt but still, in the mind of this man, had to be paid. Probably wouldn't take long and then it was done with. Until the next time.

'Get on the bed. I want you bare,' he growled. 'Turn over, girl. This is not about your face.'

A wipe of her nose, eyes filling with tears, she was so close to obeying. Then she thought of Benji, somewhere out there on the fells of Árnafjall, of Jónas in his coffin. Of the way she'd weep over both of them forever.

She stretched up and looked out of the window, saw a figure in the graveyard, felt her heart leap with hope for the first time in days.

He was on her, pulling at her clothes.

'I said—'

'Fuck you, Lars Ryberg,' she cried turning round and flailing with her fingers, her nails, her hard and bony elbows. *'Fuck you.'*

It was the first time she'd fought back. Perhaps that was why she won. It was so very unexpected. Kicking, biting, scratching, she pushed him away until Ryberg tripped over a pair of old slippers and fell hard to the bare wooden floor.

He lay there, struggling to get upright, more shocked than angry when she fetched him another boot with her right foot, then a knee to his face that left him grabbing at his bloody nose.

'Who the hell do you think you are?' Alba shrieked at him. 'Who the hell . . . you're supposed to be the priest. To look after us. Christ!'

She turned on her heels, stormed down the stairs, dashed out of the front door, stood on the steps, breathless, wondering at what she thought she'd seen. Was it real? Could it be?

Nothing moved upstairs though she thought she heard a sound nearby.

'Benji,' she cried. Then louder, 'Benji!'

Arms out, the way a mother did for a lost child always, Alba Mikkelsen ran from Lars Ryberg and the priest's house.

Something pricked her nose as she raced down the gravel path. Smoke, she thought again. Burning in the house behind.

RYBERG LAY ON THE floor, curled in a foetal huddle, not knowing whether to laugh or cry. Then he glanced at his watch. Almost six. The flight left at eight. He had to drive to Sørvágur and be on it. Højgaard said so and he wasn't a man to be ignored. Perhaps he'd delivered what the police superintendent had demanded. A reason the blame or some of it should come his way. In return the chance to jettison his present and his past and create a new identity halfway across the world.

Doing what, he couldn't begin to guess.

Didn't matter. Ryberg knew he was lucky to get out of Denmark unscathed after the girls in the congregation started talking. There could be no second chance. It was time to leave, to shed the priest's black skin and find another.

Thieving, lying, conning the gullible. He'd be good at any of those. There were always opportunities.

All the same he regretted he hadn't pushed it with Alba Mikkelsen. From what he'd heard he'd been owed that at least.

Ryberg got to his feet, found a hankie, dabbed at his face with it, wiped away the blood. Nothing broken. The caked stain around his nostrils soon vanished with a little water from the basin. When he stopped sniffing his own blood something else caught his attention.

Smoke. There'd been plenty the day before when he began burning all the papers and the pornography he thought might one day come to incriminate him. But not now . . .

He walked downstairs, still dabbing at his nose. The door was open. The suitcase stood outside on the step.

'Idiot woman,' he grumbled. 'What the hell were you thinking, Alba?'

'Not Alba,' said a voice behind him.

Smoke. There was a fire nearby.

Lars Ryberg blinked, his mind in a whirl.

'I was not expecting . . .'

Something coarse and heavy crushed the rest of the words, killed them dead as it wound a tightening grip around his throat.

Falling backwards, choking for breath, unable even to scream, Ryberg found himself glancing back at the room. The rope, the sisal rope, around the capstan seat . . .

Gone.

'SMOKE,' HARALDSEN SAID. 'You smell that?'

They'd finished their supper and had been wondering whether to go back to the laptop and try to peer into more dark corners.

Elsebeth sniffed the air.

'Yes. That is not a hearth fire, Tristan. Even if someone would light such a thing on a day like this. Why . . .?'

He was already at the door. Wooden houses, turf roofs, homes everywhere built like tinderboxes. The unexpected smell of smoke was never welcome.

Outside she joined him and the two of them scanned the low hill back to the village. A thin grey cloud hung over the sea by the Skerries but that could only be clearing mist. Nothing above the village. Nothing by the harbour.

'Tristan.' Elsebeth tugged on his arm. 'The church. That's the priest's house, isn't it?'

There was one old-fashioned fire engine in Tórshavn, manned by volunteers. Thirty minutes away at best.

'Call for help,' he said as he strode off, eyes on the rising plume twirling from Ryberg's roof.

'On the way I will,' his wife answered, grabbing a bucket as she joined him.

BALDUR GANTING ARRIVED AS they did. Then George Thomsen and some of the boat crews Haraldsen knew only by sight. Flames were licking over the front door of the timber home, wavering in the evening breeze, rising to the upper windows, red and yellow, spitting out dark smoke.

'He cannot be in there,' Ganting said, scratching his head. 'The priest—'

'Then where is he?' Haraldsen demanded. 'We must put the fire out, man.'

'With what?' George Thomsen asked. 'There is no water here. Only what the priest can pull out of his well. And I do not see a sip from there doing much.'

They had to wait on the engine from Tórshavn, Ganting said very firmly and all those around agreed.

Haraldsen glanced at Elsebeth and knew she was thinking the same: would these men be so nonchalant if the building was one of their own? If the man who lived there a native of their hamlet by the sea?

'Where is the priest?' Elsebeth asked again. 'Has anyone seen him?'

'Perhaps,' George Thomsen suggested, 'he has gone for a walk?'

'A walk?' she cried. 'When have you seen Lars Ryberg walk anywhere except to the shop and back? And the church?'

'There was a funeral,' he added, a little hurt. 'A man like him might want to think a little after . . .'

Haraldsen rolled up his sleeves and said, 'I will see.'

'Tristan!'

'I am the district sheriff, dear,' he told her. 'I have my duties.'

Then he marched off to the front door before she could say another word.

Close up he could feel the heat and the choking, noisome fumes of the flames went straight and acrid to his lungs. The fire had taken hold in what he assumed to be the living room. It had reached the upper storey and was now beginning to spark in the turf roof, sending flaming shards of burning grass high into the early-evening sky.

'Ryberg!' he cried. 'Are you in there? Can you hear me?'

Someone behind him laughed and he didn't want to know who.

'Ryberg!'

'Maybe he's in the church!' the joker at the back cried. 'Not that you saw the miserable old bastard there much except Sundays.'

To hell with them all. He walked up to the door expecting Elsebeth to come screeching at him any moment. Against the cracking of the priest's house timber, the sibilant hiss of fumes and flames, he thought he heard her voice somewhere and felt sure there would be a mention of the word 'heart'.

He paused in front of the burning house then aimed one hard kick against the black-painted woodwork. The door gave backwards on its hinges so easily he found himself falling forward, stumbling straight through into the flames and smoke, the searing heat.

'BENJI.'

She wasn't dreaming. There he was, sitting on the damp grass by his brother's fresh grave, rearranging wild flowers among the bouquets. Eyes wide, tired, hurt, she thought. As scruffy as she'd ever seen him after all those nights on the hills and he reeked to high heaven when she hugged him, not that it stopped her. Alba squeezed her son tight to her chest, kissed his filthy forehead, wept and wept and didn't think to speak, not for ages.

Something was happening back near Ryberg's place. There was smoke. She could smell it in the churchyard. People gathering too.

Not that she cared.

Benji was back. Her Benji. Alive. Come to say goodbye to his brother.

'My little lad,' she whispered into his grubby ear.

He was never one for cuddles. Neither of them were.

Grinning, sobbing, holding his face in both her shaking hands, she nodded at him and didn't say much more. There were so many questions.

Where've you been?

What happened?

Lots and lots of them but right then they didn't seem to matter.

He was staring in the direction of Ryberg's house. What happened there she'd pretty much forgotten now. The priest was a dirty old sod. Surly, unpopular, reclusive, not like the one they'd had before at all. No one liked him. No one talked to him much. He performed a function, Sunday after Sunday, birth after birth, death after death. Wedding after wedding, not that there were many of them of late.

'I will look after you, Benji,' she whispered, clinging on to him, trying to think this through. 'Better than I ever did.'

That cold bastard Højgaard would be rushing back from Tórshavn as soon as he knew. Trying to take her boy away.

'Won't happen. Won't let it.'

Still she tried to silence the nagging voice inside that kept laughing at her, telling her: Saying no was never your great talent, Alba Mikkelsen. First time ever you did was with Ryberg in his bedroom, and it was only the sight of Benji that prompted that.

'I will not let it . . .'

Benji pulled himself away from her, picked up a few stalks of ragwort from the grave and placed them in her lap.

'Did you see him, Mam?' he asked and just the sound of his fragile little voice brought more tears.

Then he took a tightly-rolled wad out of his pocket, placed it in her hand. Two hundred krónur. The money from the table.

'Wasn't letting him have that. The thieving shit. Your money. Not his.'

'See who?'

The boy just stared at her and she couldn't work out what that look was in his eyes.

'Who?' Alba asked again though the question almost stuck in her throat.

No answer.

'Benji. Talk to me. You've got to. I'm your mother. I'm . . . asking . . .'

All the questions flooded out then. Who and when and why and what. About Jónas and the Lundi Cliffs. And how he came to fall.

Her son just looked at her, mouth open, teeth in need of fixing more than ever. Silent. He didn't say a word, just turned his head and shook it, quickly, awkwardly, lost.

Looking at him, head going side to side like that, lips moving, nothing coming out, a part of her began to wonder if he was the same boy at all.

'Say something, Benji,' she pleaded. 'Just . . . talk, will you?'

Across the field there was a sound, like timber breaking. Then a brown pall drifted over and hung around them like a feeling cloud.

HANDS FLAILING, TRYING TO stop himself, Tristan Haraldsen tripped over the burning, falling door, straight into the priest's house and a cloud of smoke, flames licking close behind it.

His throat closed on the choking fumes, eyes streaming, trying to hold a hankie to his face as he called out Ryberg's name.

A cloud of crackling, swirling grey fumes and ash swirled around him like a spirit rising from the earth. Like the breath of that damned celestial pig Hildisvíni, scorching Selkie beach because a mortal had spied on his mistress.

Maybe this was stupid. But someone had to check and he didn't see any volunteers among the locals. One quick look then he'd retreat outside to some kind of safety and the inevitable scolding from Elsebeth.

'Hello! If there's anyone—'

As he staggered forward, as good as blind, his right foot banged into something trapped against the staircase, and with the way his confused mind was working he couldn't stop himself reaching down to pick it up. Haraldsen stared at the thing as the smoke whirled around him. It was a blackened, sooty poker that might have been an old whaling spear once, designed for that spot behind the blowhole he could never find. A dark, fresh liquid very like blood, sticky when he touched it, stained the arrow point. But then as the quick revulsion of that discovery set in something worse struck, swinging against him out of nowhere, so unexpected he dropped the poker as if it carried an electric shock.

'What the . . .?'

Yet Haraldsen knew straight away what it was that had bumped into him lurching around the fiery hallway. The clammy touch of a pair of cold and naked legs suspended from the bannister above, chilly skin dashing against his cheeks.

'My God!'

His hands went up to protect himself from whatever creature hung there down the stairs.

'Elsebeth,' he whispered, shaking with the unexpected rush of fear.

Something snapped. He heard the crack. Then the thing came away from whatever held it, fell down like a lead weight, taking him down to the floor in its dead white arms.

He was shrieking, wailing, trying to get the grim corpse off him. Voices came, breaking through the creaks and groans of the dying house. Hands with them, dragging him out of the burning hallway, into the light of the dying day.

'Ryberg,' he said, lying on the grass, panting as Elsebeth's worried face hovered above him. 'I saw him . . .'

A deafening explosion rocked the hot, small world. Haraldsen cricked his neck and looked. The cottage was expiring in a rush of livid flame, the timbers collapsing from the walls like fallen bones. And a dead man was still inside, sure to be incinerated in such a blaze.

'I saw . . .'

Lars Ryberg swinging from a noose as he hung from the bannister. A whaling spear with blood on it. The words wouldn't come out so he looked at his wife as she bent above him, stroking his cheek. The taste of the smoke, vile and dusty, was deep within his lungs, so bitter and black the simple thought of it started a coughing fit, and then more choking until someone, he couldn't see who, held out a plastic bottle and Haraldsen sucked desperately at the water.

'We all need to get away from here,' a voice he recognised as Baldur Ganting said. 'It's not safe.'

Strong arms came back and lifted him away from the heat and smoke, away from the dark thing he'd found inside the priest's house.

'Elsebeth.' He took her hand as they carried him. 'I believe . . .'

When the pall of acrid smoke diminished they stopped and gently eased him onto a raised mound of grass by the path back to the cemetery. Ganting, he saw, had been doing most of the carrying. Tears were running down his whiskery cheeks.

'In there . . .'

'No getting him out before that place went up. No point either. Man was dead. Rope around his neck. We all saw that.'

'There was something else—'

'Never mind the dead,' Ganting cried, and thrust out his arm back towards the church. 'Think of the living, man. Benjamin. My grandson. See.'

There he was, next to the graveyard gate, holding the hand of his mother, standing very stiffly, as awkward and hunched and pale as Tristan Haraldsen recalled.

'The lad came back,' Baldur Ganting said, choking down a sob. 'I knew he would. Never mind what that damned policeman reckoned.'

'We need Aksel Højgaard.' Haraldsen shooed away Elsebeth's tut-tuts and whines about his heart. 'There were . . . strange circumstances.'

From the Árnafjall tunnel the sound of sirens rose like the shrieks of wild birds.

'Fire engine's here from Sørvágur,' one of the crewmen muttered. 'Late as ever.'

'Højgaard . . .'

Elsebeth knelt down in front of him and stroked his face. Her fingers were stained with soot and dust when they came away.

'He'll be here soon enough,' she said. 'Tristan . . .'

'No.' He clambered to his feet, angry suddenly, and anger was an emotion that was largely foreign to him. 'Not soon enough at all.'

TWENTY

Two days later Tristan Haraldsen found himself in the office of Rasmussen, the chief superintendent in Tórshavn. Aksel Højgaard sat across the table next to his superior. In all the confusion and activity after the fire Haraldsen remembered little in the way of detail. Except that Elsebeth had, of course, insisted a doctor check him over.

The heart. The bloody heart. After an hour in an ambulance the medic had said he'd inhaled a fair bit of smoke but otherwise seemed fine. Then he was ordered home where Elsebeth plied him with tea throughout a long and difficult night. She had more discomfort from minor injuries she'd sustained in the tunnel. But she was, of course, having none of it and fussed over him needlessly for hours.

The following day seemed quite unreal. Police teams and the fire brigade set up operations in and around Ryberg's house. Højgaard had allowed no one near. Alba Mikkelsen apart, none but the police and social services people had been given access to the young boy who'd emerged from the fells. He, it seemed, had not spoken a word to anyone from the moment Alba found him waiting in the cemetery by Jónas's grave.

So, forty-eight hours after another dramatic turn of events in Djevulsfjord, Haraldsen once again knew very little indeed. Elsebeth had stayed at home, expecting a call from the policewoman, Hanna Olsen, who seemed to be kept separate from the inquiries into

Ryberg for some reason. Then Rasmussen summoned him for a meeting. With all the many doubts and questions fluttering round his head Tristan Haraldsen was all too ready to accept.

He knew the chief superintendent from the years he'd spent in the back offices of the police service. A pleasant, rather slow chap, a stickler for rules and details who hated any disturbance of his daily routine. The kind of man who regarded the job as a matter of paperwork to be processed, an activity that did not deserve to be interrupted by unpleasantness from the outside world. He was notorious for introducing discussions of food into routine meetings, so much that in some quarters of headquarters he was referred to, mostly kindly, as 'Head Chef'.

Events had clearly taken their toll. Now he looked older, careworn and visibly upset. He had, he said, asked for Haraldsen to be there in his position as district sheriff as a witness for interview, not that the post carried any formal weight. This seemed strange. Perhaps, Haraldsen felt, the man wanted someone there as a buffer against the forceful presence of Højgaard.

'Another dreadful occurrence . . .' Rasmussen shook his head in disbelief. 'I cannot ever remember such a thing in our green and beautiful isles. A priest with such filthy secrets . . .'

'He was a Dane,' Højgaard pointed out. 'Not one of ours.'

'And they send such beasts to us! The man should never have left Jutland. And to put him in that damned place.' He groaned as if the pain were personal. 'The sooner the people in that hellhole give up the ghost and go and live in civilization the better.'

'It's their home,' Haraldsen pointed out. 'The few that are left.'

Rasmussen rattled off the names of a string of abandoned villages around the islands, then pointed out that progress meant giving up on the past, not trying to breathe life into the dying. It seemed a remarkably inapposite analogy to Haraldsen and perhaps the expression on his face betrayed the fact.

'I will not argue with you,' he said. 'Since I'm here as some kind of witness perhaps you can tell me what's happened.'

Højgaard nodded and made his case.

THE OFFICIAL POLICE POSITION was simple and, it seemed to Haraldsen, very difficult to contest. The day before Ryberg died Højgaard had visited the priest as a result of information that had come to light during the search for Benjamin Mikkelsen. He'd warned him that he'd been made aware of the accusations which had dogged the man in his previous parish in Jutland.

'Had I understood the full implications of this I would have acted differently. I merely wished to rule him out of any involvement with the Mikkelsen children.'

'No need for apologies,' Rasmussen said with a wave of his hand. 'I see no fault on your part. The perpetrator is responsible for the deed. No one else.'

There, Haraldsen thought. The blame was apportioned already, and directly to the dead.

'Five, six years, the man's been in Djevulsfjord and only now you find out?'

The superintendent stared at him.

'One doesn't normally run background checks on a parish priest. When the Mikkelsen boys went missing I had to consider the possibility that they were running from some kind of abuse. That it wasn't just the unfortunate incident when the youngest pulled a knife on you.'

It seemed a plausible explanation.

'What did Ryberg say?'

Højgaard shrugged.

'He didn't deny his past. He couldn't. I had the papers. When I pressed him on the Mikkelsen boys the fellow turned quite aggressive. I had to leave it there because we were still looking for the elder brother. But . . .'

There was a folder of photographs on the desk. Højgaard picked it up and spread them out. Haraldsen didn't want to look too closely. Most were of the charred remains of the priest's house. Blackened timbers, half of the building an open shell now exposed to the elements. Then there was a second set. The dead Ryberg, burned as well, so badly it was hard to see him as a man any more. The corpse looked more like a scorched mannequin, twisted by the heat and flames into the same kind of agonised pose one saw in the dead caught in other conflagrations or one of those poor figures from Pompeii, trapped forever in lava.

'It's clear from what forensic evidence we have,' Højgaard continued, 'that he'd been burning documents in the fireplace. Most of them we've lost. There were some pornographic magazines. And this . . .'

He retrieved a photograph, the top right-hand corner blackened by fire. But the rest was clear enough. It was a naked Jónas Mikkelsen grinning on a beach, his hands in front of himself, staring at the lens.

'For the sake of the boy and the family,' the superintendent went on, 'I haven't shared this particular piece of evidence with them. I think they've suffered enough. The boy's dead. So is his abuser. I require you do not mention this, Haraldsen.'

'Tristan?'

The chief superintendent echoed the request obediently.

'Why would I? Of course not.'

Højgaard put the photo away and picked up something else.

'Ryberg had air tickets to Thailand that evening. Foreign currency. A false passport. He'd shaved off his beard. The new passport . . .'

Again, a charred document came out of the folder wrapped in a plastic evidence bag.

'It uses an old photo from his Jutland days.'

'The beast was clearly planning to flee,' Rasmussen observed.

'So why didn't he?' Haraldsen asked.

Højgaard smiled in that sly, sarcastic way he had.

'I cannot speak for the dead. But I imagine it may have been because, when I visited the fellow, I told him he was to make himself available for interview the following day. That he was a person of interest and was under no circumstances to leave Djevulsfjord. That if he tried I'd stop it and I'd throw him in a cell and want to know why.'

Haraldsen could imagine Højgaard uttering every word of that, and enjoying each syllable.

'As a result of which he killed himself?' he asked. 'Set fire to all the evidence? Hung himself off his own banister?'

Højgaard tidied the documents away and with them the life of Lars Ryberg.

'The rope was his. It came from the house. Again . . .' He glanced at Rasmussen to emphasise the point he was about to make. 'What I say should go no further from this room. I spoke to the mother. After the funeral Alba Mikkelsen went to visit him to sign off the church records.' Højgaard sighed. 'Ryberg attacked her. One last victim in Djevulsfjord, I imagine. They think that way, abusers. It's like . . . a count. A tally.'

That revelation made Haraldsen catch his breath.

'What happened?'

'She saw her son through the window and found the strength to fight the bastard off. Not long after he turned to the rope. The game was up.'

'Good lord . . .' Rasmussen could scarcely believe it. 'I shouldn't say this but thank God the man took the way out he did. The foreign papers would have made a meal . . .' He shook his head once more. 'We can keep this quiet? A local tragedy, Aksel. A simple suicide. The other details . . . they can stay in this room. That would be for the best. I gather Ryberg has no inquisitive relatives back in Denmark.'

'For the sake of all concerned we should be discreet. I agree. Haraldsen?'

'I saw . . . I saw a spear or something. A poker. I touched it.'

The superintendent frowned.

'We found no such thing. Though in the heat of the fire who knows. It may have been destroyed. Perhaps escaped our attention . . .'

'There was blood on it. I swear.'

The two police officers exchanged glances and Haraldsen realised then: he had been the subject of discussion beforehand. Perhaps there was more to his being there than he first thought.

DURING A LONG NIGHT wrecked by dreams of blood and shrieks she couldn't source Elsebeth Haraldsen had tossed and turned so much that in the end there was nothing to do but get up, go downstairs, make herself a cup of tea and sit there in a dressing gown, at four o'clock, staring at the laptop. Wondering whether to go back to the keyboard again and hunt for yet more secrets. The thing only seemed to prompt miserable discoveries, none of which made much sense.

Kaspar Ganting. Kristian Djurhuus. Søren Olsen. Two men dead, one missing, perhaps the same. And now the priest of the hamlet they'd chosen for their retirement. Did something connect them all? Or was Djevulsfjord simply a place that had suffered an unfortunate year?

The hours vanished. Tristan rose and before they could talk much got the summons to Tórshavn for reasons he couldn't fathom. She asked him, as always, how he felt, whether he'd taken his medication, and received all the pat answers in return. Seeing him choking and gasping on the ground, gagging on the smoke and fumes, outside Ryberg's house, she'd felt the sharp pain of his mortality. It was the first time that agonising panic had returned since the police doctors told him he was headed for early retirement on medical grounds. He was such a kind and gentle man, so unsuited for Djevulsfjord she now realised. His heart. There wasn't a lot wrong with it, she knew. If he was sensible it would barely affect him. Yet the idea that Tristan, *her* Tristan, was fragile in some way disturbed her. They were each other's rock. They deserved a quiet, loving withdrawal from the world of work, a delightful, slow, uncertain stumble from middle to old age. The picture postcard which greeted them when they first ventured through the Árnafjall tunnel seemed to promise that too. And now . . .

After she watched him drive off in the battered Ace Capri,

Elsebeth attempted to distract herself with more tedious household chores. Cleaning, feeding the hens, trying to avoid the judgemental stare of the three remaining sheep, all of which refused to go near the blasted shed. That had now taken on sinister connotations she found difficult to ignore.

The laptop stayed untouched. She didn't dare. So the morning dawdled, without news from Tórshavn. Across the hill, on the path back to the village, Ryberg's house was just visible, a blackened wreck. Charred timbers like the skeleton of an ancient whale rose from the field by the cemetery. No smoke any more though she could still smell some of it over the fresh tang of the salt breeze rolling in from the sea.

Just after ten her phone buzzed and she half-ran to get it, desperate for news from Tristan. Instead it was a text message from Inga Dam.

I am in New York. Which still is not far enough away from that cursed place. If you are still there you are bigger fools than I thought.

SHE DIDN'T LIKE BEING lectured. Any more than she liked Inga Dam. So her reply was less polite than it might have been.

Miss Dam. I do not appreciate your tone. There are mysteries here which both my husband and I feel deserve unravelling. You may choose to run if you wish. We do not. When last we spoke I was under the impression you had told me part of your story. Not the whole of it. If that is the case then now is the time to speak.

THAT FELT GOOD, NOT that she expected an answer.
Still it came. Just a few minutes later.

And what if my words might harm you?

ELSEBETH'S FINGERS FLEW ON the phone.

We are not children. We do not require protection. If you
have something to say then say it.

IF THIS WERE FACE-TO-FACE, Elsebeth thought, I would be screaming
at this woman by now. Almost immediately an answer flew back
and she could see those dusty sculptor's fingers angrily sending
it her way from across the grey Atlantic.

You seem intent on burnishing your foolishness. Oh well.
From my place in Selkie I have views you never see in
Djevulsfjord. I notice things.

THERE WAS A MOMENT'S pause. Elsebeth was about to prompt her.
Then:

Behind the Lundi Cliffs from my side there's a winding path
that leads up to the peak. A man has been living there. In a
cave. For the last two weeks or so. He comes and goes.

SHE COULD SCARCELY BELIEVE this.

Who?

I do not know. But I recognise furtive when I see it. Furtive
is rare in that hellish place. For the most part they do not
stoop to hiding the beasts they are.

This was unacceptable.

Those boys were missing on Árnafjall all this time and you
never said?

A couple of those cartoon faces the young used on their phones
popped up on the screen. Laughing balloons, tears of mirth in
their shining, too-big eyes.

The man came and went towards Djevulsfjord. Why tell
them something they know already?

Elsebeth struggled to find something to say. But it didn't matter.
Inga Dam still came back.

Your fool husband brought blood on you both with that
grind. If the two of you choose to pursue this, blame no
one but yourself. I have warned you. There. It's done.

Elsebeth typed automatically: thank you. Then waited five more
minutes until she realised this conversation was at an end.

She thought of Tristan but he had matters of his own to deal
with. There was only one other person she believed they might trust.

The rattle of a motorbike sounded when Hanna Olsen
answered. She must have had a headset plugged into her helmet.

'Elsebeth? How can I help?'

'You can't. But I can.'

The engine slowed then died. She must have been pulling in by the side of the road.

'There's been a man living in the fells behind us. Perhaps for weeks on end. Inga Dam knew all along. She knew and never said. I think . . .'

She hesitated to say it but the fear was there surely in Inga Dam's words, her actions. Running all the way to another continent to escape this tiny hamlet hidden away on the coast.

'I think she was frightened. She believes someone in Djevulsfjord might have known he was there all along.'

There was the sound of a throttle being blipped but nothing by way of reply.

'Hanna? Should we not look?'

It wasn't just the thought of the sheep carcass in the shed that kept her awake most of the night. It was more that Ryberg's strange death had altered matters somehow. It was hard to shake the feeling that events in Djevulsfjord were coming to a head.

'I can't. Not now . . .'

And that was that.

'HOW ARE YOU, TRISTAN?' Rasmussen inquired. 'You and the wife. I never asked. It was very rude of me.'

'I am perfectly well. Her name is Elsebeth.'

Rasmussen rolled back his chair, opened the filing cabinet behind him and took out a file marked with the stamp of the personnel department. It had Haraldsen's name on the front and seemed to fall immediately to hand.

'Your heart. They gave you retirement for your heart. You bravely made your way into that burning building I gather.'

'My heart is fine, thank you! The doctor said so after the fire. I know what I saw. A poker. Like a whaling spear. As I said . . . there was blood on it.'

Højgaard cleared his throat and added, 'I gather the one grind you've supervised was not entirely successful, was it?'

Ryberg, the Mikkelsen boys and the rest appeared to have vanished from the conversation.

'I did not come here to talk about whales. A man is dead. A child is seemingly unwell. I know what I saw in that house.'

Højgaard scowled.

'I don't deny you saw something. But amidst all the smoke and flames . . .?'

'Amidst all the smoke and flames! Is there something you wish to say to me, chief superintendent?'

Rasmussen removed some sheets from the personnel file.

'I see you were short-changed somewhat over your pension. Probably a pen-pusher downstairs trying to squeeze money out of the budget. The pittance you receive from being district sheriff is far less than they should have given you by way of disability allowance in addition to your monthly income.'

'My heart is a minor affliction dealt with perfectly well through medication.'

'Keep your hair on!' Rasmussen cried. 'I'm offering you free money!'

'For what?' There was a heat in his voice at that moment Haraldsen scarcely recognised. 'My silence?' He leaned forward and banged his fist on the desk. That was a first. 'Last year two men died in Djevulsfjord. Kaspar Ganting and my predecessor Djurhuus. Are you telling me Ryberg was responsible for them too?'

'Calm yourself,' Højgaard snapped. 'Ganting's death was accidental. As was your predecessor's. A hit-and-run. Not that we can find the culprit. Perhaps it was Ryberg. Nothing would surprise me.'

'Djurhuus had been passing reports back to this place! He said there was funny business going on! In Djevulsfjord.'

Silence. That was a mistake and he knew it immediately. He'd only found out about Djurhuus's reports to Tórshavn by taking an illicit path into the police network.

'What sort of reports?' Højgaard asked.

'I, I . . . don't know. Someone in the village mentioned it . . .'

'Who?'

He didn't answer that. He couldn't.

'Those cases are closed.' Rasmussen put the personnel file back into the drawer. 'As is Lars Ryberg's.'

'And Benjamin Mikkelsen?'

Again that look between them.

'The child's been allowed to stay with his mother for now,' Højgaard said. 'I wanted to see if it might loosen his lips. Nothing sadly. He needs specialist help. We don't have it. Denmark's the place.'

Haraldsen was aghast.

'You'll take the child from Alba? Send him across the sea where she can't see him?'

'There are flights . . .'

'She has no money! None of them in Djevulsfjord do. Not the ordinary folk . . . they're all in hock to the Thomsens. It's like . . . like the old days. When there were peasants.'

Rasmussen frowned.

'Djevulsfjord is the old days. Ten years I give that hole and then they'll give up and move to town. The sensible ones have gone already. No woman from the outside world would go there, would they? A place that can't even get itself a bride . . .'

Haraldsen couldn't believe he was hearing any of this and said so.

'Oh please, Tristan!' Rasmussen was getting mad. 'Do not overcomplicate matters. You were a civilian here, not a detective. Had you been you would realise simplicity lies at the heart of human affairs. Never convolution. It is much like when you're in the kitchen—'

'If you start talking about bloody cooking I swear I will scream.'

The man across the desk looked shocked.

'The plain fact is Benjamin Mikkelsen was responsible for the death of his brother,' he replied with a touch of coldness. 'Perhaps it was an accident. Perhaps an argument gone wrong. Perhaps the priest's disgusting habits made matters worse between them. These things happen. If the child could bring himself to speak, as an innocent might—'

'How do you know it wasn't Ryberg! If you say—'

'I know it wasn't Ryberg,' Højgaard interrupted, 'because I've done my job and established his whereabouts. We know precisely when Jónas Mikkelsen fell down those cliffs. You witnessed it yourself. At the time Lars Ryberg was in the village shop arguing with the Thomsen woman about some money he owed her. So . . .' He threw open his arms. 'We can't ignore the facts.'

Again the silence.

'Any more than we can ignore the fact you're in the wrong

place,' Rasmussen went on. 'Djevulsfjord's a grim old hole at the best of times. In winter . . . Had I known they'd put you up for that district sheriff's position I would never have allowed—'

'We chose to go there!'

The chief superintendent checked his watch very deliberately.

'You made a mistake. For your sake and ours it needs to be corrected.'

Trapped with the two of them, Haraldsen felt powerless. Had Elsebeth been here she might have torn into the pair. Still, he might try.

'As far as I'm aware it's up to us where we decide to live.'

'Indeed,' Rasmussen agreed. 'But it's up to me to decide who's district sheriff. Your appointment was an unfortunate error. No worry. The disability pension will more than make up for the loss of income. Come back to Tórshavn where you and . . . and . . .'

'Elsebeth!'

'Where you and Elsebeth belong. This rustic fantasy of yours does neither of you any favours. Birgit and I would love to have you round. I'll cook dinner. Italian. My pasta is home made these days—'

'I do not want to eat your bloody pasta, Rasmussen!'

The chief superintendent frowned at that, got to his feet and gestured towards the door.

'A resignation would be best. Say your health isn't up to it if you like. No matter. I'd rather you didn't force my hand.'

'You summoned me here for this?'

Rasmussen looked offended.

'Do you think I'd shirk from telling you face-to-face? Later today. An email will suffice. Now if you don't mind. Højgaard and I have private matters to discuss.'

Tristan Haraldsen didn't linger. Didn't waste another word on them.

There was a nip in the air. Frost might arrive early this year. Winter in Djevulsfjord would be grim. Their lives in Tórshavn had been quiet and comfortable. It was, he knew, a mistake to leave.

The Ace Capri was at the very edge of the car park, the scrape down the side from the time he nearly mowed down Elsebeth in the Árnafjall tunnel very visible.

The two men were, of course, quite right. They did not belong in a dying little hamlet in Árnafjall's shadow. But the leaving of it was theirs to decide, and no one else's. Nor was he finished with Djevulsfjord yet.

TWENTY-ONE

Two days they'd left Benji with her and all he'd done was eat, let her bathe him, watched as she ironed his old clothes now fresh from the wash, then sat by the front window watching men go to and fro on the harbour. Djevulsfjord was coming back to life after the weather and the events. Lars Ryberg, she'd been told by Dorotea Thomsen while doing that morning's cleaning, was to be shipped back to Denmark where a distant relative would see him to the crematorium, doubtless with little regret. Workers had come from Sørvágur to mend her father's boat which, thanks to Thomsen money, would be seaworthy soon, perhaps in time for one final grind. The blackfish were there. People had seen them far off beyond the Skerries. But no one felt minded to ask Baldur Ganting to lead the hunt, and he was the only one who could approach the strange district sheriff for permission.

Time and again Alba Mikkelsen had tried to talk to her son with no success. Only a grunt she got, and that to mundane questions. Did he want beans with his eggs? Was it worth darning the old clothes he'd worn out on the fells or should she just chuck them and find some more in the charity shop next time she was in Sørvágur?

Then, that first night, would he like the top bunk in the shack now it was . . .?

That last hadn't even generated so much as a sound from him as he took it.

Alba had decided she would put flowers on Jónas' grave as often as she could. Wild ones since she had no money to buy anything from the shop. But it would be a while before she felt able to take Benji with her to the cemetery. The memory of him standing by the brown earth the day of the fire was still too fresh and hurtful. There was always something blank and a little wild in his eyes, part of the way his confused mind was set to work. But that day it had been worse and she felt sure taking him back to the place his little brother's body lay buried a few feet away in the soft brown earth would only send him racing further inside himself. That was the opposite of what they needed. Benji had to talk. Had to start to be normal. There'd be questions from Højgaard and the social people soon, awkward ones he needed to answer. A few days they'd leave him with her to see what happened. That time was surely running out. She could coach him. Tell him to say that Jónas came at him with the knife and all that happened was a tragic accident, a stumble, a slip while he defended himself from the blade.

Maybe that was true. But first he had to speak.

She put a chocolate biscuit on the table. He came away from the window and ate it the way he always did: clumsily, crumbs going everywhere, not that she was going to complain this time. Dorotea wanted her back at the house in half an hour. There was kitchen muck to be dealt with and a bunch of other dirty jobs the woman would never countenance herself.

'I will have to go to work in a while, Benji. You want to come to the big house? Or stay here?'

He finished the biscuit and went back to the window.

'Don't you go walking off, will you?' She came and stroked his hair. It was clean and soft now she'd washed it. Getting the filth off him after all that time on the fells was a job in itself. 'I don't want to lose you again, Benji. Not ever.'

Don't cry. That won't help.

'You're all I got. Your dad won't be back here for a while either. And when he does . . .'

Don't cry.

'Look.' She got out some bread and some cheese, then the bluntest knife she could find. She didn't want him dealing much with knives. 'If that old bitch Dorotea keeps me working too long you make yourself some lunch. I'll get back when I can.'

He was watching the men working on the *Alberta*, sawing and hammering away. She put a tentative hand to his skinny shoulder. The boy just shrugged her off.

'I'll make you better, Benji,' she whispered. 'I'll make both of us better. They won't stop us. No one can. I won't—'

Her cheap little phone rang. The trill . . . he didn't even seem to notice.

'You wait there,' she said, not that she knew why.

The phone was on the table, shaking up and down, moving around as it rang. She didn't want to answer it. People only called with bad news, never good.

Finally Benji walked over, picked it up, gave her a hard look and placed the thing in her hands.

She answered, didn't say anything.

'Mrs Mikkelsen? Alba Mikkelsen?'

There was a woman on the other end. Cold voice, smart accent. Tórshavn. Something important.

'Speaking.'

'It's about Benjamin.'

Heart thudding she asked, 'What about him?'

'Has he said anything yet?'

They were coming. She could feel it.

'Just a bit more time. A day or two . . .'

Behind that silence lay all the agony in the world.

'We're on our way.'

Benji was back at the window and Alba knew she wasn't going to Dorotea Thomsen's, wasn't going to leave him, whatever trouble that caused.

'Don't you make a fuss now.'

She'd heard a voice saying just that a million times before. The day she ran away as a twelve-year-old fleeing something she couldn't talk about. All the same they'd dragged her back to Djevulsfjord screaming every inch of the way.

'There'll be police with us,' the woman on the line added. 'It's best for the boy, for both your sakes. You stay right where you are. You do just like you're told.'

ELSEBETH STEELED HERSELF AND went inside the old slaughter-house. Had to. The bikes they'd taken out of the Ace Capri were stowed there. She did her best not to look at the shape hanging in the corner, covered with muslin, flies buzzing round the stained fabric. The place smelled of meat and blood, with an undertow of oil from Tristan's tools and the leaky mower. As quickly as she could she grabbed the small-framed mountain bike that was hers, wheeled it out into the bright, late-summer sun and set off for the fells.

The way was rocky and winding. It was a while since she'd been out cycling. But soon she fell into a rhythm and within fifteen minutes found herself high above the corner of the mountain that divided Djevulsfjord from Selkie Bay. The place was so beautiful, even now she knew a strange kind of darkness lurked beneath the glorious surface. The wooden buildings of the village were a patchwork of different colours in the neck of the bay by the harbour. The black stumps of Ryberg's gutted home seemed insignificant from up here, like the ashes of burned timber from an old bonfire. Docked by the cobbled landing, boats moved gently on the swell. White horses rose and fell upon the Skerries and, beyond, she saw, just briefly, the black sheen of whale fins break the surface.

Another grind missed. No district sheriff to allow it even if the locals could muster a fleet without Baldur Ganting's *Alberta* to lead them.

You're wasting time, Elsebeth Haraldsen. You're on your own and you're scared.

Which was true and being frightened was not something she felt suited her. So she pushed hard on the pedals and went higher, round the path to the remote fell side she felt Inga Dam must have been describing. From here the black damp sand of Selkie shone on a retreating tide, like a giant version of the pilot whale fin she'd seen cut through the blue ocean a few minutes before.

'Where are you mystery man?' she called out loud.

No one answered. She didn't expect it. If there was someone living here it was in order to hide. Benjamin and Jónas Mikkelsen had known how to do this. So did many in Djevulsfjord it seemed. Living off the land, perhaps stealing when necessary, was hardly the most taxing of skills.

Elsebeth pedalled on for another ten minutes and saw nothing. There were a couple of caves this high up but they were empty, damp and stank of mould and algae. She was about to give up when she rounded one last knoll, right above Inga Dam's cottage, then hammered her feet onto the rocky trail and came to a sudden, breathless halt. The path here ended in a vertiginous drop, down hundreds of metres to the rocks below. No warning sign, not an inch of fencing.

End of the line. Nothing to show.

The wind eddied around her. There was a smell on it. Tobacco, strong and black. Not dissimilar to the snus that Baldur Ganting shoved beneath his upper lip in an idle moment.

Elsebeth placed the bike on the ground and looked around. The trail did end in that perilous cliff. But there was a narrow ledge running by the side of it. Cigarette ends were stabbed into the rough brown earth by the side, like spent trophies. She turned sideways and edged along the ridge, making sure not to look down. Soon the rock broadened and she could walk more freely. Ten metres along the way turned behind a spike of basalt and there it was: a cavern, the mouth half in shadow.

'Hello?' she said and walked straight in.

There was a smell she recognised. Not a pleasant one. Humanity cornered, sweat and worse. The way ahead lay in darkness and she knew what she needed. The phone again. The torch app she'd used in the tunnel when Tristan so very nearly ran her down.

'If there is someone here . . .?'

No answer. The dim light of the tiny screen cast a weak beam ahead of her. Elsebeth's foot stopped as it hit something tinny, sending it scuttling across the floor.

A camping gas stove. Next to it a sleeping bag. Some pans and a hiker's dish with a handle, food in the bottom, a dirty knife next to it. A packet of cigarettes and some clothes in a bundle. A hoodie sweatshirt with a roaring blue lion's head and the logo, 'F.C. København'.

'Oh, Hanna,' she whispered.

Whoever had worn the shirt of Copenhagen's football team had done so recently. Perhaps that very day.

She took a photo of it with her phone then, step-by-step, shaking a little, she made her way back along the ledge, never looking down again, flattening herself against the rock wall at the narrowest part, until she reached the bike.

The sun was so bright it hurt her eyes. The stink of tobacco from those extinguished cigarettes made her feel a little nauseous.

Still she took out her phone and made the inevitable call.

It took a while for the policewoman to answer and when she did there were voices in the background.

'Yes?' was all she said.

'Hanna. It's Elsebeth Haraldsen. I've been on the fells. We need to—'

'I cannot . . . I cannot deal with this now.' She sounded close to breaking. 'I have a job to do, Elsebeth. I'm outside Alba Mikkelsen's place by the harbour. Can you come, please? Can you come quickly?'

'This is important.'

A pause, then: 'So is this.'

'Of course,' Elsebeth said and climbed on her bike.

*   *   *

BY THE TIME SHE arrived a small crowd had gathered outside the tumbledown shed that was Alba Mikkelsen's home on the cobbles by the harbour. Two cars, black, shiny, new, unlike anything in Djevulsfjord, were parked along the sea wall, Hanna Olsen's motorbike with them. The policewoman was at the door looking harassed. There were three people with her, two middle-aged women and a silent man, big, with the physique of a boxer, all in grey work clothes, officialdom written all over them.

She marched straight over, looked Hanna in the eye and realised why she was there. A conflict had arisen and Elsebeth was supposed to be the policewoman's support in the fight.

'How can I help?' she asked.

'You can't.' It was the woman in grey at the front. She waved a piece of paper. 'I have a court order to take Benjamin Mikkelsen into protective custody. I expect the police to back me up in this. Not stand in my way.'

With that she banged on the door, which only generated a tirade of foul-mouthed shrieks from Alba on the other side.

'They want to take the boy,' Hanna said and didn't move an inch.

'We *have* to take him.'

'Piss off out of here,' Alba yelled from inside.

'For Christ's sake,' the woman said a little more quietly. 'These things are difficult enough without making them harder. We don't want to drag the child out ourselves.' She nodded at the crowd, Dorotea Thomsen at the front, arms folded, watching as if this were entertainment. 'Discreet is best.'

'Was Alba Mikkelsen forewarned?' Elsebeth asked. 'Did she receive legal advice?'

The women rolled their eyes. The big man with them said, 'Are you listening? We have a warrant to take the child. Take the child we will. One way or another.'

Elsebeth rapped on the door and asked if Alba would let her and the policewoman in.

No answer.

'We must talk. Please. I . . . I know this is difficult. But these people will not go away. Alba!'

There was a sound. A latch getting lifted. The door was just timber planks hammered together. You could push your way in if you wanted. But it opened and when it did she walked inside, Hanna Olsen behind her.

ALBA WAS AT THE table, eyes glistening with tears, face stony with fury. Benjamin sat on an ancient sofa, a book on his lap as if nothing had happened. Eydna, her mother, was next to him looking lost.

'They will not take my boy. I won't allow it. Benji's my son. How . . .?' She slammed a fist on the table then glared at Eydna. 'Where's Dad? He can stop them.'

'I said. Your father had to go to Tórshavn to get some things for the boat, love.'

'Those bastards waited till he was gone, didn't they?'

Hanna sat down at the table. Elsebeth didn't. She wandered round the little shack then went over to Benji, not that he seemed to notice.

'They're not taking him . . .'

Hanna put a hand on Alba's.

'They have the right. They've got papers.'

'Mum? You tell them.'

Eydna Ganting looked lost.

'Tell them what? These are big people from Tórshavn, love. You can't argue with them. You know that. We never could.'

'He's my son! Look . . .'

She went over to him, sat next to the boy. He wasn't even looking at the book in his lap.

'Tell them, Benji. Tell them you want to stay here. With me. We'll be alright.'

Silence.

'For fuck's sake, Benji, will you tell them?'

A longer silence then Hanna went to the door, opened it and spoke to the woman in grey, the one who seemed to be running things.

'I don't want to use force,' she said. 'The child has been through enough.'

'You don't know what he's been through?' Alba was halfway to her when Elsebeth intervened and held her back. 'Haven't a clue.'

The woman waved an ID card from the social services department.

'Do you, Mrs Mikkelsen? Has he said a single word since we left him with you?'

'I'm his mother.' Her voice turned weak. There was a note of defeat inside it, one they could all hear, Alba too. 'I just need time.'

'Your son is ill. He needs a secure home and specialist treatment. Edvard . . .'

The big man barged through in a flash, the other woman behind him. Before anyone could stop them they raced round the room, took hold of Benji who didn't even protest as the fellow got him in his strong arms, began to drag him to the door.

'Let me be with him!' Alba was on her feet.

'You are not part of the cure,' the woman said, blocking her way.

'I will come,' Eydna Ganting strode to her grandson. 'I will come or I will make sure those people out there never let you leave this village. Benjamin! Take my hand!'

Tight in the man's grip the boy did that. The fellow relented. Alba tried to force her way to kiss him but they wouldn't let her and nothing Elsebeth Haraldsen could do or say was going to change that.

Benjamin Mikkelsen just looked blankly at the little crowd as they led him to the car.

'When will he be back?' Alba bleated as they drove off. 'You're the police. You should know.'

Hanna checked her phone for messages. It seemed there were none.

'Why ask me? I didn't even know they were coming till the last moment. They had to notify me. Didn't mean they wanted me here.' She glanced around the room. 'I can make you a cup of tea—'

'Don't want a cup of tea. Don't want anything people like you got. If I don't have my Benji what . . .?' She screwed her eyes tight shut and clenched her fists. 'What point's there being here anyway? Just a slave of Dorotea's . . .'

Elsebeth took Hanna Olsen to one side and said what she thought was obvious: Benjamin wasn't the only one in need of care. His mother deserved it just as much.

'I don't think she should be left on her own.'

'I been on my own ever since Silas dumped me,' Alba snapped

at them from across the room. 'Before that as well. Don't think I can't hear you.'

The place was too small for a family, cramped with ancient, worn furniture so jammed together it was hard to walk around without bumping into things.

Elsebeth took hold of Hanna's police jacket and tugged her into a corner.

'We need to talk.'

'Don't worry. I won't leave until I'm sure she's OK. Or looked after.'

'Up on the fells. I found something. A man's been living up there. Maybe still is and he was out or something. Look . . .'

She retrieved her phone. There were two photos there and she switched between them as Hanna watched, wide-eyed. The football club sweatshirt she'd found on Árnafjall. And the one worn by her brother in the photo from the harbour the year before, found on Inga Dam's wall, with Djurhuus and the Gantings in the background, the remains of the grind behind them, white skeletons on the strand.

'It's the same,' Elsebeth said. 'Older but the same, surely. A man's been living there. Inga said she saw him head for here from time to time as well.'

'Søren . . .'

Hanna Olsen had a firm voice, low and hard almost, but at that moment it was close to breaking.

'Søren,' Alba repeated in a hard, sarcastic tone from the table. They turned to look at her and she stared back, an expression of defiance in her bleak, sad eyes.

'My brother,' Hanna began.

'I know who Søren Olsen is.'

She screwed her eyes tight shut for a moment. There was so much pain in this woman, Elsebeth realised, and nothing one could do to lessen it.

'Do you . . .' Hanna hardly dared say the words. 'Do you know where he is?'

Alba laughed, no joy inside it.

'Maybe.'

Nothing more.

'No games, please,' Elsebeth said. 'Where?'

'They took my boy. And you talk about games.'

'Where?' Hanna demanded.

Alba got up and went to a sideboard beneath the window, pulled open a drawer, found an envelope, brought it to them, spilled three photos on the cracked wood of the table.

It was a summer's day on the ferry to Jutland. Three selfies. Søren in that same sweatshirt. Alba next to him. Both happy, both smiling as if nothing in the world could harm them.

'Where is he?' Hanna repeated.

That mirthless laugh came again and Elsebeth Haraldsen found herself shivering in the dark, damp shed that was Alba Mikkelsen's home.

'You lot come here. From outside. Thinking you own us. Thinking you know everything.'

She spread the photos out so they could see them better.

'You don't know nothing at all.'

THE COTTAGE WAS EMPTY when Haraldsen got back. She might have left a message. He could always ring. Except the meeting with Højgaard and his old colleague Rasmussen had left him rattled. And angry, a feeling he found foreign, one he hated. Getting kicked out of the district sheriff's job didn't worry him at all. But their dismissal of his objections and ready willingness to accept facts he believed questionable in the very least – these things offended him.

Haraldsen had always believed himself a firm supporter of justice, of a kind and benevolent meritocracy in the world, one in which some prospered more than others but never at their expense. This, it seemed to him now, was nothing more than naivety. There was an arrogance in folk like the men he'd just been talking to, a superiority they felt given to them by who they were and the positions they held. The people of Djevulsfjord didn't count for much at all. That struggling fishing hamlet was nothing more than an anachronism, a hidden blight on the backside of Vágar they wished would go away.

'Dammit,' he said and knew where he was going.

The day was bright and chilly. He shivered a little as he walked to Ryberg's cottage. Two days and a long night after he'd broken down the door only to find himself stumbling against the dead Ryberg's naked legs, the investigators appeared to have finished their work. A few scraps of yellow police tape blew in the wind along the weed-strewn path that led to what was once the village priest's home. The place stank of smoke and destruction but he was surprised to see that it was not a complete wreck. True, the front was almost destroyed and the blackened staircase from which that dreadful thing had swung was now nothing more than a carbonised shell. But the back of the house, the kitchen and another room, for laundry perhaps, was almost intact though covered in the white powder of the fire engine's foam.

'I saw that thing,' he muttered to himself. 'I held it in my hands.'

A poker that looked like a whaling spear. Sticky with blood. Fire might blacken it. That's all.

A deep breath then he walked on, over the sooty threshold. The pumps of the firemen had left filthy dark puddles everywhere. The supporting timbers of the front of the house were twisted like bones from an upturned whale skeleton. The smell was intense and upsetting, bringing back those few moments when he'd burst through the smoke and flames crying out for Lars Ryberg, wondering where he was.

Then Elsebeth's kind and troubled face looking down at him as he lay on the grass in the churchyard, wheezing fit to burst from all the muck he'd inhaled. A foolish thing to do. Out of character. But necessary.

He thought he heard a noise.

'Hello?'

Just the word brought back the memory of him saying that as he fought his way into this place when it was in flames.

No answer, then or now. The sound seemed to come from the back of the house, the part that was largely intact behind a blackened wall covered in dried foam, beyond a door marked by the rips of a fireman's axe.

'Hello?'

Nothing. A dog perhaps, scavenging in the ruins.

Haraldsen looked down at his feet, rummaging with his boot end through the debris: burned carpet, shards of unidentifiable wood, broken crockery, the charred remains of curtains and sheets. A bible, the pages seared so badly it was hard to make out the print. Priests must have lived here a hundred years or more. Now there was no one to wear the dog collar. Perhaps the church would think it uneconomic to send one to a community failing so visibly. Lars Ryberg could scarcely be described as the heart of the village. But Djevulsfjord still had a church and a church needed a priest. So, he felt, did its people.

'I saw a poker,' he reminded himself out loud, and jabbed his foot through the detritus on the ground, around where he believed it might have been.

Somewhere out back there was that noise again.

'If there's anyone there please announce yourself. Police? Fire brigade? I am Tristan Haraldsen. The district sheriff.'

There was no poker fashioned out of a whaling spear. Perhaps someone had taken it as a souvenir. Or maybe he did imagine it in all the confusion and smoke and flames. Though a piece of metal sticky with blood was an odd thing for the mind to invent at such a moment.

Haraldsen wandered into what was once the living room. The fireplace he could still make out, the dark red brickwork the only thing in the room that wasn't entirely a sooty shade of black. A couple of old chairs, the collapsed frame of what must once have been a dining table, a standard lamp leaning at a crooked angle against the back wall where the pumps had finally doused the blaze. The house was made of wood. It must have gone up like tinder. He was amazed they'd managed to save this last section at the back at all.

The noise again. There was someone there. Footsteps, unmistakable.

'Hello!' Haraldsen cried and strode directly for the inner door.

It fell off its hinges when he pushed it, and just that brought back again the memory of that terrible moment he'd stumbled into the house two nights before, barging into the hanging Ryberg, suspended from his own banister.

'Who is this?'

It was the kitchen, only half-damaged by smoke. Empty, he thought, until he walked into the middle and a hand came and tapped directly on his shoulder.

Baffled, frightened a little, he turned and found himself facing a tall man of perhaps twenty-five or thirty, burly, with an athletic physique enclosed in a grubby tracksuit. He wore a beard that varied between blond and brown, eyes that were blue and seemed more than a little cruel. His mouth curled in a smile that was not pleasant at all and he possessed a strong and earthy stink to him as if he'd climbed straight out of the ground. There was something that seemed familiar, though in his confused state at that moment Haraldsen found himself quite unable to understand why or how.

'I . . .'

It was so very hard to think and his heart, the damned heart, was pounding now.

'I—'

'I heard tell you were looking for this.'

The whaling spear that doubled as a poker, now as black as most everything else in the rest of Ryberg's house, he gripped in his right hand like a weapon.

'I believe I was.'

'Well, district sheriff.' The fellow slapped the long shaft of iron hard in his left palm and then again. 'You've found it now. Haven't you?'

TWENTY-TWO

She wasn't really sure why she ran that summer. Silas hadn't been beating her any more than usual. The kids were just the same, Jónas sly and always getting into trouble, with Kaspar usually. Benjamin quiet, lovable, useless.

The Tórshavn bus was there that morning, a notice saying it was going to be thirty minutes late because of roadworks. She had money in her pocket. It only took a few minutes to sling a few clothes and some toiletries into a couple of carrier bags, then slide on at the last moment, sit at the back, head down, the only passenger the driver had.

Not that the idea was new. The week before she'd phoned the ferry company and asked them if it was possible to work a passage to Denmark. The man on the other end of the line had laughed and said: no, but if she wanted a job cleaning she could maybe then save up enough one day for the fare.

He was the same one sitting in the ferry office when she got to the big harbour in Tórshavn and told him she'd come for a job. They didn't ask for much by way of paperwork so that night she found herself tidying her things in a tiny cabin, barely a broom cupboard, down in the bowels of the Jutland ferry, feeling the thing sway in the harbour as trucks and cars and caravans drove on board for the thirty-six-hour journey to Hirtshals. She'd never been to Denmark. It sounded like an adventure.

The ship was the biggest she'd ever seen, with restaurants and bars and even a cinema. Not that she saw much of that because most of the next day and a half was spent sweeping up vomit and piss from the gangways and clearing out bedrooms that had been ruined along the way. By the time she got to Jutland she could barely stay awake. There was a twelve-hour turnaround. The crew boss, a decent enough man she thought, said she could sleep in her little metal hutch if she wanted.

Or, she thought, she could just walk ashore. Into a foreign country where the money was different, people, the way they spoke, the way they lived. Where she knew not a soul.

She slept and didn't wake until she heard and felt the trucks and cars coming back on board for the return to Tórshavn.

FOUR HOURS OUT FROM Jutland the work didn't seem too bad. The sea was calmer, the number of drunks and sick people staggering down the corridors a fraction of what it was before. The boss man said Alba had more than worked her hours on the way out so she could have a break around ten in the morning. Two hours all to herself before another long stint on the run-in to Tórshavn. They'd pay her there. She'd have decisions to face. Stay on the ferry and try to pluck up the courage to run for real. Or crawl back to Djevulsfjord, let Silas kick the shit out of her again while Benji cowered and Jónas watched and laughed.

One more trip, she thought. One more brief bout of freedom and then she'd make up her mind.

She was on the stern deck, staring at the waves, the churning wake, the blue summer sea, the perfect sky, when a hand tapped her shoulder and asked if she had a light.

His name was Søren, from Aalborg via Copenhagen. He was young, so talkative she thought he was maybe making up for lost time. Funny too, and it struck her no one laughed much back home at all. Good-looking in a battered way, with a few tattoos she didn't like and a blue-and-white hoodie bearing the name of Copenhagen's football club. Most of all, the thing that attracted her to him was he looked lost. He didn't have much idea why he was going to the Faroes any more than she understood where she might run trying to escape them. They went for a coffee. Not long after they smoked a shared joint by the railings, hair blowing in the wind, the weed, the first she'd ever tried, going straight to her head. She got her phone out and took some selfies with him, promising she'd get them printed out one day. He smiled for her, a nice smile. Then he screwed up his eyes and said he was just out of jail and she was so pretty. He couldn't remember what it was like to be with a woman. He didn't have money but he had a hunger and maybe she did too.

They had sex in her cabin in the fifteen minutes she'd left before going back on duty. It was frantic, grunting, panting, all hard and physical and so quick and desperate on both their parts. She found she liked that, liked him, liked the idea she'd just allowed a complete stranger into her after he begged so politely, with the soft, seductive heat of weed swimming all round them. If she'd said no he'd have shrugged, smiled and said OK. Which made him different from any who'd gone before.

She'd put her uniform back on and gone back to sweeping the corridors and changing the beds, still feeling the warmth of him inside her, giggling from time to time until the dope wore off. Somewhere along the way he'd said he'd been born in Vágar, left there with his sister when they were little. She must have told him she came from Djevulsfjord, not thinking it would matter. Just that one encounter had told her something about herself. Locked together in that tiny cramped cabin, mind racing into a hot dark space she'd never visited before, Alba decided there and then she'd go back to Djevulsfjord, if only for a while. Take comfort in watching Silas go about his surly business never able to guess what had happened that time she fled. And when he came for her, that quick, grunting, passionless embrace, usually with beer on his breath, she'd imagine Søren from Jutland in his place, tease out the minutes with that enticing dream.

When the ferry docked she scuttled out before the Dane could spot her, collected her wages, hid behind the fish market buildings until the Djevulsfjord bus came.

Silas hit her. She was expecting that. Then he pushed her on the bed and loosed his trousers and she was expecting that too.

The next morning a black-and-yellow bruise was growing beneath her left eye, not that she minded because Alba now had that interior knowledge that none of them could ever share. She'd run away. Weed in her head she'd taken a stranger inside her and relished every sweating second. Maybe if she was lucky his seed would take and she'd give birth to a different kind of son to the ones they bred in the place by the Skerries.

TWO DAYS AFTER SHE got back, when Silas was behaving as if nothing had changed, she went down to the harbour to take him some food as he cleaned up the boat after the grind. The district sheriff was there, a miserable old bugger called Djurhuus who everyone hated. Trying to pick holes in the grind as usual, which wasn't hard with Silas who never could get things quite right. As she handed over the sandwiches and flasks of coffee she heard Kaspar shout out her name.

When she turned to look her brother was there too, his big arm right round the shoulders of the man she never thought she'd see again.

Breathless, speechless, she watched as the two of them walked over the cobbles towards her.

'Hey sister,' Kaspar cried. 'I got a surprise. Your friend from the ferry's come to see you. All loved up he is.'

'Hi,' Søren said and looked round at the men staring at him.

He was an idiot, she realised. Maybe she'd known that all along.

'Say something,' Kaspar urged her. 'He's come all this way to see you.'

Sorry, was all she could think of.

'Can we . . .?' Søren shook himself free of Kaspar's clinging grasp. 'Can we talk?'

No, she thought. Too late for that.

Silas looked terrified. So he did what he always did when Kaspar was in that kind of black mood. He went back on his boat and started scrubbing at the deck. Djurhuus stared at the men by the quayside, shook his head and wandered off.

'Alba . . .?' Søren looked ever more desperate then.

You know what you've walked into, she thought. You know there's no turning back.

'Let's take a little walk,' Kaspar said pleasantly and put his arms around Søren's shoulders again. 'I got something to show you up on the Lundi Cliffs. That's best for us all, sister. Don't you think?'

'Suppose,' she said and that was the last she saw of him, though the memory of that frantic few minutes when the two of them locked bodies, half-dressed and wretched in their need still came back now and again.

His seed didn't take. Which was all for the best. They'd only have got rid of that as well.

TWENTY-THREE

In the shack that was her home, empty of Benji now, empty of everything that carried some meaning, the two of them listened, Elsebeth in tears, Hanna beyond them altogether. Alba finished her story, then asked if they'd like a cup of tea or something.

They didn't.

'What happened?' Hanna asked in the end. 'What happened to my brother?'

Alba blinked at her.

'Are you being funny?'

For a second Elsebeth thought the woman next to her might explode. Instead she said, 'No. Not at all.'

'What do you think happened?' Alba asked. 'Kaspar chucked him off the Lundi Cliffs. Came back here and couldn't stop boasting about it. Told Silas.' She shook her head. 'Told me like he was doing me a favour. I was theirs, wasn't I? Not meant to be shared with some foreigner. They all knew. All of them. Dad was furious. He put Kaspar on a boat to Reykjavik that same night and said he wasn't ever to come back. Silas threw me out. Called me a whore. Not that it was the first time I'd got that from him.' She stared at Hanna. 'Not my fault. What happened on the boat . . . that was there. I never asked him to come here like he was going to save me. Men. They're all the same, every last one of them. Think they've got a right somehow.'

'Where did they put—?'

Alba cackled out loud, a little mad at that moment, and the sight of her chilled them both.

'Oh for pity's sake. Some detective you are. There's a grave with my brother's headstone next to Jónas in the churchyard. Ryberg laid your brother in there while all of us watched. Except for Kaspar who was on his way to Iceland.'

She ran a finger across the table as if drawing a map on the dusty surface.

'Never show your face here again, Dad said. Kaspar didn't like that one little bit. Only world he knows is this dump.'

Elsebeth's phone buzzed. There was a message on it, from Tristan's number.

> Come home immediately. You and the policewoman.
> I need you here.

IT DIDN'T SOUND LIKE him at all.

'When do I get my Benji?' Alba demanded from the table. 'I told you about your Søren. Only fair I get something back.'

And that was it, Elsebeth realised. The only reason Alba had spoken at all. It was to plead for a bargain. Give Hanna Olsen the truth about her brother and in return pray her son might soon return.

'You could have told me,' Hanna said.

'You what?' Alba's face wrinkled up with disbelief and bafflement. She looked old. Just like her mother, worn down by years of labour and a hard life hidden away in the fjord the devil made beside the sea. 'No I couldn't. And anyway . . . what good would that have done? He's dead. Like my Jónas. Only got Benji left now. Think of the living ones. Think of us. Of me.'

Elsebeth showed Hanna Olsen the message on the phone.

'I want an answer,' Alba demanded. 'I want to know what you're going to do.'

'Did Aksel Højgaard know?' Hanna asked. 'About my brother? About Kaspar?'

Alba shook her head. She looked scared all of a sudden. Got up and stood in front of the door, arms stretched wide to stop them.

'I don't know nothing about that. I don't . . . you won't get me into trouble, will you? I never hurt anyone. I never did anything. Just want my Benji. OK?'

'I'll do what I can,' said Hanna. 'Get out of the way please.'

'He was a nice man, your brother. I liked him.'

'We have to leave,' Elsebeth told her.

As they walked off she stood on the doorstep, arms folded, hair awry, face starting to go shiny with tears.

'Don't you go blaming me!' she yelled after them. 'I never led him on. He didn't belong here.' Her voice cracked altogether as they rounded the corner to the lane out to the tunnel and the cottage. 'None of you lot do.'

TWENTY-FOUR

She rode pillion on Hanna Olsen's motorbike up the hill. The Ace Capri was in the lean-to. But the cottage was empty. Elsebeth walked all round, Hanna with her, looking for some sign of him. There was just a jacket on the coat hook and the phone on the table. His message was still on the screen when she brought it to life. Once again she thought: it doesn't sound like Tristan.

Hanna said she needed to go outside and make some calls.

'I wouldn't broach this with Aksel Højgaard,' Elsebeth cautioned. 'Not yet. Not over the phone. Not until we know . . . know what to do.'

Hanna nodded and said that wasn't what was on her mind.

'I'm going to phone my mum and tell her we're pretty sure Søren's gone. We've thought that for ages, of course. But you always kind of keep hoping. Best I . . .'

She sniffed, rubbed her nose, then walked outside.

Elsebeth checked her phone again. No more messages. Nothing on the laptop.

A cup of tea for both her and Hanna Olsen would be a good idea. What they'd heard from Alba Mikkelsen required careful consideration. She wasn't even sure it was something for Tristan's ears once they found him. Being the kind of man he was he'd simply march straight into Højgaard's office and demand some answers. If they weren't forthcoming he'd attempt to talk to someone else. Yet if Alba was telling the truth then the horror of what had happened in Djevulsfjord the summer before was shared among many. Perhaps not just those in the village itself.

And there remained the question of Jónas Mikkelsen and his brother, now in some kind of protective custody, held responsible for his demise. Where did those two fit in? Was Alba perhaps correct in believing the time had come to think more of the living than the dead?

The kettle was coming slowly to the boil, the rattling, rising sound of it comforting in the way such small, domestic rituals always were.

'Hanna?' she said, suddenly alarmed by a noise outside.

Perhaps one of the sheep, though the creatures had never made that sort of sound before.

'Hanna,' she repeated, going to the door, 'I am making us some tea. We should sit down and consider this carefully. Tristan will be back soon I'm sure. If . . .'

There was no one there. Hanna's prized motorbike had fallen off its prop stand and lay on its side by the pansies that ran down the front path, her helmet spilled awkwardly beside it.

I am not afraid. I never will be.

Elsebeth Haraldsen rarely had to say that to herself. She'd walked into the Árnafjall tunnel without feeling the slightest twitch of fear. Nearly died when she did that. All the same . . .

'Hanna! Tristan!'

There was the noise again and the sinking feeling in her stomach told her where it came from. The shed. The bloody slaughterhouse where they'd let Baldur Ganting butcher one of their sheep, primarily because it looked like the only way the man might regain some sanity. Much like her boiling a kettle in the kitchen, killing one of the animals was a routine domestic act, carried out by rote, in his case a small sacrifice to the hard season to come.

'Hello . . .?'

There was no answer.

Elsebeth went back into the house, found the cutlery drawer in the kitchen, and took out the longest, keenest cookery knife she could find. It was an old one, well worn by years of sharpening, a gift from her parents not long after they were married and were struggling with money.

It shook in her hands as she went back outside. It continued to tremble as she walked unsteadily towards the shed.

The door was ajar. There was power inside, a light switch just by the tool rack, one so well hidden you had to feel around with your fingers to find it.

She was still struggling to manage that when she heard Tristan cry out, his voice anguished and full of fear.

'Elsebeth! No! Run, woman. Run and—'

A blow, a punch, a groan. He was hurt.

Your heart . . .

She was thinking of that and that alone when the light came to dazzling life and violence turned upon her, so swift and brutal the knife fell from her hands in an instant and Elsebeth found herself swamped by strong arms, by rope and curses, fists and fury, fast feet kicking her hard to the floor.

How long the painful struggle lasted she wasn't sure. The carcass of the sheep swung above them, dripping dark blood onto Tristan's trousers as he sat, hands bound, beneath it, Hanna much the same next to him, though now she sported a bloody nose and a swollen eye.

'Elsebeth . . .' he began, only to be silenced by the figure marching between them. From the ground the man seemed so tall his head appeared to stretch all the way to the smoke-stained timber roof. He barged into the dead sheep scarcely noticing, muttered vile curses under his breath in that coarse accent she'd come to think was Djevulsfjord's alone.

'Well. What have we here?'

Kaspar Ganting. A name on a headstone in the cemetery down the way, another man buried beneath it.

'This will do you no good,' Hanna cried. 'I am a police officer. I have colleagues who will come looking—'

He roared. He lashed out with his feet. She shrieked at the shock and the pain.

Elsebeth caught her husband's eyes glittering in the shadows across the rank space between them. Tristan had no idea what to do, any more than she.

Kaspar Ganting was breathing heavily. He stank almost as much as the cold mutton rocking to and fro. Then he turned on Hanna again, fought with her jacket, found her phone, took it out and marched outside.

'Father . . .'

They could all hear him. Hear both the fear and the determination in his loud, strong voice too.

'Father . . . I am here. Kaspar. Your son came back. He had to.'

A pause then and Elsebeth wondered what Baldur might be saying.

'I had been meaning to tell you.' Kaspar Ganting's tone had

taken on the pleading whine of a child now, a bad one. 'Were it not for that stupid little shit Jónas and all this trouble . . .'

Again the halt in his speech, again her head trying to imagine the response at the other end.

'Be that as it may,' he said eventually. 'I am at the slaughterhouse of that idiot new sheriff. We have work to do. You are required.'

Silence then. The door opened. He walked in, tapped the sheep carcass so it started oscillating between them, a headless lump of meat covered in muslin, flies buzzing round the gore-stained fabric.

Then he pulled something from his jacket. Elsebeth stared at it and felt lost. It was a whaling knife, the kind she knew so well now, long and slightly curved, the surface etched with a pattern just visible in the harsh fluorescent light from the tube set in the roof.

'Work,' he repeated as he stabbed the point of the blade hard through the fabric, deep into the mutton in front of him, time and time again.

THE SLAUGHTERHOUSE WAS COLD. The walls ran with condensation from their anxious, panting breathing. Outside the sheep were baying, that low groan of fear they uttered in puzzlement when peril was close.

Finally a truck drew up, the engine beating loud for a moment. When it died a door slammed.

'Help us, man! This lunatic—' Tristan Haraldsen's shouts lasted but a second before he was beaten into silence by a sudden rain of kicks and punches.

The door opened.

Baldur Ganting stood there, eyed them all, poked some snus

into his mouth, stayed silent for a while then said, 'You reckoned you wouldn't come back.'

From the darkness Kaspar's hurt, aggressive voice, that of a child, whined, 'And where else am I to go?'

'Iceland. I found a berth for you.'

'Fuck Iceland! This is my home.'

The older man nodded.

'Jónas . . .' he muttered.

'Jónas! What of him?'

'You know what of him.'

'I thought I could trust that little bastard . . .'

'He's dead,' Tristan Haraldsen bellowed. 'A child!'

Kaspar Ganting came out of the dark and stood in the harsh light by the door, glaring at his father.

'I asked him . . . I paid him to bring me food and news till these bastards here vanished and I could come home.'

'News from who? Not me. I never knew—'

'I would have told you in the end . . . when the man let me.'

'A child,' Baldur Ganting repeated. 'What happened . . .?'

'What happened you don't know!' He nodded at the three of them silent on the floor. 'Any more than these fools.' Kaspar laughed and it was a dry, cold, dead sound. 'A man cannot live in a place like this without he kills a thing from time to time. You taught me that. I dealt with that bastard from Copenhagen coming here like he owned my Alba. I dealt with that bastard Ryberg when the man told me he was going to go pouncing on her after they laid the boy in the ground.'

His voice turned shrill and high. His arms waved crazily about him, the long whaling knife glinting in the slaughterhouse light.

'Well, Father? You taught me. Did you lie?'

More snus, more silence. Ganting looked at the three of them trussed tight on the grubby abattoir floor.

'I asked a question . . .'

'Ja. You did. Outside in the truck. I've got my gun.' He nodded at his son. 'Come, Kaspar. Let's get this done.'

WAITING ON THE COLD, dank floor, barely able to move, it was hard to think of what else to say, let alone try to do.

Hanna Olsen struggled against the ropes, then fought to work on theirs with her nimble fingers, all to no avail. Kaspar Ganting was a fisherman after all, used to tying firm knots with hemp and sisal. They were at the mercy of the man and his father.

'Baldur!' Haraldsen yelled all of a sudden. 'Come to your senses, fellow. We are neighbours. By God I thought for a while we might be friends.'

All they heard in return was the inaudible burr of distant voices, too far away to be clear.

'I should never have scolded that child on the beach during the grind,' Haraldsen moaned. 'I should have stayed in my black pyjamas, mowing the roof.'

'Oh Tristan,' Hanna said in a gentle, sorry voice. 'Do stop taking the blame for everything.'

'I can't help it.'

'Then try,' Elsebeth ordered and for some reason found herself laughing, a nervous, ridiculous response, though one which somehow seemed apposite.

She'd barely finished when there came the sound of a raised voice. A cry of fury and fear. Young. It had to be.

Then the roaring, deafening explosion of a shotgun, a single blast, short and powerful, one so loud it drove all thought from their heads so all they could do was sit there, hands tied before them, heads down, waiting.

After a minute or so they heard something being dragged away. Lugged onto the open back of the truck where whale meat and sheep and fishing gear would normally be stowed, or so it sounded like.

The engine burst into life. Then was gone.

Still they could find no words.

Perhaps thirty minutes later it was back. Tristan Haraldsen shuffled across the floor and took his wife's bound hands in his. Hanna Olsen did the same and the three of them huddled together, cold fingers, clammy skin, trying to keep each other warm, to feel the blood pulse through them, the life beating in their veins.

When the door opened Baldur Ganting stood there, fisherman's hat on, a dead look in his eyes. He wiped his hands as if clearing them of something. Then he pulled out his long whaling knife, bent down, separated the three of them and carefully cut through all their ropes.

The late-summer sun was fading as they stumbled to their feet and staggered outside blinking, desperate for air that didn't stink of blood and fear and sweat.

'There are blackfish off the Skerries,' Ganting said, shielding his eyes against the brightness over the water. 'I saw them when I was down there.'

'Baldur . . .'

The man was barely listening. A tarpaulin lay flat in the back of the truck, the shotgun back in its case upon it. A black puddle of blood pooled around the edge. When he saw they'd noticed he folded the thing in half to hide the stain.

'Do not worry, district sheriff. I am not minded for the grind today. Don't have the boat for it, not yet.'

There was a fresh fierceness in his eyes.

'Things happen you shouldn't talk about sometimes,' he told them. 'Not good for anyone. You let them die and stay there. No good chasing after what's gone. That is all I have to say on this matter. All that will be said.'

He nodded at the three remaining animals as they stood in a line behind the fence, watching him balefully as if they remembered the time he took one from the flock.

'Those beasts need dealing with before September's gone.' He took off his wool cap and bowed first to Elsebeth then Hanna Olsen and finally shook Haraldsen firmly by the hand. 'I surely will oblige there when I can.'

TWENTY-FIVE

Autumn's chilly breath was gusting round Árnafjall. Drizzle and mist curled off across the fells, along the inlet, out beyond the Skerries. Just after daylight broke through the grey shroud Tristan and Elsebeth Haraldsen walked hand in damp hand along the harbour all the way to the shingle strand.

The beach was clean of blood and bones and smelled of nothing but salt water and old kelp. The tide comes, the tide goes, Haraldsen thought, washing everything with it. In the end Djevulsfjord would return to its natural, primal state. The ocean and the people would make sure of that.

Soon the *Alberta* would be back in business, repaired, repainted, crew eager to brave the cold, hard sea. On the other, more modest boats, men whose names they'd never managed to learn busied away on the decks, mending their nets, fixing gear, intent on work, scarcely sharing a word. None so much as looked their way as the two of them passed, though from time to time they eyed the grey-blue waves, anxious to read the way the currents shifted, the flocking of the gulls around the eddying water, wondering if a black fin might break brief surface, harbinger of more to come.

Not that there'd be any appetite to chase them. Another grind would entail approaching the district sheriff to seek permission. Haraldsen knew full well that was a question which would fall to another fellow in another year. No fisherman of Djevulsfjord would come knocking at his door again, asking that he stop mowing the roof in his black pyjamas to read the rules and let the blackfish hunt commence.

It was three days since that terrible time in the killing shed. In all that time there'd been no mention of the fate of Kaspar Ganting nor had there seemed any point in asking after the fellow. The man had lain in the graveyard for more than a year, now next to his young nephew Jónas. That, as far as Djevulsfjord was concerned, was a truth as solid and irrefutable as the stories told from the pulpit of the white, wooden church across the way or the hearthside tales of old gods and monsters that mothers and fathers still recited to their young.

One hour they walked, talking, thinking, firm in their own minds, as they felt sure Hanna Olsen would be in hers. Then they returned to the cottage and found the young policewoman waiting for them as expected, her motorbike on its stand in the yard.

Breakfast followed. Toast, fried eggs and bacon for the Haraldsens. Hanna had brought her own food: two apples, a bottle of juice and a pot of skyr. A foreigner, young, she lived differently, though now they had so much in common.

It was close to nine by the time they'd finished.

'So,' he said, pushing away his plate. 'We are decided?'

'Yes,' said Elsebeth.

Hanna the same.

'Us back to Tórshavn and the world we knew,' Haraldsen continued.

A quiet, predictable life they loved and failed to appreciate as much as it deserved.

'We can be happy there again,' Elsebeth replied. 'We always were. Why we ever left . . .?'

The journey to Vágar was meant to be an adventure. Not like this.

'Jutland for me,' Hanna said. 'Home to the city for you. That feels right, doesn't it?'

'Where we all belong,' Elsebeth agreed.

He got up, kissed Elsebeth quickly on the cheek, held out his hand to Hanna only for her to race to her feet and hug him quickly before he could retreat.

'Oh.'

He knew he was blushing like a school child.

Elsebeth chinked her mug against Hanna's bottle of orange juice and said, 'Reel your man in, Tristan. Leave the rest to us.'

The words brought back memories of that day on the strand, his pathetic efforts to put the young whale out of its agonies. Elsebeth must have seen that in his face so she kissed him once again and ushered him to the door.

They were standing on the step, waving as he drove off towards the tunnel. There was such a sense of normality to Djevulsfjord on the surface. That, and the place's natural beauty, was what had lured them. Perhaps lured Søren too, chasing the unobtainable Alba Mikkelsen who would never have looked at him twice once she was back in the shackles the village threw around her.

The women thought there was something to be done on that front.

Haraldsen hoped with all his uncertain heart that this once they would be right.

★ ★ ★

'**WE WOULD LIKE TO** have a word with Alba,' Elsebeth announced as they entered the Thomsen's store. 'I gather she works here mornings.'

Dorotea shot them a vicious look.

'She works wherever I tell her. And when.'

Hanna pulled out her police ID card.

'That still good around here, is it?' Dorotea sneered. 'The girl is busy.'

A slim, hunched figure came out from behind the shelves, her eyes glazed and weary. Alba put a pile of canned vegetables on the counter and slapped her hands, stirring up a grey cloud, half cobwebs, half dust.

'Not so busy. What do you want?'

George Thomsen edged out from the back office like a man wanting to witness an argument but never a part of it.

'To make you an offer,' Elsebeth said very calmly.

'She don't need any offers!' Dorotea's temper was up straight away. 'You two are interfering with her tasks.'

Hanna waved the card again.

'We will not leave until this conversation has taken place.'

'No,' Elsebeth agreed.

'This girl works for me! Got a contract. Gets paid, gets accommodation. All signed up she is. Name on the page.'

Alba's eyes darted round the three women in the shop then settled on Elsebeth.

'What kind of offer?'

'Get out!' Dorotea yelled. 'The pair of you. This is private property. Don't care about you flashing that police card either. We all know what that's worth.'

They didn't move. Alba hovered round the counter, uncertain what to do, where to go.

'They going to give me my Benji back?'

'Course they won't,' Dorotea snapped. 'The lad's sick in the head. He's off to Denmark. Done deal, isn't it? Killed his brother—'

'I don't believe that! Never will!'

How much to say. How much to promise. Alba Mikkelsen had been offered so few strands of hope over the years. Was it fair to dangle one in front of her face?

'Tristan and I are moving back to Tórshavn,' Elsebeth said. 'We need someone to look after our cottage for the winter at least. No point in selling until spring at the earliest.'

George Thomsen came closer, interested.

'I might be interested in buying that place.'

'We got enough property, husband. Don't need more trouble. You buck out of this—'

'My money. Not yours. If—'

'Next year,' Elsebeth went on. 'Then we discuss selling. In the meantime, Alba, we're happy to let you live there rent-free, with a small income to look after the place. Enough to get by.'

'I don't want your charity,' she said, wrinkling her nose in disgust.

God, Elsebeth thought. Just like her father.

'It's not charity. We can't leave the place empty. It needs heating and cleaning and painting. Things we never got round to like . . .'

Like mowing the turf roof. A part of her regretted she'd never see Tristan finish that job.

'It's a good offer,' Hanna added. 'Fair pay for fair work. Gets you out of that shed. I can have a word with the social people in Tórshavn to see if there's money—'

'She can't leave here!' Dorotea reached behind the counter, grabbed hard at a drawer, pulled out a sheet of paper. 'Alba's mine, signed for. Room in that shack for one. Hours all done for me and no one else. See that? Her name on the bottom. Mine alongside it.' She jabbed a fat finger on the sheet. 'There in black and white.'

A long silence then Alba's eyes went back to the shelves and the cans and the dust.

'I know you mean to be kind. Nice of you—'

'Enough of this,' George Thomsen cried, storming out, cheeks red, eyes blazing, his fury aimed in one direction only. 'Good God, wife. Do you think we're slavers or something? Is there not a shred of pity in you for this poor lass?'

Elsebeth listened in amazement as he strung together as long a stream of obscenities as she'd heard since they moved to the hamlet by the water, where speech was usually slow and measured, archaic in its tone. Then he marched to the counter, snatched the paper from his wife's hands and tore it in two.

'Listen to me, both of you. Be my witness. Alba never signed anything. I was here. I saw it. Like the coward I am I said not a word.'

'Careful George . . .' Dorotea's voice was low and full of threat.

'I will not stand for this one moment longer! She forged Alba's name on this thing. I watched. You don't belong to us, child. No one does. You can't treat people like this! You understand that? I should have said something before. Won't allow it. Not anymore.'

The halves of the paper he then tore into shreds in front of Dorotea then dropped them in the bin.

'Is that right?' Hanna asked. 'Alba?'

'I do what folk ask me,' she answered with a shrug. 'Always have.'

Hanna strode behind the counter and retrieved the shredded paper from the bin. Then she took a clear plastic evidence envelope out of her jacket and placed the pieces in it before smiling very directly at Dorotea Thomsen.

'Forging a signature on a business document is fraud. A crime. It invalidates the document, naturally. But it may also mean we should continue this discussion in Tórshavn.'

Dorotea was glassy-eyed, as if she was remembering what it was like to cry, out of fury, out of shame or fear, it scarcely mattered. She mumbled something then headed off to the back office, slamming the door behind her.

HE HADN'T MADE AN appointment to see Aksel Højgaard. That would have warned the man. But the superintendent was behind his desk, sifting through messages on his phone, when Tristan Haraldsen walked in, closed the door behind him and took the chair opposite.

Højgaard put down his phone, raised an eyebrow and said, 'Rasmussen has yet to receive your resignation. He mentioned it this morning.'

'A few other things have been on my mind. Can you imagine what they are?'

A shrug, then: 'Gossip. Hearsay. Fairy stories. That place you foolishly chose to live is full of them.'

'I think unexplained deaths—'

'There are mysteries everywhere,' Højgaard interrupted. 'It's our job to keep the peace. Not hunt down every answer regardless of the consequences.'

A light went on in Haraldsen's head. He'd been asking himself, why? Why would a man like Højgaard turn a blind eye to wicked acts in his own back yard? And sometimes, though this would be hard to prove, engineer them? What possible gain might there be? Looking at him now, the whole of Vágar seemingly under his thumb from this little office in Sørvágur, the answer seemed obvious.

'That's it, isn't it?' he asked.

'That's what?'

'That's why you do this. Walk away. Sweep everything beneath the carpet. Or below the ground. Because it's convenient. You can live with the illusion that everything in Vágar, everything you feel you own, is neat and tidy and—'

Højgaard rapped his pen on the desk.

'In all my time here there's been nothing significant in the way of reported crime. Only petty matters. I keep it that way. I *like* it that way.'

'You're a police officer! What about your sense of justice!'

The man looked amazed.

'Justice must be seen to be done, Haraldsen. That's what they say. And what do people find when they look at this territory of mine? A placid, green and boring backwater where nothing of moment ever happens. A practical man understands it's the outward appearance that counts. Not the inner. The world is full of matters the likes of you would find distasteful. Better, in that case, you live with your comfortable delusions. As for Djevulsfjord . . . there's no redeeming that place. No correcting it. Those people are who they are. I cannot change that. Any more than you—'

'They are ordinary. They are small and poor and scared.'

That shrug again.

'The place is an anachronism. Lift the stone that covers it and all the world will see what unpalatable truths lurk beneath. You, of all people, should thank me for sparing them that. Truly. You got a glimpse of it after all.'

'So you will ignore what happened to Søren Olsen? To Kaspar Ganting? You refuse to dig up a grave . . .?'

'We don't do that kind of thing.'

'You will not interview Baldur Ganting and ask what became of his son?'

The man opposite laughed and shook his head. Haraldsen understood the message immediately: *don't be so naive.*

'The son is in the churchyard and has been for more than a year. There's not a soul in Djevulsfjord who'll tell you otherwise.'

'You know that's not true.'

A pause and then he said, 'What's true is what I say. What I report. Then it's done with. Think of it, man. Think of the consequences. Do you want Ganting to go to jail? What might that mean for your precious little village? For Alba Mikkelsen? Who would benefit? Perhaps . . .' He looked out of the window. The boats of Sørvágur were busy as always. 'Perhaps I should ask the people there which they'd prefer. My way or yours. Which do you think they'd choose?'

A part of that, at least, was true. If Ganting went to jail, Djevulsfjord would surely suffer. So would the man behind the desk.

'I have a proposition for you.'

That he hadn't seen coming.

'You? A pen-pusher? The man who failed as district sheriff? A proposition for me?'

'I have a proposition. A bargain if you like. Elsebeth is a party to it. As is Hanna Olsen, whose brother was murdered in that place, as you well know. Nor was he alone in dying an unfortunate death.' He paused to make sure this next was understood. 'Not that you can lay the blame for everything at the door of Djevulsfjord. Now, can you?'

Aksel Højgaard simply gazed at him from across the desk, playing with the top of his pen.

'I see you are listening,' Haraldsen added. 'That, I believe, is a start.'

IN THE SHOP, GEORGE at the counter, his wife vanished, Elsebeth reached over, took Alba's skinny arms in her hands and looked her straight in the face.

'This isn't charity. Far from it. This is work. You can move into my cottage. Plenty to do there.'

Alba glanced at Hanna Olsen and asked, 'What about Søren? Her brother? What I told you? I mean . . .?'

That was a question they knew would come, and hearing it was like a spell being broken. A name read out loud. Exorcised, a little anyway.

'Søren's dead,' Hanna told her. 'Nothing I can do to change that. Nothing anyone can do. Besides, that's my business. My loss. Not yours.'

She screwed her eyes tight shut for a moment, close to tears and said, 'I'm sorry. So sorry. I didn't ask your brother here. You can't fight this place. Don't you understand?'

'Alba.' It was George Thomsen, his voice breaking. 'Listen to me. You're your own woman. Don't belong to anyone but yourself. You've had enough misery in your life and all of us here added to that in our way. If you want to go off with these ladies . . . You have my blessing. I'll do what I can to help. Forget that . . .' He glanced at the office door. 'Forget that woman in there. She's not going to push you around anymore. Me neither. I should have . . . should have done this years ago.'

There was a touch of police in Hanna's voice just then, hard, firm, incontestable, as she said, 'You make this decision now or we leave you here. Now or nothing.'

'I can't . . . can't live in a big place like that. Not on my own. Bigger than Mum and Dad's house. I just can't.'

They'd been expecting this.

'Perhaps you won't have to,' Elsebeth said.

AS HE DROVE THE battered and somewhat asthmatic motor home over to Sørvágur, Tristan Haraldsen had planned in his head what he intended to say when he sat down to face Aksel Højgaard. Everything depended upon the man's reaction. There could be no lacunae into which the superintendent might retreat, no fault lines, no foggy uncertainties.

A narrative lay behind everything. An incomplete one he had to admit, since they had no way of asking questions of the key players. Kaspar Ganting could no longer answer to what he'd done to Hanna Olsen's brother. Lars Ryberg hadn't lived to confess to whatever lies he'd invented to allow Søren Olsen to occupy the space beneath the Djevulsfjord sods and a headstone carrying the name of his murderer.

Benjamin Mikkelsen had yet to say a word about what had happened on the fells, and how his brother Jónas had come to act as some kind of go-between with his uncle Kaspar and someone else, Højgaard he felt sure, not that he could prove it. But that last grim and frightening episode in the killing shed would remain with Tristan Haraldsen and his wife forever. He would, he thought, remember every word spoken there, and the way in which Kaspar Ganting blurted them out as they lay tethered, trussed, waiting to die.

And the words he'd spoken in the ruins of Ryberg's house. Holding the damned poker fashioned out of a whaling spear.

I heard you were looking for this.

From whom? Not Baldur Ganting or anyone else he could think of in Djevulsfjord. The father's ignorance of Kaspar's presence in the hills was obvious from his reaction in those last moments before the two men vanished, not long before the roar of a single shotgun blast.

One other thing in the shed too, spat out by Kaspar in his desperate state.

Haraldsen folded his arms, leaned back in the chair, confident in himself now, and said, 'I dealt with that bastard Ryberg when the man told me he was going to go pouncing on her.'

Højgaard's eyes narrowed and he said, 'What?'

'You heard. That's what Kaspar said when he wanted his father's help killing us. What man was that, do you think, Aksel? Any ideas?'

The pen. He couldn't stop clicking it. A rare sign of discomfort. Perhaps a small omen of hope.

'Are you well? Elsebeth said your heart was weak. Perhaps your mind's in much the same state too.'

'You know what happened that night. You know what happened

last year. You are the puppet master. The monarch of this realm of yours. If—'

'I have no complaints on my desk,' the superintendent replied, sweeping it with his hand. 'No reports of anything. What do you speak of?'

'We never made a complaint. Not me. Not Elsebeth. Not Hanna Olsen either. Not yet—'

'Officer Olsen has resigned her post. I've let her go early. She seemed . . . unsuited to work around here. I believe she's returning to Denmark.' He frowned. 'It's a shame she ever left.'

'What was the point in telling you anything?' Haraldsen asked. 'You'd have chucked our words in the bin. Just like Søren's disappearance. Just like Kaspar's supposed death on the Lundi Cliffs . . .'

Højgaard pointed to the clock.

'I'm a busy man. Make this quick then go.'

'Hanna's brother met Alba on the Jutland ferry. He came to Djevulsfjord wanting to see her. Kaspar killed him. You helped them cover that up. To keep your precious record in Vágar clean. You were the king. There was no place for a stain upon your domain.'

The pen clicked three times in rapid succession.

'Your evidence for this?'

'Ryberg helped you. Baldur, his wife, perhaps others too. Then my predecessor Djurhuus found out and tried to pass on his suspicions to Tórshavn. I imagine . . .' He was on guesswork here and he hoped this wasn't too obvious. 'The intelligence . . . you managed to intercept it somehow. Or ridicule it. Rasmussen is a gullible man. Was it hard to ensure it never went any further?'

'I repeat, your evidence?'

Not yet. Not yet.

'And here is one more interesting thing. Baldur exiled his son to Iceland as soon as he learned what he'd done. Told him never to return. Yet one week later Kristian Djurhuus dies in the Árnafjall tunnel. Mown down by someone you do not seem to have tried very hard to catch.'

He waited for a response. In vain.

'I wonder why, Aksel. I wonder . . .'

Højgaard pushed the office phone across the desk.

'If you wish to report these fantasies to Tórshavn feel free. I've nothing to fear.'

'Oh I'm sure you haven't. You're a careful man. A powerful man. Vágar belongs to you. No crime on your patch. Nothing untoward save for a village slowly dying, populated by people few care about anywhere else.'

'You should go.'

'Kaspar waited for me in Ryberg's house. He knew I'd been looking for that bloody poker. He said so himself. Just a few hours after I told you and Rasmussen I'd seen it here.'

That, at least, seemed to give him pause for thought.

'Hard to call a dead man into the witness box.'

'He told his father too. What I said. "I dealt with that bastard Ryberg when the man told me he was going to go pouncing on her." The man. You are the man, Aksel. You were the one that young rascal Jónas Mikkelsen was talking to, the go-between for his fugitive uncle on the fells, desperate to go back home, not knowing if he dared. You were the one who said Kaspar had to keep hiding on those fells until you'd allow him . . .'

No answer.

'Though I imagine that would never have happened. You'd have killed him too. Like you murdered Djurhuus. Did Kaspar suspect what you had in mind? You dispatched him to deal with Ryberg. Though I imagine he was too wary to meet you face-to-face.'

'Dead,' Højgaard repeated. 'All dead, no tales to tell. Apart from Baldur Ganting. Who'll never say a word in court to anyone. As I said, he'd be the first in jail if any of this were true. He knows the cost to that damned place of his.'

'You must have been furious when young Mikkelsen cut me and ran off into the hills with his brother. Something finally you could not control. How inconvenient.'

'Enough of this . . .'

'I could bring these walls tumbling down around your ears.'

Højgaard's face was set like stone.

'If these flights of fancy of yours had any merit that would be a very dangerous thing to threaten, wouldn't it?'

Haraldsen nodded in agreement.

'Oh, that I do not doubt. Were I like Kristian Djurhuus. A man alone, apart from a difficult lover who lived here only occasionally. But there are three of us. One a police officer. You may be king of Vágar, but even the king can't kill us all.'

Nothing but the nervous and rapid click of a pen.

Then the man opposite him sighed and asked, 'What, precisely, do you want?'

There, he thought. That was it.

'Relax, man. I didn't come here to threaten you. But to offer a bargain. A generous one in the circumstances.'

Three more taps on the desk. Haraldsen pulled out his old pipe and sucked on it. He could detect the smell of sweat, perhaps his own.

'Do it then.'

It felt as if he were standing on the edge of the Lundi Cliffs, looking out over the precipice, gazing at the endless sea.

'Elsebeth and I are returning to Tórshavn. Retirees. If it comes to it we'll have nothing to do but stand outside police headquarters every minute of the day, holding placards, handing out leaflets, calling everyone we can think of. Hanna Olsen, your former colleague, has agreed she'll be there with us. I doubt Rasmussen would appreciate such a spectacle. More to the point, the international media would surely be interested in the idea that our little corner of paradise is, in fact, steeped in blood, and not just that of blackfish alone. When they ask, I will go through the timeline of all the evidence we have. Circumstantial it may be, and in places lacking in verification. Nevertheless it exists in some quantity and there will be interesting elements to support our suppositions in the archives, Aksel. You're a careful man but no one can bury everything. You, of all people, must know the weight of accusations will, one day, become unsupportable. Your wear your precious crown so lightly. We could dash that thing from your head in a month or so I reckon. All those years of building up this empire of yours. This fiefdom full of folk you can control. Wasted.'

There was no answer.

'You seem lost for words, superintendent.'

'What do you want?' Højgaard asked again.

He hesitated. No need for haste.

'The bargain, you mean?'

'The bargain.'

'Such a small thing. A gift that means nothing to you and everything to someone who craves it.'

'*What?*'

Haraldsen sucked the pipe once more, then stashed it in his pocket.

'Benjamin Mikkelsen must be removed from wherever you've sent him and returned to his mother. To live with her without interference. The lad didn't kill his brother. Kaspar did. We heard that, as good as. When he was ranting about murdering us too. Perhaps . . .' He stared hard at the fellow across the desk. 'Perhaps running errand boy between you and Kaspar on those hills gave the lad ideas his uncle didn't appreciate. Perhaps poor Jónas asked too much. Either way his brother deserves better than you've offered him. Allow him home now. Then you will never hear from us again. That's all.'

Aksel Højgaard stuttered, 'I–I do not have the power.'

It was Haraldsen's turn to laugh.

'Oh, come, come. You have the gift of life and death here and use it when you wish. But if I'm mistaken we've nothing left to discuss.'

Haraldsen got up to go. The man was at the door before him.

'You're a strange one, Tristan. To risk so much for people who wouldn't lift a finger for you or yours.'

It seemed an odd comment.

'That is the nature of charity, surely. If there's reward in it then the thing is nothing more than self-interest. Let the boy go home. We will leave you here untouched. Elsebeth and I will enjoy our retirement in Tórshavn and never think of Djevulsfjord or this office again. Which given the blood on your hands is an offer that frankly you don't deserve.'

Højgaard frowned, scratched at his cheek, then pulled out a pack of cigarettes and lit one.

'The rules do not apply to you, Aksel, do they?'

'The rules are what I make them. Just like this place. You tread on dangerous ground, Haraldsen. This wife of yours. The Olsen girl. None of you can prove a word of it.'

'Perhaps not.' He smiled then winked. 'All the same . . . the three of us will stand out in the street night and day screaming our heads off until someone or something silences us. No proof, but by God we will hurt you in the trying.'

He reached for the door.

'A bargain,' Aksel Højgaard said quickly as he stepped forward to block the way.

For the first time in all the years Tristan Haraldsen had known the man, there was a note of pleading in his tone.

IT WAS GEORGE THOMSEN who broke the long and awkward silence.

'Tell you what, ladies. You three go sit at that table we've got out back. Sun's on it now. I'll bring you some tea and biscuits.'

It was chilly in truth but they wanted out of the shop. Sitting listening to the sea, the sound of men working on their boats, the occasional putter of an engine, was a good enough way to pass the time. Alba had no more questions. Perhaps she was afraid of the answers that might come if she pushed for them too hard.

As an old kettle came noisily to the boil inside, Dorotea slunk across the cobbled landing, back to the big house. A worm had turned, Elsebeth thought. Long years of doubt and guilt and frustration, brought to the surface by the cruel fate of Alba Mikkelsen, had finally made George Thomsen rebel against his wife's relentless tyranny. There was decency and goodness in Djevulsfjord. It was just hidden sometimes, and different in a way no outsider could fully comprehend.

When he came out he had three chipped mugs of stewed English Breakfast on a tray along with a tin of Royal Dansk shortbread.

'I meant what I said, Alba,' he said, opening up the biscuits. 'You owe us nothing. You're free to do what you like. I think . . .' He sniffed and looked at the grey ocean, anything but her at that moment. 'I think what's happened in this place of late is bad enough as it is. No need to make it worse. We need a quiet time now. No . . . incidents.'

'Incidents,' Hanna Olsen repeated, and the hurt was there, unambiguous inside that single word, as clear as the cry of the gulls hovering over the distant Skerries.

'Too much hurt already,' Thomsen added as he handed round the tin. 'Wasn't always this way but Djevulsfjord's dying, day by day. Mostly we try to ignore that. I imagine you people coming from the outside think we've got lots in the way of choices. There . . .' He blinked and it wasn't the wan September sunlight that did that. 'There you'd be wrong.'

Ten minutes later the tea was finished. No one had touched a piece of shortbread. Not a word had been spoken.

Elsebeth Haraldsen's phone rang. She walked round the corner to take the call.

★ ★ ★

'IS ALBA THERE? WITH you?'

Haraldsen stood by the Ace Capri, keys in hand, watching two boats from the Sørvágur fleet make a careful exit from the harbour like dancers trying to work out their moves.

'Close enough. Hanna too.'

'Close enough to hear?'

'Not quite.' She sounded puzzled. 'We wait, husband.'

'I know. I know.'

A bargain. That was what he'd offered Højgaard. Implicit in the word was negotiation. One side always gained but gave back too. It was only to be expected. Though the price on their part was one he had never seen coming.

'Alba will take the cottage? There's no impediment?'

'Not if they give her back her son. What hold that awful Thomsen woman had over her is gone.'

'Benjamin can come back on Friday. The social people may want to keep an eye on the two of them naturally but . . .'

She gasped, a short delighted sound.

He was glad he wasn't there, guilty as that made him feel. Emotion, open and raw, was never his forte.

'You are a wonder, husband. I must tell her.'

'Not yet,' he insisted. 'You are the wonder. Hanna. Alba too, for all her strength, if only she could understand.'

'Then tomorrow we will start house hunting. In Tórshavn. Today if you like. Perhaps somewhere near our old place. We had a few friends there. We shall make new ones. It will be good to be home. Our real home. To put all this behind us. *I must tell her.*'

He didn't know how to say it. So when he remained quiet she asked, 'There's something else.'

'Everything comes with a cost, love.'

Movement then. She was walking further away from them, he guessed.

'What cost?'

'We will not return. We cannot. To Tórshavn or anywhere in the Faroes. I'm not sure that would be safe. Or make Aksel Højgaard feel so. Which is the same thing. We must leave here altogether. Follow Hanna back to Denmark perhaps. Or . . . I don't know. Højgaard gave me an hour to decide after I said I must speak to you. The minutes tick by now. I'm sorry.'

Such news, and such a way to break it. Their time abroad had been confined to camping excursions on the mainland. The notion they could live anywhere but the Faroes was so strange they had never even discussed it.

'Tristan . . . we scarcely know what the world is like out there.'

'True,' he agreed. 'We've been quiet souls, haven't we?'

A moment, then she added, 'Perhaps too quiet. Too timid.'

'Possibly.'

She laughed and he could picture her just then, see her face, still young, still lovely.

'Well, timidity is done with now, isn't it? At least Djevulsfjord gave us that. So . . . we could take the Ace Capri and go wherever we want?'

'Indeed. Sell the cottage. Live off the proceeds and my pension. Embark on . . . another adventure. A better one. Somewhere new. Only if you want. Only if you're by my side.'

'You wish to do this?'

'There's no other way to get that boy back to his mother. But we must decide together. Though . . .'

He didn't want to say what was in his head: they'd burned their bridges with Aksel Højgaard regardless. Perhaps there wasn't much alternative. Elsebeth, being quicker and brighter, would surely have worked that out already.

A few seconds she thought about it. That was all.

'I will tell Alba her son is coming home. You shall call him. After that we must decide what to take and what to leave. For once we travel light, I think.'

He would miss the sea more than anything, he felt, watching the fishing boats leave the harbour. It was never quite the same anywhere else.

'We travel unencumbered,' he agreed. 'And for the sake of our good health . . . we travel soon.'

THURSDAY. HØJGAARD HAD BEEN better than his word, doubtless because he wanted the Haraldsens and Hanna Olsen gone. Benjamin Mikkelsen arrived in a black car driven to the harbour by a puzzled civil servant just after eight. At nine Elsebeth arrived at the shack and handed over the keys for the cottage. Baldur Ganting would turn up with his truck later that morning to help her move. Dorotea Thomsen was nowhere to be seen.

They'd booked a passage on the afternoon ferry to Jutland. The Ace Capri was half-full of clothes and personal mementoes. Two lives packed into the old van, the memories trimmed to the ones that mattered. Hanna Olsen was taking the same boat, nothing more than the motorbike and a suitcase with her.

Twenty minutes after the ship cast off, the two of them were on the back deck, the bare grey-green shape of Nólsoy to their left as the city grew smaller over the churning wake. The sky was the watercolour grey of autumn, the air chilly enough for Elsebeth to wrap a scarf tightly round her neck.

Hanna had come to say hello then invited them into the bar for a beer. Later, Elsebeth said, and of course she got the message. The islands were the only home they'd known. They wanted to watch them disappear, moment by moment. Without that memory they'd be like Hanna, burying the ghost of Søren in her head, always dissatisfied, never at peace.

Now, free of the burden of doubt about the brother she'd lost, she appeared, like them, ready to try to start life anew. Grief was a strange emotion, Haraldsen thought. It veered between pain and release, of its own volition mostly. Men and women were hostages to so much that was beyond their power to control. Like the poor fellow in Elsebeth's old myth, losing his beloved Selkie wife on Vágar because he adored her so much that one day he set her free. All acts had unforeseen consequences. Life without risk, without adventure, was not, he felt, much of a life at all. It was a shame it took such dark events to teach them that hard but important lesson, and at their age too.

'Look, Tristan,' Elsebeth said, squeezing the arm of his winter coat. 'Over there. You see the red roof?'

'I see *a* red roof.'

'The dance hall, silly. A shy young man asked an even shyer young woman to join him on the floor there once upon a time. More years ago than I care to remember.'

'Oh, yes. I do recall now.'

'I should hope so.'

'Though I do not recall you were quite so shy as you make out.'

She laughed and they held hands, much as they had that day they'd driven through the Árnafjall tunnel, found the timber cottage for sale and decided, rashly and without forethought, in part upon the poop of a chicken in the rafters, it must be theirs.

'Where shall we go?' she asked.

'Wherever we feel like.'

'South, I think. Somewhere warm for the winter. Then somewhere else when the weather turns too hot. I would like to learn a language. French. Or Spanish. Or Italian.'

'I should like to dance again,' Haraldsen said, unable to take his eyes off her. 'It's been a while. I seem to recall dancing did me great favours once upon a time.'

On the deck of the Jutland ferry, in the strong salt breeze, guillemots and gulls screeching in the vessel's wake, Elsebeth stepped back, smiled a broad smile and opened her arms.

'Well. No time, they say, like the present.'

AS THE JUTLAND FERRY rounded the Skálavík creek, Hanna Olsen hitting her third beer in the bar, on the rear deck Tristan and Elsebeth Haraldsen tight in a loving embrace, Alba Mikkelsen walked through the door of the cottage up the hill. She carried two old suitcases rammed with pretty much all their belongings: clothes and bathroom stuff. A lot of the things they'd had in the shack could get junked. They belonged to a different time.

Baldur Ganting had driven them there, then rushed back to the harbour, anxious to take the *Alberta* out on her first trip to sea since the repairs. Benji trailed behind his mother, staring at the roomy interior as if it belonged to another world. He still hadn't said a word, not since the social people delivered him, or in their care either. She was determined to be patient. He wasn't as stupid or slow as some people thought. He just didn't like to be seen sometimes, to feel people's eyes on him asking: what's wrong with that one? Every waking day Jónas had been there taunting him too, stealing attention and anything else he could lay his hands on. Benji would always feel happier in the shadows.

'Look,' she said, putting the cases by the wooden table in the kitchen. 'This is your new home. Our home.'

He wandered round the room, walked to the sink, turned on the tap, put his mouth underneath the sudden stream then yowled in shock.

Alba rushed over and stopped the gushing water.

'That's the hot one. This place has got hot and cold. See. Red, hot. Blue, cold.'

Very carefully he gave half a turn to the blue one, got a thin dribble in return and put his mouth under that.

'Let's look upstairs,' she said and lugged the cases up the steps.

There was a bedroom beneath the eaves, almost as big as the Thomsens', where Dorotea now slept alone since George had moved himself out to the guest quarters muttering a word Djevulsfjord never heard: divorce. Along the narrow corridor was a cubicle with a single bed, perfect for a child. Alba bounced on the giant mattress, grinning. The boy just watched.

'This is mine.' She pointed to next door. 'That's yours. Imagine, Benji. Your own room. Your own bed. Not a bunk. No, no . . .'

No brother to torment you. She nearly said that. She had to watch her tongue.

He didn't move and she thought to herself: for God's sake don't keep nagging him. He'll talk when he wants and not before.

'Well.' She clapped her hands. 'While I unpack you can pop outside and find some eggs from them chickens.' She winked at him. 'From what I heard you know how to do that, don't you?'

He didn't smile. He didn't grimace. Just shambled down the steps.

Five minutes later he still hadn't returned and she was starting to get worried. Alba went to the back door and called out, 'Benji! Where are those eggs? Time to eat.'

She found him standing by the sheep pen looking at the three remaining ewes, the creatures staring back at him, too woolly for their own good, she thought. The Haraldsens didn't have a clue.

'You find any?'

He held up a wicker basket he must have found in the kitchen. Four brown eggs, straw around them, alongside a bunch of wild flowers, ragwort and daisies and something blue she couldn't name.

'You are the sweetest child,' she said, close to tears, and kissed his hair, then thought, he needs a bath and some shampoo. But food first. 'Let's go inside. Our new home, Benji. Our new home.'

The eggs were so fresh they hissed and spat as she fried them and one of the yolks broke and ran. She took that, and passed the perfect pair over to Benji.

He'd got a knife and fork and something else too. A kitchen blade, long and sharp with a wooden haft, almost big enough for the sheep.

'Eat up. Then we'll try the television. They've got a big one here. After that a bath. Hot water out of the tap. Don't have to boil it like the old place, you sitting in that old zinc tub.'

The eggs and toast went down in no time. She was only halfway through hers when he finished and started playing with the knife.

Still no words. Still he wouldn't look her in the eye.

'Benji.' She took his hand. 'Look at me.'

He did but at the same time he jabbed the point of the big knife into the soft wood of the table and carved a lump out, as big as a hazelnut.

'Don't do that, love. This place. It's not ours really.'

He held the knife, point down, ready to prod at the wood again.

'Just us now,' he said and she wished she'd felt more glad to hear his voice. But she didn't. There was something odd in the hard, dead tone. Something new.

'Just us,' she agreed and squeezed his hand.

He shrank back at her touch and jabbed the kitchen knife deep into the wood. Splinters flew out of the crack he made like shards of shattered bone.

'What happened . . . what happened on the fells . . . it's done with. We don't need to talk about that now.'

'I know, Mam. Not stupid.'

'Of course you're not.'

The knife rose and fell.

'We'll make things right now. You and me.'

'Just us.'

Another blow. More splinters.

'What Kaspar did,' she said and wondered whether this was right. 'What Uncle Kaspar did . . . that was down to him. Not you. Never you, Benji. You're a sweet boy. Always were.'

Not like Jónas. Though she'd never say that. They were both her sons, for better or worse.

The knife bit into the table more furiously.

'Kaspar was . . . difficult,' she went on. 'Not an easy brother.'

'Like Jónas.'

It wasn't a question.

'Like Jónas,' she agreed. 'But I was a girl. You won't . . . you won't understand. Your uncle . . . what he did that day up in the puffin hide . . .'

His face creased in the cruellest sneer, just like his brother's.

'Kaspar, Kaspar, Kaspar. Cut it out, Mam. You sound like Jónas. Anyway Kaspar's dead for real now, ain't he? Jónas too. Just as well.'

The room felt cold all of a sudden or maybe that was her.

'You don't need to say anything—'

'Jónas reckoned that bastard Højgaard didn't want Uncle Kaspar back in the village. Not until he allowed it. Policeman gave Jónas a phone for him and Kaspar wasn't to do nothing till he got told. Just had to stay out there, living like a pig. He was . . .' He screwed up his face to say it. 'Bloody furious. Said Jónas was jerking him around. Said all kind of things . . .'

Stop, she thought. Just stop.

'Your brother always told a lot of lies. Your uncle too.'

That was all she could think of.

'Who don't round here? Jónas started yelling when Kaspar took a pop at him. He reckoned . . .' That pause again, as if he was trying to get this straight. 'He said Kaspar was his dad. His real dad. And Silas mine. That was why he was what he was. And me . . . why I was me.' He peered at her. 'Uncle Kaspar went all red in the face. Didn't say nothing at all except he was buggering off and Jónas could go screw himself now he'd got Højgaard's phone.'

'Benji—'

'Then that policewoman turned up and Kaspar snuck up and clobbered her. Dead mad he was. Is that right, Mam? Is it? Did we have different dads? Or is that a lie as well?'

Don't cry. He'd see.

'No. Course not. And if he was he wouldn't . . . he wouldn't hurt his own son now, would he?'

A quick, sharp grin and then, 'Who said he did?'

The silence between them seemed to go on forever until finally she managed to say, 'Want some yoghourt? Or maybe we could watch the TV. A bath or—'

'Jónas kept running over the fells, like a little rat between Kaspar and old man Højgaard. Been doing that for days he reckoned. Uncle Kaspar didn't need Jónas after he got that phone, did he? Told him to piss off.' He squinted as if trying to remember something, then shrugged. 'Soon as he'd gone Jónas turned on me. Said it was my fault they fell out. You're to blame, goat! Always me, wasn't it? Always . . .'

The blade went into the table. Down a split between the planks the point dived and stuck there, like a whale knife in a blackfish hide.

'I love you, Benji,' she whispered through the tears. 'I love you and if you love me back that's all the two of us are ever going to need.'

The Haraldsens' cottage was nice. A refuge from the village. A place they could try to heal. Both of them. With time.

'That brother of mine had it coming.' One last hard stab in the table. The blade quivered in the shattered wood as he let go and laughed at it in triumph. 'Bloody Jónas. Just us now, Mam, ain't it?'

The boy reached out with grasping fingers, smiling his bent and funny smile, then stroked her straggly blonde hair.

'Just you and me.'

Author's note

This story comes from the imagination and in no way is a depiction of life in the real Faroes Islands. In addition to much outright invention I have greatly simplified everything from the highly complicated system of Faroese family names to fishing, hunting and agricultural practices. Readers seeking a local insight into feudal Faroese society, the nature of the whale hunt, and the pressure on young islanders to abandon older ways of life more than half a century ago, should track down *The Old Man and his Sons* by Heðin Brú, one of the few original works of Faroese literature translated into English.

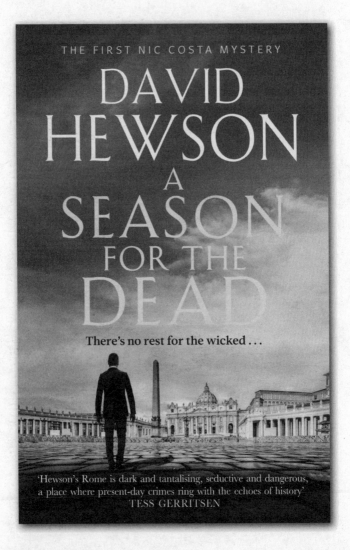

THE FIRST NIC COSTA MYSTERY

DAVID HEWSON

A SEASON FOR THE DEAD

There's no rest for the wicked . . .

'Hewson's Rome is dark and tantalising, seductive and dangerous,
a place where present-day crimes ring with the echoes of history'
TESS GERRITSEN

'Keeps the reader guessing . . . relentlessly
tightening the suspense until the end' *Telegraph*

CANON█GATE

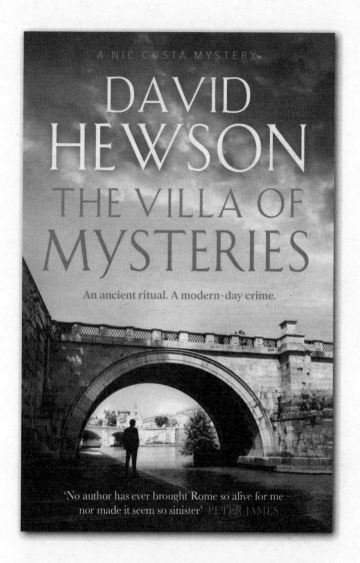

A NIC COSTA MYSTERY

DAVID HEWSON

THE VILLA OF MYSTERIES

An ancient ritual. A modern-day crime.

'No author has ever brought Rome so alive for me –
nor made it seem so sinister' PETER JAMES

'A riveting and fast-paced thriller'
Booklist

CANON■■GATE

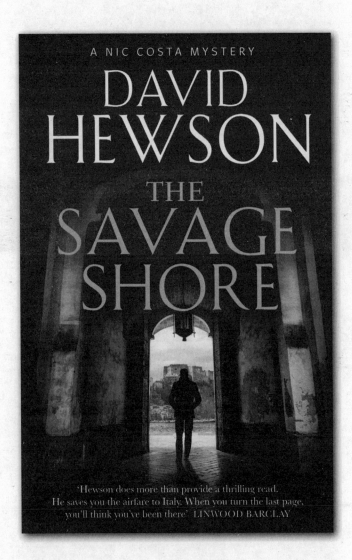

A NIC COSTA MYSTERY

DAVID HEWSON

THE SAVAGE SHORE

'Hewson does more than provide a thrilling read.
He saves you the airfare to Italy. When you turn the last page,
you'll think you've been there' LINWOOD BARCLAY

'A tense, thrilling and atmospheric read'
Simon Kernick

CANON🮥GATE